Wycaan Master: Book Three

A Novel

ALON SHALEV

Tourmaline Books
Berkeley, California

ASHBAR

Ashbar
Wycaan Master, Book 3

Tourmaline Books, Berkeley, California
http://www.tourmalinebooks.com

ISBN: 978-0-9884428-7-0
LCCN: 2013944793

First Edition: October, 2013

Published in the United States of America

Dedication

Each summer for three years, a family gathered around a campfire, deep in the ancient redwood forests, to hear the story unfold and bare witness to the tales of Odessiya and the summoning of the Wycaan Masters.

But at these magical moments, the family was not complete.

It falls upon the elders to pass the stories down. Our elders did not live in the age of elves or dwarves, but they witnessed the rise and fall of tyrannical powers. They saw a society emerge from the ashes of war and claim their freedom. They witnessed the transition into the technological age so many of us take for granted.

This book was written for my children but is dedicated to their grandparents: Trudy & Harry Fellerman, Sondra & Bernard Krakower–the elders of our tribe, who continue to enrich our lives with their own stories.

The Wycaan Master Series:

At The Walls Of Galbrieth–Wycaan Master Book 1
The First Decree–Wycaan Master Book 2
Ashbar–Wycaan Master Book 3

Acknowledgements

–To Monica Buntin, my editor, for once again making sense of an awful lot of words.

–To William Kenney, my book cover artist, for your amazing ability to continually transform my jumbled ideas into such beautiful pieces of art.

–To Jeny Lyn Ruelo and her team at The Fast Fingers, for the interior design and formatting, and always being willing to deal with my tech-challenged questions.

PROLOGUE

Hear my words, my people, and hearken to my warnings. For I have seen a vision of the future and it will surely come to pass.

The Age of the Great Alliance will end with such blood spilt that it will drench the mountainsides, gushing down in a river of despair, and flow from the battlefield into extinction. And it shall be that when all civil society collapses, so, too, will the standings of many races, but none will fall so low as the elves.

Many of our people will lie still forever on the battlefield, their bodies and dreams decomposing among the weeds, while those who live will become a pitiful people, a social underclass. Dignity will be lost, hope forgotten, and the Elf Code only a myth, spoken in the rambling of fools.

The Age of Man will be upon the land, its values forged by greed and power; enforced by iron and steel. And the humans will breed and spread, taking all they desire and leaving mere scraps for the other races to carve out a humble and demeaning existence.

So hearken to my word, proud elves, for you are the most ancient of peoples; the founders and custodians of the Great Alliance. Take your sons and daughters and head into the west, to the great forest of Markwin. Fortify its magical boundaries and close yourselves off from the madness that will erupt.

Preserve the Elf Code, learn and develop the magic of the earth. And wait. For though many Wycaan warriors will fall in defense of the Alliance, others will survive and pass on their teachings.

Wait and be patient, my people. For I have seen that one will come from the East–a Wycaan of our own ears, pointed and proud. But he will be young and unstable, all too ready to fall by the way. Teach him, then, our heritage and values. Train him to find the strength at his core and help him prepare for what must be done.

For it falls to him to reforge the Alliance, and he must not fail. For his failure will be the end of the elves, and the dwarves, and all the races, save man. Then nothing will stand between man and his greed, and the earth will destroy itself rather than be subjugated. Life as we know it will end. . . forever."

Wycaan Master Tansu
From the Book of Prophecies

Chapter One

H ad it been weeks? Months? Seanchai had no idea–nor did he care. If the sun had risen, it had not reached inside him, for the mourning elf was consumed with darkness.

Since he had buried Ilana, nothing mattered. He had left his heart with her on the mountainside where she had died in his arms. He cared little for the dwarves' victory at the battle of Hothengold, and had ignored the pleas of their king to remain and help them raise an army.

He silently packed his bags and left the dwarf capital while Hothengold slept. Using his Wycaan stealth training, he crept past the sentries and out through the tunnel. In the darkness, he stretched his cramped limbs, though he was numb to the pain. He turned to head north and jumped with surprise, almost colliding with Rhoddan.

Seanchai glared at his friend, even while knowing that loyal Rhoddan deserved better. But he didn't care, because to care involved feelings, and Seanchai was numb.

He saw Shayth, the human, and Sellia, the beautiful, dark-skinned elfe, sitting on a rock to his right, bags prepared next to them. He gave them the same glare, and then purposely tried to circle around Rhoddan on the narrow path.

"I go alone," Seanchai growled.

"Of course you do," Rhoddan chirped, "and we're going alone with you."

"I don't want your company," Seanchai mumbled.

"We know," Rhoddan responded, not budging.

"Maybe you didn't understand. . ."

"Oh, I think you've made your intentions pretty clear," the big elf replied. "Now, unless you want to stand here and futilely discuss—"

"LEAVE ME ALONE!" Seanchai screamed, loud enough that even the usually unshakable Rhoddan flinched.

Seanchai wiped spittle away from the corner of his mouth and felt momentarily ashamed. Then he unsheathed one of his Win Dao swords and drew a line in the dust.

"I'm not in control of myself," he hissed. "It's dangerous to be around me."

"We know," Rhoddan said again, his tone more guarded.

"But we're still coming." Shayth added, standing and combing a hand through his spiky, black hair.

"No," Seanchai said. "Anyone who crosses this line. . ." he raised his blade in front of him and, though it shook, it gleamed even in the hazy light of the dawn.

Rhoddan didn't hesitate. He stepped forward over the line, and the sword point touched his stomach. His expression was rock hard, his eyes locked on Seanchai's, who started shaking his head. Sellia moved gracefully to Seanchai's side.

"Let's reach an agreement," she said into his ear, her deep voice calming him. "You walk alone and camp alone. We won't bother you until it is time, but you'll let us track you."

Seanchai thought for a while. He began to nod, but stopped. "Until it is time?"

"You have set things in motion, Wycaan, that cannot be stopped. All Odessiya awaits your next move."

Before he could snap back at her, she put her hand on his shoulder, her long, thin fingers pressing gently. He needed all his willpower to stay his response.

Sellia continued. "You want space. You want to run, and you need to do this. Go. We'll follow behind. Go." She leaned forward and gently kissed his cheek, her voice breaking as she whispered, "This is how Ilana would have wanted it."

Seanchai turned and walked, soon breaking into a run. *Ilana. Ilana.* His breathing fell in with his stride and, as he exhaled, he cried her name. It felt good to run, good to say her name. He embraced the burning in his lungs, and his eyes filled with tears. He let them roll down his cheeks.

Ilana. Ilana. Ilana.

Sellia scooped rabbit stew into her bowl and sat on a rock. She blew on the steaming liquid and watched Rhoddan pacing as he looked outwards, halfheartedly guarding.

"Shayth?" he asked.

"Yeah, Rhoddan."

"How long are we going to let this go on? We've been following him for almost two moon cycles."

"I don't know," Shayth replied.

"How long did it take you to get over your parents' death?"

Shayth abruptly looked up from the stick he was whittling. Sellia could see the human's glare, ominous in the flickering firelight. His father, the Emperor's brother, had died suspiciously in an ambush. His mother had supposedly committed suicide shortly afterwards. Shayth blamed the Emperor for what he was convinced were two murders.

"I still haven't," Shayth growled. "You never get over that."

"Did killing Tarlach not help at all?" Rhoddan asked.

Shayth's whittling became harsher, and the stick snapped. Sellia realized that Rhoddan, with his back to them as he guarded, was unaware of the effect his questions had on his friend.

"It never gets any easier," she ventured. "Avenging the death of a loved one doesn't fill the void."

"It helps," Shayth murmured. "Killing Tarlach was exhilarating if you must know. But I have one more name left on my list."

"Even if you do kill the Emperor," Sellia said, "nothing can give you back what you lost."

"How would you know?" Shayth snapped.

Sellia never flinched. "I had a mate once. Dyrovas died in an ambush on an army convoy a week before we were to be bonded. I have never had anyone since. Do you think I've been short of suitors?"

Sellia was beautiful, tall and thin, but there was nothing frail about her build. Her bone structure was exquisitely defined. Everything about the elfe exuded speed, agility, and ruthlessness.

There was silence after this, broken only by the burning wood crackling. Sellia thought of her oath with Ilana, to help Seanchai overcome Ilana's death, and maybe in time to mate with him. *Ashbar.* She had sealed her oath with the binding word of the ancient language, but she was puzzled how it could ever come to pass when Seanchai was clearly so dedicated to Ilana.

"I'm sorry," Shayth broke her thoughts, his voice calmer. "I knew about your. . . your mate. I just. . . I'm sorry."

"That's okay," Sellia replied. "It's Seanchai we need to be concerned with right now."

"He needs time," Shayth said. "Perhaps he should have been the one to fight Tarlach. Ilana was his mate, and the general the one who killed her."

"No," Sellia replied. "That is not who Seanchai is."

Again, they fell into a despondent silence. Though Seanchai had been Ilana's mate, they had all been close to her and each deeply mourned her loss.

"But how much time?" Rhoddan persisted after a while. "The Emperor has just suffered a massive defeat–his first ever. He won't take this easily. He has huge resources at his disposal, and when he decides to strike, it will be devastating. He'll want to send a very clear message."

"Do you think Seanchai is capable of leading a resistance right now?" Shayth retorted. "Can he command the respect of his soldiers? He is liable to charge ten thousand of the Emperor's finest by himself and kill as many as he can while desiring only that they take him down."

Rhoddan turned to face his friends. His muscular arm clenched the pommel of his broadsword, even as it remained sheathed.

"Seanchai is my best friend. I was with him almost from the beginning of his journey, when he couldn't even hold a sword. I have stood with him in battle and would die for him without a moment of regret. Such have I sworn upon my sword. All this you know. But he needs to recognize that he has set powerful changes in motion that will impact the lives of all the races in Odessiya. He has a duty. . ."

Rhoddan stopped at the sound of footsteps approaching. Instantly, he drew his sword, while Shayth and Sellia slipped behind rocks, their bows already strung and taut. A young man ran into the camp, and the three immediately relaxed.

"Jermona," Shayth said, standing up and loosening his bow. "How nice of you to drop in."

Jermona stood for a moment to catch his breath. Sellia knew that the young ranger was exceptionally skilled at tracking and would have found them even if they had tried to conceal their tracks.

"Have some stew," she said, emptying the last drops of her bowl on the ground and refilling it for him.

Jermona thanked her and then turned to Shayth. He had always been in awe of the young prince. "Word came to Hothengold. The Emperor's army attacked the province of Ulster. The dwarves of Clan Dan Zu'Ulster have called for help." There was silence, and Jermona looked around. "What is it? Where's Seanchai?"

No one answered, and after a brief moment, Sellia stood up and sighed. Her eyes went to her friends. "You should both return to Hothengold and ride out with the dwarf army."

"What about Seanchai?" Jermona asked again. "Won't he lead us?"

"No," she replied. "But I will go to him." She put a hand on Rhoddan's arm. "Perhaps it is time after all."

Chapter Two

Deep breaths. In and out. Seanchai's stomach filled with the energy he drew up from the wiry trees around him and the ancient rocks at his back. He sighed loudly. This was the only time he felt a semblance of control–really, the only time he felt anything.

When he slept, he dreamed of her. Ilana was everywhere his imagination took him. And only there could he reach out and join her. But no matter where the dream took him–whether to the deserts in the south, the great forests, or underground with the dwarves–somewhere, Seanchai would lose her, his precious Ilana, and he would wake every time to the sound of his own sobbing.

During the day, he ran and ran. There seemed no other option. His sole goal was to exhaust himself so that he could sleep and be with his beloved. If he saw an especially beautiful tree, lake or mountain, he would imagine seeing it with her. And then he would turn in pain from the beauty and run. Running was the only way.

In the mornings and evenings, he practiced the standing exercises that replenished his store of energy out of a dim sense of responsibility. This was the break between the physical drive to exhaustion and the brief mental solace of his dreams.

And when he could tear himself away from thoughts of Ilana, he reflected on the many elves, humans, and dwarves who had died for him. No, he corrected himself. They had sacrificed their lives for their people, for freedom, for the land of Odessiya. Ilana had been his soul mate, his completion, but she had not been the only one who had touched him. Though his mind filled with her face, his nostrils with her scent, and his heart with her love, another voice called to him from the abyss of his grief.

His teacher, Mhari, the Wycaan master, who had died bringing down the walls of Galbrieth to allow Seanchai and his friends to escape, remained the lone voice of sanity in Seanchai's raging mind. Mhari, white-haired and resilient, whose sparkling, slanted eyes had garnered enough wisdom to see him through many trials; who could say just the right thing at the right time.

"Always return within," she had told Seanchai so many times. "Go back to your exercises to replenish lost energy and hope. Keep your body and mind clean and vibrant. When you begin to lose yourself, your exercises will be your anchor."

So Seanchai broke the monotony of dreaming and running with all that was left to keep him in touch with his inner warrior. It was a branch to grasp in the endless swirling rapids of pain and despair. It was hope, and no matter how desperate he felt, no matter how lost, Seanchai clung precariously to the branch and his sanity.

Deep breaths. In and out. The energy rose in his body. As he inhaled, he drew the vibrating warmth up through the soles of his feet, fresh from the earth, and, exhaling, sent it up into his stomach, arms, chest, and head. Only his heart seemed to resist. It remained closed, numb, hard as stone.

He sent a wave of warmth into his head, relaxing the muscles around his eyes and nose. Then a rich, earthy scent brought him out of his reverie, and his stomach rumbled involuntarily.

He quickly grounded the energy and stretched his cramped muscles, realizing when he saw the sun above the treetops that he had been standing for hours. It was the first time that he was aware of the passage of time, though he cared little for the revelation. But, his stomach reminded him again, it was time to eat.

He turned at the crackle of wood burning behind him and saw Sellia crouched over a pot, stirring whatever was emanating that seductive smell. Seanchai's stomach growled again.

Despite the promise of food, he did not move. He stared at the elfe, instead. She was tall and well-built, her body hardened from a life in the resistance. She was the only dark-skinned elf he had ever met. Her eyes were a beautiful, haunting brown, her ears finely pointed. He knew that her voice, smooth and deep, could calm, and her down-to-earth wisdom had kept the hot-headedness of Shayth and Rhoddan in check.

Seanchai had been aware of Sellia's beauty since she had first intimidated him when they had met in Uncle's camp. As the only two young elfes in the camp, she and Ilana were natural best friends. Sellia was an incredible archer and hunter, but had also proven herself ruthless in close combat when they had defeated General Tarlach's army at Hothengold.

Staring at the dark-skinned elfe in front of him, Seanchai felt the anger rise. She had promised they would leave him alone if he allowed them to track him. He glanced around, trying to sense if Rhoddan and Shayth were nearby. They weren't. Something had happened.

"Hungry?" she asked, looking up for the first time.

He approached and took the steaming bowl she offered. The soup was thick and dark. There were some roots in it and thin slivers of mushroom. He felt the warm liquid flow through his body and didn't refuse a second or third bowl.

They sat together in comfortable silence. When he saw her rub her arms, Seanchai added some more wood to the fire and stared into the flames. He found he appreciated having her with him and, oddly, his silence made him feel guilty. He looked up. Sellia was watching him as she sat on a log across from the fire.

"Thank you for the soup," he said.

"You're welcome. What's our next move?"

"Our? You think one bowl of soup makes me yours?"

Sellia smiled. "I counted three bowls. Rhoddan and Shayth have returned to Hothengold. The province of Ulster has been attacked. The king requests your presence."

No reply.

"Seanchai," Sellia's voice was mellow and rhythmic. "You need to take action."

"Why?" He snorted and immediately regretted it. "I'm sorry. You can go back and report that I'm not much in the way of company."

"I'm not going back alone," she replied. "Either I stay with you out here, or we go together to Hothengold."

Seanchai was on her in a flash, knocking her from the log to the ground. He had the dirk he kept in his boot at her throat, which he had exposed by yanking back her long, curly hair. She was breathing heavily, but made no attempt to stop him.

The elf could feel his eyes bulging and summoned all his strength to pull the knife away. He rose and offered her a hand. As he pulled her up, he took her tightly in his arms. He was shaking.

"I don't want to harm you," he whispered in her ear. "It's good that Rhoddan and Shayth have gone back. You must leave, too."

Sellia pulled him closer. Her voice quavered. "Not without you. I can't."

"You must. I might kill you."

"Either way, then, my destiny is to die."

He pulled away from her and stared.

Sellia took a deep breath. "I gave my word to Ilana. I swore in the ancient language. Ashbar."

She slowly pulled out the green stone that hung around her neck. Ilana had insisted she take it. It was half a dwarf-stone. Seanchai had the other half, and the old dwarf priestess had told Seanchai and Ilana it would help them find each other even over great distance.

"You cannot fulfill your destiny alone, Seanchai. Ilana knew that, and she knew that I care strongly enough for you that it would not be a burden."

He took a step back and shook his head, still staring at the stone. "I-I release you from your oath, Sellia."

The elfe's laugh was throaty. "You have many talents, my Wycaan warrior, but that's not one."

"When did she give you the stone?" he asked, his voice shaking.

"Before the battle for Hothengold," Sellia replied. "She knew then. I don't know how—"

"The old priestess foresaw it. Ilana made me swear to continue to struggle to free Odessiya and even to open myself to finding a mate if something happened to her." He pulled out his own green stone and brought the two halves together. They connected perfectly. The sobs erupted, so violent that a flock of birds launched themselves from a nearby tree. Seanchai fell into Sellia's arms and stayed there until his crying subsided. When he finally drew back, he saw the rivulets Sellia's own tears had carved in her cheeks.

"You mourn her, too," he whispered, realizing for the first time that Ilana's death hadn't affected only him.

"We all do," she replied, "everyone who knew her."

Seanchai turned and crouched by his bags. He withdrew a thin, metallic shirt and fingered it. Then he looked up at Sellia. "I will return to Hothengold, but won't go with them to Ulster. I must return this Kings Mail to Thorminsk's family."

"But it was given to you freely," Sellia replied. "Kings Mail is almost impervious to a blade or arrow. Quite handy, given your propensity for combat."

"Yes, but it's extremely valuable, and Thorminsk's children are without a father. He died for me and this was meant to be his son Orenminsk's inheritance. Orenminsk won't ever know his father, but I will ensure he knows his father's handicraft."

Sellia decided not to pursue it. "What then?" she asked. "Will you go to the elves and finish your training in the west? Wasn't that what Mhari counseled you to do before you came to rescue us in Galbrieth?"

"I can't," Seanchai replied. "They won't accept me, not like this. There's no point."

"Won't accept you?"

Seanchai sighed. "If they even exist, and if they even still practice the powers of old, the Elves of the West will not blindly accept me because my hair is Wycaan white. They'll see my instability and refuse me."

"Even if that means the downfall of Odessiya?"

"Have they shown any concern for our people up 'til now?"

Sellia was quiet for a while. She took a stick and played with it in the fire. "Then what?" she asked.

Seanchai took a deep breath. "I will go to Ilana's father. I must apologize to Uncle."

CHAPTER THREE

As Seanchai and Sellia entered Hothengold, the giant cavern buzzed with activity. Where houses had stood before the Emperor's army had razed them to the ground were now tents. Having lived out in the wild by himself for months, the sounds of an army preparing to move seemed deafening to Seanchai.

He walked slowly past the encampment without acknowledging anyone, even Shayth and Rhoddan. In his peripheral vision, he saw dwarf soldiers steal furtive glances at his long, flowing white hair and massive build.

He and Sellia passed through the stone gates of the exterior wall, and then the second and third gates. Each time, Seanchai felt his lungs constrict even more. This was where Ilana had made her last stand, leading the dwarf army and hoping to hold out long enough for Seanchai and his troops to return. He had not returned quickly enough. He had failed her.

He climbed the steep, narrow streets, struggling not to stop as he passed the hall where Ilana had been held prisoner and fatally poisoned by General Tarlach. He clenched his jaw and resisted the desire to demolish the building with his bare hands. He could have done it and flexed his hands as he felt the power rise within him. But deep inside he knew it was a power borne of rage, and that could become the first step on a long, dark path.

He entered the hall of council and approached the guards standing outside the king's chambers.

"I desire an audience with the High King of Hothengold," he said tonelessly, his eyes locked forward.

Seanchai didn't move a muscle as one guard disappeared inside and returned minutes later. "Please enter and take a seat," the guard said stiffly.

They obliged, and Seanchai stood before an empty dais. Sellia took a pitcher of water and filled two glasses. She sipped from one and brought the other to the Wycaan, who took it without a word.

A dozen dwarf soldiers entered and flanked either side of the throne. The King entered, his crown on his head and golden axe in hand. He walked slowly and settled on his throne. Seanchai stared at the guards' unsheathed axes.

"I must take the necessary precautions," King Hothen said unapologetically. "But know we are deeply in your debt, Wycaan, and consider ourselves as friends."

Seanchai nodded. "You are wise to take such steps, Your Majesty."

There followed a silence in which King Hothen seemed to want Seanchai to speak. When he didn't, the King cleared his throat. "I would ask after your welfare, but you wear your grief plainly, and I suspect words could not do it justice.

"I will not lead your army to the Ulster province," Seanchai said flatly.

"Are you capable of controlling your emotions and leading troops into battle?" the young king asked, concern clear in his tone. Seanchai stared at him mutely, and King Hothen nodded, his crown shaking slightly. "Then I reluctantly release you of your duty." When Seanchai frowned, confused, he continued.

"As a member of Clan Den Zu'Reising, you swore fealty to me as king. But Ballendir will lead our army, and I am glad that Shayth and Rhoddan will ride at his side.

"However, I will not pretend that I am unconcerned for your state of being–or what it means for ours. There is a path before you, and, while we can hold out for a while, we will need you to lead us in the end."

"And what if I can't?" Seanchai's voice was sharp, and the soldiers bristled. This was their monarch he was addressing.

But King Hothen only smiled. "Then we will all die gloriously, and you will live the rest of your life with the guilt."

Seanchai glared at him, but the King met his stare without flinching. "Why did you return, Wycaan, if not to lead our troops?"

Seanchai nodded, took the King's Mail from his bag, and stepped forward. Immediately, four soldiers closed in front of him, denying him access to the king.

For a fleeting moment, Seanchai considered drawing his blades and slaying them, but Sellia's hand was already on his shoulder and he stilled his anger. He handed the mail to the nearest soldier.

"What is this?" King Hothen asked.

"This is the King's Mail given to me by Thorminsk of Clan Dan Zu'Ulster. It was his, and he refitted it for me to wear in battle. Thorminsk died fighting the pictorians, a small, talented artisan against eight-foot killing machines. I saw him fall to their First Boar, Umnesilk. As Thorminsk drew his final breaths, I promised to make sure his son would learn of his father's skills. The King's Mail should return to Ulster so that Thorminsk's family may have the resources denied by his sacrifice."

The King took the chain mail and examined it closely. "This is indeed fine work. Thorminsk's death is a loss to our entire nation." He handed the mail to the soldier and signaled with his head that it should be returned to Seanchai. "This gift was given to you freely so that you might serve a higher purpose than Thorminsk could ever have hoped to achieve, even with his considerable talents. I am sure the sight of you wearing it helped him pass smoothly to the halls of our ancestors.

"I will not dishonor him by taking it back. You will wear it and fulfill your destiny so that Thorminsk's family can live in freedom. I will ensure that his family receives a tribute from my treasury to ease their financial burdens."

"But—"

"But nothing," he replied. "I am your king, and I have spoken."

Seanchai bristled and, again, Sellia squeezed his shoulder. He nodded, and then bowed his head. "Then, with your majesty's permission, I will take my leave."

"Go rest," the King said. "I do not want you to leave in front of my troops as they prepare for battle. Tonight you will set forth under cover of darkness. I will order four horses and adequate supplies prepared."

"*Four* horses?" Seanchai knew the dwarves did not have vast numbers of horses at their disposal.

"You will travel as hard as you physically can. Alternate the horses and keep them fresh. Do what you must and complete your training. But remember, the longer you take, the more innocent people like Thorminsk will perish.

"You carry a heavy heart, Seanchai Elf Warrior. But you also carry the hopes of all who live in servitude. Wherever your destiny takes you, it takes us all. Go find yourself and return to us as the Wycaan Master that all Odessiya cries out for."

CHAPTER FOUR

P hineus, the Crown Prince, heir to the Empire of Odessiya, retreated under a storm of vicious blows. He parried with his sword and shield as he took one step back and then another. The flash of the broadsword as it whistled through the air in another deadly arc brought the prince to one knee, and a wave of panic stirred and immediately dissipated in his stomach.

The next blow splintered his shield, so he threw it at his adversary and rolled away. As he sprung to his feet, Phineus heard the Sword Master's whistle to stop, but his opponent came on, oblivious to the order.

Phineus crouched, his breathing heavy and his sword before him. As his adversary whirled his sword for another attack, a huge man crashed into the soldier, sending him sprawling to the ground.

The prince watched as the soldier rolled fluidly back on his feet, but this time a sword tip at his throat stopped him advancing. The soldier stood, panting, then ripped his helmet off and flung it to the ground. It rolled to Phineus who stopped it with his boot.

The Sword Master lowered his sword and slapped the soldier across the face. "Are you mad, Ahad? Do you think killing the Crown Prince will avenge your father? Would the great General Tarlach have approved of such behavior? When you are in my academy, I don't care if you are the Emperor's favorite, or the Crown Prince's best friend. I don't care if you spar the Crown Prince or a common soldier. You will obey my orders. Is that clear?"

Still panting heavily, Ahad nodded and slid his sword into its sheath.

"I didn't hear you, soldier," the Sword Master bellowed.

The young man just stood there, his chest heaving, a dark scowl marring his face. The Sword Master slapped him again, and Ahad's face whipped to the side. Phineus made to intervene, but the Sword Master flashed a hand at him.

"I am the Emperor's Sword Master, entrusted to train his finest. I will have order in my academy. I will have discipline. When I tell a soldier to stop, he stops. When I tell him to jump, he jumps. You will obey my orders. Is that clear?"

Ahad turned his dark eyes to the burly, gray-haired man.

"Yes sir," he said, his voice flat and devoid of emotion. "You are correct. I apologize."

Phineus watched the veteran officer's shoulders relax. Now his raised hand went to the boy's shoulder.

"Ahad," the Sword Master's voice was softer now, "your father, General Tarlach, was a great man, the finest soldier I ever trained. Perhaps he was the greatest fighter that passed through my tutelage, but that was not what made him the Emperor's most trusted officer. Your father possessed a brilliant mind. He could out-think his enemy, whether it was one man or a whole nation. He brought the Galbrieth province to heel—not with bloodshed, but with strategy. He brought enemies to the court and turned them into allies.

"I see your skill with the sword. It's impressive. You may yet surpass your father's ability. The gods alone know that with your continual growth spurts, you will certainly surpass even his stature.

"The Emperor has shown his faith in you. He has allowed you to train nonstop with the finest teachers. He has allowed you to study with the assassins and, most of all, he has trusted you to spar with his only son, the Crown Prince of Odessiya.

"But if he were to ask me today, I would have to tell him that you are not fit to serve. Even the greatest warrior must have calmness and perspective inside of him. He must have self-control at all times. Your mourning for your father, your hate for the scum that cut him down. . ."

"Shayth," Ahad hissed, and even the Sword Master was momentarily stopped by his virulence.

". . . and your very desire to kill Shayth is preventing you from advancing toward that goal. The Crown Prince here is your equal with the sword, yet he defends and retreats so that you can vent your rage. But he could finish you off because, in your rage, you expose yourself.

"Perhaps that is how Shayth defeated your father, by preying on whatever loyalty and emotions the venerable general still held for Prince Shindell."

"I've heard all this," Ahad snapped.

"You have heard it, but you have not accepted it. You want the Emperor to let you ride out and find Shayth and the elf, but you will only be allowed to go when you are ready."

"I *am* ready," Ahad jerked his head, and his hand moved to his scabbard.

"You are not. Hear the words of an old, experienced warrior. I tell you that you are not. You have the skills that I have taught you, and, in another month, you will conclude your training with the assassins. Then you will need to prove that you are ready here." The Sword Master tapped Ahad's head. "You still have plenty of work to do. You are dismissed."

Phineus noticed that, though the Sword Master had dismissed Ahad, it was the old man who turned and walked away. As Ahad stormed off in the other direction, Phineus sighed. He knew that the Sword Master was correct.

He had met Ahad a year ago. General Tarlach's son was a scholar then, an academic, and possessed only a passing interest in combat. The Crown Price was the opposite: a fine soldier at the age of fourteen, but a terrible student. When General Tarlach had gone in pursuit of Shayth and the elf, and Ahad's mother had left the capital to tend to her ailing mother in some remote province, the Emperor had brought Ahad into the palace to study with and tutor his son.

Phineus had initially resented his new babysitter, but Ahad had been creative in helping the prince find new ways to learn that worked for him. In return, Phineus had arranged for Ahad to study under the finest trainers in weapons, horsemanship, and strategy. Now they were nearly inseparable as they studied and trained together, and the Crown Prince conceded that Ahad had grown into a formidable soldier.

He knew how much his father had enjoyed the trust and loyalty of his finest general, and Phineus wanted to bind Ahad to him in a similar way. Surely Ahad would possess the strategic mind of his father. He would be a powerful asset when the Crown Prince took the throne.

Phineus headed toward the showers. He knew where to find Ahad, but he also knew that his friend needed to calm down. A hand on his shoulder pulled him short of his next step. He didn't turn around. He could smell the pipe weed that caught in the Sword Master's bushy moustache.

"I can teach him many things, my prince, but what he needs most right now, only you can give him."

Chapter Five

"It's me, Phineus," the Crown Prince said softly as he neared the huge tomb in the cemetery.

Ahad stared down at his friend from atop the stone cube where he was perched. The Crown Prince hated his name and rarely used it. He was making a conciliatory statement, and Ahad knew he should appreciate it. His legs dangled over the side of the oversized tomb as he stared down on the plot where his father was buried, the earth still free of weeds, still fresh.

There was no tombstone yet. Traditionally, the grave remained unmarked for a year. But there was a mass of flowers and ornaments, constant reminders that the great General Tarlach had many friends and admirers. At first, Ahad had come and read the notes left behind by fellow officers, soldiers who had served under his command, and commoners who felt they owed him their lives.

In the streets, people had approached him to offer condolences and tributes to his father's generous deeds. It irked Ahad, as much as he hated to admit it, because these people seemed to know his father better than he did. He soon began to walk the streets with a hood on, his head hidden deep within his cowl, and he stopped reading the letters left on his father's tomb.

"My father is worried you might try to leave on your own." Phineus said. "I would counsel you against this. Even when you finish your training with the assassins, you should wait for his orders."

Ahad did not reply. The Crown Prince jumped nimbly up onto the tomb and sat beside his friend. He waited a while, but the silence irked him.

"You have not visited your grandfather of late. He is recovering well and has the finest physicians. But he misses you. He has lost his son. You should not deny him his only grandson while you are still in the capital."

No reply.

"Ahad, I'm talking to you . . . as your friend."

"I know," Ahad whispered. "I appreciate your patience, and the Emperor's. It was a nice gesture to bring my grandfather into the palace."

"Then you should thank him for it yourself," Phineus replied. "He will return in a week or so, and you should seek out an audience with him."

Ahad nodded, but did not respond. Then, as he digested what the Crown Prince had said, he stopped dangling his legs.

"I didn't know the Emperor was abroad."

"He doesn't advertise it. In fact, he has doubles wandering around the palace and replacing him in ceremonies so that no one knows. He fears his enemies might try to take advantage of his absence."

"Where does he go?"

"Not sure. But before he leaves, he is grumpy and short-tempered. When he returns, he is more relaxed and has more energy. He even looks younger. It's kind of cool."

Ahad stared at his friend. He wondered how well Phineus knew his own father. The Emperor had revealed to Ahad that he was a Wycaan himself and that only he could now defeat the elf who rode with Shayth. He had ordered Ahad never to reveal this secret, so Ahad couldn't even ask Phineus if he knew.

The Emperor had given him permission to kill Shayth, the Emperor's nephew and sent him to study with the Emperor's assassins. His training was almost over and Ahad pondered whether he would be allowed to leave and track his father's murderer. But his thoughts went to his grandfather.

"I have not been to see my grandfather because I am ashamed that his son is dead and I stay in the palace doing nothing," he conceded to the Crown Prince.

"There is another reason, is there not?"

"Yes," Ahad sighed. "I fear that when I leave, he'll give up the will to live."

"Then," the Crown Prince said enthusiastically, "you should go and seek his permission to leave, and then ask my father to let you go. I think you will show respect by asking."

"Why should I try to please your father?" Ahad snapped, and then felt chagrined by his outburst.

"Well, to begin with, he's your Emperor," Phineus replied patiently. "But there's another reason. You're about to make him very angry."

"How is that?" Ahad smiled despite his mood. The Crown Prince knew how to make him laugh.

"By taking me along with you."

Ahad turned to his friend and laughed. "Is this a joke? Okay, you made me laugh. I credit you. Right now, that is no easy feat."

But Phineus' face was serious. "Do you think I would let my best friend march alone into battle against a violent psychopath and an elf with strange, formidable powers?

"Your father was part of a secret, tight-knit group led by my uncle. My father knew of this group and was both threatened and impressed by it."

"He *knew*?" Ahad was shocked, but quickly recovered. "How interesting. Why, then, did he allow it?"

"Ironically, the group never threatened my father as long as he took care of them. Once they lost their leader, they had no motivation to rebel or challenge their emperor. They were all his best officers, so he promoted them and won their loyalty."

"He's. . ." Ahad searched for the word to reflect his emotions. "He's very impressive."

"Yes," Phineus agreed. "He's always several moves ahead of everyone else. I think sometimes that he possesses special powers." He laughed. "When I was a boy, I would beg him to tell me his secrets. He always promised he would, but he never did, and I stopped asking as I grew older."

"You cannot come with me," Ahad said, returning to their bone of contention. "You are the crown prince and must be groomed, ready to take over one day."

"Am I a horse to be groomed?" Phineus laughed. "My uncle learned that you bind people to you through good leadership and bravery in the field. That is why he was so often abroad and in the thick of military campaigns. I plan to be out there, too, with a small band of our best soldiers and future generals. And you, my friend, will be first among them."

"I appreciate your strategy," Ahad replied, "but you won't slip that past your father."

"I actually don't plan to ask," the Crown Prince replied.

"But what if he confronts you? You cannot lie to him. None of us can."

"I will tell him that I, too, want to kill Shayth and the elf. He killed the man who was a close friend of my father, an honored general of the Emperor's army and, most importantly, the father of my best friend."

Ahad put his hand on his friend's shoulder. He knew he was not supposed to touch royalty, but he did it anyway. "I shouldn't be encouraging you, but thank you," he said, and actually smiled.

Chapter Six

Sellia missed Rhoddan and Shayth. They had not been together for long, but during such intense times they had bonded, and she found them to be good company. Rhoddan was funny when he was not trying so hard to be a great warrior. Shayth was more enigmatic, and this made him intriguing. The time they spent together, when not killing or fleeing soldiers or pictorians, had been comfortable.

For now, she stared across the smoldering fire pit at Seanchai. He was standing, his eyes closed and his arms in front of him as though hugging a tree. She had hugged him a lot, herself, in these past weeks. She would wake to his quiet sobbing and go to him. Now she slept next to him and when he reached for her, she pulled him close. There was nothing sexual, nothing romantic. Seanchai's grief was all-consuming.

During the day they rode without conversation. When he spoke to her, it was to ask the way or inquire after her needs. But otherwise, the steady trotting of their horses was the only sound they made.

Sellia rose and picked up her bow. Her only enjoyment and escape was hunting. She was good at it; her aim was deadly, her stealth impressive, and she much preferred it to killing humans and pictorians.

Sellia walked for about ten minutes before she heard running water and made a mental note to replenish their water skins before leaving. She saw that the narrow stream widened as it rounded a bend, and there was a patch of earth free of bushes and trees.

She gasped at the beautiful stag sipping at the water's edge. His long tongue elegantly rolled water into its mouth. He stopped regularly and looked around, ears flicking, on constant alert. There was no wind; he could not possibly smell her.

The stag kept up its watchful state and several times seemed to look past Sellia toward their camp. Perhaps he had seen or smelled them earlier. She quietly removed her bow and nocked an arrow. The stag looked up again and turned its head. A doe exited the brush and joined him. She was beautiful, a light brown color with white spots. She came to the water and drank while he looked around. When she raised her head, the stag nuzzled her face, and the doe leaned in.

Sellia lowered her bow and watched. She caught herself recalling how she often slept these days with her head on Seanchai's chest, and how in his sleep, she was sure, he bent his head to encompass the crown of hers. . . like the stag was doing to his doe.

Sellia was joined with the elf; she had sworn to be so, and believed she could love him, but still, she was lonely. She was in Seanchai's presence, but found no entrance into his mind or heart.

The stag and doe jerked their heads in her direction in unison and fled. She stood, stretching her cramped muscles. Had they discovered her or... The realization hit her, and, as she swung around, a fist sent her sprawling.

When she came to, a man was on top of her, holding her hands above her head. A second human, also male, held her bow and knives.

"A pretty one we 'ave 'ere, eh 'ubert?" said the one straddling her.

He reached down to touch her cheek, and she bared her teeth.

"Oooh, she 'as spirit, too," he laughed through crooked, yellowing teeth. "'er ears are pointed. Look, 'ubert, a dark-skinned she-elf. Ain't never seen one o' them."

"Elfe," Sellia snapped. The term she-elf was derogatory, and her reaction automatic.

"Shut up," the man said and squeezed her mouth with a big, greasy hand. The other trapped her hands. "You'll use that mouth fer kissin', sweet'eart, nothin' else."

He bent forward, lips puckered, and Sellia jerked her head to the side. This made the man laugh. His friend leaned forward. "Maybe she jist fancies me, Kullan. You c'n unnerstan' why."

Both men laughed and leered at her, and then Hubert put his knife over her throat. She could feel the coldness of the blade against her skin, and he leaned forward.

"Not a word, she-elf," he warned. "We can be nice t' ya if yer nice t' us."

He turned the blade and cut the string at the top of her shirt. He put his knife between his yellow teeth and slid his hand inside. Sellia gasped and felt rage rising. She was panting now, trying to control both her fear and anger.

The man stopped, leaving his hand where her chest began to swell. "Kullan? What if she ain't alone? Don't think a beauty like this, even wiv a bow 'n blade, would be out by 'erself."

"You should have thought of that before," said an icy voice behind them, and the crisp rasp of swords leaving their scabbards sliced through the air.

Sellia felt the man on top of her shift his weight. Pressing her feet into the ground, she bucked and he fell off. She rolled away from him, but neither man gave her much thought now that they faced a huge, white-haired elf holding two thin, curved swords.

"All a mistake," said Kullan, apparently deciding that their tag team wouldn't have quite the same power over Seanchai as over Sellia.

"Won't do that again," said his friend, backing away.

"No," Seanchai growled. "You won't."

Kullan had backed into Sellia, who grabbed a dagger from his belt, jerked his chin up, and cut his throat, all in one smooth and swift movement. Blood sprayed in a fan as he swayed before toppling over. Hubert held his sword in front of him, jerking it from side to side, facing first Seanchai and then Sellia. He feared them both now, and the tip of his sword shook as he glanced down at the blood still trickling from his crumpled partner's throat.

"All a mistake," he said backing up. "Big misunderstanding."

He turned and fled. Sellia retrieved her bow and swung her quiver over her back. "I need to hunt," she said coldly and disappeared after the fleeing man.

When Sellia returned to their camp, Seanchai had packed everything up and strapped their bags to the two horses that today would not bear the elves. She walked over to one of the horses and began checking the knots.

Seanchai moved behind her and gently turned her around. He pulled her against him and held her tightly. Suppressed emotions welled up, and she burst out crying. Her whole body shook, and she pulled him tightly to her.

"I'm sorry I wasn't there for you," he said quietly into her hair.

"You're never there for me," she snapped back between breaths, and they were both surprised at her vehemence.

Seanchai, after a moment of hesitation, pulled her tighter.

"How long until we reach Uncle's camp?" he asked.

She pulled away from him, shocked that he had ignored her revelation. "Two days," she snapped.

He reached out, gently cupped her face in his hands, and looked with great intensity into her eyes. "I must face Uncle and beg his forgiveness. It will be one hundred days before we leave his camp, the end of my mourning. Then," his voice quivered, "I will be there for you. I'll try and give you what you deserve. However, you may choose to stay with Uncle and reclaim your place with his group."

"I took the oath to Ilana," she reminded him in a whisper. "I swore in the ancient language."

Seanchai's eyes welled with tears.

"We will never forget her," Sellia said. "I promise."

Chapter Seven

S eanchai lay awake. They had entered the forest where Uncle's camp was. Sellia knew every tree. She had lived here for most of her life as one of Uncle's resistance fighters. But Seanchai had stayed for only a few days, and when he left, he took Ilana, Uncle's only daughter, with him.

Now he was returning to break the news that the great man, who had already lost his wife, had also lost his daughter. Seanchai would rather fight a hundred enraged pictorians than give Uncle this news.

He could have saved her. Tarlach had poisoned Ilana, but he had an antidote. The price he demanded was Seanchai's surrender to the Emperor. Mhari, Seanchai's teacher, had warned him that the ruler of Odessiya was more powerful than him. How could anyone be more powerful than a Wycaan?

He would have gone, though. To save Ilana's life, he would have freely sacrificed his own. But she had made him swear. *Ashbar.* He had given his word in the unbreakable ancient language.

Sellia stirred in his arms. It was cold, and her body sought only warmth. He leaned in and smelled her hair. Though they traveled, the rich, musty scent he had come to associate with her still emanated from her hair and skin.

Sellia had also sworn a binding oath to Ilana. She had sworn to stay with Seanchai, to be his companion and his consort. He wondered how she felt about that. For now it didn't matter, because they both mourned Ilana and anything else seemed a million leagues away. But what had she said? *You are never there for me.*

She stirred and mumbled something indistinguishable, and he drew her tighter to him.

Uncle, he thought. He would get no sleep tonight.

Seanchai knew they would be seen long before they reached Uncle's camp. The rebel leader was vastly experienced and would have sentries posted in every direction. Seanchai wondered what he should say and sighed deeply. His lungs filled with the smell of the forest, of leaf and moss, and his mind suddenly took him back to his home village.

Seanchai was ashamed that he rarely thought of those who had shielded him all his childhood and sent him into the night to escape the grips of the army. He had been told it was so he could escape conscription, but it occurred to him that they had known. They had known and paid for it with their–

He felt rather than heard the sudden presence. He reached out with his mind, scrying to distinguish friend or foe. If soldiers or rangers were tracking him, then he could not lead them to Uncle's base.

He pulled his horse up and told Sellia in an unnecessarily loud voice that he needed a moment of privacy. He dismounted and gave her both horses. As she took the reins, their eyes met. Seanchai knew that she understood. As he turned to disappear into the brush, he saw her carefully loosen her blades.

Seanchai skirted the area and came up behind where he had sensed the man. But there was no one there. He began to scry again, but when he heard Sellia laugh, he relaxed and returned to her.

"Seanchai," she called as he exited the bushes, "do you remember Chamack?"

"Well met, Wycaan," a tall, dark-haired elf said, extending his arms in the universal sign for peace. "You rescued me, Sellia and Luvial from the wolfheids."

"Well met, Chamack," Seanchai replied, his voice steady. "Did we not also fight together outside the walls of Galbrieth?"

"Indeed, my frien. . ." Chamack stared at his face. "Life has been hard on you." This was not posed as a question.

"Where is Uncle?"

"I don't recall you being a particularly chatty elf. Come, we are near."

Their small entourage grew to six as they entered the clearing of Uncle's camp. Chamack offered to take the horses when they dismounted.

"Where is Uncle?" Seanchai asked a gray-haired elfe.

"Go to the fire pit and eat," the elfe replied, her voice high, "I will call him."

They had hardly sat when an unusually large elf approached with two plates of food. "Aah, Sellia, my beauty," he said. "You never could be bothered to eat at meal times."

"Is this fresh, Dvural?" she responded. "Or leftovers from last time I was here?"

"If it was still from back then, it would have sprouted legs and walked to you unaided," came the retort.

They both laughed and hugged awkwardly, careful not to spill the food. Sellia took a plate, but Seanchai shook his head. When Dvural tried to insist, the Wycaan rose and walked away.

"You were too honest with him about my cooking, I fear," Dvural said, but this time his laughter was muted.

Seanchai had his back to them, but was sure an unspoken conversation was taking place behind him. He walked further away from them, but turned as he heard Uncle's gruff voice to his left.

"You come alone?" The huge elf demanded, thick, hairy arms protruding from the short sleeves of a green shirt.

"N-no Uncle," Seanchai replied. "Sellia is with me."

There was silence as Uncle stared into Seanchai's eyes. He sighed deeply, and then said almost in a whisper: "Walk with me."

Uncle turned around and strode off. Seanchai followed, but since the big man made no attempt to wait for him, he kept his distance. They climbed a steady slope for a long time. Uncle's pace never faltered, but rather quickened. They broke from the forest, and Seanchai saw Uncle now running up to a peak. When Seanchai met him at the summit, he heard a sound that tore his heart. Uncle was sobbing. This bull of an elf, this brave and fierce leader, was absolutely crushed.

Seanchai sat down about twenty hands from him and gave Uncle his space. He peered across the vista where the plains unfolded from the base of the mountain. He could see the outskirts of Morthian Wood, his home. His realized his village was but a few days at a fast pace.

It would be easy to stand up, run down the mountain, and keep running until he was home and safe. Safe? He snorted to himself. He would not be safe ever again. Was his village even standing, or had the Emperor razed it to the ground as a punishment? Perhaps his parents were still alive. Perhaps they sat at night by the fire, wondering if their son had somehow survived.

Even if they were alive, Seanchai thought, the village was no longer his home. The only homes he had known as a Wycaan were with Mhari, and in the arms of his beloved Ilana. As Ilana's face filled his mind, he buried his face in his arms and wept silently.

"Seanchai."

The elf started as he raised his head and peered into Uncle's red eyes. Seanchai had not heard him approach. They stared at each other, and then Uncle spoke.

"Tell me everything. Tell me how it was between you. Leave nothing out, even how she died."

CHAPTER EIGHT

A had had to wait through a very long week. He had gone to see the Emperor's clerk, who promised to pass on the request for an audience. From the Crown Prince, he learned that the Emperor was still abroad, and so he refocused on his studies and the impending assassin's exams.

His training with Lord Hervarty had been intense. He understood the Assassins Master had objected to training him because he deemed Ahad mentally unsuitable. The Emperor had instructed Lord Hervarty to not only allow Ahad into the assassin's academy, but to personally train him and condense his training into one year.

Phineus had told Ahad that Lord Hervarty was furious. He had never been ordered to take a student, much less to compound that student's studies into a third of the normal time.

"You have never taught a student so smart, so talented, and so bent on succeeding," the Emperor had apparently replied.

The Assassins Master had piled on the studies, always pushing the boy, testing him, and very early on, had sent him on simple but increasingly deadly missions.

The other students kept away from Ahad. He was favored, had come from the palace, and, most of all, was a scarily brilliant student. Many of those who were already two years ahead of him watched as Ahad devoured their lessons, mastered their exercises, and then came back demanding more.

He had learned many weapons, including the miniature crossbow and how to fit a variety of poisons to the tips. He learned to use different throwing knives and discs. He excelled in stealth and strategy to such an extent that even his teacher was stretched to outthink him.

And so it was that Ahad found himself summoned to an audience with the Emperor just a week before his graduation. He bathed and wore his freshly washed assassin's apprentice clothes–brown cloak, shirt, trousers, and boots. When he graduated, he would wear black, the color of a master.

He waited for the Emperor in the antechamber, recalling how he had sat here not so long ago, squirming with fear. Now he was calm, even if apprehensive. This time his father was dead and he was a resident of the royal palace. Ahad could not wait to be dismissed–to leave and kill those responsible for killing his father. He was ready.

As the Emperor held his audiences from behind a veil, Ahad was aware that the Emperor was present, but had no way to distinguish how the Emperor looked. He had seen his ruler only once, when the Emperor had revealed his Wycaan heritage.

The Emperor's clerk came into the antechamber and bowed formally. "Are you well, Master Ahad?"

"Yes, thank you."

"I hear good news about your training. You follow in the footsteps of your father. He would have been proud of you."

Ahad did not answer. As often happened, he felt a well of anger and noticed the clerk smile. This had all been planned, a warning perhaps. A bell rang.

"Come. The Emperor of Odessiya awaits."

Ahad walked into the room and bowed in front of the veil. He could see silhouettes of figures scurrying about. A wave of a hand from the throne emptied the room. When the last servant had left, the Emperor spoke.

"Open the veil, Ahad. You may look upon me."

As he pulled the heavy material back, Ahad gasped. The Emperor's skin was smooth and his hair a shiny white. He looked twenty years younger and seemed to be glowing with health. He was also smiling.

"What can you tell me of my son's studies? Come sit here and report." The Emperor signaled to a stool considerably lower than the throne.

"My lord, what does he tell you?"

"Aah. We are both equally curious. He is happy in your company. But I need to know whether he is mastering the basic knowledge that the ruler of Odessiya requires to hold court and make sound decisions."

"He would probably not excel in academic tests in the traditional sense. But he is smart, my lord, and he understands his destiny."

"How, then, should we test him? How do I know what you say is right?"

Ahad thought for a moment, unsure how his answer would be received. He took a deep breath.

"My lord. You should engage him in conversation and maybe involve him in ruling."

The ruler of Odessiya stared at Ahad, contemplating deeply.

"You know what you are saying?" he said after a few moments.

"I do, my lord. Am I so remiss?"

"Not as long as you remember your position. But I wonder: whose best interests do you serve?"

Now it was Ahad's turn to ponder. "Can I not serve both of you?"

"As long as it remains in the interests of our empire. Do you serve us both in the same way?"

"No, my lord. I serve you out of duty and privilege."

"And my son?"

Ahad didn't answer.

"And my son?" the Emperor repeated more emphatically.

Ahad looked up. "Out of loyalty and friendship, my lord."

"I applaud your honesty, though I question your strategy."

"I am sworn to tell you the truth, my lord, and in that alone lies my strategy."

The Emperor smiled. "And what is your strategy regarding my son after you graduate?"

"My lord?"

"I know about my brother and his little group that included your father. I believe my son might think to follow in his footsteps."

Ahad tried to conceal his surprise. "Would it not be strategic for him to bind the best of his generation to him?"

"A bit young, wouldn't you say?"

Ahad's voice went icy. "And the elf, my lord? And Shayth?"

The Emperor nodded and sighed. "Would you, in my place, send the Crown Prince of Odessiya to take up arms against a Wycaan or Shayth?"

"I would not, my lord. You told me that only you can defeat the Wycaan, and you know I live only to kill your nephew. Shayth murdered my father. He will die by my hand."

Chapter Nine

"**M**ove back and draw the veil between us," the Emperor said.

When Ahad was again seated, the Emperor rang a bell. An attendant brought a ceramic pot of steaming tea. The Emperor ordered a second cup.

"Rejoin me, Ahad," the Emperor said after they were again alone. "Drink with me."

Ahad returned and took the cup from the tray. He waited for his liege to drink first and shuddered at the bitter taste. The Emperor laughed, not unkindly.

"This is dangseng root. It is a rare plant that I have an army of herbalists foraging for all over Odessiya. A Wycaan drinks it to build his strength and facilitate the flow of energy between the earth and himself."

"I know little of the way of Wycaans," Ahad replied when the silence suggested he was expected to respond. "I remember all the children's stories, of course, but. . ." he swallowed hard. "My lord? Can you not train me to be a Wycaan? I can then fight and kill the elf for you."

"Children's stories," the Emperor nodded, giving no indication that he had heard the question. "Ahad, bring the book that sits on the table there. Keep the page open and read to me exactly what you see."

Ahad moved to the table and, though this book was beautifully bound and the pages gilt-edged in gold, he recognized the story and illustrations.

"I had a copy of this in my nursery," he said quietly. "My father would read it to me when he was home."

"Which was not often," the Emperor replied. "That was my fault, I'm afraid. I would apologize, but he was my best general. I am only sorry you did not spend more time with him. Please read."

Ahad looked down at the open page. "I call out to the Wind Spirit. Wind Spirit, where are you?"

"Is that what you see, Ahad? Wind Spirit?"

"Yes, my lord. That is the story."

"Thank you. Please return the book to the table and sit with me again."

Ahad returned, puzzled, but did not question the instruction. The Emperor sipped his tea and thought.

"Would that I could train you, Ahad, but it cannot be so. No one knows for certain why one man is called to become a Wycaan and another passed over. Even the son of a Wycaan is not necessarily destined to become one, my own heir included."

"Might I request something else?" Ahad felt emboldened. The Emperor nodded, and Ahad cleared his throat. "Give me leave after the graduation. Let me seek out Shayth and the elf. I don't want to wait any longer."

"You will go as soon as the next batch of information arrives, assuming you pass your exams. I do not want you gallivanting around the empire needlessly."

"Thank you. When we last spoke, you told me that when I find him—the elf, I mean—I'll be able to summon you. How?"

The Emperor leaned over and picked up a small wooden box. It was intricately carved dark wood. "What do you know of the dwarves, Ahad?"

"They mine. We buy their ores and gold. They live underground in clans. Is this where Shayth and the Wycaan are?"

"I am unsure," the Emperor replied. "They were, but now I think they might have gone. I am fairly certain that the Wycaan has left Hothengold, their capital. Dwarves mine not only gold, but also powerful stones. These stones are imbued with the earth magic that the dwarves use. They can be very effective."

He offered Ahad the box, and the lad opened it, surprised as he withdrew a smooth, dull stone on a worn leather cord.

"I could have made it more ornate," the Emperor said, as though reading Ahad's thoughts, "but I would rather someone overlook it if they ever waylaid you."

Ahad nodded. "Very wise. How do I call you, my lord?"

"You will take it in a closed fist. The stone will read your intent and do the work. Now, return to your studies."

Ahad stood and bowed. He began to withdraw, but stopped. "My Emperor? May I ask one last boon?"

"He will be well looked after, Ahad. As long as your grandfather lives, he will have a home in my palace. But you should go to him and share your news."

Ahad bowed low. "I appreciate everything you do for me and my family."

"You are the son of the great General Tarlach. Your grandfather and great grandfather both served my father with distinction. You have nothing to thank me for. But serve me well, Ahad. That is all an Emperor can ask for in return."

Ahad wrapped his hand around his grandfather's withered fingers, steadying the cup at the old man's mouth. His grandfather slurped, and some of the wine spilt down his face.

Ahad tenderly wiped it away.

"I'm so sad," the old man muttered after a while.

"You know I must go, grandfather. My life cannot move on until I have avenged my father."

His grandfather nodded. "Would that I could stand by your side; that the long swords of three generations of the House of Tarlach could. . ." Ahad saw the old man's lips quiver. "Three generations no more. Better you leave me to fall into the mists of my mind, where my dreams are not incarcerated like my body. Oh, Ahad, I am sad because you will remember me like this, and not as the general I was.

"I led many campaigns throughout Odessiya, often against an enemy that boasted greater numbers. Only the Swords Master could defeat me with the sword, and I made him sweat heavily for the privilege.

"Your father, my son, was the greatest of generals. Still, his genes came from my loins." The old man closed his eyes and, after a few minutes, Ahad rose quietly to leave, thinking his grandfather had fallen asleep.

"Ahad." The old man's loud, authoritative voice stopped him in his tracks. He turned to see the old man summoning all his strength to rise and stand straight. His emaciated body shook from the effort, and his face grimaced with pain. "Stand in front of me."

Ahad returned and stood in front of his grandfather. They were now the same height.

"You have a weakness, Ahad. I see it. You are not a cold killer like Shayth. You are driven by hate and revenge, but it has not consumed you, and it should not. Recognize this as your weakness. Shayth will see it and try to exploit it. You must hide it well."

"I will, grandfather," Ahad said, and they hugged.

Through blurred vision, Ahad looked upon his grandfather one last time. The old man, teeth gritted, stood even straighter, every ounce of energy pouring into the effort. He pointed to his shield and sword hanging on the wall.

"Bring me my sword."

Ahad did, and his grandfather slowly drew it, rasping, from its scabbard. He held it up, the jeweled hilt glittering in the light of the torches while the blade shook in his grasp.

"Yes, I am your grandfather," he said, his voice began softly, but then it hardened. "But I am also a general in the service of the Emperor of Odessiya until the day I die. Show me respect by remembering me this way."

Ahad's fist moved across his chest and rested on his heart. The last living General Tarlach stood to attention and raised his sword. His withered fist moved the hilt to his chest. Ahad saw that it no longer shook. He stared and nodded. This is how he would remember his grandfather.

He turned and left the chambers of the great General Tarlach, his grandfather, for the last time. He did not, could not, look back.

Chapter Ten

When Sellia awoke, she felt a brief wave of contentment. She could hear the familiar calls of her friends, the only real family she had ever known. She could smell Dvural's oatmeal gruel that she had eaten every morning of her childhood, and yet, today, it felt as if she was smelling it for the first time.

She looked up from her bedding and stared at the canopy of leaves quivering gently in the soft wind and sunlight. A deep sigh escaped her lips. She wanted to remember and treasure this moment.

She turned to see if Seanchai was awake, remembering that he had sat up late with Uncle and probably wouldn't appreciate her contentment. Seanchai wasn't there. He was probably doing his exercises somewhere. She rose and stretched her body, curving it first one way and then the other.

It was still chilly, and she put her cloak around herself. Seanchai's cloak was missing. So was his bedroll. She turned sharply and scanned the eating area. When she caught Uncle's eyes, he looked away, and she knew.

She ran to where the horses were corralled. This resistance cell kept only a few for emergencies, and she quickly saw that two of the four horses they had ridden in with were gone. Her temper rose and she turned, sprinting back to the eating area.

Uncle was staring into his bowl. Elves and men sat around him in deferential silence. Their leader was grieving, and though many owed him their lives, they had nothing to offer at this moment except their presence. And there were many too who shared his grief for the playful calhei who had grown up among them.

Sellia could not help herself. She kicked the bowl from Uncle's hands. Still he did not move or look up to acknowledge her. Others rose, perplexed and angry. Sellia had grown up here under the great elf's protection. She was family.

Chamack moved between her and Uncle, gently pushing her back from the seated leader. She glared into his eyes and he met her gaze, eyes locked. When he spoke, his firm voice was meant only for her.

"He grieves, Sellia. What possesses you? Ilana's death is still fresh for us, if not for you."

"I grieve for her every day," she hissed back, knowing that all were listening. "I curse the gods every night for taking her and not me. I have no father and no lover–only a dear friend who is denied to me, as well."

"He's her father," Chamack said, his voice soft and bewildered.

"And he is a leader. What has he done? What did he concede to the Wycaan?"

Chamack stood there, clearly confused.

"Move aside," she snapped and pushed the big man away.

A surprised Chamack stumbled and fell over another elf, bringing two more down with him. He sprung up instantly, eyes burning. His hand moved to his short knife, but a thick, hairy arm clamped onto him.

"Enough," Uncle growled. "Sellia. Walk with me."

He moved away from the others, but did not speak. After a few minutes, he sat on a thick log on the ground. Sellia sat next to him, and, as she looked at his face, her anger dissolved.

"I'm sorry for what I said back there," her voice was soft again. "She's your daughter. She's my. . . It's so hard."

Uncle forced a smile and opened his massive arms. As she had many times as a young elfe, she fell into his strong embrace.

"You're like a daughter to me, too, Sellia. You and Ilana grew up together, and you are my blood in thought, if not reality."

"I need to be strong," she said, her voice muffled in his chest. "He is the most powerful person in Odessiya, an elf who can set our people free, who can bring down mountains and emperors. But he is so fragile. Do you know what gave him the strength to continue, what was the anchor he clung to when madness raged around him?"

She pulled back and stared at Uncle. "It was Ilana. She was–still is–the world to him. She gave him confidence, vision, morals, strength, and bravery. She gave him everything, and now, she gives him me."

"You're wrong," Uncle said and put a huge finger to her lips when she tried to respond. "I spoke with him deep into the night. There are no secrets between us, I believe–not concerning my daughter. And I have determined that it was not Ilana who fueled him.

"She was merely the carrier. It was love. A young, elven healer destined to kill many thousands more than he will heal needs more than air, food, and water. He needs love, and, through love, he receives the values and strength that you mentioned."

Sellia stared at him. "She made me swear."

"I know."

"I'm not Ilana."

"I know that, too, and so does Seanchai."

"I cannot replace her. I'm very different."

"In many ways, yes, you are. I speak as the one who watched you both grow from wailing brats to fine young elfes. You *are* different, but not where it matters. You both strive for honor, embrace duty, and crave freedom."

He rose and gently pulled her to her feet. They walked away from the camp, arms around each other.

"If you go to him now, you go by your own choice. If you wish to stay with us, with your family here, and prick pins in the butts of the Emperor's army, you're very welcome to, and you may do so free from your oath."

"But . . . I swore in the ancient language. I said the word: *Ashbar*."

"One cannot be compelled in matters of love, and neither can the ancient language hold you in servitude. Love is too pure. Seanchai knows that. He told me."

"He said that?"

"Yes," Uncle stroked his beard. "He's a Wycaan. He knows that kind of thing."

Sellia stopped walking and stared at him. "But Ilana didn't. And neither did I when I spoke the word. Why did he not tell me?"

"I suspect he wanted to bring you home and it is right that from here, where you are most tempted to stay, that you should make your decision."

Two big, powerful hands rested on her shoulders. His swollen eyes stared at her. "You may stay and we'll welcome you back to our group, though you might need to let Chamack push you to the ground a few times."

They both laughed. Chamack would take an arrow for both of them without a second thought. He was a noble and brave elf.

"But if you go, then you go freely to Seanchai with my blessing. Know that he's stronger than you think, Sellia. He will survive and fulfill his destiny with or without you, if the gods so decide.

"The Wycaan has decreed that you cannot go to him out of obedience to an oath that never was, nor out of guilt for Ilana. Now I tell you, as the father I want to be for you: if you go to Seanchai, go in love or friendship, not pity. There's no room for guilt and self-recrimination for those of us who rise again from the depths of our sorrow and continue to fight."

"Is that how you survived when your mate was taken from you?"

"There is not a day or night that I do not grieve her, and now Ilana will be by her side in my thoughts every day for the rest of my life."

Sellia took a step back. "I must go to Seanchai."

"Why?"

She thought for a moment. "Because I want to be by his side. Because I want to help him fulfill his destiny. Because I want to restore the elven pride and set the other races free."

She saw Uncle smiling.

"What is it?" she asked, her hands on her hips.

"My other daughter said that to me when she followed the Wycaan. I pray that you find the love that she did. It is as precious as freedom itself, more precious even than life."

And Uncle turned his back on her and walked away, his shoulders shaking with grief.

Chapter Eleven

Seanchai had spent his youth foraging in Morthian Wood with his mother, the village healer. He knew exactly where the burdock roots, the sages, and the artemisia grew.

He stopped to fill his canteen at the river by a deep gully. It was a favorite fishing hole that his father had shared with him and where he had caught his first trout. He smiled to himself as he remembered the strain on the rod. The fish had been enormous to his five-year-old eyes, though it had barely been enough for him to snack on. Still, he had been so proud.

As he led his horses along, he glanced over his shoulder. He had been right to release Sellia from her obligation to Ilana. He didn't want her to be bound to him out of duty instead of desire.

He was sure he had hidden his feelings from her. Perhaps she was attracted to him, but it would not have been appropriate during the mourning period. It occurred to Seanchai that Ilana might have known of their mutual admiration. Sellia was beautiful and graceful. Her dark skin; flowing, black hair; and arched cheekbones made her exotic. Her demeanor made Seanchai want to run from her and to her at the same time. Ilana had joked with him about her friend on many an occasion. She was secure in his love and Sellia's sisterly bond, but as she foresaw her own death, she earnestly encouraged them to be together if they both wanted to.

He was recognizing every tree now and knew he was near his village. A pit formed in his stomach. The decision to come here had been impulsive. Facing Uncle and bringing him the tragic news, had consumed Seanchai. He had not realized how close he was until he had seen the borders of Morthian Wood from the mountain peak where Uncle had sat with him.

Since leaving Uncle's camp, Seanchai's thoughts had dwelt almost entirely on Sellia and his decision to release her from her oath. Now, as he walked along the road to the mouth of the village, he began to realize exactly what he was doing.

He stopped in his tracks and stared. Everything in the small village was smashed and burnt almost to the ground, marked by charred bricks or a corner of a foundation. He walked slowly to his own house near the edge of the village. It had been totally flattened and the debris removed—the only property that had been so completely obliterated. The message was clear: Seanchai and his family had never existed.

He stood there for what seemed a long time, trying to remember how the small hut had looked. There had been three rooms: the living area with kitchen, fireplace and an area to both relax and treat patients, his parent's room and the tiny room that had been his. He wanted to remember it all. It was the least he could do.

A small green shoot poking out of the ground caught his attention as he surveyed the remains. He stared at it. Garlic. He had helped his mother plant herbs and food, and the garlic had always been the hardiest. He smiled to himself. They had not succeeded in erasing his past life in its entirety. The earth had not allowed it. He began to laugh and suddenly was laughing hysterically, without reserve. He was alone and didn't care. He laughed and laughed and laughed. . . until he cried.

He fell to his knees and sobbed. His cries echoed eerily through what was left of his village. He found himself propelled back on his feet by a wave of anger. He looked up to the sky and screamed.

"You missed me! You bastard! I escaped, so you destroyed all these innocent elves. You killed my parents. Did that make you feel powerful? It's the act of a weak bully. But I'm back. This is where it started. Here, come finish it. Come and get me now, if you dare. You coward!"

He closed his eyes and brought his heavy breathing back under control.

"It be better they not hear you," a female voice said.

Seanchai turned, startled, to find an old elfe in rags, a thin shawl over her head. She held a skin of water and offered it to him. He felt suddenly ashamed.

"Marta? I'm sorry," he said. "I thought I was alone. How did you. . ."

He knew the old woman but not well. She had, he recalled, always been old.

"My husband and I be away visiting our daughter to help with the birth of her first child. When we returned, it be like this. The wood be still charred and smoking, but no one be here alive.

"We buried everyone by the river where the earth be soft. No one be spared."

"My parents?"

"No one. I be sorry. Please come with me. I recently buried my husband there as well, may his soul find peace with his ancestors."

She turned and shuffled to a house at the other end of the village that he had overlooked. She went in and came out with two bowls of a watery stew. Seanchai rummaged through his bag and produced some bread and cheese. They sat outside in the shade of the house.

"A feast," the old elfe said, and cackled. After a few bites, she sighed. "Winter be soon coming when we returned and we rebuilt our house from the rubble of the others. At first, I be feeling guilty, using their property, but now it brings me comfort. As we continued to build, I made sure to take something from every one of our neighbors, so there be a little of each of them in our house with us. There be only one house where we couldn't find anything, where nothing be left."

"Why do you stay?" Seanchai asked after a few moments of silence broken only by the old elfe slurping her soup.

"There be nowhere to go now. The Emperor's taxmen don't bother me because they don't know I be here. It be peaceful, a good place to die. I be with my husband and our village folk.

"And you, Seanchai? Why you be coming back?"

He shook his head. "I don't know. Maybe I hoped. . ." He did not finish the sentence. There was nothing left to say. "I'm sorry I brought this on you, on the village. I didn't know. It seems like such a waste, such a waste."

"Seanchai. Will you bring freedom to the elves and the other races as the legends be telling?"

"I'll try," he replied. "I must unite the races into an alliance and learn how to defeat the Emperor."

"But you be doing it?" she persisted.

"I think so," he replied, feeling the weight of the expectation.

"Can you do it?" she asked again, her voice earnest now.

Seanchai looked into the eyes of the old elfe. He did not see hate or resentment. He saw only hope.

"Yes," he said with as much determination as he could muster. "Yes, I can and *will* free Odessiya."

"Then all this be not in waste, I think," she said.

They smiled at each other and Seanchai felt contentment emanating from the old elfe.

"We are very similar," he said. "We are both alone."

"I think not," the old woman said. "I be having my husband and friends buried nearby, and you be having that beautiful, young elfe over there, who be waiting patiently for you."

Seanchai turned and saw Sellia standing outside the gate into the old woman's garden. He stood and stared at her.

"Are you sure?" he asked.

"I am," she replied. "I come of my own volition."

Seanchai threw his arms around her and drew her close, though the gate was pressed between them. His voice quivered. "Then you are most welcome."

Chapter Twelve

Ahad rode steadily through the Great Valley, vast fertile land that fed the capital. It took two days to pass through, even with two horses and the minimal breaks he allowed himself. Nobody stopped him, though he carried papers from the Emperor in case an alert sentry demanded identification.

Only Masters wore black, and Ahad knew that his blackened Assassins Master clasp and his small crossbow were enough to suggest to anyone who got close enough that he was not one to be trifled with.

The Great Valley ended at the Forest of Delweith. Still a mighty gathering of trees, the forest was now carefully cultivated to provide wood for the Empire, and, in particular, the ever-growing capital. Ahad, ever the academic, had studied this area as part of a school field trip, learning about the ecology and how to sustain the natural habitat while still taking from its resources. He remembered being impressed with the people who lived and worked here. Now he realized that the Emperor had cultivated not only the land, but also the people here, to serve him. He felt a wave of admiration.

He also felt that he was no longer riding alone. He did not look around, but was able to determine three riders from the hoofbeats. He eased out the clip of his sword and his dirk in slow, unobtrusive movements. He shook his sleeves slightly to loosen poison-tipped stars in one and dart-like blades in the other.

One rider, hooded and armed, was now trotting alongside Ahad. A knife handle protruded from a boot, and a light green gem glinted from its hilt.

"Well met, Prince Phineus," Ahad said, grinning with pride that he had identified his friend's disguise so easily, "though I was beginning to wonder if you would ever join me."

"How?" the Crown Prince's voice was sharp.

"Your green-gemmed dirk." Ahad tried to curb his smile, which he was sure oozed smugness. "Was it hard to get away?"

"No, surprisingly uneventful. My father went away this morning. He even deigned to give me an audience first and made the point that he might be detained a while." Phineus laughed. "If only he knew."

"He knows," Ahad said with ease.

"How? You told him?"

"No. But he anticipated it and told me so. He asked if I planned to request your company. I told him I wouldn't; that I think it wrong you come, given the danger of the mission."

"Do you still think it wrong?"

"Yes. But I'm glad you ride by my side."

"I am the Crown Prince of Odessiya, Master Assassin Ahad Tarlach. *You* ride by *my* side."

Ahad turned his head and smiled. "I think out here, your majesty, we should not flaunt your title."

"Good point, my friend. We ride together, then."

They both laughed with bonded ease. But after a few moments, Phineus spoke. "Still, what makes you think he suspects I would join you?"

"He told me about your uncle's secret society and that he believed you would try to form such an organization, yourself. I told him that if you did, then I'd be honored to be the first enlisted."

"That was very brave, Ahad, or very stupid. Did he get angry at you?"

"No. He thanked me."

"What?"

"Don't underestimate your father, Phineus. He is always several moves ahead of everybody else. Did you not advise me several times with these very words?"

Phineus laughed. "Yes, I did. If I recall, the first time was just before your first audience with my father. You were almost wetting yourself with fear." He laughed some more, but then stopped abruptly. "But you aren't as many moves behind him now, I suspect. You're very smart, Ahad–very smart, indeed."

"Thank you. I believe that this was the reason the Emperor brought me to serve you. Shall I test you on some botany while we ride?"

"Only if you want this gem-hilted dirk thrown at you," Phineus joked. "You are no longer my tutor, Master Assassin."

"I think," Ahad continued, "that your father would be happy for you to bind the best of our generation to your side. He looks ahead and probably sees great strategic value in you creating your own power base as long as it doesn't challenge him. What say you, Phin–" he paused a moment and looked around. "We should give you a different name, and suggest in our interactions with people that I am the leader, if only because I'm older."

"I want an impressive name, especially after the one I've been stuck with these past seventeen years."

"Shadow," Ahad suggested, and they both nodded. "Not sure it will attract the ladies, though," he added.

"That's never been a problem," the prince boasted.

It occurred to Ahad that while his friend was fairly good-looking, he wouldn't have his crown to fall back on here outside the Empire's walls. From his friend's sudden brooding, he suspected Phineus was thinking along similar lines.

"Come now, Shadow. You're a strapping lad," he said and laughed.

Thankfully, so did Phineus. He certainly looked regal. He had very dark–almost black–hair, which he cut to shoulder length in the fashion among the young at court. He actually looked similar to a painting that Ahad had encountered in the palace of the late Prince Shindell. Ahad had never mentioned the painting, but had spent hours studying it. By the prince's side stood a five-year-old boy with dark spiky hair and dark eyes. Shayth. Ahad had taken in every feature of the lad, but especially his cold, black eyes. It had always been a strange feeling that Phineus and Shayth, cousins, looked so strikingly alike.

A thought occurred to him. Would the ambitious Crown Prince try to bind his cousin to him if he found it advantageous, despite knowing how Ahad, his declared best friend, felt about the murderer? Suddenly, Ahad was not quite so happy that his friend rode beside him.

Chapter Thirteen

Ruel and Crefen, the two young men who accompanied Ahad and Phineus, rarely spoke. They took their turns guarding and hunting. In fact, they took on more than their share of the work, never seeming to desire to be part of a group on an adventure.

As they sat around a fire enjoying a young boar that Phineus had killed, Ahad studied the two. Phineus was guarding while the others ate, so it was just the three of them.

They were twins–not identical, but almost. They were a year older than Ahad; both large and muscular. They had also trained in the academy, but Ahad knew nothing else about them besides that they were formidable in physical combat. As Ruel packed a pipe, Ahad spoke to him.

"What's your bond to Shadow?"

Ruel stared at him and continued to pack his pipe. Crefen swigged ale from a skin and wiped his mouth on his sleeve.

"We trained with him at the academy."

"I know that," Ahad snapped. "You trained with me, as well."

"Yes," Crefen acknowledged. "And you've improved greatly since our first lessons. Still, it was most entertaining to bruise you then."

They both laughed, and Ahad scowled. He wanted to remind them that he was now a Master Assassin, but it seemed impetuous. He resented that they had even made him scowl in the first place.

"What is your bond to him?" Ahad repeated.

"We serve at the pleasure of the Emperor of Odessiya," Crefen said.

"The Emperor sent you?" Ahad was stunned.

"No, not exactly," Crefen replied. "He charged us with the safety of his heir."

"How come I never see you in court or at the Pr–Shadow's social events?"

Ruel spoke, deeply and menacingly. "Our family name is not seen with honor like some."

Ahad frowned at him, and then to Crefen. When neither twin spoke, Ahad decided to drop it.

"Tell him," Shadow said from behind Ahad. "Either that, or he'll accost me at the earliest opportunity."

Crefen took another swig of ale, and then screwed the top back on the skin very deliberately.

"Our father trained at the academy and served under Prince Shindell and your father, the great General Tarlach. He was disgraced, framed he always said, and finally took his own life."

"Or so we were always led to believe." Ruel added.

"Tell him," Shadow repeated, his voice regal and authoritative. "He should know with whom he rides."

"We believe our father discovered Prince Shindell's secret society and tried to join. Your father persuaded the prince to reject him."

"Why do you think that?" Ahad asked.

Crefen stared at him. "Our fathers were close until the day they both laid eyes on your mother. They were both fine men, and your mother took her time to decide with whom to mate. But losing a woman can cut deep, very deep. . . and perhaps winning her was not enough for the victor either."

"You think my father had yours killed because of my *mother*?" Ahad couldn't hide his skepticism and he spoke sharply. "My father was a great man. He would not belittle himself with—"

"Maybe he felt insecure about being away all the time," Crefen sneered.

"Or maybe this has something to do with the secrecy of the group?" Shadow said.

"So it could have been Prince Shindell?" Ahad added quickly.

"More than likely both," Ruel spat. "They were very close, from all accounts."

"Anyway," Crefen said, "they did something much worse than kill him. They disgraced him, took away his honor, his dignity. Honor meant everything to our father. He was a walking dead man long before they finished him."

"I'm sorry," said Ahad. "I really am."

There was a heavy silence as each boy stared into the fire. Then a thought occurred to Ahad.

"If your father was disgraced, how is it you were both allowed into the academy, and then entrusted with the life of the Emperor's heir?"

"We were admitted to the academy by the Emperor himself." Crefen replied, rather too quickly. "Perhaps he saw the injustice, but whatever his reasoning, we are loyal to him, so we will protect his son with our lives.

"He knows he can trust us to keep an eye on you too. Maybe he has planted us to destroy any secret society that you try and form. History repeats itself and the rotten apple never falls far from the diseased tree."

Shadow spoke from behind Ahad. "My father is always. . ."

"Yes," Ahad snapped, "several moves ahead."

"You need not fear us," Ruel said. "We are here to protect the prince. We won't sacrifice our lives for you, but neither will we stab you in the back, either physically or figuratively, as your father did to ours."

"You don't know anything for a fact," Ahad snapped. "Sounds like a lot of assumptions."

"Maybe, maybe not." Crefen was cleaning his fingernails with a thin blade and did not look up as he spoke. "But when you grow up with the stories—hear them every night, see them on every noble's face—they become very persuasive."

Ahad stared at him and then turned to Ruel. He mustered as much authority into his voice as he could. "I'm sorry for your loss, but I had nothing to do with it."

"You understand revenge. You want to kill Shayth."

"His blade killed my father," Ahad snarled, his temper rising. "That's different. He held the sword in his hands."

"We all define our distinctions," Crefen said.

"Define them well," Ahad stood. "I am very focused in my mission. Give me any reason to doubt you, and I won't hesitate to dispense with you."

"You see?" Crefen smirked without amusement. "The rotten apple never falls far from the diseased tree."

Ahad glared at him, then turned toward the Crown Prince. They walked a minute into the darkness.

"I trust them, Ahad," Phineus said. "They strive to regain their family honor and will achieve that by protecting me. I'll bind them to me as I have bound you. I promise. And I'll try—*try*, I say—to keep them back from my cousin Shayth so you can take him down first."

"It's not just Shayth I'm thinking of. Tomorrow we'll reach the command post of General Shiftan."

"Was he one of them?" Ahad hesitated, and Phineus smiled. "Understood. I'll tell them not to kill anyone without my approval. They're loyal."

"Are you sure that loyalty is to *you*?" Ahad asked, and spent the rest of the night trying to interpret the Prince's expression.

Chapter Fourteen

Seanchai and Sellia rode out from Morthian Wood the next morning, traveling much lighter. Seanchai had given the old elfe a considerable portion of their supplies. Sellia knew it was useless trying to persuade him otherwise.

They returned the way they had come through the woods, but Seanchai turned north when they left the trees behind. Sellia stopped him.

"Seanchai, either we go aid the dwarves in the east, or find the elves of the west. You have pointed us north."

"I know," he said. "We head for neither the dwarves, nor the elves."

She stared. His face seemed more relaxed than it had in a long time. "Where are we going? I'm not sure a vacation is a priority right now."

Seanchai laughed out loud, and Sellia realized how she had missed that sound.

"North?" she asked.

"I want to find the pictorians."

"You're kidding me. They aren't known for their hospitality."

"Actually, I'm counting on their lust for war," Seanchai replied. "An alliance with the pictorians could create a second front for the empire and take the pressure off the dwarves. This would give us time to turn west and allow me to complete my training."

"I've been thinking about that," Sellia said. "Do you feel that you need more training? I've seen what Mhari has taught you. There can't be many who can stand up to you."

Seanchai shook his head. "They will need only one. There are higher levels of Wycaan energy that I have not discovered. The Emperor has mastered this and I have not. My hope is that the Elves of the West will be able to teach me what it is and how to counter it. Mhari and Master Onyxei either could not or would not."

"Why?" Sellia asked.

"I don't know. Mhari put great emphasis on me training with a Wycaan elf, saying that each Wycaan has an ability unique to his or her race. This might be what she was referring to. Master Onyxei was just too old."

A few moments later, she pointed at a flock of circling white birds–a sure sign of nearby water. Once they started to climb out of the Turkian foothills toward the great mountains, water might become scarce. It would also become colder.

"We need to fill our water skins," Sellia said.

"Perhaps we can bathe there, as well," he said, reflecting on the uncomfortable, itchy feeling he had.

A short while later, they crested a small hill and found a waterfall feeding a lake nestled in the hill like a bowl. They dismounted, unloaded their supplies, and tethered the horses. Seanchai scanned for the birds.

"I'm going to check what's happening over there. Perhaps we can eat some fish tonight. You bathe."

He was confused at the disappointment he thought he saw in Sellia's face as he gathered his swords. She had sent him away while she bathed after he rescued her from the wolfheids, but things were different now–very different.

Still, he felt compelled to hunt. He removed his shirt and walked away.

Sellia watched Seanchai leave and sighed. This was a beautiful setting, with the lake, the waterfall, and even the snow-capped peaks high above. She liked them better at a distance. She suspected her appreciation would wither when negotiating those high passes.

She approached the edge of the water near the soapwort reeds she would use to lather her body. She shed her clothes and washed them before hanging them on the thickest reeds to dry. Then she entered the water with a handful of reeds, wetting her shoulders and hair. She washed herself and leaned back until only her eyes were above water.

She sighed again, staring up at the mountains. The journey would be arduous and, though Seanchai had succeeded once with the pictorians, persuading them to withdraw their support of the Emperor and leave the battle they were waging on the dwarves at Hothengold, Sellia was worried how he would fare with those who had not served the Emperor.

With her ears under water and thoughts elsewhere, Sellia did not hear the horses' braying, but something instinctive stirred her. She raised her head and saw six shaggy bears. She swam to the shore and grabbed her bow, naked and shivering.

One huge brown bear faced Sellia. It reached her chest even on all four legs, and was a she-bear with hanging teats and two cubs peering out from behind her legs. The bear grunted at the cubs who scampered into the bushes. One tripped and rolled, and Sellia laughed, despite the danger. The bear looked at her and grunted.

Sellia glanced along the shore. Seanchai was standing there with several fish on a cord and one of his swords. She know he could fish, but wasn't sure how he had caught them with those tools alone. But this wasn't the problem.

The bear pack stood between them, so they couldn't join forces. But the she-bear grunted and nodded toward Seanchai, as if telling Sellia to go to him. Sellia obeyed, walking slowly and the bear paced alongside her. She was shivering and regretted not grabbing her clothes. The bear had a fur coat, but all she had was pimples from the cold. She shook her head in disbelief that this was what was worrying her.

As she watched, Seanchai extended his arms in the universal sign of peace and began speaking to the biggest bear, which stood nearest to him. She watched as Seanchai offered it the fish, surprised at the unspoken conversation the bears seemed to be having among themselves. Seanchai somehow understood the instruction to have another bear to inspect the offering, and when it had, the largest bear approached Seanchai, rose on two feet to tower over the tall Wycaan, and raised a claw above its head.

Sellia gasped under her breath as she realized Seanchai was not about to defend himself.

Chapter Fifteen

The giant bear stood with its paw in the air above its head. Sellia could see Seanchai's lips moving as he talked to the bear, but could not make out what he was saying. The bear lowered its paw to Seanchai's chest and scratched four lines, one from each claw.

Seanchai did not flinch, though Sellia could tell it was painful. Blood dripped from the wounds. The bear lowered back down onto four legs and turned away. One by one, the bears approached Seanchai and smelled his body from tip to toe. Only when they were clearly leaving did Seanchai move. He fell to his knees, and his hand went to his chest. Sellia ran to him.

"We must clean that," she said.

"Yes," he acknowledged. "And they have consented to us eating their fish. Please bring it."

He rose and began walking back to the horses. Sellia gathered the fish and jogged to catch up to him. When he stumbled, she put his arm around her shoulder to support him. They walked awkwardly and she suddenly realized her breast was rubbing against his torso. She pulled away without thinking when she saw his blood on her.

Seanchai smiled, though Sellia didn't know why. He removed the rest of his clothes and waded into the water. She came after him and cleaned his wound. Then she rubbed some reeds and washed his entire body. When she finished and stood straight in front of him, he gathered her in his arms and pulled her tightly to him.

"You're shivering, Seanchai," she said after a few moments.

"So are you," he replied.

"Let's go make a fire."

He let her go and she left the water, lit a fire, and set the fish on smooth stones, another gift from the lake.

A short while later, as they sat eating, Seanchai looked up at her, his face beaming.

"I could talk to them—the bears," he mused out loud. "They aren't normal bears. Bears don't stay in packs like these do. I talked to the leader and. . . he understood, I am sure."

"What did you say?"

"I'm not exactly sure. It just came out, in the ancient tongue."

"You speak the language of our ancestors?"

"I learned certain words in my training, but this was different. I connected to him, Sellia. It was amazing. I could feel what was in his mind, rather than individual words or thoughts. I could tell that he was listening and consented to us being here and passing through their territory."

"Is this a Wycaan thing?"

"Maybe. I don't know. There's so much I don't know. But something very important just happened. It wasn't just accepting me in their territory. It was. . ." he wrinkled his face trying to comprehend. "I was accepted into a family."

"Their pack?"

"Not exactly. It's bigger than that. I don't fully understand. . ." He looked at Sellia earnestly. "We must finish with the pictorians and head west. I have a lot to learn about being a Wycaan; a lot to learn about myself."

By mid-morning, it had already gotten considerably colder. They were riding steadily uphill and had entered the Turkian Range. The mountains were dark granite and, as they rode higher, the peaks disappeared into the clouds.

"How do you know where we're going?" Sellia asked as they rested and fed the horses in the mid-afternoon.

"Uncle has records of an expedition that set out to meet with the pictorians. An elf and a human left and returned to camp after the elf got sick halfway up. The others disappeared. Maybe they were killed by the elements, but many believe it was at the hands of the pictorians."

"That's encouraging," Sellia said. "Either we find pictorians and they slaughter us, or keep looking for them and die of exposure."

"Still happy you joined me?" Seanchai grinned.

"You've become very confident," Sellia replied. "I like it."

"Receiving Uncle's blessing and seeing my old village feels like a closure of sorts. Losing Ilana was very difficult and I was never quite sure I could continue. But it feels like a fresh start. I feel this is what Ilana would have wanted."

"And having to choose between a violent enemy or death by freezing doesn't curb your enthusiasm?"

"I don't think we'll freeze to death."

"Why?" Sellia asked.

"Don't look up," Seanchai replied, "but we're being tracked."

"By pictorians?"

"I believe so. It's looking good."

"How so?" Sellia had to fight the urge to look around.

"Well, they haven't attacked us yet. We're still alive. Perhaps they're interested in why we have come."

They stood up, checked the straps on their horses, and then led them through a narrow passage onto a flat plain. A huge spear whistled through the air and landed at Seanchai's feet. He looked up to see more than fifty seven-foot-tall pictorians gathered in a large semicircle, massive axes and spears at the ready.

"Still feeling optimistic?" Sellia asked.

Seanchai, unfazed, walked toward the largest boar and approached, hands outstretched to his sides, palms facing the giant.

"I am Seanchai, a Wycaan warrior." He removed his hood, but received almost no reaction from the pictorians. "I am known to some of your people. I have fought against them, but parted from them with mutual understanding and respect."

Seanchai stopped a few feet away and looked up into the pictorian's face.

"I must speak with your leaders. Where is Umnesilk?"

There was a silence that seemed to Sellia to last for ages. Then the boar said something and another translated.

"If you fought our people and lived, you must be strong. But if you think this earns our respect or lenience, you are wrong."

The leader growled, lifted his axe, and stepped forward. Seanchai heard the blade cut through the wind, but quickly stepped close and pounded the pictorian with his fists under his armor and through the sides between the front and back plates.

The pictorian staggered back, his axe dropping behind Seanchai. But the boar only smiled and drew a massive broadsword. Then it charged. Seanchai instantly had his two curved swords out to parry the blows, but he was forced backward by the intensity and strength of his opponent.

He stepped to the side, ducked under the pictorian's swing, and stabbed twice into the boar's unprotected thighs. Now behind his adversary, Seanchai kicked the wounded leg, and the leader grunted in pain as he fell to his knees.

Seanchai came in front of him, but turned to the pictorian who had translated. "I haven't come to kill you or fight you. I seek an audience with your leaders. I believe I've proven my worth as a warrior."

He was aware that the pictorian behind him was struggling to rise. The translator glanced between them. "Not yet," he said. "NuGavack has risen. You have not proven yourself."

Seanchai sighed as he swung round with amazing speed and kicked the rising pictorian in the head, sending him sprawling. Again he turned to the translator. "Now can we finish this? There are those of your people who fought at Hothengold; they can vouch for me."

"No," came the reply from behind.

Seanchai looked over to his opponent, who was on his knees and trying to rise, clearly dizzy.

"What do you want me to do?" Seanchai shouted. "Kill him?"

"Do you have the heart of a warrior?"

"A warrior does not kill senselessly."

"A warrior does not dishonor his opponent by leaving a fight unfinished."

"That's absurd," Seanchai snapped. "Can I not pass without killing your boars?"

The translator replied slowly. "Only through a fight to death or a Viehdigct can you pass. For Viehdigct, a First Boar must vouch for you."

There was a deep growl from behind the translator, and pictorians were pushed aside. In a blur, a huge creature passed Seanchai and decapitated the wounded pictorian with one fell swoop of its axe. A rich, deep, purple fountain of blood spouted from the dead pictorian before the headless torso toppled over. Then the eight-foot, horned giant turned back to face the translator.

"I vouch for Wycaan," boomed First Boar Umnesilk, and, as he walked away, the other pictorians bowed their heads and made way for their most feared warrior.

Chapter Sixteen

I t was late afternoon when Ahad and the Crown Prince–
with Ruel and Crefen trailing silently behind–arrived at the
fortress of Skiliad in the province of Ulster. Any discussion
in the two days since the discussion around the campfire focused
around guard duty, hunting, and other such necessities. There
was no mention of their previous conversation.

Skiliad was perched on the side of a mountain by the same
name. The stones of its fortification were as gloomy as the
mountains around them, and the only color was the flag that
flew from its mast. There was only one way in, as the rest of
the fort either backed against the rock face of the mountain or
faced a sheer drop into a deep ravine.

"How did they build that?" Ahad marveled aloud.

"You don't want to know," the Crown Prince answered, and
Ahad grimaced at the thought.

As they began their ascent to the castle, a large group of
soldiers galloped up from behind them. An officer shouted for
them to move aside. "We have wounded," he cried.

Ahad watched the passing brigade. There were about thirty
able-bodied soldiers and six more either tied to their horses or
hanging on to another rider from behind. He saw raw wounds
exposing bright pink flesh, bloody bandages, and two dead.

He felt his and his riding companions' mood, not great to begin with, plummet still further. When the party had passed, Ahad led them back onto the path. A mounted soldier with a banner in his hand galloped down from the fort to them, and they stopped.

"Identify yourselves in the name of the Emperor," he demanded.

"I am Ahad, son of the late General Tarlach, and I come with documentation. I will introduce my friends to General Shiftan. He knows me." Ahad reached into his pouch and offered a sealed scroll.

"The seal of the Emperor," the man said, clearly impressed. Then his eyes returned to Ahad. "I never served under your father, but I know he was a great man. Our own General Shiftan speaks of him with the highest regard."

"Thank you," Ahad replied tonelessly. "Please take me to the general."

They followed the standard bearer through the gates and were directed to the stables. The man soon returned.

"Master Tarlach," he said and saluted. "General Shiftan attends his wounded and receives information from the company head. He instructed me to lead you to the halls for refreshments. If you leave your bags there, they will be taken to your rooms."

Seeing the youngsters hesitate, unsure what to do with their weapons, the man spoke again. "Here, we always carry our swords and"—he glanced at the insignia of the assassins that Ahad wore—"whatever other blades are upon us. Your bows and heavier weapons can be left here with your bags."

They soon found themselves in a large hall lined with tables and benches. There was a low-burning fire in the fireplace. Bread, stew, and ale were set out for them.

When they were seated alone, Phineus mumbled to Ahad. "It's strange that the general doesn't run to greet you, no?"

"Not at all," Ahad answered. "The soldiers here are loyal to General Shiftan for good reason. He has gone to first tend his wounded and honor his dead. He knows many of their names and about their families. I have heard that any soldier who dies under his command can be assured that any kin will be well looked after, beyond the pension they receive from the army. He is a good man and a fine officer."

Ahad studied Ruel and Crefen as he said this, but their mouths were too full to react as he thought they might. A few minutes later, the standard bearer returned with a young boy at his side.

"Master Ahad. I am instructed to bring you to General Shiftan. The squire here will escort your friends to their rooms and bring them to dinner shortly after." The man stared at Phineus, who had made a face at Ahad being called "Master."

"Is there a problem, sir?"

Ahad didn't wait for the Crown Prince to reply. "It's fine. Please, just give me a moment with my friends." As the solider backed away, Ahad leaned in close and spoke quietly.

"Time to decide, my friend. If you want to let it be known that you're here, come with me. But if you do, General Shiftan or one of his staff will send word back to the capital."

"You go," Phineus replied. "Do not announce me unless you feel there's a very good reason to do so. I trust your judgment."

Ahad rose and followed the standard-bearer from the hall.

"Have you ever met the general?" the soldier asked pleasantly.

"Yes," Ahad replied without elaborating.

"Was he expecting you?" After a moment's silence, he spoke with more restraint. "I'm sure your business—the Emperor's business—is your own, sir. My apologies if I overstepped my mark. I'm at your service."

Ahad didn't look at him when he said, "Thank you."

As they approached a building that Ahad suspected might serve the healers, General Shiftan exited. His sleeves were rolled up, and there were bloodstains on his forearms.

"Thank you," he said to his standard-bearer. "Please check that Master Ahad's guests are well taken care of. Come, Ahad. Let me show you our fortifications."

He turned and walked away, and Ahad followed. Their conversation would not take place near prying ears. They climbed onto the walls and up to a tower. Once there, Shiftan closed a heavy, wooden door behind them. They stood, just the two of them, on the parapet.

"You've grown, Ahad. I would not have recognized you as the man who stands before me."

"Life moves us along quicker than we expect." Ahad replied. He remembered General Shiftan as a man with a dense bush of red hair, but now it was thin and predominantly gray. Time had not been kind to him either.

"You're probably tired of condolences for your father's loss, but I was one of his closest friends. I cannot let this moment pass without expressing what a great man he was. Your mother aside, there is no more than four or five others who knew him as well as me."

"Thank you," Ahad said. "Is it true he died by Shayth's sword?"

Shiftan nodded. "And I bear shame for that, too."

"How so?"

"I met Shayth in battle and singled him out for my own personal attention. I knew your father was. . . attached. . . to the boy, and wanted to save him the confrontation."

"What happened?"

"Shayth is good. He is fast; balanced; and, above all, ruthless. He has no discernable fear, seeming to welcome death. He took control of our confrontation, as though he, not I, had thirty years of field experience. When he recognized my rank, he smashed my knee, but let me live. He wanted me to deliver a message to your father that he was coming for him."

Ahad sighed. "Does your intelligence tell you where he might be?"

"I don't need intelligence. The dwarf king sent reinforcements here from Hothengold to Clan Dan Zu'Ulster. The son of Prince Shindell leads them."

"You have seen him?"

"Not personally. But the troops that return talk of him. They speak with awe and fear. I plan to ride out and confront him in the next few days."

"Why have you not done so already?" Ahad demanded.

"I needed my second-in-command to return from leave. He arrived yesterday, and I have been briefing him so that he can assume command if needed. I'm experienced enough to know when I'm facing a better soldier."

"If you think Shayth will kill you, why go out to face him? Send younger soldiers and greater numbers."

General Shiftan smiled. "My age and experience may have made me a wise commander. But the boy killed my best friend. I will avenge his death."

Ahad stared at the general. "Then it was well you waited until now."

"Why?"

"I will ride with you and face my father's murderer. The rite of vengeance is mine."

Ahad expected gratitude from General Shiftan, but instead the man just sighed and shook his head.

Chapter Seventeen

"What's the matter?" Ahad asked.

"I'm not sure that you're ready to face an adversary like Shayth, and I don't know how your mother would fare losing you, too."

Ahad's tone was haughty. "The Emperor has deemed me ready, or he wouldn't have sent me."

"Perhaps," Shiftan replied dismissively. "What else has he instructed you to do?"

"Find the elf and track him. I have a way of contacting the Emperor when this happens."

"Interesting." General Shiftan looked around to check they were alone. "Tell me, Ahad, can you imagine that the Emperor might find it equally to his advantage to have you removed? You're very close to his son, likely closer than the Emperor himself. I'm sure he draws parallels between you two and Prince Shindell and your father.

"Perhaps the Emperor sees you as a potential threat. You carry the legacy of one of greatest generals, his memory still fresh in the minds of soldiers and peasants."

"I am no threat to the Emperor," Ahad snapped, not liking how everyone around tried to manipulate him. He smiled. "And of course the Emperor sees parallels between the Crown Prince's strategy and that of Prince Shindell."

General Shiftan gasped, his mouth hung open. Ahad continued, glad to shock his father's friend.

"I have spent considerable time with the Emperor and learned much from him. For instance, the Emperor eats very healthily. When he eats meat, it's only the leanest cut, and he makes a point of keeping tabs on this."

Shiftan stared out across the battlements, taking his time to collect his thoughts. 'The leanest cut' was the password for the group of men, many highly ranked now, that Prince Shindell had gathered to him as a secret society.

"He knows?" Shiftan whispered. "Yet he never acted against us?"

"There was no need as long as you never threatened his reign. You were all loyal and competent. The Emperor admired his brother's ability to distinguish the best and bind them to him. Since you all continued to serve the Emperor with distinction, it wasn't in his interest to destroy you."

General Shiftan turned and smiled at Ahad. "You've grown up a lot, boy. Your father would have been very proud of you. And very worried."

"Why?" Ahad asked, pleased to have finally elicited a response.

"It frightens me that the Emperor sees fit to lay such heavy responsibility on the shoulders of an unproven–"

"Heavy responsibility! You mean Shayth?" Ahad jerked his head around, aware that he had raised his voice.

"No," Shiftan replied, his voice still scarcely more than a murmur. "While Shayth might be your death, I'm more worried that the Emperor puts his heir under your protection."

"I was just his tutor."

Shiftan turned sharply, but kept his voice low. "I am a congenial man, Ahad, but never let that fool you. Tell me:

what did you tutor him on while you traveled the long road to Skiliad?"

They left the fortress early the next morning, how long after dawn Ahad could not tell. He was unable to see the sun through the pregnant cloud cover. A deep, foreboding fog swallowed the peaks of the mountains.

He wrapped his cloak around his body and tried not to show others that he was shivering from the cold. Snow flurried but did not settle. The Crown Prince rode next to him while Ruel and Crefen followed behind.

General Shiftan led the patrol of three sixers and Ahad's group. Their mission was to meet with a trade train and escort it through the mountains. It contained arms, wood, grains, and other supplies–all essentials to maintain a large military presence, and Shiftan had confided to Ahad that they had allowed word to spread of the train. They were waiting to be attacked. With winter approaching, denying the fortress precious supplies would make a lot of sense to the resistance.

When they rested that night, Ahad's cold, stiff muscles were sore. He was ready to sleep when a sergeant with a long, braided beard approached.

"Master Ahad, sir. I am to assign you and your men to guard duty."

Ahad saw Phineus stiffen and quickly spoke. "We'll of course take our share," he said loudly.

"Does everyone share?" Phineus asked through his cowl.

"Everyone," the man answered edgily. "Senior officers take the first and last shifts, but everyone takes one."

"I said we would guard," Ahad repeated, stiffening his own voice. "Which shift–"

"I would prefer to split you up. There are four shifts, and you'll each be assigned to one."

"Do you not trust us?" Phineus snapped.

This time the sergeant glared at him, and Ahad was relieved that the sergeant could not see at whom he was glaring.

"How long have you served with General Shiftan?" Ahad asked the sergeant, anxious to move the attention away from his friend.

"Five years, sir. Before that, I served for fifteen with your father. I'm proud to have drawn swords and fought with the great General Tarlach."

Ahad turned to his friends. "This man has served the Emperor's officers for two decades, more than any of us have lived. . . and he's alive to tell the tale. I think we should trust his judgment and learn from his experience." He turned back to the sergeant. "Shadow here will take the first shift, Crefen the second, and his brother, Ruel, the third. You may assign me to the final shift."

"The last shift is often the most dangerous," the sergeant warned. "Perhaps you should give one of–"

"I'm aware of the dangers from the dawn shift. It is mine to claim."

A smile crept across the soldier's face. "Ha! You're your father's son, Master Tarlach, and that's the highest compliment I can offer." He turned to Phineus. "Okay, Mr. Shadow, put your things over there and grab some food while it's warm. I'll introduce you to your shift captain."

When the Crown Prince had moved off, the sergeant tuned to Ahad and spoke quietly. "The lad will have a hard time if he brings an attitude. I almost cuffed him for his insolence, and the other soldiers will be less forgiving. He might have an unpleasant discovery about life on the frontlines, if he crosses them."

"I'll talk to him," Ahad said, and turned away so that the sergeant couldn't see his grin. If any soldier hit the Crown Prince, he would also have an unpleasant discovery, and remember it for the rest of what would no doubt be his very short life.

So he would talk to Phineus. The army couldn't afford to lose too many of its battle-hardened soldiers.

Chapter Eighteen

First Boar Umnesilk led Seanchai and Sellia away from the group and across the flat plateau. His brisk pace meant their horses had to trot to keep up. He didn't seem to notice, or, if he did, then he didn't care. They climbed between two mountains until the path flattened onto another plateau.

When they reached more mountains, Umnesilk stopped. They were about to enter a gorge, barely wide enough for the four horses. He signaled for them to dismount.

"Pictorian villages destroyed by elves, dwarves, and humans. Pictorians not give birth much. Often mates have one or two pictorye. We fight much, pictorians die. We guard village. You come first to my hearth. Then I ask to bring you to clan hearth, to council. Understand?"

"Yes," Seanchai replied. "Thank you."

"You swear in elf tongue never tell where our homes. You have word for this, yes?"

"We do," Seanchai replied. "I swear to never reveal your villages to my people or the races of Odessiya without your permission. *Ashbar.*"

Umnesilk nodded and then looked at Sellia. She nodded back.

"I swear also to protect the locations of your villages. *Ashbar.*"

Umnesilk grunted. "You fine warrior," he said to Sellia. "Remember fight at little people's hearth. You good as mate for Wycaan?"

"We're working on it," Sellia replied and glanced at the blushing Seanchai.

Umnesilk stared at her and then shook his huge head. Whether he understood or not was unclear, but he signaled for them to follow through the narrow passage. As they progressed, the path wound left and then right. Seanchai could hear muffled voices and smelled food cooking on a fire.

"Not easy way," Umnesilk called back. "Not trust all the way."

"That's okay," Sellia replied. "You protect your family. We understand this."

Finally, they were standing on an inverted plateau, surrounded by rock that rose more than forty feet above them. It protected from the winds, Seanchai thought, but could not be very defensible if attacked from above.

As he scanned all the way around, he realized that Umnesilk was watching him.

"What you think?"

"Isn't this a difficult area to defend?" Seanchai asked.

The massive pictorian nodded. "I First Boar. Few challenge me, but challenge must come before council. We not grow, I say before. Pictorians not attack mates or pictorye. Fear armies from Odessiya, fear wolves and bears. They not come down here. Scent of pictorian rise straight from here. Fire from pits not seen."

Seanchai nodded. "I understand. You chose a place where you won't be noticed rather than a place to defend."

The First Boar stared for a moment. "Pictorian not hide," he snarled. "Fighting is our way, but pictorians must grow to be more. See Emperor and dwarves have many in army. Talk more with food. Come."

Seanchai noticed that there were several stone houses, all with doorways that were at least eight feet tall, and one bigger structure, possibly a meeting place. But Umnesilk led them to a hole in the rock wall, a small cave. They all had to bend and climb through into a spacious cave.

"Not good," Umnesilk said, "but not have house, and not winter."

"It's fine," Sellia said to him. "Better than where we have been these past months. There's air and a place for a fire. This is good."

"Umnesilk," Seanchai said. "I didn't see anyone else."

"All in houses. Pictorian warriors guarding or out hunting with party that stop you. I call them. You come soon when I tell."

Seanchai nodded. He went over to a pallet with a thick skin on it and lay down. Then he jerked his head up.

"What is it?" Sellia asked.

"This is a bearskin. It feels. . . wrong."

Sellia looked at him. "Perhaps you're just tired."

Neither of them believed that.

Seanchai dozed while Sellia unsaddled their bags from the horses. Umnesilk returned.

"My family meet and feed you. But they not know to speak not-pictorian. Most never seen, only our race. Will look, smell, and maybe ask questions. Our way."

They stepped outside, and Sellia immediately looked around, startled. "The horses."

"We take," Umnesilk answered. "Give water and take to grass, but we not know to brush like see soldiers do in army."

"We'll groom the horses," she replied. "Thank you for taking care of them."

They walked to a big fire adjacent to the biggest house. Seanchai smiled as he met the females. They had no horns and were smaller in stature than the males, but Umnesilk had once told him that they could hold their own with males in combat. He also noticed the pictorye. There were several of them.

"You have sired several children?" he asked.

Umnesilk translated, and they all laughed. A female rose and stood by her First Boar. She spoke to Seanchai, and Umnesilk translated. "My mate, Onywei, say that I not as old as looking. Need be very old for seven pictorye. But four are mine. I am First Boar. Others from brothers. I had two and their families live at my hearth."

He introduced the wives, and Seanchai dared not ask about their mates. He himself had killed a number of pictorians over the past year—more than any other man or elf. He feared the possible answers.

They seated themselves and were served by the pictorye. It was a heavy, meaty stew. Seanchai typically ate only fish and vegetables, but decided it would be disrespectful not to. And he also happened to be really hungry.

Onywei spoke to Sellia though her mate. "Do you have young elf of your own?"

"No," she replied. "We're both very young and have only been mates for a short while."

"You want children-elves?"

Seanchai looked at Sellia. They had never discussed such things. It was all very new and seemed so not part of the world in which they existed.

"Yes," she said at last. "But only if they can live as free elves."

Once translated, this was greeted by many nods around the circle. Onywei spoke again through Umnesilk.

"Onywei say: we look different, but inside," he tapped his heart with a massive fist, "we are very same."

Chapter Nineteen

*H*e stood upon a great hill, a green cloak wrapped around him and his white hair flowing in the gentle breeze. He held his Win Dao swords without fear of battle. To his left was a great, white, frozen flatland, and to his right, a mighty green forest. Behind him rose huge mountains, their peaks hidden in cloud. In front of him was a plain that ended at a massive expanse of water as far as his eyes could see.

He stood alone, waiting, and expectant. He knew they would come. He had summoned them, though he held no dominion over their race. His call was for help, energy, and power. They would come.

As the sun reached its zenith, he began to make out movement on the horizon. He smiled to himself, secretly relieved. From the four winds, they were coming, from all the lands of Odessiya.

Four great ice bears were the first to arrive, all white but one, subtly pink–a sign of pregnancy–with clear, blue eyes and black snouts in sharp contrast. They sniffed him all in turn–a greeting, an examination. Time passed, and six black dots became sleek, black bears suggestive of great speed and stamina. They too approached and sniffed.

And finally, seven brown bears emerged on all fours from the forest. They were somehow familiar. One, with hanging teats, glanced furtively back into the trees, where she had surely left her cubs. When they sniffed him, they knew him. The biggest came last and slowly rose on its hind legs. It put its mighty paw slowly on the Wycaan's chest wound, and *a wave of warmth passed through the elf. The bear stared into his eyes with recognition.*

When it had returned to its pack, all eyes went to the Wycaan. No—they were looking beyond him and he felt a great shadow behind him and turned slowly. Standing there was a great grizzly, twice as big as most of those gathered. The Wycaan glanced toward the looming mountains for others, but this creature had come alone.

It stood on its hindquarters, and the tall Wycaan barely reached its chest. It had wild chestnut fur and huge paws. It was a majestic beast, and the Wycaan could not hide his admiration.

The bear lowered itself onto its four paws and moved past him, brushing the Wycaan gently, filling his senses with musty and powerful bear scent. Then the mountain bear moved to the ice bears. They all stood and the biggest stepped forward. Scents and grunts were exchanged and then the mountain bear did the same to the others. When completed, it moved again in front of the Wycaan. It rose again on its hind legs and spoke in deep, throaty grunts. The Wycaan understood.

'When the gods created the world, they built the land and seas. They created the mountains and forests, the desert and the great ice plains.

When they inhabited the world, they could not decide to whom dominion should be given.

"The great firebreathers were fierce and strong, but the gods feared their unbridled rage. The wolves were favored among many for their focus and intelligence, working in a pack. But they were independent of spirit and only concerned themselves with their own future. The great eagle was wisest and fastest. Its deadly accuracy with its talons earned it the respect of all the beasts of the land. But it sought solitude on the skies and rarely came among the animals. It lived on the high peaks and kept its council to itself.

"Then there were the bears. We were strong, fierce in battle, deliberate in council, and loyal to our packs and those in our midst. We were not

as powerful as the firebreathers, as intelligent as the wolves, or as fast as the eagles, but our strengths brought balance to the lands.

"In time, alliances were formed between firebreather, wolf, eagle, and bear, and it was the bear that nurtured this fusion. And so the gods saw fit to share power among the four species.

"Time passed, and the two-legged walked the earth. Four races there were: man, elf, dwarf, and pictorian. The pictorians gravitated toward the souls of the firebreather, man ran in packs like the wolf, and dwarves sought excellence at the ends of the earth with the eagle. The elves brought balance for many centuries by nurturing their culture and people, but seeking always to hold together the four races. For this reason, bears and elves have always held common ground and common cause.

"But as the firebreather, wolf and eagle, so different bears have different traits. Some bears stay together, a close-knit family, their cubs always near," He nodded towards the forest where the brown bear cubs now dozed, too exhausted to take note of what was happening. "The mountain bears live solitary lives, coming together only to mate and fight. Some wolves thought of the greater good, and some eagles were companionable creatures.

"So it is with the two-legged. Some are good, others bad. Some fight, others think. The similarity of creature, four or two-legged should never be assumed."

The huge mountain bear turned to face the Wycaan. "It is the Wycaans who understand best the connection with the animals and have sought our help to enhance their powers and duty.

"And so we stand with you, to offer our help as our ancestors did for thousands of years. An Elven Wycaan walks among us with a difficult path before him. We come to offer our paws to run with you. Will you accept?"

The Wycaan unbuckled the clasp of his cloak, and it fell to the ground. He removed his shirt to reveal the scarred claw marks on his *chest—the giant bear paw now a badge of honor. "I am proud to run with the bears."*

And run, they did. Five of them—the Wycaan and one of each pack—ran across the plains, through the forests and across the great ice sheets. They ran to the peaks of the highest mountains. They ran deep into the night. The Wycaan felt no fatigue, but only fusion with the brown bear in the forest, the back bear on the plain, and the white upon the glaciers. They were no longer running next to him, but inside of him.

When he stood upon the mountain peak staring out upon the land of Odessiya, he was alone with the great grizzly. "Thank you," he said to the mountain bear. "Thank you all."

"We are one now," the grizzly replied. "Even when you stand alone, never will you stand alone again."

And the great grizzly stepped into the Wycaan.

Seanchai woke with the smell of the great bearskin covers filling his lungs. He could feel their furs against his naked chest. Sellia was awake and watching him. He pulled her to him and held her tightly.

"That must have been some dream," she remarked, offering no explanation.

He smiled. "It was momentous. And I must discover its meaning. It might just hold the key to everything."

Chapter Twenty

During the uneventful day's ride, Ahad had requested a private conversation with General Shiftan. The general had nodded, but there was little to do about it at the time. They rode without breaks, needing to reach the entrance to the mountain range before the caravan entered.

That night, the bearded sergeant requested Ahad join the general on the first watch. They patrolled the perimeter of the camp in twos, three pairs of soldiers at different distances. Ahad matched General Shiftan's casual pace.

"I haven't heard of many generals who participate in the guard duty," the young assassin said.

The General smiled. "Most don't, but we each have our own style. Spending a couple of hours with a man gives me a chance to learn who he is, and what motivates and scares him. I don't want my men's loyalty to derive from fear. I'm alive today because a dozen men gladly put their bodies between mine and a blade or arrow."

"Was my father like that?" When General Shiftan didn't answer, Ahad added: "Please don't feel obliged to suggest he was perfect. I want to know my real father. There'll be plenty of books, plays, and songs written about the myth. Tell me about the man."

"Very well," Shiftan replied. "Your father was very different from me, though we loved each other as brothers. He would mock the manner in which I treat my soldiers—not out of spite, but I think a lack of understanding.

"Your father was brilliant, but brutal. There are certain campaigns that I'm glad were assigned to him rather than me, if you understand my meaning. But it took a toll on him, which is why he requested Galbrieth."

"I didn't know he requested it," Ahad said. "I resented that he was assigned a place so far from the capital."

"He conquered Galbrieth ruthlessly, but then built a loyalty among the men of rank, many of whom rose to power because your father killed their lieges. At that point, he could rule without too much violence—or so we thought."

"How about when it came to competition for women?"

General Shiftan was quiet for a moment. "You ask because of the brothers in your entourage?"

"You don't miss much, do you?" Ahad laughed.

General Shiftan smiled back. "As I've said before: I'm a congenial man, Ahad, but never underestimate my drive to succeed and win. What I miss could make all the difference between victory and defeat, between life and death. I take care of my soldiers, but I don't suffer their failure or lack of discipline.

"Yes, your father pursued your mother with the same single-minded mentality. He probably frightened other suitors, but she's a strong woman. You haven't seen her since she traveled from the city after the funeral, have you?"

Ahad didn't answer.

"Good. She does it for your safety. She loves you very much, Ahad. It's hard for you, but excruciating for her, to be sure. And whatever you heard from those two sons of Lord Morogen is probably embellished, but not so far from truth as to be unbelievable. Does that make sense?"

When Ahad did not answer, General Shiftan stopped and tuned to him.

"There is something very important I want you to understand. You might be, in time, as good as your father, but you will never be him exactly. You're more like your mother and should draw on her strengths. If you try too hard to walk in his boots, it'll be your downfall. Do you understand?"

Again, Ahad didn't answer.

"Your father never hesitated to destroy an entire village, Ahad. He was feared throughout the land as much as he was admired. He did what needed to be done, when it needed to be done, and achieved it by any means necessary."

"The fortress at Skiliad is impressive, as I'm sure you noticed when you arrived. What if I told you that more than four thousand men died building the fortress? Your father would reply that if that was necessary, so be it. But you're different and must think for yourself. When you face Shayth, the elf, or any other enemy, you must know who you are facing. But you must also know who you are. Do you know, Ahad?"

Ahad looked down at the ground and kicked a stone with his boot cap. Shiftan resumed walking.

"This, son, is why I fear for you if you do face Shayth."

The attack on the supplies train came the next day. General Shiftan's troops heard the attack while still a mile away from the rendezvous. The supplies train had halted as planned at the Mouth of Ulster, where the plains met the mountain range.

General Shiftan turned to his troops, his voice clear and authoritative. "We ride in formation. No one breaks without my order. On my mark, be ready to form a cavalry line and charge."

They set off at a gallop, and Ahad found the thundering rumble of hooves exhilarating. He looked over at the Crown Prince, who grinned back. Ahad nodded. When he drew his sword, he was surprised to hear a battle cry escape his mouth.

But the joy was short-lived. A torrent of arrows fell upon them from the mountainside to his left, and as they veered aside, a second wave came from their right. Several men fell from their horses, a few rising to their feet, while others lay still.

Those still mounted continued, following General Shiftan's red armor, his sword now high above his head, his banner man behind him. Then the General's mount jerked into the air and collapsed to the ground, a line of bright scarlet blood oozing out of its neck from the trip wire that had been strung across the path. The horse whinnied from pain and then lay still. Shiftan rolled away and sprung to his feet. Ahad was impressed.

Arrows were directed now at the fallen General, and his soldiers immediately surrounded him. One soldier jumped from his horse, and the General took the offered reins.

"Form up," he cried, spittle and blood gathering at the sides of his mouth. "We ride slowly. Keep watch. On my command, we charge, and the gods' vengeance be upon them."

Ahad moved into line, his breathing heavy with anticipation, and the cavalry moved at a slow gallop.

As the steep rock receded on either side, Ahad saw the wagons, halted as instructed before entering the narrow mountain passes. A strong military escort accompanied them, but these soldiers looked on helplessly as pitch-laden arrows rained down from all sides and were lit by accompanying burning arrows.

The dwarves and their allies did not seem intent on fighting the disciplined soldiers, only on destroying the supplies. The officer in charge of the convoy sent two forays into the thick forest from where the arrows came, but these cavalry lines were cut down with deadly accuracy by archers firing from high up in the trees.

One sixer succeeded in entering the forest, holding their shields together, but never returned. The sounds of combat echoed against the mountainside. Ahad glanced at the General, seeing his indecision.

"From Geenauld to the end, you ride to the wagons and save the supplies," Shiftan called. "The rest will charge with me into the forest. If you see archers in the trees, raise your shields. Hit the trees with your horses.

"On my mark," Shiftan raised his sword, but as he did, fire snaked across the entire path from both edges. A thick, black smoke filled the sky as flames leapt up.

The general's curses were as angry as his soldiers' as his horse reared.

The Crown Prince slapped Ahad's arm with the side of his sword and pointed up to a mountain peak.

"Recognize?" he called.

Ahad saw a tall, thin man dressed all in black, his spiky, black hair distinct in the sky. "Go home, Shiftan," he cried. "These mountains belong to the free dwarves. Go home 'fore the winter feeds you to the crows, if I don't finish you first."

Chapter Twenty-One

A had stared up at Shayth. He felt rage grow inside him and pulled his horse round. He backtracked and rode up the first gorge he could find. He could sense others behind him—he guessed Phineus, and therefore Ruel and Crefen.

General Shiftan had barked something, but Ahad ignored it. When they reached a dead end, he jumped from his horse and began scrambling up the rocks and scree.

"Ahad," Phineus shouted, his voice sharp.

Ahad stopped, ready to snap back at his sovereign not to interfere, but Phineus spoke first, his voice calm and authoritative.

"Curb your emotions. Remember your training."

Ahad heard the words and took a deep breath. He nodded and turned again to ascend the mountainside. This time, his footing was measured and surer. He was a Master Assassin and had trained in the academy. He admitted to himself that his friend might just have saved his life.

He waited near the top to catch his breath and for his companions to join him.

"Ruel guards the horses," Phineus whispered when he had joined Ahad.

Crefen was about twenty yards to their left and threw a pebble that hit Ahad's shoulder. The boy pointed to his left and tried to signal a number, but his thick battle gloves made it difficult to decipher. There were possibly ten men above them.

Phineus leaned in. "I'm not sure these are great odds," he said. "Even if most are dwarves, we have the disadvantage."

Ahad nodded. He drew out a long throwing knife. He would take one shot, but Phineus put his hand on Ahad's arm.

"Do you have a plan?"

Ahad hesitated. "Let me throw, and we can run back to the horses. One throw. You can start back. If I cannot join you, I'll hide. I know how to disappear."

Phineus frowned. "We'll be near," he said and began to retreat.

Ahad waited several minutes and then crawled to see above the rock face, where he found mainly dwarves and a few men and elves retreating, chortling at their victory. They had destroyed most of the supplies. Mission accomplished.

Ahad felt the anger. Was that Shayth laughing, mocking the memory of his father? Mocking Shiftan, his father's best friend? He began to run silently behind the disappearing group, tracking them through a narrow gorge and then suddenly on flat, open ground, totally exposed. Facing him stood a dozen dwarves, short, but broad and well armed. Each held an axe and shield, except for two who had nocked bows aimed at him.

Next to them was a well-built elf holding a sword and long knife. His face was hard, but puzzled. Shayth stood next to him, bow in one hand, arrow in the other.

"Are you trying to defect, man, or do you just have a suicide wish?" Shayth asked.

"I've come for you, Shayth," Ahad replied.

A voice from behind Ahad called out: "All clear. No one else follows."

"Either you are very stupid or. . ." the elf paused in his mockery of Ahad. ". . . Or very, very stupid."

The dwarves laughed, but Shayth raised his hand. "You look familiar. Name yourself."

Ahad actually did feel stupid. All this training, and he had acted like a petulant boy. He lowered his eyes, and then slowly turned and began to walk back the way he had come from. Surprisingly, they allowed him. He did not look back, suspecting that if he did, they might change their minds.

He was in the narrow rock corridor and felt confused.

"Stop," a voice said from behind. Shayth sounded authoritative, but not insistent.

He stopped, but did not turn.

"Face me," Shayth said.

Ahad did.

"Who are you?" Shayth asked for a second time, but now with wonder in his voice.

"Do you know him?" the elf asked when Ahad did not answer.

Shayth began to approach.

"Careful," the elf warned. "He may not be as dumb as he seems."

There were just the two of them, it seemed.

"I know you," Shayth whispered, keeping his bow and arrow taut. "You did come for me, didn't you? You're from the palace? An assassin. But why one so young and green?"

"Mebbe the Emperor still underestimates yeh, Shayth," a burly dwarf, now standing next to the elf, said.

Shayth ignored Ballendir and spoke again to Ahad, his voice quiet, but his dark coal eyes blazing. "You came to avenge him?"

Ahad realized he was holding his breath. This is not how it should be. He had imagined their confrontation a thousand times, and no scenario came even close to this.

Shayth's voice turned to ice. "There is nothing to avenge, Ahad. Your father betrayed me after he pledged to protect me.

He poisoned my friend to capture the Wycaan, and let her die while he held the antidote. He was a bad man, Ahad—a tool of a violent Emperor, my uncle."

"Who is this ta yeh?" Ballendir asked, but Shayth continued.

"I thought rotten seed passed through a family. That's why I became what I became—a killing machine, feared throughout the land and hated by all. But it's not true, Ahad—for either of us."

"You killed my father—stabbed him in the back when he loved you."

"He never loved me, Ahad. He loved the man who conceived me, and he loved what he defined as duty. He murdered tens of thousands. Men, women, children, humans, elves, dwarves; he didn't care. And my sword pierced his chest as we fought, not his back. I looked him in the eye and fought him."

"You lie," Ahad said, feeling his chest constrict. "He. . ." But he didn't continue.

"I hated him, Ahad—hated him after I had loved him as my own father. But I learned that a man is measured by his actions, his values. Go back to your books and studies. Become a beacon of learning in these dark times. You don't have to follow in his footsteps."

"I swore to avenge him. . ." Ahad heard the doubt in his own voice. "I have trained to fight, all for this day, this moment."

"If you fight me, there'll be no way back. I will hurt you. If you are a real threat, I will kill you. I see the badge you wear and won't take your attack lightly. Go back to Shiftan and talk to him. He was your father's best friend after mine was murdered. I hear Shiftan is a wise man, as well as a worthy general. Seek the truth. If you come again to fight, I shall kill you, albeit with a heavy heart.

"For I have changed, Ahad, and so can you."

Ahad drew his sword. "You lie. You murdered my father, and now you dishonor his name. Fight me if you call yourself a man."

Ahad took a step forward, only to fall into darkness with a blow to the back of his head.

Chapter Twenty ~ Two

Seanchai and Sellia set off with Umnesilk after a hot breakfast. They scrambled to keep up, having left their horses to rest at the First Boar's advice.

"We go up," he said while they ate. "No place for horses. You return, they fresh, ready to run many miles."

"How long will it take to reach the council?" Sellia asked.

"We go your pace or mine?" the pictorian asked and laughed in a throaty way that made both elves smile.

"We can run," Seanchai said. "Not as long as you, but we can run."

The pictorian grunted. "We see. Ready now?"

They rose and thanked Onywei for the meal. Umnesilk signaled with his head for them to go ahead. When Seanchai peeked back, he saw the giant pictorian and his mate touching foreheads and holding each other.

"Turn around," Sellia snapped. "They don't want an audience."

He frowned at her. "You okay?"

"Sure," she said curtly. "I don't like the cold, and I'm not sure we're making the best use of our time."

He stared at her and a thought occurred. "Do you want children, Sellia? Did that conversation upset you? Do you want a family?"

"You heard my answer last night. Right now, I just want to win a war and live among elves, free elves."

"You want to be among our own kind," Seanchai replied, "back in the forests where our kind belong."

Sellia tightened the strap on her bag and readjusted her bow. "I made my decision. Let's go," she said, and set off briskly.

Umnesilk came running up to them, his gait thumping the ground. "Good to makes haste," he said, "but go wrong way."

The temperature soon dropped further, and the air thinned. Seanchai eventually called for a rest and was glad to see he wasn't the only one sweating and breathing heavily. They drank and stared at the path before them.

"The snow line," Seanchai said. "How long do we have, Umnesilk?"

"Tomorrow we arrive, when sun is highest. Another go on to tell of us coming. No good to surprise pictorians. Rip off heads if surprised."

"How will they receive us?" Sellia asked.

"Not sure," Umnesilk replied. "Maybe rip off heads."

"But we have the First Boar with us," Seanchai said.

"First Boar for fighting. Council for smart?"

"I think you're pretty smart," Seanchai replied. "If General Tarlach trusted you, then so do I."

Both Sellia and Umnesilk stared at him.

"That's kind of weird," Sellia said. "Shouldn't you be hating him?"

"Can hate *and* admire," Umnesilk said. "Best if so, know enemy."

"He killed your mate," Sellia said to Seanchai. "He murdered Ilana."

Umnesilk looked from one to the other.

"Not now," Seanchai snapped and jumped abruptly to his feet. "Let's run."

"I'm sorry," Sellia said in his wake. She wasn't sure if he heard her.

"Wycaan!" Umnesilk shouted, and Sellia glanced up, fearing an avalanche. "Wrong way. Go this way."

That night, they slept in a cave. There was wood piled in a corner, ready for a fire. This was a way station, it seemed, for there was also water and a shovel.

They ate dried meats and hard root vegetables they had packed earlier. Umnesilk told them that the food here was best left for an emergency.

They lit a small fire, wrapped themselves in furs and sat in the cave by the fire, staring into the flames.

"Umnesilk? Do your people tell stories?" Sellia asked.

The great pictorian nodded. "Stories are beautiful and long. Many battles and blood. In tongue of Odessiya, not sound good like in our language."

"Share one with us anyway," she said. "We need to learn more about each other's past if we're to build a future together."

Umnesilk nodded. "Female pictorians always smarter. Elves, too?"

"Of course," Sellia replied.

Umnesilk laughed and nudged Seanchai playfully with his boot. Seanchai almost toppled over.

"I'm smart enough not to respond," the elf said, and this only made Umnesilk laugh more.

After a while, he brought out a flask. "You have?" he asked.

Seanchai reached into his pack and brought out the gift he had received from Thorminsk, the young dwarf craftsman from

Clan Dan Zu'Ulster. He sighed as he passed it to Umnesilk, and the pictorian admired the intricate handiwork. Then he looked up at Seanchai.

"Is very beautiful. A gift? Why sad then?"

"It was a gift, yes–from a young dwarf. But he'll make no more."

"Dead?"

"Yes. You killed him."

Umnesilk frowned, clearly thinking back. "I remember. When we chase to swamp, he not dwarf warrior, but he try to fight."

"Yes," Seanchai replied, and his voice wavered.

Umnesilk filled the flask and gave it to Seanchai. "We drink to dwarf's memory. We honor him now."

Seanchai took a sip and shuddered. Dwarf draft was strong, but this was far more intense. He offered it to Sellia, who declined.

"You gave me a pretty good idea of how it tastes," she said.

"No, you drink," Umnesilk insisted. "We honor Seanchai's friend."

They both stared at him, but he was absolutely serious. Sellia took the flask and drank.

Umnesilk spoke. "Pictorian and dwarf should not fight. When gods made world, made two brothers. One big and strong. He very brave and fought creatures and hunted. Other son small and slow. He angry not to be strong like brother. No good. They fight with words; they fight with fists. No good.

"Mother take small son to gods, who send him on journey under earth. Here he learn to find great stones: some of beauty, others strong for build, and still others for magic. Small brother could walk underground because small. He use magic and learn to make beautiful flasks, and weapons, and jewelry. Become famous, become rich.

"Older brother fight, make enemies. One day, mighty king come to fight and challenge older brother to Kuntai, fight by blows. King stronger than brother, even though brother eight feet tall. King bigger, wider, stronger. King say if win, he take mountains and family be slaves.

"Small son come to see brother. Give him thin vest of many, many very small metals. Older brother say it beautiful but not help. Younger son say: we are different. You fight, and I create. We must trust. I trust you tomorrow to win Kuntai. You trust me with metals.

"Older brother put on under shirt, feel light and not strong. Meet king and king punch first. Punch so loud, echo through mountains and valley. Older brother stagger back from force, but not hurt. Punch king hard, and king fall but rise. Trade many punches. King very strong, but not hurt older brother.

"Brother win victory for family and mountain. Thank younger brother for magic shirt. Then two brother live as family: one under earth, other on mountain. One hunt and fight, other mine stone and create beauty. Both different, but brothers forever."

He stopped and drank from his flask. "You see, Wycaan. Pictorian fight dwarf, not good. Understand?"

"I do," Seanchai replied. "Thank you. I want to show you something. This was made by the same dwarf."

He stood up and let his blanket fall to the ground. Then he unfastened his shirt and removed it. Underneath, shining in the light of the fire, was the King's Mail, small and intricate as Umnesilk has described.

"This was the greatest achievement of Thorminsk, artisan of Clan Dan Zu'Ulster, his finest work, and his last."

Umnesilk stared at it and nodded. He removed a glove and his great hand moved to touch it and look closer. "Odessiya

poorer for loss of dwarf. I sorry for his death." Then he picked
up his flask again. "I give honor to fallen foe, shame he ever
became my enemy."

Seanchai took a swig of his own flask and said, "Tomorrow,
at the council, I need you to say that again. For this is why I
have come: to ask the pictorians to come to the aid of the dwarf
nation."

Chapter Twenty-Three

The following day, Umnesilk led the elves higher into the mountains. After an hour or so, they were walking on ice. Seanchai found it particularly difficult and slipped a number of times.

"How much longer?" he asked Umnesilk, exasperated.

"Soon," the pictorian replied, and then, a few minutes later: "Stop here and wait."

They stood, trying to spot whatever Umnesilk was looking for. He seemed to sniff the air. After a while, they saw two figures in the distance, gliding on the packed snow. As they came closer, Seanchai could see that they were sliding down the mountain on flat, tapered pieces of wood.

They were much smaller than Umnesilk, and Seanchai thought it was because they were female until they drew up next to him. They were pictorye.

The youngsters exchanged words with their leader, and then pulled what looked to Seanchai like crudely made bracelets from their bags and offered them to the elves. Umnesilk instructed them to strap one to each of their boots. There were sharp studs on the bottom.

Now, with these grips, they were able to walk at a more comfortable pace. The pictorye stole furtive glances at the elves and tried, through the First Boar, to ask questions. But Umnesilk was not interested in translating, and they soon fell silent.

It was another hour or so before they entered into a big snow tunnel. Seanchai pulled his hood over his head. They walked for about ten minutes, while a steady drip of water echoed around them and set their pace. Seanchai marveled at the beauty, but the cold, white tunnel soon began to feel like it was closing in, and he was glad when they made it through to the other side.

"Close your mouth," Sellia whispered to her agape companion. "This is the first time the pictorian nation is seeing you. Try and look reasonably intelligent."

"This is amazing," Seanchai marveled, and closed his mouth.

They were in a huge basin, with the surrounding rock walls reaching up at least forty feet. Burrowed into the walls were rooms, maybe homes or storerooms. Seanchai gasped when he saw the round ice houses on the basin floor. On some, he could distinguish the shape of the blocks each with unique carvings. Each house had windows and a doorway.

Seanchai and Sellia followed Umnesilk past a number of houses, and pictorians of all ages and sizes came out to stare at them. Many were clearly uncomfortable, but the First Boar ignored all their comments and kept his eyes focused ahead.

Seanchai, peering through his cowl, began to realize that Umnesilk was tense. The First Boar was taking a risk bringing elves into what he had called the City of the Elders. He led them to the center of the village where a huge tent was erected, covered on all sides by animal skins. Seanchai was relieved to see that they were not from bears.

The huge tent area was lit by torches on poles, and around the perimeter hung decorative skins of many colors. In the middle was a semicircle of nine wooden chairs with armrests.

On the floor in front of the chairs was a row of wooden benches, where Umnesilk signaled for them to sit. When the big pictorian sat next to him, Seanchai turned and spoke.

"You've taken a big risk bringing us here," he said. "I appreciate what you've done. Know that."

Umnesilk nodded and turned to reply, but before he could, a pictorian stood before the nine chairs and began to pound on a big, flat drum slowly and rhythmically. Umnesilk rose, and the elves followed his lead. Seanchai saw that the tent was full behind them.

Nine pictorians wearing purple sashes walked slowly to the front and took their seats. When the drumming ceased, Umnesilk signaled for the elves to sit, but remained standing himself.

He addressed the council and the crowd of people behind him, explaining why he had brought Seanchai there. Then he sat again and leaned in to Seanchai. "All council female, our wisest. They understand your language, some more, some less. One coming who will share between tongues, but speak slow and many will hear your voice. Ah, he come. Thycad serve with me. Trust well."

Seanchai rose and drew back his hood. There was a murmur around the hall, and he waited for it to subside. "I am Seanchai, son of Seantai, a wood elf from Morthian Wood. I am also a Wycaan, and I serve those who would rebuild the alliance and allow all who live in Odessiya to be free.

"Your legends tell how the gods put two brothers on this land, how the brothers were driven apart by their differences, but how eventually their differences helped them work together to defeat an evil king."

He paused a moment. "I come to you today because your brothers who walk under the mountains have taken a stand against the evil Emperor. They defeated him at Hothengold, and now he pursues them across the land.

"I come to ask that you ally with dwarves, elves, free humans, and the Aqua'lansis. This alliance will be guided–not led–by a Wycaan Order, and we will see a peace that once flourished for hundreds of years reborn.

"In your legends, your brother came to you in your darkest hour and gave you the King's Mail." He stopped and pulled off his cloak and shirt in unison. A gasp rose around the hall.

"The dwarf nation–your brothers–honored me with this gift. I bring it to you as the short brother did in the days of old. It is a symbol, but it is also a plea for help. The craftsman who made this died at the hands of Umnesilk, First Boar of the Pictorians.

"Umnesilk paid his respects to this dwarf, who, though not a soldier, died with honor by the First Boar's axe. Now I come and ask that you repay the debt to your brother who lives under the earth.

"Go forth and help the dwarves. Buy me the time that I may go to the Elves of the West and bring them back; that I might find time to train and learn how to defeat the Emperor."

Seanchai looked slowly around the room and then at each of the nine council members. "I come to ask that you stand again with your brother under the mountain, and help free the people of Odessiya. Your boars understood the value of freedom and so left the Emperor's servitude. You are already involved because the Emperor will not forget their departure. Don't wait for him to come to you. Don't face him alone, but in an Alliance with dwarves, elves and others. Take your rightful place once more in the fight for freedom. Thank you." Seanchai held one more gaze with the council, and then slowly sat down.

Chapter Twenty-Four

The first thing Ahad felt when he woke was a pounding in his head. He opened his eyes long enough to note that he was back in the fortress of Skiliad before letting them close again. The darkness was comforting, but the throbbing would not allow him to return to sleep.

He heard two hushed voices in the room.

"He'll wake with a real headache, judging from the lump," said a voice he didn't recognize. "What happened?"

"We found him unconscious on the road," Crefen replied. "Reckon he slipped on the scree."

"You get used to it 'round here," the other replied. "Whole land is bloody rocks. Still, seems clumsy for a Master Assassin and all that. Are you sure that's what happened? You sure—"

"You think I'd make up something?" Crefen snapped. "How long have you been stationed up here?"

"No offense, friend, please," the man replied. "Been here too long, I guess. If the cuts open again, call for me. If he wakes and complains about the pain, give him this."

"Will it help?" Crefen asked.

"No," the man admitted. "But it's disgusting enough that he won't complain again after drinking it."

They both laughed, and Ahad heard the door screech open and shut.

"You can open your eyes now," Crefen said. "I know you're awake. And whine about the pain just once, and I'll gladly force this drink down your throat."

Ahad tried to laugh, but winced instead. "Thanks for covering there. I owe you."

"You owe me nothing. I follow Shadow's orders. If he told me to stick my dirk into where your heart should be, I would without hesitating."

"That's comforting," Ahad replied.

The door opened, and Phineus entered and sat on Ahad's bed. "How're you doing?" he asked. "You look terrible."

"Be up tomorrow," Ahad replied, though he doubted he would.

"Yes, you will, whether you want to be or not. General Shiftan is moving many men out of the Ulster Mountains. He doesn't want too many mouths to feed when the snows hit, if we can't do much to attack the dwarves."

"The supplies?"

"Destroyed," Phineus replied. "But that doesn't matter. I'm sure there are enough supplies. Shiftan's smart. He was probably bringing supplies in another way or something. What does matter is that he's furious with you. You broke from the line; that's insubordination. Either he punishes you or dismisses you. That wasn't subtle, Ahad. I'm surprised at you."

Ahad sighed. "I didn't plan it. I saw Shayth and. . ."

After a few moments of silence, the Crown Prince spoke. "At least they didn't recognize you. Lucky they didn't, or you would be either dead or captive."

Ahad opened his mouth to respond, but then decided not to share the conversation he'd had with Shayth.

"Help me up," Ahad said instead. "I need to speak with General Shiftan."

Rising into a seated position required considerable effort, and Ahad already felt dizzy. "Crefen, let me have a swig of that potion. If it kills me, say I died bravely."

Crefen came over and handed him the bottle. "With pleasure."

Ahad was made to sit outside General Shiftan's office for what seemed like hours. The bench was hard, and there was nothing to lean back on. When he dozed, his head bobbed, and he woke each time from the pain. A rotund man eventually stepped out and stared at him.

"Oh, my," he said, his hands wrapped around his stomach.

"Don't tell me," Ahad snapped. "I look like my father and you fought with him."

The man stared at him momentarily without blinking. When he spoke, his voice was crisp and clipped. "I served as your, um, father's secretary for over twelve years, until he died. I never took up arms with him, but I loved him and served faithfully.

"And if you are half the man he was, Master Ahad, then you will never grow tired of hearing people, um, praise him."

"It won't bring him back," Ahad snapped. "It doesn't serve me."

"Your father's legacy doesn't serve you?" Bortand frowned. "It is the only thing that has kept you alive and, um, provided you with the friends you have, and, um, the education you've received. You take much for granted, but that is beside the point.

"It serves those who wish to tell you how he impacted their lives. It allows men who served with him; risked their lives with him; and killed, mourned, and celebrated with him, to console themselves. Fighting alongside General Tarlach was the single greatest honor they will ever experience.

"It is not always about you, young Ahad. That is what we call, um, leadership. General Shiftan will receive you now."

As the man began to shuffle away, Ahad looked up. "Bortand," he called, and the man stopped and half-turned. "My father spoke highly of you. Thank you for serving him and for being his friend."

Bortand looked at Ahad and finally smiled. "Thank you," he said, his voice no longer terse.

Chapter Twenty-Five

"Y ou were not invited to sit," General Shiftan snapped from behind his desk when Ahad began to droop into a chair.

Ahad stood quickly back up and took a deep breath. He was determined not to show weakness, but his head was pounding.

"Soldier," the General said. "We were in a battle situation, and you disobeyed my orders."

"I'm sorry," Ahad said. "I should know better, but I saw him and momentarily lost all sense of . . ."

"You're lucky the rocks felled you. I can't imagine what Shayth would have done. He cares nothing for you, as he cared nothing for your father. He's been killing for ten years—not soldiers in honorable combat, but in barrooms and alleyways. He wouldn't have hesitated to kill. . ."

The General stopped abruptly. He had seen something in Ahad's face. "What is it? Not used to being chewed out by a higher ranking officer?"

Ahad didn't answer.

"I asked you a question."

"I've apologized and admitted I was wrong," Ahad said. "Punish me as you see fit."

"Punish you? Yes, maybe I should, at that. But will you learn from the punishment?"

"I've learned from the mistake," Ahad retorted. "I am lucky the others–"

He stopped abruptly. Shiftan had risen to his feet. "You didn't fall, did you, Ahad? You wear good boots. You trained as an assassin to move on all terrains. You didn't fall."

Ahad didn't answer.

"Do I need to remind you that I am a considerably superior officer?" He still received no reply. "Guards!" he shouted, and two burly men entered immediately. "Escort this young soldier to the holding cell. Let him relieve himself on the way and see that he receives the bare minimum of food and water. Lock him up for twenty-four hours by himself."

The soldiers saluted. Ahad nodded. "I accept my punishment and again apologize."

He turned and walked out with a guard on either side.

"Bortand, stay, if you don't mind," General Shiftan said, and then turned to the healer he had also summoned. "You examined Ahad after we brought him back to Skiliad, correct?"

"I saw him when we found him on the road, as well, General, though I only checked him briefly in the field."

"What did you find?"

"The swelling was small when I got to him. The skin had a cut on it. Why do you ask, sir? I decided there was minimal danger to lift and bring him back here, given the circumstances. We could have been attacked if we had stayed longer."

"You saw evidence of a single cut and a swelling beginning to grow around it?" General Shiftan asked.

"Yes sir, that's correct. Are you worried about. . ."

"Be at ease man," the General interrupted. "I'm not questioning your actions. When a man falls down the side of the mountain, he'll bang his head several times, no?"

The healer stared at him. "I get what you're asking, sir. Yes, he would have numerous cuts and scrapes, and probably a number of bumps. What I saw, now I come to think of it, was the result of a single blow."

"Yes, that's what I thought. Thank you. You serve the Emperor well."

"Thank you, General," the healer saluted. "I only looked quickly 'cause we were in the field."

"I understand. You're dismissed. Thank you."

After the door was closed, General Shiftan turned to Bortand. "Let's talk to the soldiers who went with him."

"Is that wise, sir? You'll need to acknowledge the, um, young prince."

"Yes, you're right. We need to question them more subtly."

"With respect, my General, I tried that. One of our men questioned the boy named Crefen. He stuck to this story. What are you thinking, sir?"

"Bortand, you know Shayth, at least through Tarlach's eyes. If Ahad had confronted him, would Shayth have killed him?"

"Good question, sir," Bortand rubbed his ample belly, deep in thought. "His reputation reflects the time before he joined the Wycaan. It might be that Shayth has changed. He was so young when everything happened, so perhaps being around this elf has, um, stabilized him."

"You have sympathies for him?" Shiftan was annoyed at himself for even asking the question.

"General Shiftan, I am a loyal servant of the Emperor. The boy killed General Tarlach, and you know how I felt about him. My job as your advisor, however, dictates that I answer your question as best I can."

"I'm sorry," the General replied. "I want to kill Shayth for what he did. I also have the eye of the Emperor on me for my role at Hothengold. I don't curry his favor as well as your former superior did. But I feel a responsibility for Ahad, my best friend's son, and if he confronts Shayth, I'm not sure he'll survive."

"There's an additional problem, too, begging your pardon," Bortand said. "You have the, um, Crown Prince to consider."

"Hmmm, yes. We cannot remain complicit to his being here in disguise for too much longer."

Both men sat in silence for a while. Then Bortand cleared his throat.

"You think Ahad and Shayth met but did not fight?"

Shiftan nodded.

"And that worries you because it suggests that Shayth might have, um, changed?"

"Yes, and also because Ahad is lying. Why would he not tell us that he confronted Shayth?"

Bortand suddenly looked up. "They're changing roles. Ahad suffers for the loss of his father and is perhaps becoming unstable because of it. Shayth has passed through this stage and. . ."

Shiftan leaned forward ". . . and might just become the leader that his father was. Put the two together, and the Emperor might be facing a far more serious threat than he anticipates."

Bortand smiled. "And that's without considering the Wycaan, my lord."

General Shiftan rose and went to a flagon of wine nearby. He poured two cups and brought one to Bortand. "A powerful alliance. Now add the Crown Prince to all this."

Shiftan sipped his wine and stared into his cup. "What if Shayth and Ahad spoke? What if Ahad hesitated because of things Shayth said?"

He rose and took his cup to the window. After a moment, he turned to Bortand. "In the morning, we'll confront Ahad and the Crown Prince. They must not be allowed to make a connection with Shayth. Bring them to my office first thing in the morning."

"Before breakfast, my General?" Bortand asked, rubbing his stomach as he contemplated the next day.

"Yes, before anyone has time to act."

General Shiftan entered his office in the cold, fresh morning air. Bortand was waiting for him, his hands clasped tightly across his stomach. Shiftan glared.

"Gone?" he roared.

"Gone," Bortand replied.

"And the other three?"

"Gone, as well."

"We must inform the Emperor."

"I have already prepared a message. If you approve, I have a hawk waiting."

Chapter Twenty-Six

One of the elders nodded to Umnesilk, who called a young boar to him. They exchanged a few words before Umnesilk turned to the elves.

"This Gruenisk. He serve with me in Emperor's army, speaks common tongue. Go with him for eat and wait. When council ready, horn will blow and all come hear council's decision."

"How do you think it went?" Seanchai asked. "Is there anything else I can do or say?"

"No. This pictorian decision now. Go, eat well."

With that, Umnesilk turned his back on Seanchai. Sellia took Seanchai's arm and guided him away. He noticed most pictorians filing out of the huge tent toward a big fireplace where meat was cooking. No one paid them much attention until they were sitting on a log in a semi-circle with about fifteen pictorians.

Most seemed content to just eat, but one began to talk loudly and pointed at Seanchai several times. He turned to Gruenisk, but Gruenisk had already begun arguing with the female pictorian who sat opposite him. Though Seanchai could not understand what either was saying, it was clear they were becoming increasingly agitated.

Finally, an old, bent, pictorian banged his staff on the ground. It had a metal base and made a loud thumping noise.

Both pictorians stopped, and all looked at the elder.

"Torimisk here instructs me to translate what we before say," Gruenisk said to Seanchai. "This one not happy you here. Pictorians live in these. . . these far away areas because we not grow. We—I know word—breed, we breed slow. When boars die in war, we more weak.

"In last three ten-years we see more pictorye because boars stay to breed. She say going to fight for Emperor lots wrong and she thinks going to fight for you lots wrong too. She blame Umnesilk. Say he too hot-blooded."

Seanchai looked at the old female and nodded. "Gruenisk, please translate for me. Tell her that I understand her legitimate concerns. Tell her that she has every right to feel as she does, but I have a responsibility for all the races of Odessiya."

He stopped while Gruenisk translated. When he had finished, Seanchai continued. "Pictorians are an honorable race with a rich heritage and culture, their noble past interwoven into the histories of Odessiya. Your time of isolation is past no matter what this council decides.

"The pictorians left the Empire during the battle of Hothengold, a battle that the Emperor lost. He will not forget the betrayal by your people, and he will come for you all, including your females and your pictorye."

When Gruenisk translated, there was a hum around the circle, but Seanchai immediately raised his hand to indicate he hadn't finished. "The question isn't whether or not you fight in the struggle for the freedom of Odessiya at all; it is whether you fight and succeed with the other races, or stand and die alone. The days of pictorian isolation are already over. . . forever."

A horn blew, and all put their plates down and returned to the Tent of the Elders. One old pictorian rose and spoke, her quiet voice carrying throughout the tent. The only other sound was Gruenisk whispering a translation into Seanchai's ear. The leader spoke about how this day had been anticipated, how they knew the decision to side with the Emperor had effectively ended their isolation. She paused for a moment and took a deep breath.

"The council has decided. We set events in motion long before the Wycaan came. When we agreed to fight for the Emperor, the die was cast. We chose wrong, but now history affords us a second chance. We will once again stand with the elves and the dwarves, as we did in days of old. We will join the Alliance."

There was a ripple of discontent around the room and a comment that included Umnesilk's name. The First Boar rose sharply, his huge body looming over all, and the tent fell instantly silent. Gruenisk leaned closer to Seanchai to translate.

"Have we forgotten proud history? Once, pictorians members of the High Council of Odessiya. Once, we respected for principles, feared for strength, and admired for courage. We once warriors.

"It took elf on battlefield at Hothengold to remind what I forgot. We not hide in the mountains while others are enslaved. When Emperor came, we thought we joined side of right. We mistaken. Now we have chance to rectify mistake. Not only blood of pictorians been shed. We never flinch at spilt blood of our warriors or the warriors of foes. But we killed innocents. I slew little brother that made King's Mail. He barely hold axe, yet he accepted his death. But combat with little craft brother not honorable. Now we right the wrong."

The tent remained silent as Umnesilk sat down. Seanchai saw Sellia lean closer and, with his heightened elf hearing, heard her say: "A First Boar proves himself a leader not just on the battlefield."

Seanchai thought he discerned the twitch of a smile from the huge leader. As the meeting closed, Umnesilk rose and led them from the Tent of the Elders. Three others, including Gruenisk, fell into step around them, and Seanchai noted their hands near their weapon hilts.

They walked in silence, and Seanchai was relieved when they were again soon out on the snowy tundra. They reached Umnesilk's village by nightfall. Dinner was again communal as Gruenisk told everyone what had transpired. The First Boar sat in silence, eating and staring into the fire. Onywei sat next to him, an arm around his shoulder. Though he had won, Umnesilk seemed to take no satisfaction.

After dinner, Umnesilk growled something to Gruenisk and rose together with his mate. Seanchai glanced at the young pictorian.

"We join him soon. Onywei traveled far before they had pictorye. She has great knowledge of land here in north."

"Maybe Umnesilk needs some time alone with her, too," Sellia said. "That was a heavy decision to make."

"No," Gruenisk replied, his voice harder. "Our numbers not as small as you might think, but our peoples scattered, and when great horn blows, we shall hear how many will answer. Also, what is pictorian if he not connected with past, with his *khundai*, his warrior heart?"

The rest of the evening was spent in Umnesilk's tent. Seanchai told Onywei where they were heading, and she drew a route that she became less sure about as it led farther away. An older pictorian came in with a knotted length of string and measured Seanchai. He fretted as he measured Sellia and shook his head.

"He look for clothes in pictorye supplies, but not hopeful," Umnesilk chuckled gruffly. "Says you eat whole boar before tomorrow. Now you go bed. In morning, we have supplies ready."

Seanchai rose and bowed. "Thank you, Umnesilk, and you, Onywei."

Onywei answered and her mate translated. "Best for pictorians that you go fast and return soon. Onywei thinks mate most happy when fighting with you at side."

"I'll be as fast as I can," Seanchai promised. But as he left their home, he wondered whether he would be fast enough or, when he returned, good enough.

These thoughts kept him awake. Just as he began to doze, a great horn blew. It was deep and vibrated through his body. Three times, it blew: long, drawn out notes. A few minutes later, a second horn blew from further away, and then a few minutes after that, a third, more distant again. This went on until Seanchai only heard the faintest of sounds. The horn blower blew again and the response came. Then a third time and once again came the response.

He rose and stepped outside to where a group of pictorians stood looking up to a pictorian on a hill with a huge horn. When they saw Seanchai, they parted so that he faced Umnesilk. The First Boar looked at him solemnly.

"Great horn sends message across snow plains. Pictorian nation called to war. We march to free Odessiya."

Chapter Twenty-Seven

U mnesilk led Seanchai and Sellia out onto the tundra in the early morning dew. They followed a flat path that snaked between imposing mountains. The wind whipped up fine, icy dust, and all three covered their mouths and noses, exposing only their eyes. Seanchai was sure his eyelashes were going to freeze.

They walked for a long time in silence before Umnesilk called for a break in a small cave that gave some shelter from the wind. Onywei had stayed up deep into the night preparing their packs with wood, water, and other supplies. These were secured onto a sleigh with furs that was being pulled by the horses.

Seanchai wondered whether the creatures could possibly survive the journey. They were to climb through a pass in the next day and then walk across a vast ice pack.

Onywei believed this was the shortest and least obtrusive way into the west. They would encounter pictorian hamlets and, even though they had answered the call to war, Umnesilk was worried about their being able to pass through. He planned to take them as far as the ice flow.

"When at ice, try to ride horses," he said. "Not know how long they live, so ride hard and feast on them when die."

Seanchai made a face and then looked at Sellia. When he had rescued her from the wolfheids, the beasts had killed her horse, and the elves had eaten its remains in tribute and as a good source of food.

"Sleigh can be pulled by pictorian," Umnesilk continued. "Maybe you pull for while, too. Less supplies, less heavy."

"What about you?" Sellia asked. "You will return to what?"

"Other tribes have three days to gather food and weapons. Then must come before elders and march. Will head for Ulster as you ask."

"Will anyone challenge you as First Boar? It didn't seem that everyone was in agreement."

Umnesilk shrugged. "Maybe young boar, but if so, soon dead boar."

It was after midday, judging by the position of the sun, when they came through the mountains and to the edge of the ice plains. Seanchai stared ahead at a flat, white sheet that appeared to go on forever.

"Close your mouth," Sellia suggested. "We part here from Umnesilk."

Seanchai turned to the pictorian. "You have done me a great service. Thank you, First Boar Umnesilk."

Umnesilk shook his head. "No, Wycaan. It is you who done great favor. Help me find *khundai,* heart of pictorian. Help remind people of great past so we have great future. I thank you, Seanchai of the Wycaan."

I am a wood elf, Seanchai thought to himself. *What am I doing here?* His feet crunched on the ice, one foot and then the other. He was thankful for the nailed soles that gripped the ice. He looked around. Nothing but white under blue. The land was flat and cold and empty.

One of the horses nickered behind him. They shared his fear, he was sure. Seanchai tried not to think that he was leading them to their death, but he felt that they knew it anyway. There was straw on the sleigh, and the pictorians had covered the hooves of the horses with cloth for protection.

When they camped at night, they tethered the horses and kept them close to the fire, but still, in the morning, they were stiff, and the elves spent time massaging their legs. Seanchai tried to transfer some energy through his ryku training, but it was draining on him, and he felt cold and spent each time. Sellia told him to stop and save it as a last resort.

The first horse fell on the fifth day. It rose and continued for a few hours, but as dusk approached, Sellia told Seanchai to lead the other three on and camp once she was out of sight. She remained behind with the fallen horse, her bow and arrows, and a burlap sack for the meat.

They ate well that night, though neither elf took any joy in the horse's final sacrifice. It didn't help that Seanchai felt convinced the other three horses were glaring at him.

"Sellia, do you think we made a mistake coming this way?"

"No," she replied. "We need to maintain as much secrecy as possible for as long as we can. Once the Emperor realizes you're heading into the west, he'll make life very difficult.

"He'll not only send armies to stop you from getting through the pass, but also might decide he must crush any uprising before you return with a free Elven army."

They both went quiet for a while.

"Do they exist?" Seanchai asked.

"I hope so," she replied. "For you, for the land of Odessiya, and for myself."

"You?"

"Have you noticed I look different than the rest of you?" she laughed. "I'm the only dark-skinned elf I know."

"I have seen pictures of them," Seanchai replied.

"So? Am I the last of my kind? If not, where are my people?"

"We *are* your people, Sellia. An elf is an elf. Skin color doesn't make you any different."

"I need to know," she said.

"And you hope the Elves of the West can tell you?"

She shrugged. "Let's just find them, huh?"

"Find them and persuade them to train me. And then expect them to give up the peace they have protected and march into Odessiya."

"I think my skin color might not be our highest priority," Sellia replied, smiling.

Seanchai rose and went to her. He drew her close. "After we topple the Emperor and bring peace, you and I will go looking for an answer. We'll take Rhoddan and Shayth and search until we find one."

She laughed. "And who will lead the new, free Odessiya? The people will need a strong leader—one with morals, and principles, and a vision."

"That's not me, Sellia. I'm just a wood elf. I want to learn healing as my mother did and live among trees. Maybe I can train at a Wycaan school like the one Mhari described."

"I wasn't thinking of you, Seanchai. The people need a king or emperor."

Seanchai stared at her. "Shayth?"

"He was born to rule, and the more I get to know him, the more convinced I become."

Seanchai realized he was not blinking or breathing. "Are you serious? Shayth?"

Sellia met his stare, and her intensity left no doubt. "Yes," she replied. "Shayth Shindell, once Crown Prince of Odessiya."

Chapter Twenty-Eight

"Get them out of here," Shayth yelled.

He and three dwarves had been leading an army patrol toward an ambush. They had run through a small clump of trees and over a ridge. The soldiers chased them as they scrambled down the other side, but a small group of refugees—about twenty dwarves, young, old, and shorn of their fighters—were making their way on the road below. Shayth needed to cross the road and draw the soldiers onto the incline on the other side.

"No, wait. This way." He ran to his left, moving in front of the refugees, who had stopped in their tracks. "Don't move," he yelled at them.

"Shayth! Yeh're moving away from the am—" Callestar, the oldest of his companions, cried out.

"We can't run through them. The soldiers will cut them down as they pass."

"We're dwarves," he shot back. "The soldiers'll catch us on flat ground. Yeh head for the ambush point. Bring them through here as we planned."

"But then you're just three of you against eighteen of them."

"Better us than old women and children."

"One of you go. I might be able to—"

"No. Ballendir told us to guard yeh," another dwarf interrupted.

Shayth spun round. "What?"

The three dwarves all stood with their hands on their knees, panting. Dwarves were tough, but not cut for running fast over long distances. They all looked at him with trepidation in their eyes. Shayth glared at Callestar.

"He did, Shayth," Callestar said. "It's true. He also told us not to tell yeh."

The soldiers appeared on the ridge. Shayth watched them look from him to the refugees.

"Go hide among the refugees, and then head for the rendezvous. Tell Ballendir that I will bring the soldiers round to you in the canyon. Then tell him I'll want a word with him." Shayth glared at them. "*Several* words."

He ran well ahead of the refugees to divert the soldiers. As he did, he loosened his bow. The first soldier to reach the flat ground was rewarded with an arrow through his throat. The second fell, clutching the arrow that pierced his heart. Then Shayth ran north into the wood.

He heard a shout directing the sixers to follow him, and hoped the entire troop was on his heels. He ran through the trees, trying to keep track of where he should turn east toward the ambush. He couldn't stop to see if they had indeed left the refugees alone.

A few minutes later, he came to a brook and began to run alongside it upstream. He could hear his pursuers, but they were not getting any closer. The terrain began to ascend, and he scrambled to get up to the top. If he couldn't find his way to the rendezvous point, then he would need to lose his pursuers.

He didn't like the idea of jumpy soldiers wondering around these parts. The area was home to many wandering dwarves who had fled their villages.

Shayth flew down the other side of the ridge, but in his haste, his foot caught a tree root and he tripped, rolling head over heels. He faintly remembered cold spring water as his head crashed against a rock and everything went dark.

Shayth's head was pounding, and he felt close to throwing up. Two hushed voices spoke close by. He moved his hands very slowly and determined he was not bound.

He heard a third arrive, skidding on the ground. "I have his arrows—all that I could grab." The voice was very young, and either elf or human. "But there might be more. They're black feathered and easy to find, I fear."

"Nothing we can do about it now," a female, also young-sounding, whispered. "They're out there looking. Hiding the tracks while dragging him here was the best we. . ."

There were shouts getting closer and boots crunching the ground.

"So what if 'e fell," came a soldier's voice nearby. "Prob'ly got up and kept running. Ain't got no brains, them scum."

"This one 'as, Jocknan. 'e's from the Emperor's family. Must be brainy if 'e's royalty. Them all 'ave babies among 'emselves to keep the brains."

"We're the ones wifout brains if we keep 'aving to look 'ere."

"Yeah? An' if we go back empty 'anded, it's our brains they'll stew."

Three men's laughter faded as they moved away. Shayth lifted his head and turned slowly, but a hand went over his mouth and a knife to his throat. The knife worried him because the hand holding it was shaking.

He slowly nodded and the hand over his mouth withdrew, though the knife remained precariously close. Shayth shut his eyes and lay his pounding head down. He actually dozed off and when he woke, it was dark.

He couldn't make out the others in what he now thought might be a small cave, but he could sense they were there. His throat was dry and raw. "Water," he whispered.

Out of the darkness came a hand at the end of a thin, young arm, and a water skin. Shayth took the skin and drank slowly. As his eyes adjusted to the darkness, he saw two faces staring at him. They were young, much younger than him—maybe eight or ten. A third, even younger, was curled in the corner, asleep.

"Are the soldiers still around?" Shayth whispered.

"Maybe," the girl said, but her expression suggested otherwise.

"I-I think you saved my life," Shayth said. "Thank you."

He tried to sit up. The girl again brought the knife out and pointed it at him. He rubbed his head. "May I sit up and lean against the wall? Please?" he asked.

She nodded.

"You saved my life," Shayth said. "I won't hurt you. Ouch!" He rubbed his forehead. "I don't think I could even if I wanted to."

The boy and girl exchanged glances. She began to lower the knife, but the boy shook his head, and she raised the blade again.

"I'm going to guess that you're running from the soldiers," Shayth said quietly. "So am I. You saw that."

"We know who you are," the boy said. "We 'eard them soldiers 'n we've seen wanted parchments wiv your face on it. You murder innocent people 'n kids. You're Shayth, the traitor."

"I am Shayth, that's true," Shayth took another gulp of water. "But remember that the people who call me traitor are the same people you're hiding from. Why are you running?"

"Soldiers came to our village. Our mum's a blacksmith 'n they gave 'er work to do shoeing 'orses. She's the best blacksmith in Odessiya 'n when they moved on, they told 'er she'd 'ave to join 'em. They threatened to burn the 'ole village if she didn't go. They're short of blacksmiths 'ere 'n said it was for the Emperor."

"I'm very sorry," Shayth said. "But why did you leave the village?"

"We're going to rescue 'er," the girl said.

"The three of you?"

"We 'ave knives," she said brandishing the blade, "and now we 'ave you."

"Am I a prisoner, or one of your gang?" Shayth tried not to smile.

They hesitated and looked at each other. Then the girl looked at him, her eyes hopeful and innocent. "You decide," she said.

Chapter Twenty ~ Nine

Shayth led the three children through the forest. The older two chatted about their mother and life in the village. The youngest followed behind and said nothing. Shayth had to keep glancing behind to make sure that he was still there.

Only when they were near the dwarf's resistance cell did it occur to Shayth what he was doing.

"Let's rest here," he said, and promptly sat down on a log.

"But we 'ad a break just before," the girl protested.

"Maybe the prince gets tired 'cause 'e's royal," the older boy said.

"I'm not royal," Shayth snapped, and then felt bad when they cringed. "I'm sorry, but I don't like being reminded of my past. Let's just take a moment, okay?"

"I think 'e's just weak," the youngest said.

"Are you ganging up on me?" Shayth asked, trying to lighten his own tone.

"Why don'tcha like bein' called a prince?" the girl asked.

"I wanna be called a prince," the youngest said, sitting next to Shayth, their legs touching.

Shayth ruffled his hand through his hair, making the spikes rebel and stand up even straighter.

"I lost my father and mother, and I'm convinced that the Emperor murdered them."

All three children were staring at him now. The youngest
shook his head. "But wasn't the Emperor your father's big
brother? He wouldn't 'ave. . ." he glanced over at his own big
brother, his expression wide-eyed.

"Anyway," Shayth said. "That's why I don't like being called
a prince. I gave it up and ran away from the palace forever."

"You were our age when y'ran away, weren'tcha?" the girl
asked.

Shayth nodded.

"And then. . . and then you. . ." she didn't know how to
continue, so Shayth did it for her.

"I was hurt, and angry, and afraid. I had no one to guide
me—not like the three of you, who have each other. I did some
very bad things, and I'm ashamed of them now. I was an angry
boy—mean, and looking for a fight. But when I met the Wycaan,
I found a fight for a cause nobler than anger and revenge. Can
you understand?"

He stopped. He himself was shocked at this revelation. The
four of them went very quiet. Then the girl moved and sat next
to Shayth. She put her thin hand on his arm.

"Our mother says people can change, 'specially when
they're young," the girl said quietly. "I think you're a better
person now."

"I'm not sure I—"

"And maybe y'are still the prince," she continued. "You just
need a chance t' let the prince-ness come out. Maybe fighting
for the Wycaan will do that."

Shayth patted her hand. "Thank you," he said, and meant it.
"You're very kind, but I don't think I'm meant to be a ruler."

"Would you take a mother away from three little children?"
the smallest asked. Shayth shook his head, and the little boy
continued. "Then I think you can be a prince. Those soldiers

took our mummy 'cause the Emperor wanted 'em to. They said so. I think you'd make a nicer Emperor."

"Me, too," his brother said.

"And me," said a voice from behind them.

The children jumped, but Shayth didn't move. "This is my friend Rhoddan. He's an elf, and they have very good hearing. Sometimes too good."

They all rose and found the big elf in a green cloak that only partially concealed his hefty broadsword. Rhoddan never felt comfortable around children.

"Greetings," he said with a stiff smile that somehow made him look fiercer. "I need to speak to you, Shayth."

They moved to the side, away from the children.

"A scout has been tracking you and Ballendir is adamant. You can't bring these children to the camp. Once they join us, we cannot let them leave and give us away. You have to leave them here, now, or take them back to wherever you found them."

"They're going to rescue their mother, who was conscripted as a blacksmith."

Rhoddan glanced back at the children. The girl smiled and waved. He leaned closer to Shayth. "I'm not sure I fancy their chances. Let's get them back to their village."

"Are *you* going to persuade them?"

Rhoddan walked over to the children, rubbing the stubble on his chin. "Listen, brave humans, your mother is safe."

"'ow do you know?" the older boy asked.

"Because the army desperately needs a good blacksmith, and she's good, right?"

"She's the best," the youngest said, almost offended by the question.

"You can't rescue her," Rhoddan said, raising his hands as he saw them bristle. "It's not because you're not brave. If she runs away, the army will come to the village and take revenge. They do that, you know.

"Your mother would never want that to happen. She'd prefer for you to live safely in the village until she can return for you."

"But who'll look after us?" the little girl asked.

"We'll take care of that," Rhoddan said. "Shayth, um—the *prince*—and I will escort you back and take care of everything."

"We will?" Shayth asked, glaring at Rhoddan for calling him a prince.

The children looked from one to the other and agreed. They immediately set off back the way they had come. That evening, they camped near the spot where the children had found Shayth. As they sat around the fire, the children peppered Shayth with questions about the palace and royal life. Shayth answered them with truth when he could and stories when he couldn't. He didn't remember much from his childhood; neither did he want to dig into his past to try. But he humored them.

They walked the whole of the next day and camped in a deep wood. Shayth hunted and caught a young deer, which they cooked over a spit. Again, the children plied him with questions, often the same ones and he spun more stories.

The following morning, they walked until nearly midday, when they passed through rough, but cultivated fields. Another day and a half of walking and questions, and then they were passing thatched huts and small enclaves for animals.

"That's our house," the girl exclaimed, and pulled Shayth inside. The place was empty, but nothing inside had been touched. The children all gravitated toward toys and the single table.

Shayth went back outside to stand with Rhoddan. A few villagers were approaching them, all wearing stern expressions.

"I hope you have a good idea," Shayth said. "It doesn't look like anyone worried too much when these children ran off."

"Put your hood on," Rhoddan replied.

The big elf crossed his arms and stared at the ragged bunch, now numbering at least thirty. Some held scythes, pitchforks, and other agricultural tools that could be used for tasks other than what they were made for. The sight of two big and well-armed men didn't provide much inclination to be hospitable.

"Who is the council here?" Rhoddan demanded, his voice deep and clear.

From the crowd, two elderly women stepped forward. "There is another," one said, "but she's poorly right now."

"The two of you speak for the village?"

"Yes, milord."

"We brought back these three children. You know who they are?"

The two women nodded, almost in unison.

"And you know who their mother is and why she is not here?"

Again they nodded.

"There are two solutions," Rhoddan continued. "Either you agree to care for the children until their mother can return, or we'll go get her and bring her back here to take care of them herself. You should know that if we take her from her conscription, we'll be followed by a very angry regiment of the Emperor's finest, who won't be happy at losing such an accomplished blacksmith."

There was a murmur among the crowd. Then one of the old women looked up. "How do we know you would do that?"

"I am, indeed, a very pleasant chap," Rhoddan said, peering down at her, "and it might be hard to imagine that I'd do such a thing. But my friend here has a bit of a reputation. He's been known to be a little crazy."

As Shayth removed his hood, the little girl, who had followed him out, announced: "Do you not know who this is? 'e's Prince Shayth Shindell."

And then, in one movement, the thirty or so villagers went down each on one knee and bowed their heads.

"You 'ave our word," one of the old women said. "We will do the bidding of the prince."

Chapter Thirty

S now swirled around Seanchai and Sellia. They kept their
faces covered and the pictorians' fur coats wrapped tight.
But nothing could stop the penetrating cold. Their eyes
watered, their ears rang, and their hands and feet were numb.

The storm had been raging for hours and there was no sign
of it abating. When two horses fell to the ground, Seanchai took
out his swords and ended their misery. The final horse pulled
the sleigh, but it, too, fell shortly after. Seanchai barely had the
strength to drive his blade home this time, and his muscles
screamed against the movement.

He wrapped the thick leather harness around his shoulders.
Slowly, he began to drag the sleigh, but Sellia shook her head
when she saw him struggling. He took off the harness, undid
the furs that covered the sleigh and helped Sellia inside. He
crawled in with her and closed the furs around them. Clumsily,
they clung to each other desperate to share any body heat.

"S-s-s-s-so c-o-o-o-o-o-ld," Sellia chattered.

Gradually, the furs above them pushed in, weighed down
by accumulating snow. Seanchai thought he felt warmer, and
dozed off to sleep.

Seanchai woke to the sounds of scraping and bear grunts instead of howling wind. The furs were pressing in, and it occurred to him that the skins that had saved them might have also attracted their guests. Then he could make out sunlight filtering through the snow. The bears were digging Seanchai and Sellia out.

A few minutes later, the sounds stopped. Seanchai waited a few moments, and then pushed his way out. He fell onto the ice, his body stiff and uncooperative. Pulling himself up with help from the sleigh, he saw that the horses' carcasses had been ripped clean. As his eyes adjusted to the sunlight, he could make out four ice bears nearby. They were pure white, except for the red staining their mouths and paws.

The bears grunted as they gnawed bones. When Seanchai stumbled, they looked up from the carcasses and sniffed the air. A few more grunts and they lumbered away from the dead horses and the Wycaan.

"Thank you," Seanchai whispered, unable to speak any louder. He hoped the bears had heard.

He rose and staggered over to wake Sellia and dig her and the sled out from under the snow. She didn't stir, but he could see steam escaping her nose as she exhaled. He looked up and saw they were near the end of the ice sheet.

With renewed hope, Seanchai put the harness around him and began to pull the sleigh. It moaned in protest, but slowly he was able to pull it. He felt around for a source of energy to give himself strength, but there were no trees or water or plants.

He heard a growl behind him and focused his thoughts on the great ice bears. Left foot, right foot, left, right. The image of the great bears, bloodstained and staring at him with their ice-blue eyes, filled his senses and gave him the energy as his legs slowly pulled the sledge forward.

Seanchai finally pulled the sleigh off of the ice by a rock hill. There was no wind, so he untied the fur from the sleigh and pulled out the remaining wood. It was damp, but he piled it into a small mound and, channeling considerable energy, lit it. He pulled Sellia over to lie next to it. He removed her furs and rubbed her arms and legs, breathing heavily from exhaustion. He turned her toward the fire on her side and rubbed her back.

Finally, he elicited a sigh from her, and it was the most beautiful sigh he could imagine. She moved her body closer to the fire without opening her eyes. Seanchai added the remaining wood and collapsed on the other side. He quickly fell asleep.

He woke to Sellia pouring a warm liquid down his throat. He coughed and struggled away.

"Easy, boy," Sellia said. "I've been trying to warm you some, but the wood is almost gone, and I don't have the energy to give you a rub down. Drink this. We need to move on."

Seanchai sat up with considerable effort and tried to open his eyes. He took the mushroom drink, with its spiraling steam, and brought it to his mouth. It filled his insides with warmth, and he began to feel better.

"We made it, Sellia," he said. "I wasn't sure we would."

She smiled at him. "That was crazy. I thought we were dead. I kept having strange dreams of ice bears hugging me and rubbing me to stay warm. Ice bears. Weird, no?"

"Yeah," Seanchai said, clutching the cup and staring back toward the ice and the bears. "Weird."

Chapter Thirty-One

Seanchai was able to pull the sleigh up a gentle incline for the next day with relative ease. But the path became considerably steeper on the second day, and, by lunchtime, they were also seeing tracks of other travelers.

"We need to leave the path," Sellia said when they saw some mounted horses ahead of them. "What is left in the sleigh?"

Most of what remained was dried food and fur. They repacked their bags to accommodate the extra supplies, and Seanchai rolled up the fur skins.

"You planning to carry that?" Sellia quipped. "I don't want you holding me back."

Seanchai laughed as he stroked the rich fur. Almost every night now, in his dreams, he ran with the bears, fished with them, and once had hunted down an elk. It was exhilarating.

"We have ten days of fast walking," Sellia said. "We're going to follow a path across the ridge there. I want us off this trail. It's not supposed to be well used, but Umnesilk thought we might encounter refugees trying to remain unobtrusive."

By late afternoon, they had climbed up near the ridge and would soon make it onto the narrow path Sellia was aiming for. As she turned a tight bend, she stopped abruptly, and Seanchai almost knocked into her. There were shouts coming from the main path beneath them.

A man laughed, and then a woman screamed. Children and another woman cried out for the man to stop whatever he was doing. Seanchai began to move forward, but Sellia grabbed his arm.

"There's only one way through, and we're going to have to pass troops stationed there already. If they find out you're here now, these hills will be swarming with battalions, and the pass filled with soldiers.

Another female scream pierced the air and was followed by two men laughing.

"I can't walk past whatever's happening down there," he hissed. "They're females, Sellia."

She flinched, remembering the two men who had caught her on their way to Uncle's camp. "Let's see if we can stop them without you being seen. Come."

Sellia threw down her bags and ran along the path, bow in hand. Seanchai did the same, and when he caught up with her, she was leaning against a rock.

"Let me go alone, Seanchai. I might be able to deal with this. If not, you can jump in and swirl your swords."

He nodded and watched as she made her way down from one rock to another. She was so graceful, so balanced. She stopped behind a tall rock and peered around it. Seanchai moved along the ridge above her and now saw the scene below. There were three men, humans in dirty uniforms. Deserters, he guessed, too desperate or stupid to even change clothes.

One of them was still mounted on his horse, but the other two were circling a family. They had already tossed the rickety cart over and rifled through some boxes. Clearly annoyed that there was nothing worth stealing, they had turned their attention to the family. The man was lying on the ground with a deserter's foot on his chest and a sword held carelessly at his throat. The other soldier was grappling with the woman, while the children sat on the grass, crying.

Sellia took aim with the arrow taut on her bow, a second in the same hand. She aimed at the man on the horse, and then at the man standing over the father.

She released and, with great calmness, nocked the second arrow and fired at the deserter on the horse. Both men grunted and fell, but the third man sprung to his feet and pressed his knife to the woman's throat, his spare hand gripping her to his chest.

"She dies if you don't show yourself," he yelled, his voice squeaking with fear. He stumbled two paces forward and stared at the hill, his eyes darting from side to side. "I mean it. I'll count to three."

Sellia needed the man to turn to afford her a clear shot. Seanchai turned his palm toward a nearby rock and, digging his feet into the ground, pushed forward with his hand. The rock was a long way off and barely vibrated. He tried a second time, to no avail, so he picked up a smaller rock and threw it. It missed, but created a small avalanche. The man jerked around to see where the noise was coming from, and Sellia didn't miss her chance. Her arrow pierced him through both his ears.

She quietly ran back up to Seanchai, and they retrieved their packs.

"Hey," the woman called. "Where are you? Let us thank you."

Her echo was the only response.

It was another half hour before Sellia stopped and took a drink.

"You were amazing," Seanchai said. "I've seen you shoot, but that was. . . that was special. The speed that you nocked the second arrow, and then. . ."

Sellia was laughing, her teeth a bright, white contrast to her dark skin.

"What's so funny?" Seanchai asked, folding his arms.

"You're cute when you forget who you are," she replied. "I guess I forget who you are too."

"And what does that mean?" Seanchai was unsure how to take this.

"I forget how young you are, Seanchai. You've had to grow up so fast. I remember the lost and somewhat pathetic *calhei* that stumbled into Uncle's camp. I was so glad that Uncle didn't pick me to teach you."

She laughed, and Seanchai couldn't help smiling.

"I bet you're sorry now that you never got to teach the Wycaan anything," he jabbed good-naturedly. "Wouldn't you have liked to be able to boast to your grandchildren? But maybe it's not too late."

"What do you want?" Sellia asked, arching an eyebrow.

"Teach me to use a bow. I mean, you probably can't teach me much, but even a rudimentary level so that when I reach the—"

"Hey, I was amazing just a few moments ago."

"So you'll teach me?"

"For a price."

"What?"

"I get both bearskins when it gets cold."

Chapter Thirty-Two

Rhoddan followed Shayth out of the village and back onto the narrow forest path. Both had to keep their eyes on the rocky, root-riven ground, which forced them to rely on their ears to warn of anything suspicious. They walked briskly and in silence.

A couple of hours later, they crossed a brook and took turns filling their water skins.

"Do you think there are army patrols anywhere nearby?" Shayth asked, peering into the brush.

"Maybe, but I doubt it," Rhoddan replied, crouched at the water. "The brush is too thick here, but you never know. The army *did* find the village and take the blacksmith. I hope she was a blacksmith. . ." he mused.

"What do you mean?"

"I hope the reason they took her was because she was a blacksmith, and not something else," Rhoddan explained.

"Yeah," Shayth replied. He went silent for a few moments and then spoke. "No one can hear us right now?"

"Seems like that to me," Rhoddan said, rising and stretching a few cramped leg muscles. "But I wouldn't go out of my way to make a noise. Why?"

He turned just in time as his friend's right fist slammed into his chin. He wheeled around and fell, banging his head on a protruding rock, and lost consciousness.

When Rhoddan came to, he was lying with his head on his cloak. Shayth crouched nearby, looking at him.

"W–what happened?"

"Here," Shayth took the elf's hand and pulled him to a sitting position. When Rhoddan groaned, he offered his water skin. "How do you feel?"

"Like some pictorian just punched me in the face and the back of my head."

"Thank you, but the rock there takes the credit for the back of your head."

"And the front?"

"A pissed off prince. I suggest you refrain from calling me that again."

"Ow," Rhoddan rubbed his head and winced. "What gives, Shayth? Did it occur to you that we're in hostile territory?"

"Yeah, but if I waited until we returned to the dwarves, then I might have changed my mind."

"Wouldn't want that," Rhoddan muttered.

"Well, I didn't mean for you to hit a rock on your way down. Kind of spoiled it, in fact. I had planned to pommel you a few more times."

"Is that your way of apologizing?"

"Maybe we should camp here tonight. I'll hunt and then make a fire. You relax."

"So you're sorry?" Rhoddan's attempt at a grin quickly became a wince.

"Don't push it." Shayth growled and disappeared into the forest.

Rhoddan leaned back and slept until the smell of rabbits over a fire woke him. He sat up and stared at Shayth, who was turning the meat on two spits. He reached over to his water skin and drank some more. Shayth passed him one of the spits.

"Um, this is good. You make such tasty dishes with so little to work with." When he received no response, he returned to eating. He knew that brooding silence.

"What's going on, my round-eared friend?" Rhoddan asked finally. "You whacked me. Why aren't you moving on?"

"Did you see them all go down on one knee?"

"I did."

"After everything I've done, people still want. . ."

"Why shouldn't they?" Rhoddan said. "The Emperor gives them nothing but fear and despair. They have a right to dream of something better. You might just be what–"

"I'M NO KING," Shayth yelled.

"Yeah, I don't think there are any patrols around," Rhoddan replied evenly. "What's really bothering you, Shayth? You can't be surprised people recall your lineage. You garnered a lot of attention before you joined us. And people are hanging by a thread. They're desperate. Remember what the little girl said her mother told her? People change. Has it ever occurred to you that she might be right?"

Shayth didn't answer, and Rhoddan ripped another mouthful of meat off the spit. He chewed, watching his friend.

"You've thought about this before. How could you not? What is it Shayth? Do you really think I wasn't okay to play that card? I didn't have any other ideas. We've been through a lot together, my friend. Tell me."

Slowly, Shayth finished chewing his meat and stared into the fire. Rhoddan waited. Then Shayth took a big sigh and turned to the elf.

"It stays between us?"

Rhoddan nodded. "I promise."

"When they went down on one knee," he gulped and struggled to continue the sentence. "When they went down on one knee, I felt that it. . . I felt that . . . it felt right."

They went silent again. Finally, Rhoddan spoke.

"That's okay," his voice was quiet and hesitant. "You were born and trained for such a role. It's there under the surface. No point denying it. You can decide against it. But it exists.

"When we rode out from Hothengold with Ballendir, at the head of the dwarf king's army, it was you who rode alongside him." He put up a hand to stop Shayth interrupting. "It was fine. I know you didn't do it intentionally. But that's my point. There's a path there that you could choose to walk.

"For now, let's just keep ourselves alive, okay? And perhaps find yourself another punching bag?"

"Thanks, Shayth said, "and I'm sorry about. . ." He signaled a swinging a fist, then rose to his feet and threw the skewer behind him. Rhoddan could see he was struggling with something else. The human rubbed his spiky hair and shook his head. When he turned to his friend, his voice was scarcely a whisper.

"There's something else about when the villagers went down on their knees, Rhoddan. When they paid homage, I-I wanted it."

CHAPTER THIRTY-THREE

B allendir called his commanders to a meeting as soon as Rhoddan and Shayth returned to camp. He was not interested in their fatigue and made sure they knew that he disdained their little detour.

"There'll be one more major attempt ta bring supplies ta the troops in Ulster 'fore winter. A large regiment of troops'll escort the supplies 'n possibly stay ta replace the soldiers at the fortress.

"We'll attack again near the mouth o' the mountains, but this time further in. Clan Dan Zu'Ulster has prepared a second site with a few surprises. We're fortunate that, though his clan is steeped in the ways of craft 'n not battle, Clan Leader Dugenminsk saw fit ta prepare several lines of defense. We move out in the morning."

As the group broke up, Rhoddan approached Ballendir with Shayth alongside.

"Ballendir, what happens after this operation?"

"When we ride out for this fight, some'll stay behind 'n pack up the camp. I think this'll be our last offensive 'fore the winter."

"Will you march back to Hothengold?" Rhoddan asked.

"No. We'll winter in the mines of Ulster."

Shayth and Rhoddan glanced at each other. "We'll take our leave after the battle, then," Rhoddan said. The dwarf frowned, but Rhoddan pressed on. "Our place is with Seanchai. We must return to him."

"Yeh have no idea where the lad is," Ballendir snapped. "Nobody seems ta. Do yeh think now's the time ta go wandering 'round Odessiya in search of an unstable young elf who can traverse great distances?"

"We'll start at Hothengold," Shayth suggested. "We'll try and pick up his trail from there."

The plan was similar to the previous ambush, but General Shiftan was ready this time. To begin with, the troops accompanying these wagons were four times stronger than the time before. Shiftan had also employed a group of rangers, expert trackers who could uncover what lay ahead, long before the army arrived.

Ballendir was especially dismayed to discover that Shiftan had called for regiments of dwarves who were trained to fight in the tough mountain terrain. These dwarves did not march with the main body of the caravan, but swarmed over the crags and peaks nearby. So the battle never reached the wagons in the gorge, because the conscripted dwarves pushed Ballendir's troops back.

Unable to force their way through with the traps that had been prepared, Ballendir watched with growing frustration as Shiftan's caravan progressed. Desperate to halt the supplies, the dwarf led his troops out from the cover of the steep slopes and confronted the caravan just beyond a trail that led to a closed gorge.

He had left his archers in the rocks above to guard against the Emperor's dwarves, and to attack from above if he could drive the main force into the gorge.

It was a mistake, as Shiftan immediately sent wave after wave of disciplined cavalry against the dwarves. Then, inexplicably, the cavalry ceased its charges and pulled back to the caravan. Ballendir roared at his troops: "See how they cower? Prepare ta charge."

"No!" Rhoddan cried and stepped forward. "Ballendir, wait. It might be a trap. Wait! Think about why they're doing this."

Ballendir roared back. "Never question mah orders in battle. If something has happened we press our advantage. Now lead the charge, Rhoddan, and I'll forgive yeh. . . yeh insubordination."

Rhoddan stared at the dwarf. Ballendir was not usually like this, but Rhoddan had seen the battle rage before. Ballendir's eyes were wide, his armor dented, and his axe held high. He was fueled solely by adrenaline. Rhoddan glanced at Shayth and saw the same worry reflected in his eyes.

"Are yeh a warrior, Rhoddan? If not, step out of mah way," Ballendir bellowed.

Rhoddan turned, drew his long broadsword, and raised it high over his head. "*Rharghastii*," he cried in the dwarf tongue. "After me!"

Shayth charged forward with the dwarf forces. They rounded the bend and saw their enemy in formation further up than they had expected. As they passed the entrance into the dead-ended gorge, Shayth realized General Shiftan had the same plan as Ballendir: to drive his enemy into the gorge where there was no escape. Shayth looked over to Rhoddan, who was clearly having the same realization.

Furious fighting was happening on the ridges above them. Not only would the dwarves not be able to count on cover from the archers that Ballendir had placed there, but also they themselves would now be vulnerable to attacks from above if Shiftan's dwarves seized control.

When the cavalry charged, Ballendir formed his men into a tight wedge. Dwarves did not carry spears, so their best defenses were their shields and their height. It was hard to strike a dwarf from high up on a battle charger.

Ballendir called to Rhoddan and Shayth to stay protected in the middle and drop to their knees. He took the point position. The great chargers smashed into the interlocked wall of shields, which stood the charge.

The cavalry reformed on the other side and the wedge pivoted to face them. The thunder of heavy hooves shook the ground, masking the sound of the foot soldiers as they crept up from the wagons and attacked the rear of the defensive wedge.

The formation broke as dwarves in the back turned to fight off the attack, and the battleground became desperate mayhem. Horses charged through the ranks of dwarves, kicking up dust and cutting down all in their path, regardless of which side they were on.

Ballendir had no choice. As the cavalry passed by for another run and the infantry continued to push, he called for his soldiers to retreat into the gorge.

"It's a trap," Rhoddan yelled in his ear as they moved.

"Yeh think I don't know that, elf? I planned for this ta happen ta them, remember? But we can't survive attacks from both sides. With our backs ta the rocks, they can only attack from one direction."

"But they hold the ridges. The caravan will pass."

Ballendir glared at him. "Do yeh have a better idea, other than ta run? Dwarves don't run."

Rhoddan didn't have an answer. He raised his sword and let out a cry as he charged the line of infantry at the mouth of the ravine. Shayth joined him, and, together, they pushed the soldiers back from the mouth, allowing most of Ballendir's forces inside.

Once in the gorge, they formed up to face the line of cavalry horses that assembled. As the rhythmic thunder of hooves pounded the ground, rocks flew down on the dwarf shields and sent many to their knees. The wedge did not hold.

The battle should have lasted only a short while, as the fighting increased in desperation. The horses retreated to allow the infantry to finish the mission, keeping in close line to cut down any dwarf who might try to run. No dwarf ran.

Rhoddan felt a surge of energy as he battled multiple soldiers at a time. The battle rage took him. This was a good way to die. He barely registered when the intensity of the fighting dropped. The horse line was broken; the foot soldiers had turned to face another enemy. Rhoddan continued to swing his blade, though his arms were numb.

Then he vaguely heard Shayth shout. "Rhoddan, stop. Hold!"

He lowered his sword and stared. Pictorians swarmed into the steep enclave and were hewing their way through the cavalry. In the middle, towering over all, First Boar Umnesilk roared his battle cry, and it echoed against the three rock faces around Rhoddan.

It was the most beautiful sound Rhoddan had ever heard.

Chapter Thirty-Four

S hayth moved among the wounded dwarves. He had little to offer but a few words to some and eye contact with others. Still, he followed orders from the healers to bring water, tie a splint, or help a wounded dwarf to the wagon they had procured.

When there was nothing left to do, he helped the pictorians pile bodies onto two pyres. On one was stacked with dwarves of the resistance, the other with uniformed dwarves. Shayth didn't think any pictorians had died; their impact had been so sudden and decisive. There was a lot to say for surprise, he thought.

Rhoddan came alongside him. "It's crazy to see them as allies," he said quietly.

"I met their first boar," Shayth replied, staring at Umnesilk. "Seanchai reached out to him when we were leading them away from Hothengold. I could have killed him."

Umnesilk looked over at them and, recognizing Shayth, lumbered over.

"We meet before," he said in his deep, melodic tone. "You friend of Wycaan."

"I am," Shayth said and stood straighter, noting that he barely reached the

First Boar's chest. "This is Rhoddan, also close companion to the Wycaan."

"Well met," Rhoddan inclined his head. "Your timing is impeccable. Thank you." Umnesilk stared at him. Rhoddan cleared his throat, thinking of what else to say. "Last I recall, you led your boars from the battle at Hothengold. Have you returned now on our side?"

"It decided by Council of Elders. Wycaan come to our home, address my people."

"Seanchai?" Rhoddan and Shayth stared at each other, dumbfounded. "When?"

The First Boar looked at them untrustingly and did not reply.

"Umnesilk," Shayth said. "Rhoddan and I plan to leave the dwarves for the winter. We must return to serve Seanchai. It might help if you could give us a direction."

Umnesilk shifted uneasily.

"Listen," Rhoddan said, grabbing the pictorian's arm, then promptly releasing it when Umnesilk glared. "Sorry, but we don't have time to wander the length of Odessiya. If I guess right, will you tell us?"

Again, Umnesilk visibly struggled. He shook his huge mane, trying to decide. Rhoddan deliberately returned his hand to the pictorian's massive forearm. Umnesilk looked at him, and their eyes locked for a few heartbeats. Then Rhoddan leaned forward, speaking in almost a whisper.

"He's going through the Cliftean Pass and out to the Elves of the West."

Shayth watched as the elf and pictorian, their faces almost touching, stared at each other. Umnesilk's stare bore into Rhoddan. Beads of sweat rolled down the elf's face, but he returned the gaze without blinking.

After a moment, they both straightened up.

"Thank you," Rhoddan said quietly.

Umnesilk didn't say anything. He just turned and walked away.

General Shiftan glared at Ahad. "Why have you returned?"

"I must find him."

"Where's your friend?"

"Nearby." There were rings under Ahad's eyes, and he looked gaunt.

"What makes you think I won't drag you back to Skiliad and throw you in the cells myself?" General Shiftan demanded.

"Because we share the same desire: to kill Shayth and the elf."

"Well, we haven't done a good job of that yet. I lost a lot of men down there, and I was so close. . ."

"Is it true?" Ahad interrupted.

"What?"

"The pictorians," Ahad's voice was quiet. "Have they joined the fight?"

"Yes, on the wrong side. Damn it!"

"How did it happen?"

"We had it worked out perfectly, got the dwarves into the—"

"No. How did the pictorians decide to join the fight?"

General Shiftan stared at him. "What are you getting at?"

"Shayth is here. The warrior elf that my father held in Galbrieth, the one we thought never leaves the Wycaan's side, is here, and we are chasing shadows in the mountains of Ulster. It's all a ruse. That's why I returned to you."

Shiftan nodded and stroked his beard. "While we are all here, the Wycaan is somewhere else making alliances. We have just seen his handiwork. So where is he now? Who else is he talking to?"

They both fell silent. Then a man dressed in a dull green and brown approached. The ranger stopped a short distance away, but Shiftan beckoned him forward. Any general was anxious to receive updates in the field, especially from those so highly-regarded as the rangers.

"You can speak in front of this man. He's an officer of the Emperor and a Master Assassin."

"Yes, sir," the ranger said, and bowed courteously to Ahad. "The rebels are disbursing. You instructed me to keep an eye on the young prince and–"

"He's no prince," Ahad snapped.

"Quiet," General Shiftan ordered, and glared at Ahad. Then he turned back to the ranger. "Please continue."

The ranger seemed unperturbed. "The dwarves return to their mines, sir. The prince and the elf who serves him have left the main group."

"In which direction?"

"West."

"They're being tracked?"

"Yes, sir. I have only two rangers left with the main body. If the pictorians separate from them, I'll need more help. But I sent two separate triads after the pr–after the one called Shayth."

"Why two?" Ahad asked.

"In case Shayth and the elf separate, sir."

"Thank you," Ahad replied and offered a conciliatory smile. "Please excuse my outburst before."

"We're all very tired, sir, and distressed by the battle. It is forgotten. And I know you, sir. Or, rather, I knew you when you were small. I served your father, and it was a great honor to do so."

Shiftan felt the boy tense and quickly thanked the ranger, sending him to eat and sleep. When the man was out of earshot, he turned to Ahad.

"Your father always showed a deep respect for the rangers. It was he who created this whole relationship. We pay them for their service, but they could easily make it elsewhere."

"I understand," Ahad said. "I need to hold my tongue better."

"You do," Shiftan said and smiled. "Your father had a hard time with discipline in the academy, too, and often found himself on the wrong end of a punishment." He laughed at the surprise on Ahad's face, but turned serious. "Ahad. By the time we were commissioned in the field, *he* was ready."

"I'm going to head west," Ahad said ignoring the hint.

"I imagine that most of us are. Will you travel with me?"

"Thank you, but I think it unwise," Ahad glanced around to ensure no one was listening, "given the company I keep."

"Ahad," Shiftan spoke quietly, as well. "I am worried about the others with whom you ride? I'm referring to the brothers."

Ahad nodded.

Shiftan continued. "I was disturbed to see them enter my fort. Do you know why?"

"Because their father did not partake of the leanest cut?" Ahad said, referring to Prince Shindell's secret society.

General Shiftan betrayed no shock. "I'm less worried for myself. But you'll ride with them far from a guarded fort, sleep while they guard you, and fight with them at your back. We've talked about your father's history with that family."

"Was my father really that ruthless?"

"Just remember: in matters of war and love, there are no good or bad guys, Ahad—only winners and those who seek retribution. Sleep lightly on your travels, and with a dirk in your hand."

Chapter Thirty-Five

S eanchai was content for Sellia to set the pace through the mountains. These were darker, more ominous rocks that those he had known near Galbrieth and on his journey to find Mhari. They seemed entirely made of sharp edges and ready to join an avalanche if someone sneezed. His nose itched.

He had come a long way since the day he had fled the village where he had grown up. It occurred to him that, were he still there, he would soon be graduating from his apprenticeship with his mother, the village healer.

Now he wondered if she knew how little time she would have with him. Had the other villagers known? He hadn't thought to ask the lone survivor when he returned a few months ago, and now regretted the lost opportunity. But there had been many involved in his escape. He was convinced they did.

"What are you thinking about?" Sellia asked, interrupting his thoughts.

They had stopped by a little waterfall, and she was filling her water skin. As Seanchai emptied his own, he told her. "I plan to finish that apprenticeship one day," he concluded. "I want to heal, not kill."

"They're both part of the same life cycle," she replied. "We must go through times of strife to reach times of peace. How else can we appreciate the peace, if we're never without it? Were the ten thousand years of peace not preceded by chaos?"

Seanchai actually didn't know, and shrugged. "I'm so good with weapons, and, yet, so detached from them." He drew his Win Dao swords, and they sparkled in the sunlight reflecting off the waterfall. "They're so beautiful, so deadly, and yet I can't wait for the day when I can discard them."

Sellia nodded. "I don't know if that day will ever come," she said, her voice grim. Seanchai turned and stared at her. "All my life, I've been trained to fight. As soon as I could draw a bowstring, I was given an arrow and pushed to learn. All I remember of my time before Uncle was weapons training."

She frowned. Seanchai thought that even the creases that lined her face were exquisite. "I have no recollection of a permanent home. There was a caravan and horses, always horses. I was passed from family to family. I recall an elf—old—with long, crinkly, gray hair. He was the head of our caravan. There was an elfe who insisted I call her my mother. I have many images of her face, though little recollection of anything else. I think she was very kind.

There were a few moments of silence. Seanchai waited for her to speak and when she finally did, Sellia had a faraway expression on her face.

"She would call me her *shaythelfe zinge.*"

"*Zinge?*" Seanchai asked.

"*Zinge* is a princess in the ancient language. And shayth, of course, for the rare black stone. I was their dark elfe, their princess. I loved that name. I've thought of it often after I met Shayth."

"These elves were not dark-skinned, then?"

"No," she smiled at Seanchai. "That would have been too easy, huh? No. I don't know if the elfe I remember was my mother and my father was shayth-colored, or if they were just another holding station for me. Still, in my fantasies, at least, my father was a great warrior who loved my mother and had me before going off to perform acts of great heroics."

Seanchai leaned against a rock. "So, what happened?"

"Remember how you told me that your parents drilled your escape into you, knowing that the day would come when you'd have to run? Mine's a similar story, a sign of the time we grew up in. I was very good at climbing, and encouraged to hide in trees, I guess, because it seemed very natural. I was also taught to keep my bow and arrows with me at all times. It was the only thing I think I was allowed to treasure. I never went to bed with a doll or a blanket. I hugged my quiver.

"So the day came, and I knew I had to hide in the trees and not come down until I was called by my nickname, *shaythelfe zinge.* A few times it happened as a false alarm, and I was always called down. Then the last time, no one called."

She went quiet for a while and then, holding her quiver to her chest, turned and leaned back against Seanchai. It was a strangely vulnerable move, and Seanchai wrapped his arms around her, wordlessly offering comfort and protection.

"It got dark, and I slept," she recalled sadly. "Then I had to relieve myself, but I knew that if I peed from the tree, the droplets might give me away. I thought I was being tested and would be punished. I held it and finally fell asleep again. When I woke up, there were strange voices below me.

"Someone called to me, but I wouldn't budge because I had been taught not to. After an hour or so, a huge elf came and stood under the tree. He held a plate with sliced apples and honey. He told me that this was lunch for him and me, and he was very hungry. Then he came and sat against the trunk of the tree and began eating.

"He made all these funny remarks about how tasty the apples were, about how hard the bees had worked to make the honey, and that he hoped they wouldn't be upset that I wasn't going to eat any.

"Finally, I came down and sat opposite him." She laughed. "He had another apple that he sliced for me. He told me that I wasn't allowed to look behind me, and I promised not to. When we finished, he told me that he had a daughter a little younger than me, and wondered if maybe I would come and play with her.

"I agreed. It sounded very exciting. Then he picked me up and told me to bury my head in his chest and close my eyes. He made me promise not to open them until he told me.

"As we walked, I smelled things burning. It was a sick smell, and it scared me. The huge elf kept talking the whole time—about his home, his daughter. After a few minutes, he told me I could open my eyes. We were on a road with a few horses, and some elves and humans.

"He climbed onto his horse, and a man passed me up to him. As we rode, he continued to talk about his daughter and how happy she would be to see me. I asked about the woman who was caring for me and he explained that she and all her friends had gone to a better place and would know safety and good food. She would be watching from the clouds. He gently told me that he would be my family now: him and his daughter.

"I asked their names. He told me his daughter was named Ilana, and that I should call him Uncle."

Chapter Thirty-Six

They continued walking along the mountain ridge until they came to a small field. Before Seanchai could move, Sellia whipped round her bow, nocked an arrow, and let loose a single shot into the tail end of a herd of arawat mountain goats.

A small newborn fell, and the others vanished. Seanchai and Sellia crossed the opening, and Seanchai knelt before the creature. "You offer us up your life for food and nourishment. We celebrate your existence and look forward to your rebirth as the gods choose." When he knelt to scoop up the small animal, he gasped. It was shot straight through the eye.

"My arrow first, please," Sellia said. "I don't want to bend it."

"Did you aim for this arawat?"

She glared at him. "Yeees. I aimed for its eye."

Seanchai pulled the arrow out and handed it to Sellia. He slung the animal over his shoulder and stood. Sellia pointed to a small clump of trees by the foot of the mountain on the other side of the clearing. The late afternoon sun bathed the spot.

"Let's camp there tonight," she said.

"It's a bit early, no?"

"Maybe, but those are tundraish trees and I see many young saplings."

"So?"

"So, I have an idea. You set up camp, gather wood for the fire, and prepare the meat."

They pulled their packs off, and Seanchai began to collect wood. He watched Sellia draw her short knife and walk toward the forest.

"Are you okay?" he asked.

"I'm fine," she replied. "Please thinly cut any meat we aren't eating tonight and cook it. Then wrap it in the skin of the arawat and put it beside the fire. Do not burn it."

She was staring into the woods and sounded distracted.

"You sure you're okay? You shared a difficult story with me before."

Sellia nodded and disappeared into the trees. Seanchai watched her go before busying himself lighting the fire. He skinned the small goat, and prepared the haunches to roast on spits; the rest he cut into thin slices to dry.

He didn't enjoy this work and was uneasy eating animals. In his village, they ate only fish and fowl. He used to fish in the nearby river with his father and longed to do it again. He had learned to identify the bulbs, tubers, fruit, and mushrooms that the forest offered, and helped grow the vegetables by their house.

But eating animals like this was unsettling. It felt wrong, but he knew it to be a necessity. He had to maintain his strength, and he was aware that he was still growing. Away from the water and constantly on the move, he had to take what the land offered.

Seanchai closed his eyes while the meat sizzled, leaned back against the rock and enjoyed the warming rays of the sun on his face. He must have dozed, because he became suddenly aware of the sound of whittling. He opened his eyes to find Sellia working a long, thin branch of wood. There were two others next to her.

"I should turn the meat," he sighed, and then saw that it was not over the fire anymore. "You took care of that?"

"Here," she said, tossing him a piece. "You deserve the most charred."

She retuned to whittling as Seanchai sliced off the burnt skin and gnawed his dinner. He watched her work on the sticks, remove the bark and taper the ends. He was distracted, though, when she took off her outer shirt and sat with her arms, shoulders and face glowing in the rich, red light of the sun.

"What are you thinking?" she asked.

He felt the tips of his ears redden, but courageously recovered. "Wondering what you are doing with the sticks."

She looked up at him and smirked. "Uh-huh," she said, and Seanchai felt his blush deepen.

Sellia held one stick at its end and peered up the length. Then she gently bent the other end to test its flexibility. It straightened back when she released it, and she smiled.

"What are you doing with those sticks?" Seanchai asked.

"We have a deal, Wycaan. It's chilly up here, and I plan to sleep in those bearskins you carry."

"You're making me a bow?" he asked, oozing excitement.

Sellia rose. "Sort of. This is an ancient craft that takes years of apprenticeship to master. What I'm making for you is merely a toy, but you'll be able to practice with it." She picked up her small knife and went back into the forest.

Seanchai cleared away the remnants of dinner and then began his standing exercises. With muscles sore from walking all day, he did not greet this with the excitement and diligence he had felt in the past. But the routine felt as though he was honoring Mhari, his teacher. It was a way to ensure he always remembered her.

When he finished, he stretched and breathed deeply. He opened his eyes and saw a small pile of rough arrows by a rotting wood stump Sellia was setting up for target practice.

She stood about ten feet from it, nocked one of the practice arrows, and shot into the heart of the stump. Even though the arrow swerved, it hit the center.

"You have potential with the bow," Seanchai quipped, sipping some water. "You just need a little practice."

She turned her head and smiled wryly. "Come here."

Seanchai took the bow. Sellia stood tightly against his back and adjusted his form and hand on the bow. She instructed him how to latch and draw the bowstring. Her other hand came around his back, guiding his other hand to hold the arrow's crude nock.

Seanchai could feel the tension in the bow gut and the strain of the arrow. As he listened to Sellia's instructions, he steadied his breathing. His deep inhalations took in the smell of her skin, her hair. He became acutely aware of her skin against him, and her voice sang in his head.

With Sellia pressed to him, Seanchai shot six arrows. He missed the target every time, but it never bothered him.

Chapter Thirty-Seven

Sellia sighed deeply, cozy in the warmth of the bearskins. She woke to the lazy crackle of a few sticks–enough heat to boil water. She was used to the routine. Seanchai would either be doing his standing exercises or brewing his sustaining mushroom tea.

But not this morning as different sounds penetrated her thoughts. When she opened her eyes, Sellia found a shirtless Seanchai practicing with the bow and arrows. She sat up and leaned against the rock, hugging the bearskin around her. The morning sun encircled the Wyccan with light as it peeked over the mountains from where they had come.

She sighed again. Sellia had not expected to actually experience these feelings of intimacy again. She never thought she would love another. But somehow, the memories of Dyrovas, her deceased mate, seemed less painful now and her growing affection for Seanchai had surpassed simply a binding oath made to Ilana.

As Sellia watched, Seanchai jumped into the air in celebration.

"Did you actually hit the target?" she asked.

Seanchai blushed, startled. "Caught," he admitted. "There is some bread and meat warming for you by the fire."

She crawled out from the skins, disappeared into the trees and, when she returned, sat by the fire. Seanchai gave her a steaming mug of tea. "You're not going to cast a spell on me with your Wycaan potion?" she declared, relieved to smell aromatic leaves rather than his bitter mushroom tea.

Sellia glanced at the target she had set up. There were five arrows protruding from it. "That's quite an improvement. Have you ever used a bow before?"

Seanchai nodded. "I had a simple one for hunting that could shoot a light arrow about twenty or thirty feet. It was meant for kids. I tried to show my prowess to Uncle when I met him. It didn't work. I put a few arrows in a target standing still, but then he made me run and roll before shooting. I missed every one, I think. You *never* miss. Whether you are in motion, or under pressure, or you're taking a reflex shot like what took down our dinner last night. There is something almost spiritual about it."

They finished eating, packed up their possessions, and were soon walking through the trees.

"Tell me more about archery," Seanchai said after a while.

"Tell you more? Okay. The arrow has a pointy bit and you try and pierce that into whatever you are aiming at."

Seanchai, who was leading, pulled back a branch he passed under and let it flick back toward Sellia. She ducked with ease and continued laughing. Seanchai was smiling.

"We have a long walk," he said at last. "Humor me."

"Okay," Sellia replied. "Those who make bows are known as bowyers, and those who make arrows are called fletchers. In the bigger cities, they have shops and often work together under one roof. Sometimes there is a tanner working with them, making the quivers. When the city has an archery competition, the winner's bow and arrows are a great advertisement for the bowyer and fletcher.

"Ideally, you have everything custom-made to your exact build and needs. Even the quiver can be made to fit your specific build. And since they serve different purposes, the bow and arrows used in war are not usually the same as the ones used for hunting."

After a few minutes, Seanchai asked another question. "Did you win your bow?"

Sellia's bow was a dark red wood, and Seanchai had seen the care she used with it. "Some of the bowyers travel around the country selling their wares. When I was about sixteen, I already had a reputation with a bow that Uncle had given me. A few of us were returning from a very successful ambush and were in high spirits.

"We came across a trader caravan under attack by bandits, and Dyrovas led us against them. I shot one who was attacking the bowyer's daughter. When we had driven them off, the traders were very appreciative. They told Dyrovas to choose anything from their wares as a sign of their gratitude.

"He picked out a beautiful bow and asked if it was suitable for me, but the bowyer said it was not a good match for my build. She made me shoot some arrows with the bow I had and watched. Then she produced this one that she had kept wrapped in leathers. She told us that it was the finest work she had ever done. Dyrovas. . ." Sellia stopped and Seanchai turned to face her. "Dyrovas told her that he would be honored to offer it as his bonding present to me. That was how he proposed."

"Did he give it to you at the bonding ceremony?"

"No," Sellia's voice had gone quiet. "He died a week before our celebration."

"I'm so sorry," Seanchai reached out to hold her, but she drew back, her eyes glistening.

"Please, let's keep walking."

Sellia took over the lead and set a strong pace. They walked throughout the day, stopping only to refill their water skins. Seanchai asked several times if she was okay, and she nodded or replied that she was. There was no other conversation.

As the sun began to set before them, they found another open area, a junction with a path that ran north/south. They moved to the eastern edge of the field to enjoy the setting sun. Seanchai found an upended tree stump and prepared it as a target.

Sellia collected firewood, and Seanchai gave her space. As he shot each of the six arrows that she had made for him, he reflected on the dark elfe.

They had both grieved Ilana, but Sellia had never opened up about her mate. Clearly, those wounds were still open four years later. Seanchai wanted to be there for her. He wondered if Ilana had only been thinking of him when she had made Sellia take her oath. Was she maybe also looking out for her stepsister?

It was intense, this traveling just the two of them, Seanchai thought as he nocked another arrow. He pulled back the string and, without much thought, shot his arrow straight into the bullseye. A big smile crossed his face, and he wondered if this was a good time to show Sellia.

Suddenly, another arrow, heavy with black feathers, zipped past him and thudded into the center of the target, splitting his spindly homemade arrow. Seanchai whirled round, the grin on his face growing even wider.

"Shayth!" he cried. "Rhoddan!" He ran over and hugged them both in one swoop. "Well met, my friends. Well met."

Chapter Thirty-Eight

A had watched Ruel crouch to feel the ashes. There was no smoke coming from the fire pit, and Ahad knew they were still many leagues behind. Two of their horses had gone lame—a consequence of being ridden relentlessly through stony mountain passes.

Now they walked with all the speed they could muster, stopping only to hunt and sleep. Twice, they had bought food. The peasants seemed surprised to receive payment, but Ahad had insisted.

Ruel and Crefen kept mostly to themselves. The Crown Prince was happy to talk with Ahad and, in truth, Ahad treasured their time together. If he needed anything from Ruel or Crefen, he would ask respectfully, but with authority. His requests were always within reason, and neither boy argued.

"How long, Ruel?" Phineus asked.

"Too long," the boy replied. "It's stone cold. We could be days behind, and we have no idea if they're going faster or slower than we are."

"We need horses," Crefen growled.

"Agreed," Ahad replied. "Any ideas?"

"There was a road back there," Phineus said. "How about we follow the road and hope to catch some travelers?"

"And then what?" Ahad asked warily.

"We'll pay for our steeds if that makes you feel better."

It took a while to find the road. Almost immediately, they heard horses–many horses–and Ahad signaled for everyone to hide. At least two hundred cavalry rode hard with General Shiftan leading the banners.

"I'm glad we decided to head out by ourselves," Phineus said to Ahad, just loud enough to be heard above the horses. "At least we had a head start on them."

He laughed, and Ahad frowned at him. Sometimes Ahad wasn't sure the Crown Prince cared at all about catching the elf. "We weren't sure whether the General had told your father you are here and how the Emperor might respond."

"I know," Phineus replied, and punched his friend lightly on the arm. "Take it easy. Come, let's move fast now that we're on the road."

They walked quickly for another hour and came to a small village. The cavalry were literally just leaving, a cloud of dust from the other side of the village punctuating their departure.

The village had several stores and houses set back from the road. There was a stable on the left, and they entered the rickety barn. There were three emaciated horses that perked up their ears as the young men entered.

"Take them all," the Crown Prince said. "We'll rotate them."

"Doubt they'll last long, anyway," Crefen said as he opened the paddock.

"Hey there!" An elderly voice called from the entrance.

They all turned to face an old man with snow-white hair protruding from under a straw hat, his hands on his hips.

"Can I 'elp you, gentlemen?' Them be my 'orses."

"We need them in the name of the Emperor," Ahad said. "We'll pay you well."

"Them 'orses must plow our fields. I make good money out o' them. I does, and I 'as the plow, too. 'ow am I to make money wiv no horse? And who's to say that a scruffy bunch the likes of you work for the Emperor, anyways?"

Crefen towered over the old man. "Be glad the Master Assassin here offers you coin. He doesn't need to."

The old man stepped back and glanced at Ahad's cloak. Though it was dirty from the road, the farmer recognized the insignia. Still, he shook his head. "I-I needs the money. I needs to plow."

"You don't need to plow," the Crown Prince snapped at him. "Are you simple? We're giving you more money than you'll ever earn from plowing."

"But all I knows is plowing," the old man whined.

Phineus swore in frustration, and Crefen swung a fist that sent the old man reeling. He dropped and didn't move. Crefen went to help his brother with the horses. Ahad stared, his mouth hanging open. Then he went to the old man and checked for a pulse. The old man stirred at Ahad's touch.

"Don't move, old man," Ahad said. "We must take your horses because the empire is in great danger. I'm leaving you enough money for a few winters and to buy more horses. Perhaps you can even hire a boy to plow for you so you can rest more.

Ahad pushed some coins into the farmer's jacket pocket and patted his chest.

"Why don't you go tuck him into bed?" Crefen jeered and laughed as he passed Ahad leading a horse.

"Shame we're short on time. You could've plowed a field for him," his brother added, following behind with the other two horses.

"There's no fields here," Crefen called over his shoulder, "only rocks and dust."

Phineus laughed as he followed them. Seeing Ahad frowning, he patted his friend on his shoulder. "You have no sense of humor," he said.

Ahad grabbed his arm and hissed, trying to ensure the old farmer could not hear. "Crefen and Ruel are cruel thugs. That is one of your subjects lying there. You are the Crown Prince of Odessiya."

"You paid him, and we're in a hurry. You did him a favor, I'm sure. He might never have to work again."

"We didn't just take his horses. We took his livelihood and his dignity."

"We need his horses," Phineus said, now serious.

"And there was a better way to take them. He could have lived out his days telling people how he helped a royal family member." Ahad stared at him, fighting to keep his voice low. "Be the Crown Prince, Phineus."

"You need not remind me of my station, Master Assassin," Phineus replied, his voice suddenly cold and his face twisted in anger. "Now, you are touching royalty. That is forbidden. Take your hand off of me."

Phineus stalked out of the barn, mounted a horse and galloped off by himself.

Chapter Thirty ~ Nine

A had mounted the other horse and rode with Ruel and Crefen after the Crown Prince. Phineus had not gone far when he stopped, seeing the army settling down to camp ahead. It was almost dusk, and guards would soon be posted.

The Crown Prince dismounted and led his horse on a path that stretched between two hills. The others followed suit without question. It took them an hour to go around the army camp, and now they had to decide whether or not to camp so close to the soldiers.

Ahad was going to suggest that they keep going, as General Shiftan might send out scouts, but he was not consulted on the matter. Phineus jumped back on his horse and spurred it forward. When Ahad jumped back on his, Crefen looked over.

"Let's follow at a distance. Whatever stupid thing you said, he needs space."

Ahad nodded and let Crefen set the pace. They rode in the darkness, keeping their eyes on the road. He began to doze in his saddle, until shouts and the sound of steel on steel jolted him awake.

Crefen's horse was already at full gallop as Ahad and Ruel spurred their horses on. Without regard for danger, they charged into a group of men who had Phineus backed against a rock.

In the moonlit darkness, Phineus's blade flew at great speed. Already there were three men down, and the two others were having a hard time. Crefen crashed his horse into one of the men, sending him flying. The other hesitated long enough for Phineus to pin him against the rock and headbutt him. There was a loud crunch and Ahad was sure the man's nose was broken.

Ahad moved the Crown Prince away and held his blade to the man's throat.

"You okay, Shadow?" He asked Phineus, glancing to see if his friend was wounded, but though Phineus was panting, and beads of sweat poured down his head, he was smiling.

"I was just asking these gentlemen for information. I told them they would be paid well, and they thought they could take all my money without a transaction." He glanced at the bloody man. "Not a good business model, as you can see."

"Do you even carry money?" Ahad asked.

"No."

"Did you tell them that?"

Phineus just smiled. "I neglected to tell them that I don't carry the money, and I neglected to tell them that you were all behind me." Then he turned to the man, and his voice went cold. "Tell me how far we are from the Cliftean Pass, and I might spare your life."

"N-not far, my lord," the man gasped, and told them it was reachable with two days of hard riding. "S-spare me. I will tell you more. You ain't the o-only ones who asked."

"A man and an elf?" Phineus asked immediately.

"N-no sir. A youth with s-spiky black hair, two pointies, one was female and dark-skinned, beautiful i-if you go for 'em. There was a fourth. He was huge and wore his cowl tight so I couldn't see his face. Well-armed, they were too."

"How far ahead of us are they?" Phineus asked.

"Was a c-couple of days back, but they's on foot, master."

"Thank you," Phineus said, and slit the man's throat.

Blood spurted onto the rock while the man gurgled and fell to the ground. Ahad stared at his friend.

"You told me to act my part, Ahad. He dared to attack royalty. This is it. Some may have tortured him first for fun. I was being royally civil."

As the sun rose behind them, Seanchai, Sellia, and Shayth crawled up onto a ridge and looked down into a valley. No one looking up would have seen them through the blinding sunlight. Rhoddan had retraced their route to see if they were being followed.

There was sheer rock on the other side, except for the opening directly across from where they lay. They had reached the Cliftean Pass, the westernmost point of Odessiya.

The group had been here before, but Seanchai had not crossed. Instead, he had headed north and discovered the dwarves. He glanced toward the Bordan mountain range. It was dark and sinister, the peaks engulfed in cloud.

This time, however, Seanchai was determined to get through the pass. He was absorbed with the idea that he would meet free elves. He was convinced there would be at least one other Wycaan there. Otherwise, why would Mhari have instructed him seek them out? But he had not considered how to get around the soldiers.

"There are so many," Sellia whispered.

"I reckon at least two thousand, judging by the tents and fire pits," Shayth said, squinting to see as well as the keener-sighted elves.

"There's more beyond," Seanchai said, scrying, his eyes glazed and his voice distant.

Rhoddan ran up. "We need to move," he panted. "There are soldiers on their way. Come. I've found a cave."

They crawled back off the ridge and jogged behind Rhoddan. He backtracked about ten minutes, and then moved north. A short while later, they sat in a small cave, eating dried meat and apples and discussing how to get through the pass.

"What about a distraction?" Rhoddan asked. "Shayth and I attack them, and they chase us. Easy."

Sellia stared at him. "How are you going to get thousands of soldiers to jump up and chase your shadows?"

Rhoddan shrugged.

"Wait!" Seanchai stared at Sellia. "What did you just say? Chasing shadows?"

"It's just a phrase, Seanchai," she replied, but he was curling up his lips and mouthing something. "What is it?"

Seanchai looked up. "There's a rock over there, about a hundred paces from the mouth of the cave. I want you to wait here for at least a half hour. Then come looking for me. I won't be far from there. If you don't see me, hoot like an owl a few times. You can hoot, right, Rhoddan?"

Rhoddan nodded. "I'm not sure there are many owls that would agree with you."

Seanchai was too excited to laugh. He took a long swig of water and then went out to the rock, his cloak wrapped around him. Closing his eyes, he went through his meditation exercises, relaxing his body and emptying his mind.

After a few minutes, he began to whisper a word over and over again. *Chashichot. Chashichot. Chashichot.*

Chapter Forty

*C*hashichot. *Chashichot. Chashichot.* Seanchai kept his focus firmly on the word. He had once whipped up a sandstorm to hide himself from wolfheids and joined with the water element when he had submerged into the underground lake on the day of his Wycaan transformation.

If he could harness wind and water, then why not light and darkness? He recalled the word from the ancient storybook Mhari had instructed him to learn by heart. As Seanchai repeated it, energy swirled up around him. He could sense a cone of power, intense but nonthreatening. He built it, layer by layer, until he felt encased.

Shayth and Rhoddan's muted voices reached him, though he could not make out the words. He saw them, and Sellia behind them, blurred and distant. They were looking for him and passed so closely that Rhoddan's sword brushed the cone of energy and met resistance. Rhoddan glanced in Seanchai's direction and then at his own blade. He frowned, but walked on.

Sellia was close to Seanchai now but looking in the other direction. Suddenly, all three ran back toward the cave and disappeared. To Seanchai's left, four mounted horses approached. The young elf almost panicked, but instead filled his mind with Mhari's face as he summoned his discipline to focus and maintain the dark cone.

The front two men halted their mounts just past Seanchai, and one called out in a hushed whisper. "Stay close to us, Shadow. We're not far from the sentries, and there may be scouts out."

"What about my dear cousin?" the hooded one asked.

"The scum is stupid, but not fool enough to take on a thousand soldiers."

"Shayth isn't stupid," a second youth admonished from behind. "Neither is the elf. Do not underestimate them."

"Have you decided whether to enter the camp, Ahad?"

"We will camp to the side," Ahad replied. "In the morning, I will seek information before General Shiftan arrives."

"Let's camp here," said one of the front riders.

"No, Crefen," Ahad replied. "We don't want the army to see us. There might be officers from the capital, and someone might recognize Shadow."

The party moved on, though the mumbles of the men in front made it clear they were not happy with either the decision where to camp or the one called Ahad.

Ahad? Not a common name, Seanchai thought. Then a chill coursed through his body. *What about my dear cousin?* he had heard one say. Shayth's cousin was. . .

Seanchai glanced to see that they had gone before he grounded the energy he was using to summon the darkness. He quickly made his way back to the cave, hooting as he approached.

Once inside the cave, he turned to Shayth. "One of those riders is called Ahad. Who is he?"

Shayth stared back, his tone grim. "The son of the late and great General Tarlach. He seeks revenge on the one who killed his dear father. We confronted him in the Ulster Mountains."

Seanchai nodded. "Another in their group is your cousin. Who is that?"

Shayth creased his brow. "What makes you say that?" Seanchai repeated the words, and Shayth tussled his spiky hair. "Are you sure?"

Seanchai nodded. "They called him Shadow. Who is it, Shayth?"

"The Emperor's son. The Crown Prince of Odessiya."

"He wants to kill you, too?"

"Probably," Shayth admitted. "But I suspect he's more intrigued with defeating you."

"Nice to know." Seanchai shrugged, trying unsuccessfully to make light of the situation.

"How close to them were you?" Sellia asked.

Seanchai beamed. "I was sitting on the rock that you walked past, and they rode right up to me." The others looked confused. "Rhoddan, when you passed the rock, you felt something with your sword. Do you remember?"

"I do," Rhoddan replied immediately.

"It was me. Or, rather, the darkening energy around me."

"The what?"

Seanchai explained what he had done. "I think I might be able to walk through the camp. I need to practice, but. . . maybe I can extend the cone to include you all."

They all absorbed this in silence, glancing furtively at each other. Finally, Sellia touched Seanchai's arm.

"The most important part," she said, "is that *you* get through. If we jeopardize that, then maybe you should go alone."

Seanchai hoped the darkness in the cave concealed his fear of such a situation. He was on his way to becoming a full-fledged Wycaan warrior, but he knew he was still a very young and unsure elf.

"Try it," Rhoddan said, "Sit next to Sellia and see if you can conceal the both of you."

It took several tries, but Seanchai finally succeeded. The others could see he was physically drained. Shayth passed him his water skin.

"Seanchai should sleep," Rhoddan said. "Let's split the guarding among the three of us and wake him before dawn for another hour of practice. We'll see if he can cover all four of us and then decide who goes."

"All four of us?" Shayth was surprised. "No–just three. I never intended on coming with you."

"Why would you not come with us?" Seanchai asked. "You came all this way. Why?"

"To get you through. That's the priority. But you're going to meet some very reclusive elves. Do you really think they'll want to see a human with you? And a tarnished one, at that?"

Seanchai opened his mouth to argue, but there was truth in Shayth's words. He yawned and was sent to sleep. As he lay down, he heard Rhoddan's voice.

"That's not the only reason you want to stay here, is it Shayth?"

Seanchai could feel Shayth struggling with his answer, and barely heard it when it came.

"I cannot leave Odessiya. My place is here with my people and my land."

They woke Seanchai in time to practice. He managed to extend the shadow cover to another person, but not to a third. By the time it was light out, he was again exhausted. He used the last of his energy to heat water for his mushroom tea, but after that he went back deep into the cave to sleep.

He lay there for a few minutes, listening to the others. They were deciding that Seanchai and Sellia would go. Shayth was resigned to facing Ahad and the Crown Prince. Rhoddan swore to stand by Shayth's side, but Seanchai could hear the disappointment in his voice. Rhoddan, like most young elves, had grown up dreaming of the free Elves of the West.

"But you should be the one to go with him," he heard Rhoddan say to Sellia. "He needs you. If you *do* find the elves of Markwin, I believe Seanchai will face a number of tests. My sword will be of no help then, I fear."

"But you were there from the beginning," Sellia said. "He needs you, too."

Rhoddan countered. "Shayth and I are family for him, yes, but you have done something that neither of us could," Rhoddan lowered his voice even more. "I didn't think he would recover from. . . from losing her. But I see the way he looks at you–the energy that is between you. Your love has helped heal him."

"No," Sellia hissed, trying to keep her voice down, too. "I have given him a part of me, but I'd never presume to replace what Seanchai had with Ilana. Some wounds never heal. I should know that. Dyrovas will always have a place in my heart. We just move on the best we can, because we must."

Seanchai closed his eyes and allowed the tears to trickle down his cheeks. He poked a finger into the dusty ground and wrote Ilana's name with his finger. Then, as he thought about Sellia, he wrote Dyrovas, too. He mourned for the elf he had never met.

Chapter Forty~One

They decided to postpone passage through the camp for another day. Seanchai needed to practice and build his strength. He made stronger potions of the mushroom tea, much as Mhari had increased the dose of danseng root prior to his entering the ley lake.

Shayth and Rhoddan hunted and returned with a small doe that Shayth cooked in the twilight hours when the smoke would be less visible. It was still a risk, as the smell would be inviting, no matter when it was roasted.

Sellia decided to scout a route through the camp and hovered behind a large rock looking down on hundreds of white tents and banners. In true military fashion, the camp had one main thoroughfare down the center and various paths that went off it at regimented right angles, one leading straight into the Cliftean Pass.

Deciding she had seen enough, she considered trying to make out where the sentries were posted, but it would be difficult to do this undetected and, if Seanchai's plan worked, it would make little difference.

As she rose to go, she heard voices frighteningly close to her. She pulled her cloak around her and loosened her long knife. It was too risky to swing her bow round and nock an arrow.

"This is absurd, Ahad. I could walk into the camp and demand a feast."

Another voice laughed. "That you could, Shadow, but while you stuffed yourself with venison and boar, they would be sending a message back to your dear father. Maybe Shiftan already told him and has orders for when you surface."

"Do you think they are also here?"

"Who?"

"The elf and Shayth," the first voice replied. "Aren't they scouting out a route to get through the pass?"

"They could be behind the next boulder, for all we know. They understand stealth, I imagine. If it was me, unless I had magical powers like some say the elf does, I would be climbing the peaks to go around the camp–not through it."

There was silence for a while, then the first voice, Shadow, spoke. "Ahad? Are you sure you can take him?"

"The elf?"

"No, Shayth. I know you can't take the elf."

"Listen, Shadow. When I find the elf, I'm to alert the Emperor. He's given me a way to do this so that *he* can fight the elf. You need to know that. I'm ordered to do so and won't disobey a direct order from my liege."

"You've gone against him already by bringing me, and he'll discover that when he arrives," Shadow laughed and Sellia thought how young the voice she now knew to be the Crown Prince sounded.

"I think he knows you're here and approves. But do you understand what I just told you?"

"Yes, yes. You're so serious. We'll leave the elf to my father. I'd like to see him in action, though by the time he organizes his retinue and travels here, it won't only be the elf with white hair, and he will probably be long gone. Have you thought of that?"

Ahad replied, "I believe you'll discover that your father has secrets of his own. He'll be here on time."

Sellia felt the atmosphere tense as the prince brooded. The Emperor's secrets were apparently not his favorite topic. When he spoke, his voice was more serious. "What about Shayth?"

"I'm a trained officer of the Emperor's army."

"As was your father."

"I'm also a Master Assassin."

"Your father had experience that you don't, and he was considered one of the greatest swordsmen in the land. It worries me that you are untried."

Now Ahad's voice was hard. "My father had feelings for Shayth. I fear the traitor used that against him. I'm not vulnerable in this respect. Now come. If you want to eat, we should hunt. Tomorrow we will look for the elf and Shayth."

Back at the cave, Sellia shared the conversation that she had heard.

"It really is the Crown Prince then?" Rhoddan was excited. "Are you sure?"

"Yes. He referred to the Emperor as his father."

They all looked at Shayth who was sharpening the dirk he kept in his boot. "Then the Crown Prince is here," he confirmed. "His name is Phineus which he hates. I once got slapped a few times for using it. Admittedly, I knew exactly what I was doing."

"Weren't you the charmer," Rhoddan said.

"You've no idea," Shayth replied and actually smiled.

"We should assume that he is as proficient as Ahad," Rhoddan said. "He must have received the best training. This changes things, doesn't it?"

"A lot," Shayth admitted, and all they heard for a long while was the methodical scrape of his dirk blade on the sharpening stone.

"I have a suggestion," Sellia said at last. "Don't confront them. There are probably more highly-trained men in his entourage. The Emperor wouldn't allow his only son to wander around unguarded with another boy like this. It's too much for you. Let them think that Rhoddan is Seanchai. He's done it before. They'll give chase to the two of you. Lead them back to the dwarves. Hopefully, you'll get an opportunity to capture or kill them."

"I'm tired of running," Shayth said, his voice somewhat distant. "I'm ready to face them: Ahad, my cousin, and after that the Emperor."

"That's not a fight you can win," Sellia replied, staring at him. A pregnant silence descended before she spoke in barely more than a whisper. "But you know that, don't you?"

Shayth nodded. "I said I'm tired of running. Defeating Ahad, even if I can, won't solve that."

"You'll take Rhoddan down with you," her tone was icy. "Have you considered that?"

"I assumed he would go with you. It was supposed to be just me and Ahad, as it should."

"I will stand by you," Rhoddan said, his voice firm.

Shayth didn't answer. He returned his dirk to his boot and unsheathed his sword. It sparkled, and Sellia know it was already sharp. But Shayth went to work on it with a vengeance. "I told you when we met that I'm not good at working with others."

"But you swore to join me," Seanchai said, appearing behind Sellia. They had assumed he was asleep. "If you don't swear now that you will never willingly let yourself die, then I will stay here and fight with you instead of going through the pass."

"Don't guilt me," Shayth snapped, jumping to his feet.

Seanchai stepped closer. "Swear to me," he said, his voice quiet but firm.

Shayth glared into Seanchai's eyes and they locked on each other. It was Shayth who finally looked away. "Your ancient language doesn't bind me," he snarled.

"No, but your honor does," Seanchai replied. "You have a destiny, Shayth. You are seeing it unfold before you. You cannot give in now. Swear to me."

Sellia had never heard Seanchai speak like this. His voice was iron, and he never flinched from Shayth's glare. She looked over at Shayth. His chest was heaving, and he clenched his sword with white knuckles. Finally, he turned from the Wycaan and stared down at the fire.

"*Ashbar*," he said quietly, and they all knew he had bound himself.

Chapter Forty-Two

They decided that Seanchai and Sellia would cross the army camp about two hours before dawn, when there wasn't much activity. Shayth and Rhoddan had spent a cold, cramped night watching to see when the sentries swapped out. There was only one guard change, so those on duty when Seanchai crossed would be especially tired.

Seanchai spent most of the day sleeping, drinking his mushroom tea, and doing his standing exercises. He was not interested in practicing the darkness exercise any more. He had to prepare himself as best he could and trusted his attunement with the elements.

He and Sellia filled their bags carefully, packing as much food and water as possible. No one had any idea what the terrain would be like—whether it would be cold or hot, arid or with fresh water. They could only hope to be able to hunt.

On the other hand, if they were forced to run, any weight would be a disadvantage. But at that point, Shayth said, they should drop their bags and flee. Rhoddan and Shayth accompanied them to the road that led into the camp.

"There is no time for goodbyes," Shayth said quickly.

Seanchai stared at him. "I will be back, and we'll fight side-by-side to free Odessiya and find you the peace you crave. I promise."

"Get out of here before I make you swear oaths," Shayth said, but he did not object as Seanchai suddenly reached out and hugged him.

"You are important to me," the elf whispered in his ear and then loudly, about Rhoddan: "And try to keep this chump out of trouble."

"Now you ask too much," Shayth replied.

Seanchai turned to Rhoddan. "I'm sorry you can't join us. I wish you could, for both of us."

"Just do what you have to do," Rhoddan replied. "I'd hate for you to miss all the fun on this side of the pass."

They hugged, and then Sellia and Rhoddan hugged. Sellia turned to Shayth and held out her arms. He hesitated.

"You want me to say what I have to say out loud?" she asked. Shayth shrugged, and she pointed a finger at him. "Be the person you were destined to be, Prince Shindell, and stop wasting so much energy trying to deny what everyone else sees so clearly."

Seanchai was stunned by Sellia's audacity, but he noted Rhoddan nodded in agreement and Shayth actually didn't scowl. Seanchai put his pack on his back and then his swords. He watched as Sellia adjusted her bow and quiver over her pack.

He and Sellia walked a short distance away so Seanchai could summon the energy around them. He closed his eyes and began to call the darkness. *Chashichot. Chashichot. Chashichot.* He could feel the connection even though he couldn't see it, and held to it fast. He nodded to Sellia, whose eyes were wide with wonder, as he soundlessly repeated the word.

"Can you see us?" Sellia called out.

"I can't see Seanchai," Rhoddan said, "but I think I can see a bit of you."

Seanchai tried to project the darkness, and a minute later he heard Rhoddan. "That's better. I can't see anything now."

"Go," Shayth said. "May the gods walk beside you."

"I didn't know you were religious," Sellia remarked.

"Only tonight," Shayth replied. "Come, Rhoddan. Let's move to a better place to watch." They would create a distraction if anything went awry.

Seanchai continued to murmur the word and summon the darkness to them. Taking Sellia's hand, for reassurance as much as anything else, he led her forward.

Two guards stood at the entrance to the camp. There was also a clumsy barricade of logs that one could bypass on either side.

One guard was sitting on a tree stump on the left, smoking a pipe. The other stood by him, staring out toward the two elves. A wave of panic rose inside Seanchai, but Sellia gently stroked his hand and guided him across the road. The sentry showed no sign that he had noticed them.

They passed by the logs around the other side and continued walking. Seanchai squeezed Sellia's hand in excitement, but never ceased to mouth the word: *Chashichot. Chashichot. Chashichot.* He began to feel comfortable with the energy and how it responded to his voice and his direction while he mentally maintained a field around them.

They passed a series of tents, and Sellia guided him into the middle of the road. They did not want someone to exit a tent and bump into them. As they reached the center of the camp, they crossed the main road. A group of cavalry galloped up and stopped a few feet from them.

Seanchai froze, and again, Sellia guided him away from the horses. They stood listening. The officer gave orders to his troops, and then told them that he was going to General Shiftan's command tent to report in.

After the horsemen had passed, the elves continued. This area was more crowded making it particularly difficult to negotiate. There was an infirmary on their left and considerable activity within a big white tent where the officer entered. Inside was an eating area with dozens of tables and benches. Smoke rose from a connected tent, probably the kitchens.

As they passed the mouth of the tent, Seanchai saw a table with a model on it. There were many men in armor, and a white-cloaked figure, deep in discussion, who abruptly turned his head. Seanchai could not see anything inside the cowl, but he was convinced the figure had seen them. He felt his blood freeze.

He quickened his pace, and Sellia squeezed his hand. They both looked back. The white figure and an officer had stepped outside. The officer was still talking, but the white-cloaked figure was staring in their direction.

Seanchai continued to murmur the word with greater vigor, hoping that the blackness would deepen. They were in the Cliftean Pass now, the rock face rising on both sides and the well-worn road giving way to a stony path.

The elf could see soldiers sleeping in various holes in the rocks. He led Sellia past two tents from where a cacophony of snores exited. There would be more soldiers ahead.

He glanced back over his shoulder. The white-cloaked figure was now walking after them with two huge soldiers on either side of him. It didn't seem that he was chasing them, but. . . Seanchai *knew* the figure had felt his presence.

He dared not increase his pace for fear that either Sellia or he would trip on the stony path. One of the soldiers behind him barked out.

"Sentries! General Shiftan wants you on your feet, pacing. Quick to it, men!"

Two soldiers stood up immediately and began pacing. Two more crawled out of blankets and jumped to their feet when they saw the entourage behind Seanchai. The elf was sweating, his hand clammy in Sellia's grip.

Seanchai timed their walk past two guards perfectly, and they were through. He looked back and saw the officers had reached the sentries. He breathed a sigh of relief. They had made it.

"Archers!" came the cry from behind him. "Light the tips of your arrows. Watch them fall and report anything strange in their trajectory."

Chapter Forty-Three

"**A**rchers! Fire!"

Seanchai quickened his pace. He could hear the arrows whistling behind him and the thuds as they landed. He had no idea whether this darkness would be impervious to fire, and it was ruining his night vision.

Sellia gasped quietly as an arrow landed very close. A second passed just over them. A third landed on top of them. It bounced off and extinguished. Surely they were almost out of range now, but the arrows seemed more concentrated in their direction than they were before.

When a second arrow hit and bounced off of them, they heard the cry. "Over there! Shoot in that direction." More arrows. Were the archers moving forward?

Seanchai heard pounding hooves and, again, his blood went cold. Suddenly, he hit against something in front of him. It felt like a barrier, cold and flexible, but firm.

"Keep summoning the darkness," Sellia hissed.

She must have sensed it, too. He repeated the words and sent the darkness up against the barrier. There was a feeling like two energies fusing together. More arrows screeched overhead, and hooves continued to gallop.

Instinctively, he threw back his hood, revealing his hair. He flicked it behind his ears, exposing their tips. He turned and did the same to Sellia. Nothing happened, though he felt a shimmer in the energy of the barrier.

The arrows had stopped, but the cavalry's hooves were getting louder. Seanchai's mind raced. He had to keep up the darkness, but he needed to get in.

Go back to the stories, Mhari had told him. *In times of stress, go back to the stories.* Seanchai stopped calling the darkness and, as the energy shrank from him, he lifted his head. He didn't understand the words that came from his mouth, but he knew what he was saying. They were from a famous story he had heard dozens of times from his mother when he was a child going to bed. But now he spoke them in the ancient language.

Here walks one of the Wycaan Order. I bring the peace of my people, the wisdom of my teachers, the healing of the land. I. . . will. . . enter.

And with absolutely certainty, Seanchai walked through the barrier and pulled Sellia after him.

"Do you think it was him, my lord?"

"Yes, General Shiftan, I do."

"How do you know?"

"It is difficult to explain. The earth is a web of magic and energy. When something disturbs that web, the shimmers ripple out like a drop of water in a lake."

The Emperor continued to stare into the dawn light, and General Shiftan tried to fathom his thoughts.

"My lord. With your permission, I will lead a regiment after him. He'll not go far under such cover, will he? It must take effort to conceal himself like that. I could continue to track him–"

"Thank you, General Shiftan. But you know not what lies beyond."

"Someone needs to find out, surely? Has anyone tried to go beyond?"

General Shiftan looked up into the white cowl that covered the Emperor's head. He wished he could discern his lord's expressions. But the Emperor kept himself concealed, as always.

"Across this plain, few have ventured and even fewer returned. There's a barrier woven of powerful and ancient elf magic, where we lost track of them. Only the selected pass through. I, myself, ventured forth in my younger days."

The Emperor went silent, and Shiftan waited patiently. A soldier approached and asked if he should call up reinforcements. A slight shake of his ruler's head told the soldier what he needed.

"Leave a security detail," General Shiftan instructed, "and tell them to retreat another fifty paces."

"General Shiftan, sir," the soldier responded standing straight. "Begging your pardon sir, ain't safe t–"

"You have your orders," Shiftan replied in a voice curter than he would have wanted. He softened his tone. "I appreciate your concern, Janos."

"Yes, sir." The soldier saluted and turned away.

"They're extremely loyal to you, General Shiftan. It is a rare trait. General Tarlach had his soldiers' respect, but they also feared him."

"General Tarlach was a close friend of mine and a most capable officer," Shiftan replied.

"Yes. But his mistakes allowed the Wycaan to get to where he is. And that, my good general, is a most worrying predicament. If they accept him, then he may well return a powerful adversary. Too powerful."

"Let me go after him, my lord?"

"He is beyond your reach now."

Shiftan thought for a moment. "Who are *they*, milord?"

"Good question, General Shiftan. Good question."

"But you said that you have passed through the boundaries. Who did you meet?"

"That is difficult to say. I never saw anyone, but I was aware of them, and they communicated with me. It felt as though the trees were talking, but I think those living beyond the pass spoke through the trees—through the entire forest. Have you heard of the Elves of the West, General Shiftan?"

"Children's stories, no?"

The Emperor did not answer and they stood together a while longer, each lost in thought. Finally, Shiftan spoke. "What are your orders, milord?"

"Fortify this pass, my friend. Prepare to repel an invasion. Whether it will be a whole army or one elf, we must be ready. I will leave that to you. Now, I want to find my son before he and Ahad confront my nephew."

"Do you think Shayth can best Ahad *and* the Crown Prince now that he doesn't have the Wycaan with him?" Shiftan was surprised.

The Emperor turned and though he could not see his liege's eyes, Shiftan sensed a father's fear for his son. When the Emperor spoke, his voice was harsh and cold. "I have no intention of finding out."

Chapter Forty~Four

Seanchai led Sellia across the wide valley floor in silence. It looked similar to other places on their journey, but it felt different. It seemed cleaner, somehow, Seanchai thought–less inhabited, less spoiled.

They headed for a mass of dark green forest before them. Seanchai was excited at the prospect of being back among trees–a place where he had felt safe as a child.

"Seanchai, look!" Sellia said from behind him. He turned and saw she was pointing at a huge herd of. . . what looked like very big, brown cows. Their hides were covered in thick, shaggy fur, and many had horns that spread out wide before arching forward.

Sellia began to take off her bow, but Seanchai stayed her.

"We don't know the rules yet," he said, "and we're being watched. This might be a test."

Sellia looked around and saw no one. "How do you know we're being watched?"

"I just do," he replied testily.

"As you wish." Sellia shrugged and replaced her bow on her shoulder. "But I hope the test includes refreshments at some point."

"We have food in our bags," Seanchai said.

"Yes, but anything that won't spoil should be kept for when we're on the run and don't have time to hunt."

"I know." Seanchai continued walking. "For now, I think we can make the forest by nightfall."

He was wrong. After a couple more hours, the ground became increasingly marshy. Seanchai was still leading and stopped a little way in. A mist was coming out to meet them and, while wispy on the edges, it seemed thicker and more imposing in the middle.

"Sellia," he whispered, though he did not know what compelled him to keep his voice down. "This might be a test, as well. It feels strange and. . . wrong."

He took a small cord out of his pack that he had hoped to use for fishing at some point. He turned and told Sellia to tie it to the front of her belt and the back of his, connecting them. Sellia frowned but did not argue.

As they walked further into the dark marsh, the fog engulfed them. Fire flared and just as quickly disappeared, playing with their vision. Seanchai decided to follow the flames in the hope that they were beacons meant to lead them through the marsh.

He began to hear voices pleading for help from. . . underneath. He looked down and then jerked his head up again. He turned and saw Sellia staring down, transfixed on the voices.

"Sellia! Sellia!" He touched her chin, but she did not respond. Her skin felt cold and clammy. He shook her face, and she glared at him. "Don't look, and don't listen."

"I can't help it," her voice was distant and weak.

"Hold my hand," he encouraged. "Try humming a song."

Seanchai felt a cold chill as Sellia squeezed his hand and began mumbling a tune to herself. But she was shaking now and incoherent. He stopped again and ripped an edge off his shirt and stuffed two crumpled-up pieces into her ears. Then he tied a longer piece around her eyes.

She tried to stop him, but her attempts were feeble, and he kept speaking gently to her even though he didn't think she was focused on what he was saying.

His fear rose. He took a deep, grounding breath and, holding Sellia's hand, kept moving forward. The voices around him were desperate, frightened, resigned, and defeated.

Go back. Go back now while you still. . . Take me. . . Don't leave us, we can't. . . Go back. . . It's not too late, but it will be. . . You cannot get through. . . You aren't welcome. . . Go back. . . Take me with you. . . Help me. . . Help me.

Seanchai fought not to look down, not to stop, not to turn around. He focused on the face of his teacher and her gray-silver hair, wrinkles, and piercing blue eyes.

This worked for a while, but gradually, the desperate cries around him seeped through. He tried to recall Mhari's lessons, and when this failed, he focused on his breathing exercises. Pulling energy up from the marshes felt different, almost alien.

He felt a cold current course through his body. He considered stopping, but the sensation helped block out the voices, and he became increasingly certain of their direction.

Seanchai squeezed Sellia's sweaty hand, and she responded, gripping him tightly. She was struggling, and he tried to stroke the hand he was holding with his thumb.

At one point, she tried to let go of him, and he tightened his fingers around her hand. Sellia whimpered. Whatever she was going through must be intense. Usually, Sellia was so tough.

Seanchai stopped walking and turned around. He reached out with his mind and felt her telepathically grab him in a desperate hug. He embraced her, pulled her into his mental grasp, and quieted her. They stood still for a few minutes, Seanchai pouring energy into her. Her breathing calmed, her grip became less frenzied, and she cleared her throat.

"Thank you," she panted. "I'm ready to go on."

They continued for another hour before the ground became firmer and the voices disappeared. It was still gray around them, but now it felt like a natural dusk instead of artificial darkness. The forest loomed up before them. Seanchai untied Sellia's blindfold and the cord that connected them. She fell into his arms, and they held each other tight.

"That was intense," she said when they pulled back. "You were amazing. I feel like. . . I feel," she chewed her lip, searching for the right words. "You were so strong, so constant. How come you weren't afraid?"

Seanchai stroked her cheek and smiled. "Come," he said. "I think the worst part is behind us."

He was wrong.

Chapter Forty-Five

In the forest, they quickly chose to camp under a huge tree with a flat, tuberous trunk. The tree had smooth bark, and Seanchai felt it exuding great energy as he stroked it. He felt safe and suggested they both sleep without posting guard.

"No," Sellia said. "We almost had our lives sucked out of us back there. I'm not convinced whoever's watching us is on our side."

"We had better hope they are," Seanchai replied, "because this forest is ancient and imbued with energy. I think those who live here draw their strength from this powerful source."

"Well, that's a comforting thought you've used to send an elfe to sleep."

Seanchai laughed as he spread out the bearskin. "Okay. You sleep first shift. I will do my exercises and try to learn some more about what we might encounter and where we're headed."

"Are you going to be able to stay up?" Sellia asked, failing to suppress a yawn.

Seanchai patted the bearskin and she came over and lay down. He kissed her forehead as her eyes closed. "You were amazing back there," she mumbled as she fell asleep.

Seanchai rose and assumed the first standing position, scrying the perimeter of their camp. There were many signs of life, but they seemed to be small animals, birds and insects. He let go and allowed his body to direct him through the positions.

As his breathing deepened, he felt his body regenerate as though it was growing a new layer of internal skin. He felt energy pulsate through his legs, into his loins and stomach, and up through his chest to his arms. His mind became both calm and invigorated. Thoughts and fears crystallized into understanding.

When the moon was above him, he stretched and came out of his exercises. He was brimming with energy and drew his Win Dao swords to make the most of it. He went through the moves that Mhari had taught him, and then through others that he had developed on the road. As his blades moved faster, they moved almost of their own volition in ways he had never used them. It felt as though the swords were directing him, and he felt as though he could do anything.

At one point, as both swords came swirling down to his left, he kicked his legs out first with the right and then the left. It was a move he had imagined doing but never thought he actually could. Now it had come to him unbidden and he felt exhilarated.

Panting from exertion, he began to wonder if this was due to the vibrancy of the trees or another test. He felt a strong instinct to ground the energy and, though tempted to continue, went through his series of stretching exercises to center himself. Then he sat on a log on the other side of the clearing from where Sellia was sleeping and took out the pipe he had received from Thorminsk. He had not smoked it often. While on the run, the scent of burning herbal leaves could give away their position, and among the dwarves underground, he had shied away from the stone caverns filled with the dense smoke of hundreds of dwarves puffing on their pipes.

He woke Sellia after the moon began to dip behind the big tree. He was now very tired and ready to sleep. He waited while she disappeared into the trees, and when she returned and took out her waterskin, he wrapped himself in the bearskin.

He walked along a river. Mighty, tuberous trees lined both banks but kept a respectful distance in deference of the eroding persistence of the river. Behind him were tall, snow-capped mountains.

He loped along, conscious of his huge paws sinking into the soft, damp earth. By his side was a great white bear, but Seanchai felt bigger and shaggier. The great white stopped and moved into the water, looking intently under the current. One paw rose slowly, and the sun glinted off its claws. It struck swiftly, and when its paw emerged from the water, it had a small, pink fish that wiggled desperately in the few moments it took to disappear into the bear's mouth.

Seanchai joined the white and felt his companion smirk. He struck twice and failed to catch a fish. The white pulled a second with little effort and tossed it at the young grizzly, who snapped it between his powerful jaws.

Seanchai heard laughter from behind and turned to see a slender chestnut bear, the likes of which he had never seen before, on a smooth rock about six feet above the river. The bear sat on its back haunches, its two muscular front legs planted straight on the rock.

"Not a mighty hunter yet, I see," the chestnut said.

This was the first time Seanchai had heard a bear speak in his dreams, other than the grizzly, and he eyed the chestnut suspiciously.

"I'm not a bear," the chestnut said, "not even in the way you are."

"But you have entered my dreams," Seanchai said. "How?"

"Do not be alarmed. You are in no danger from me. Usually I seek permission first, but since you are an outsider. I need to vet you. I apologize."

"But how—"

"I am a dreamwalker. Once, every tribe had one, but I guess things are different beyond the boundary. I can enter an elf's mind

and communicate with him, learn of his needs, and give healing and council."

"You're an elf?" Seanchai was excited.

"Yes," the bear replied. It licked one of its paws. "Why do bears do this?"

"To keep their paws clean so they don't lose their grip. Don't elves over here wash their hands?"

The chestnut laughed. "Yes, we do. How did you know that?"

"Know what?"

"About cleaning paws?"

"I'm not sure," Seanchai said, puzzled. "I haven't been connected to the bears for very long, but somehow, I just knew."

"You intrigue us," the bear replied. "We wish to know why you have come, how you passed our tests, and who the old human was that you summoned to guide you through the swamps."

"Bears don't usually ask that many questions."

The chestnut laughed. "Who is the elfe? Does she share your powers?"

"No. But she shares my destiny and my heart."

"Oh. I'm not sure if she'll be allowed. As it is, we're suspicious of you. You're the first in a few hundred years to pass through. Only a firebreather succeeded in my lifetime, and he was finally turned away."

"A firebreather?" Seanchai was confused. "One who was a firebreather like I am a bear?"

"Indeed."

"Why was he turned away?"

"He failed the tests. We felt his bad intentions. He is out there still, and if we had embraced him, he might have subjugated us to his will. You also have come with a request, have you not?"

"This is not the time for that," Seanchai said "What did you mean, my companion might not be accepted? Would you send her away?"

"No. We would kill her to preserve our secret existence."

The white bear turned to the chestnut and growled, baring his teeth.

"Are you here to protect me?" Seanchai asked the white. It looked back at Seanchai, and he was sure of the answer. "Thank you, my brother."

"What about the firebreather? Why did you not kill him?"

The chestnut shuffled his paws. "He may have been too powerful already."

"But you would have if you could?"

"Yes."

Seanchai glared. "Do your people dole out life and death so easily?" He knew his tone was harsh, but the chestnut showed no anger.

"Do not be so quick to judge. We came here in desperate circumstances and have survived because our location is secret and our barriers stop all but a few."

"Why not all?"

The chestnut bear rose. "Because we wait for one to come, and we think it might be you."

"And if I'm not the one?"

"We will kill you, too, and no pack of bears will be able to stop us." The chestnut turned and jumped down from the rock on the other side and disappeared.

CHAPTER FORTY~SIX

Seanchai and Sellia ate breakfast and packed up their camp in silence. Seanchai could feel Sellia looking at him, but he didn't want to meet her stare. He had to make a decision, and fast. Finally, as they stood with their packs on their backs, he turned to her.

"Sellia. Do you know how to find your way back?"

The look on her face went from concern, to hurt, to fear.

"What happened in the night?" she asked, her voice softer than usual. "I heard you cry out and saw you toss and turn."

"Do you know your way back?" Seanchai asked again.

"I do. I just have to cross a talking swamp, get through a magical barrier, and face General Shiftan and his army by myself. Directions are the least of my problems."

"If you continue with me, I might not be able to save you."

"Whereas if I head back, you will? I never have understood your powers, Seanchai, so forgive me the feeling of utter abandonment."

"Abandonment? I'm trying to save you!"

"Definitely feels like it." Sellia's cheeks were flushing hot. "When you finish, meet me at the swamp. Remember to look down or you might miss me. If I'm not there–"

"Stop!" Seanchai's voice was sharp but there were tears welling as well.

Sellia sighed. "What did they tell you?"

"That you aren't welcome here." He looked down at the ground, poking the mat of fallen leaves with his toe. He was suddenly small and vulnerable, the young forest elf once more. "And I'll only leave alive if I'm the one they are waiting for."

Sellia moved toward him and took him in her arms, one hand guiding his face into her neck as she had done so many times when they had mourned for Ilana. "You need to learn from them, Seanchai. If the only way to do that is to sacrifice me, then I understand. You must become the Wycaan Master. All Odessiya waits for you."

Seanchai jerked his head up. "I can't be the Wycaan that Mhari was, or Master Onyxei. I must be the Wycaan that only I can truly be." He took a step back and looked at her, feeling power rising inside him. "The races of Odessiya accepted me for who I am," he said, and he turned to the trees surrounding him, power coursing into his voice as he shouted: "and so will the Elves of the West."

He took her hand and led her on. Within a few minutes they reached a sharp ridge. The drop was almost straight down and afforded them a magnificent view of a huge forest that stretched to a thin, blue line an even deeper shade than the sky that met it.

With the sun on his back and his long, white hair billowing in the wind, Seanchai drew his Win Dao swords and held them above his head. He cried out in a deep, booming voice.

"I am Seanchai, son of Seantai, and a Wycaan warrior. I am the student of Mhari the human, of Master Onyxei the dwarf, and I come to study with the Wycaans of the West, the Wycaans of my own people. I walk with Sellia, my mate, and I will walk with her by my side."

He listened to his echoes become distant rumbling.

"Very well," said a cheerful voice from his side. "If that is what you have decided. We should go."

Seanchai turned to see a small, dark-skinned elf with bright red hair sitting on a rock only ten feet from them. He was clothed in loose beige trousers and a brown shirt that hung on his skinny body.

"You are the dreamwalker?" Seanchai asked.

"Indeed." The elf jumped down from the rock and approached with his hands held wide to his side in the universal sign of peace. "Am I doing this right? I have never done the hand sign before, having traveled in your lands only in the dream world."

Sellia smiled. "Your palms should face the person you are addressing," she said, "like this." She demonstrated.

"Very good," the elf replied. "So, Sellia, mate to the Wycaan from the East, well met, I say. In truth, I am not sure whether you will be welcomed or not, but for my own part, I am happy to meet you. Tell me, if this is not too imprudent, are the elves from the east pale like Seanchai and dark like you?"

"I have never met another dark-skinned elf until now," Sellia said. "This is exciting."

"That means you are probably the first not to immediately notice the color of my hair!" He laughed. "Forgive my manners. I am Denalion, Dreamwalker of the Markwin Forest, as Seanchai discovered last night.

"Come. We have a long walk, and there will be no more tests for now. You should enjoy the journey."

Denalion led them north along the ridge for a long time. They stopped at a small path that Seanchai could have easily overlooked. Denalion turned to them.

"Drink water and tighten your packs. This part can be challenging if you are not used to the terrain."

Soon, they were walking down a steep, narrow path. Denalion kept looking back at first, but when he saw that both elves easily kept their balance, he focused on the view.

Seanchai and Sellia, while fairly confident in their ability to negotiate the path, still had to look down and concentrate on their steps. They stopped once on a little plateau to drink, but otherwise continued their walk with increasing agility.

As they approached the height of the trees, Sellia called out for them to stop.

"Take a moment, Seanchai, and see the forest," she said. "You are home."

Denalion peered around the Wycaan with a puzzled expression on his face. "What do you me. . ." He trailed off at the blissful expression on Seanchai's face as he absorbed the canopy of treetops, smiling widely. "Very well. Welcome home, then, Wycaan from the East. Welcome home, I say."

Chapter Forty ~ Seven

As at home as he felt, Seanchai did not recognize any foliage from his childhood in Morthian Wood, or of the other forests he had passed through. This was an ancient forest, and the tree trunks were huge.

He scooped up a handful of rotting leaves and twigs from the ground and, closing his eyes, inhaled their scent and sighed deeply. He touched the trunks and stared up at the height of the trees.

"Denalion," Seanchai said, gently rubbing the bark of a tree. "This wood is as red as your hair."

"And I hope when I reach their age, my hair will still match. These are bloodwoods, my friends. They are the largest trees this side of the Great Ocean—the oldest and most majestic."

"I feel humbled in their presence," Seanchai said, and both Sellia and Denalion smiled at his sincerity. "These are powerful trees."

"Indeed they are," Denalion replied. "Did you not feel their power when you practiced your energy exercises."

Seanchai exclaimed, "I did. I can't wait to try more!"

"You shall have your chance soon, but I would like to continue for a few hours. We will camp in the woods and reach Bloodwyre by midday tomorrow."

"Then let's go," Seanchai said, and Sellia thought he might actually take off sprinting by himself.

"Steady up, green ears," she chided quietly. "Denalion will set the pace."

They followed the red-haired elf into the forest. Seanchai kept stopping him with questions about the trees, the plants, and any tracks he spied.

Sellia followed behind, laughing to herself. She had not seen Seanchai this happy for a long time. Whatever tests lay ahead, she was pleased for him now. They eventually arrived at a small river, and Denalion took off his pack.

"We will rest here tonight, my friends. And if we are lucky. . ." He moved over to a small wooden box on an upright log and fiddled with the catch. When he opened it, he peered inside. "Well, not a feast, but food, nonetheless."

"What is this place?" Sellia asked.

"Throughout the forest are little camps like this. We prefer travelers use them and so refrain from spoiling the forest. You would be surprised how much plant life, insects, and small animals are unintentionally harmed when you stop to camp. People take what they need and leave supplies for others.

"I will forage a bit—see what's in the vicinity. Oh, look at this." He held a pole with a series of thin lines getting smaller towards the hook. "We can also fish."

"I can do that," Seanchai exclaimed, and took the rod Denalion held with great enthusiasm. He reached into his pack and baited up with a piece of cheese. Then he moved to the riverbank, dropped the hooked end into the water and sat on a rock, watching the cheese closely.

"I say. What does he think he's doing?" the elf asked Sellia after Seanchai hadn't moved for a few minutes.

"Fishing?" Sellia ventured.

Denalion frowned. "Hmmm. I see." He walked over to Seanchai. "You know, I really am quite tired. Do you think you could collect some wood instead? It can get somewhat chilly once the sun sets. Only dead wood, mind."

"No problem," Seanchai jumped up and passed the rod. "Try and keep the line taut but flexible." He walked past Sellia, whistling.

Once Seanchai was gone, Denalion took the cheese off the line and ate it. "Very good," he said to Sellia as he retrieved a dried bug from a small wooden box.

Then he moved back to the river's edge and stared into the water. Sellia watched, fascinated, as he carefully chose a spot and swung the rod gracefully in front of and behind him. The line arced easily until, under Denalion's movement, it settled on top of the water and floated down. He did this several times.

When Seanchai returned, he stood by Sellia, his mouth agape. When he tried to go to Denalion, Sellia stopped him.

"Wait," she said. "Watch and absorb. You're in a different world and must be respectful. The river and trees are forgiving. Denalion, as well, I think. But you must show restraint when we reach his tribe."

Seanchai nodded and, moving to one side, squatted on a rock, his chin in his hands, his elbows on his knees. Sellia shook her head. Still very much a boy, she thought. It was a wonder after all he has been through.

A flurry from the river snapped her back to attention. The water was churning, and the droplets on the thin line of the rod glimmered in the rays of the setting sun.

Seanchai rose to help Denalion. Sellia felt compelled to join him. The fish was tugging hard, and the rod bent and quivered under the strain. Denalion patiently drew in the line, trapping it to the rod as he wrapped the slack around a buckle on his belt.

The fish rose out of the water and smacked back down. Denalion responded by lowering the tip of his rod to the water, his face unflustered and relaxed.

Sellia noted how completely at one Denalion was with his surroundings, with the fish, with his role in life. In contrast, Seanchai was erratic, emotional, and doubtful.

Seanchai might garner practical skills like fishing and archery while he was here, but at that moment, Sellia understood that he had something far more profound to learn.

CHAPTER FORTY-EIGHT

Rhoddan winced at the pain in his arm. He was near exhaustion, and every time he tripped, which was happening with increasing frequency, he knew he might be giving their position away. Shayth would jerk his head round, but knew Rhoddan was not being careless.

A sixer of long-swordsmen had ambushed them earlier in the day, and the fight had been intense. Rhoddan and Shayth had won, but as Rhoddan dispensed with the final soldier, four more armed men appeared on the ridge.

An arrow had hit Rhoddan in his sword arm. It was very small, and he had ripped it out with one stroke, but he quickly sheathed his sword as the pain numbed his arm. Shayth tied a quick tourniquet under the shoulder.

Shayth had glanced up at the four and swore. "Come, we must run," he commanded.

Rhoddan had quickly followed, and they spent the rest of the day one step ahead of their pursuers. His arm wound made him feel unbalanced, and as the day wore on, he became weaker and less focused.

Shayth found a small cave, and they quickly moved inside. While Shayth did his best to hide their tracks, Rhoddan lay back against the cave wall and realized he was sweating profusely. Shayth returned, rinsed one of his fingers, and touched Rhoddan's wound. He licked it, grimaced, and spat on the ground.

"That bad?" Rhoddan asked.

"Tastes disgusting and the tip of my tongue is now numb. I want you to drink all the water we have and roll yourself in both our blankets. If it's poison, we've got to try and flush it out of your body."

Rhoddan finished his own waterskin and took Shayth's. Water dribbled out of his numb lips and, despite the circumstances, Shayth couldn't help grinning a little.

"I guess this is how we'll end up when we're old," he said.

"I'm very fond of you, Shayth, but I hope to settle down with a comely elfe and not spend the next fifty years running from cave to cave with you."

Shayth sobered. "What if he doesn't come back? What if he fails there?"

Rhoddan leaned forward and stared hard at his friend. "He will succeed. And if he doesn't come back, we'll head over there and create some serious problems."

"Oh, you mean like we're doing here?"

"I'm surprised we're getting this much attention now that Seanchai has gone."

Shayth stared at his friend. "That mini arrow was shot from nearly two hundred feet. Only a Master Assassin would be able to do that. Ahad is tracking us and I'm sure his men are just as formidable."

"You worried?"

"It's more that I don't want to die without knowing what happened to Seanchai. It's probably the first time I haven't welcomed death."

"Well, if you want to leave me here. . ."

Shayth laughed. "You're joking, but even if you weren't, you know I can't."

"Why not?"

"Because if Seanchai does return, he would seriously kick my butt if he found out I left you behind, and double kick me if I die too."

They both laughed at the thought.

"Shayth?" Rhoddan said after a while. "Does the Emperor ever go out and fight battles himself?"

"The Emperor is a mystery, my friend. Even those who live in the palace don't know him. I suspect that even my royal cousin has very little understanding of his father.

"I remember people gossiping about his frequent forays out of the capital when I was a child. My nanny said that the Emperor turned into an eagle and flew across Odessiya, checking that everyone was behaving themselves. She used to say that if he got angry, he could grab a child with his long talons or burn them with fire.

"I would point out that eagles don't breathe fire and that humans can't transform into great beasts. But she was pretty adamant. Said those born to royalty could. . ."

Shayth stopped and they stared at each other. Rhoddan was the first to speak.

"Shayth, can humans, emperors especially, turn into animals?"

"Not that I know," Shayth said, his voice now quiet and hesitant.

Rhoddan was agitated. "Mhari said that even if Seanchai could unite the races tomorrow, he still wouldn't be able to beat the Emperor. I've been thinking about this a lot, and maybe your nanny wasn't that far off. Does your uncle have white hair?"

Shayth stared out into the void, sifting through painful, buried memories. In the silence that followed, Rhoddan began to doze, jerking awake when his head bobbed.

He woke to a different silence. No crickets or nocturnal animal stirred. It felt like calm before a storm, and Rhoddan saw Shayth crouched against the rock face, an arrow strung on his bow.

Rhoddan crawled to the entrance and took position on the other side. He drew his sword quietly, with great effort. He was sweating again, though the prickly feeling crawling up his spine told him that this time, it was from fear.

The first sounds were rhythmic whooshes of air that became increasingly louder. Mesmerized from the steady beat, Rhoddan suddenly realized it was flapping.

The night sky blazed from a stream of fire. Rhoddan crouched under cover of a rock and tried not to stare at the bright flames. All he could think right now was that it would destroy his night vision, and that might prove deadly.

Though the creature passed above them and into the distance, its roar of frustration shook the rocks in the cave.

Chapter Forty-Nine

After they had dined on smoked fish, Seanchai moved away from the fireplace and stood among the bloodwood trees to complete his exercises. He had noticed that they tended to grow in circles, and decided on his own that they were rings of energy.

He stood, breathing deeply and allowing his consciousness to fill his body. Planting his feet firmly on the earth, he drew energy up from the ground, and wave after wave swept through his body. Seanchai felt cleansed from within. The old energy was being replaced by something new, something vibrant, and something powerful yet pure.

At one point he became aware of Sellia leaning on a nearby tree and reluctantly grounded the energy that swirled around him. He stretched and took deep breaths before finally opening his eyes.

"Denalion suggested you sleep some tonight. It's important that you're fresh when we reach the city. I said I would wait up until you finish your exercises, but I'm falling asleep, myself." Sellia yawned in unintentional emphasis.

Seanchai smiled, feeling both relaxed and energized. "What's he worried about? Does he think I would keep this up all night?"

"It's well past the middle of the night, Seanchai," she laughed.

Seanchai looked up to find the moon, but the canopy of branches and leaves denied him. He began to realize that he was, indeed, stiff. He nodded to Sellia and glanced over at Denalion, who was snoring softly.

"Okay," he said. "Are you going to wake our red-headed friend to guard?"

"He says there's no need to guard. We're being taken care of."

Seanchai frowned as he stretched his cramping muscles. "I hope I can fall asleep, knowing there's no guard."

He didn't even recall putting his head on the pillow.

Seanchai woke to the smell of fish sizzling on a fire. He rose and went to the river, where he dunked his head, immediately gasping from the icy water.

"You have come to learn our ways, Wycaan," Denalion said. "First lesson, then: Check what you're sticking your head into before you do so."

Denalion and Sellia laughed, but Seanchai winced. He had once done the same thing at Mhari's camp, and received almost the exact same admonishment. He missed Mhari and that moment reminded him of Ilana too. He sighed.

"Let's go," he said, striding back to his bedding.

Denalion continued to prepare the food. When Seanchai looked at him, he said, "These fish sacrificed their life to sustain us. We must honor their gift."

Seanchai sat down, suppressing his impatience as best he could. He didn't have long to wait before they were walking. Denalion led them downstream to stepping-stones that crossed the river. They easily jumped from one rock to the next and were soon the other side of the water.

Denalion looked back. "The river is a source of food and water. It is also a barrier, and can become impossible to cross if we are threatened. We are grateful for its generosity."

Seanchai wasn't sure if this was a thank you to the river or information for him, so he bowed slightly to the river, just in case.

As the sun reached its zenith, Seanchai noticed that the trees were getting even bigger, their trunks two or three times the girth of those he had first seen upon entering the forest. Above him was an impenetrable canopy of green.

He touched the smooth, shiny bark on one trunk and, as he gazed up, he saw two figures balancing on it, watching them. They made no effort to hide and Seanchai saw no weapons. They were wearing green and blended with the trees.

When they were closer, Seanchai saw that they were *calhei*, young elves, and his pulse quickened. They were healthy; nourished; and possessed vibrant, dark skin. Enslaved *calhei* were often hungry, dirty, and jaundiced.

Denalion walked past them with a short nod of acknowledgement, but Seanchai and Sellia stopped.

"Greetings," Seanchai said, and waved.

The *calhei* stared at him, and then jumped down elegantly and ran off ahead of them.

"They're shy," Seanchai said, and then saw the look on Sellia's face.

"They're dark-skinned," she whispered. "Like me."

Denalion stopped when the *calhei* ran past him. "Elves come in all shades," he said to Sellia. "You will find dark elves to be common here. Behold! We have arrived at the capital. Welcome to Bloodwyre."

Nothing but huge trees surrounded them. Seanchai looked back at Denalion. "I see mighty trees and little clearing. Where is your city?"

The elf pushed back his red hair and smiled. "Look up, my friend."

Chapter Fifty

Seanchai obeyed, and his mouth fell open. For a moment, he thought he might actually be dreaming. He set his backpack on the ground and lay down, using it as a pillow.

From here, he could see that nearly every huge trunk was a stairwell into the trees. Branches crossed in a sensible, orderly maze. Elves had gathered to look down at him. They were pointing and laughing. As more elves congregated, descending from hidden areas above the platform they stood on, Denalion cleared his throat. When Seanchai looked at him, their guide nodded with his head.

"Bloodwyre is far more impressive from above," he said, a big smile across his face.

Seanchai rose and picked up his bag. He and Sellia followed Denalion to one of the tree staircases. They reached the first platform quickly. It was wide enough for several elves to walk together.

The path connected the tree trunk out to another branch. Denalion led them up, across, and up again.

Seanchai noticed that the elves here kept a respectful distance, their eyes darting at him and Denalion. Sellia was hardly noticed. As they moved higher and further across, they passed elf dwellings of differing shapes and sizes, but always appearing as part of the trees and branches. Tightly braided vines and thatch appeared to be the main construction materials. There were regimented gaps that functioned as windows.

Seanchai wanted to look closer, but Denalion led him to where huge branches and trunks converged to form a square with small buildings around the edges. The dreamwalker pointed to the other side of the square, at a larger building with a roof of logs and living vines.

Green leaves stretched out and up from it, seeking the light. Before he followed Denalion into the structure, he looked around and saw that a large number of elves of all shapes, sizes, and colors had gathered and were watching the newcomers. Sellia gently pushed him inside.

The hall was taller and wider than he had anticipated. It was cool and well lit, and there were many elves gathered. They were buzzing with conversation as Seanchai had approached, but now they all stared at him in silence.

Denalion walked toward a long table at the opposite end from where they entered. It sat on a platform made from a huge trunk split down the middle. The flat part of the tree trunk was smooth while the rounded part nestled on wooden stands. The table that sat on the platform was constructed in much the same fashion.

There were seventeen elves seated along its length, and there was a chair for one more. Two elves had bright white hair. They were female—one old, and the other about Seanchai's age. He bowed to them and they inclined their heads.

Denalion cleared his throat. "Greetings, members of the High Council," he said, his voice projecting clearly to all in the hall. "I bring guests, the first in many years. They have passed through our barriers, survived our tests, and come to us now in dire times for their people."

He pointed to Seanchai. "This is Seanchai, son of Seantai. He is a Wycaan studying to become a master. I have met him in the dream world, and I am comfortable vouching for his honesty."

Then he turned to introduce Sellia. "This is Sellia. She knows not her roots, but is deadly with the bow, whether hunting or fighting. She is sworn to the Wycaan."

"Have you met her in the dream world?" One of the council asked, an older elf with a dark complexion.

"I have not," Denalion replied.

"Then you have brought one among us whose way is hidden."

"She is the consort of the Wycaan." Denalion's voice remained firm. "It is enough for me that the Wycaan vouches for her."

"Why have you come to us, Seanchai, son of Seantai?" one councilmember asked. She was wrapped entirely in green cloth, so much so that Seanchai could not make out her age or features.

"I seek training," he said. "My master, Mhari, whom you know, has passed into the spirit world. She died bringing down the walls of Galbrieth to save my friends and me. I swore to Mhari that I would come here to complete my training with Wycaan elves."

"Does a Wycaan ever complete his training?" the older Wycaan replied. "I think not. And we would need good reason to train one already so old as you."

"You are right. Master Mhari believed that I could never reach my potential as a Wycaan until I had learned from a Wycaan of my own people. As for good reason, consider this: A cruel human despot, one who will soon strive to gain entry into—and conquer—your land, rules Odessiya. He places many elves, dwarves, humans, and pictorians into slavery. Many others are serfs, living in great poverty without rights or protection.

The elves, especially, are considered an underclass and suffer the most.

"I have come to ask that you help free the races of Odessiya. The dwarves have risen, but though they are large in spirit and bravery, they are small in number. The aqua'lanis and the pictorians, too, have pledged to help, but they are also small of number.

"It is with the Elves of the West that our hopes lie, for you are a free and powerful people, and you live and breathe our heritage."

"You have wasted your time," the female in green said. "Our people left Odessiya in order to protect ourselves and our heritage. The sad story you tell of the eastern elves vindicates this decision."

A murmur of agreement ran around the hall.

"I am sorry to bear you the bad news, and am surprised Mhari didn't save you the trouble or teach you our history during your training, It would have saved you a long journey," she added.

Seanchai didn't falter, and instead took a deep breath. "These are the words of Wycaan Master Tansu, written in the Book of Prophesies. He brought you to this place from the brink of extermination.

"Wait and be patient, my people. For I have seen that one will come from the East—a Wycaan of our own ears, pointed and proud. He will be young and unstable, all too ready to fall by the way. Teach him, then, our heritage and values. Train him to find the strength at his core and help him build the foundation he will need.

For it falls to him to reforge the Alliance, and he must not fail. For his failure will be the end of the elves, and the dwarves, and all the races, save man. Then nothing will stand between man and his greed, and the earth will destroy itself rather than be subjugated. Life as we know it will end. . . forever."

Seanchai turned and slowly surveyed the entire hall. Then he turned back to the council member who had admonished him. "I know your history. I learned from the Book of Prophecies and the wisdom of Wycaan Master Tansu. I have come to claim my own heritage as a Wycaan Master.

"And I have come to fulfill the prophecy he spoke of. I have come to save *you*, proud Elves of the West."

ChApter Fifty-One

When Seanchai finished, the silence in the Great Hall was palpable. No one moved or spoke for some time. Then the two Wycaans rose together from their seats. The older one turned and addressed the council.

"Wise members of the High Council, Elves of Bloodwyre. There is much to digest, much to discuss. We warn against haste and impulsiveness. Whether our decision is judged right or wrong in the tomes of history, let it not be said that the High Council's decision was rushed and fueled by long-buried emotions and fears we have tried so hard to suppress.

"Let the High Council break for the day and each meditate upon what has occurred. We will take the young Wycaan to our school and begin to train him. Let the High Council reconvene if and when the young elf is ready to be tested.

"We have trusted in the wisdom of the trees, and they have never failed us. Dig deep into your souls, my friends. The path will be revealed."

As one, the entirety of the Great Hall rose and stood in silence. Some had their eyes closed. Others held their heads or hands facing upward.

Seanchai soaked in the energy exuding from these hundreds of elves. He glanced up at the shimmering leaves above and heard a great creak in the trunks of the bloodwood trees. The people exhaled. They had been answered.

"Follow us," the old Wycaan said as she and the younger one walked past Seanchai. He turned to Sellia, but Denalion was ushering her off in a different direction. "We are taking you to the home of the Wycaans. There is no entrance tolerated for any but those who walk our path." The old elfe glanced at Seanchai. "Denalion will take care of her. Come now."

Outside the Great Hall, the two Wycaans put their hoods over their heads. Seanchai did the same, but kept his head at the front of the cowl. He did not want to miss anything.

They passed different dwellings, and an area of workshops: blacksmiths, wood workers, metalwork, and many artisans. Soon, they were walking on paths with only the tree trunks surrounding them. They reached an abrupt end at a sturdy vine.

"Do you have gloves?" the older Wycaan asked him.

Seanchai took out his riding gloves, and she examined them and fretted.

"Hold on, but not too tight. Here—go first."

Seanchai put his gloves on and firmly grabbed the vine. He twisted his feet around it and looked down. He couldn't see the forest floor.

"Ready?"

He nodded, still looking down. . . and shot upwards to another platform, where he skipped off. The others followed him, both grinning. Seanchai rolled his eyes, but smiled as well.

They walked for a long while, and by now, even the muted light was darkening. The path descended to the forest floor and Seanchai was happy to be on the ground, forest elf or not.

They approached a big clearing where a number of elves wandered around, sparring, meditating, and performing the exercises Seanchai recognized from his own teachings. They all paused and stared. Seanchai's Wycaan guides stopped abruptly and turned to him.

"If your story is not true, if you are an imposter or bring evil in your heart, you will not be able to walk five more paces. You have been warned."

Seanchai nodded. "I am who I say I am. You know what my heart desires."

He walked forward and felt his body thrum. It was uncomfortable, but not painful. When it stopped, so did he.

"Did I pass the test?" he asked, smiling.

"The tests," the elder frowned, "have not yet begun. But you will know if you have passed them, for you will still be alive. Come."

She led him to a tree with a hole in it. Like a living cave, he thought.

"This will be your dwelling while you are with us. It is sparse, but all you will do is sleep, read and meditate here. I will have food brought to you. Then exercise and sleep as you see fit. We will send for you early tomorrow."

"Thank you," Seanchai said, bowing to both of them. The younger had not spoken at all, but Seanchai wanted to show respect, nonetheless.

He put his bags inside. There was a small pallet for sleep and a hole for light, but he was happier outside. He exited the tree, went through his stretching exercises, and then began his standing meditation. The energy surged through him, and again he felt waves of invigoration.

When he opened his eyes, a young elfe sat, leaning against his tree. She wore brown trousers and a shirt that showed, even on her small body, defined muscles. He also noticed her green eyes and the fact that she was smiling at him.

"I have brought you your dinner, Outlander. We aren't sure what you eat. I hope this meets your taste."

"Thank you," he answered. "What is your name?"

"Pyre," she replied, and offered him the clay pot she cradled.

The pot contained a thick, brown soup. Seanchai smelled its rich, earthy scent, and then tasted it. It was sweet and smooth.

"This is delicious," he said, and the young elfe's smile broadened. "What is it?"

"Bloodwood nut soup," she said. "I'm glad you like it. We tend to eat little else." She giggled behind her hand, looking to either side to see if she had been heard.

Seanchai smiled back. "So, tell me about this place?"

"I can't," she replied. "I was forbidden to say anything but exchange pleasantries. But. . ." She glanced around again before continuing. "They said nothing about you talking to me." Her giggle was infectious and Seanchai smiled.

They sat together while Seanchai finished his soup. He consumed all the soup in the bowl but declined more when Pyre offered to go and refill it. Finally she rose.

"I should go," she said, standing and taking the pot. "You don't seem as threatening as they say."

"Threatening?"

"Yes. Some say that you're the harbinger of our destruction. But I think you're rather cute." She giggled again. "Sleep well, Outlander."

"You too, Pyre, *calhei* of Bloodwyre."

Chapter Fifty-Two

A had and Phineus sat on a rock near their campsite. It was dark, and they were staring at whatever flew above them, billowing fire. They had lost Shayth's trail two days ago, and Ahad was uncertain of their next step.

Ruel approached with two mugs. Steam floated up, and, though it was not yet chilly outside, it was a welcome sight. He gave one to the Crown Prince and sipped from the other. Ahad pretended not to notice the slight.

"What are those streams of fire, Shadow?" Ruel asked. "What beast trails us so?"

"What do you think?" he replied.

"Black magic of the Wycaan, milord. Crefen thinks that maybe they did not cross as we thought. The traitor we chase was a distraction to draw us away from the Wycaan."

"Do you agree with him?"

Ruel shrugged. "My brother is smarter than I, milord."

Which isn't saying much, Ahad thought. He was fed up with having the brothers beside him, guarding while he slept, and glaring at him whenever he addressed them. They never questioned his authority, but also left no doubt what they thought of him. It occurred to Ahad that if Phineus was ever harmed or killed, they might then try and kill *him*. Not a comforting thought.

"What do you know of the Wycaans?" Phineus asked Ahad. "Do they have such an ability to transform?"

"There are so many stories, so many legends, that it's hard to separate fact from tale. No one even thought they existed until this elf emerged. Now we know there are others, and that many of our nannies' stories were truer than we imagined.

"The power of the Wycaans comes from the earth, as I recall. It is said that they have the ability to control the elements. Or maybe it was channel the energy of the elements. If this is so, why could they not also control an animal?"

"Even a firebreather? I thought they were extinct." Ruel said.

"We thought the Wycaans were, too. I suspect that many animals we consider extinct have just moved beyond our borders," Ahad said. "We don't know anything of what is outside Odessiya."

Ruel had nothing left to contribute, so he grunted something and returned to the fire.

"Shadow," Ahad said when they were alone. "Has it ever occurred to you that your father's power might also come from this magic?"

"You think my father has Wycaans working for him?"

Ahad knew what the Emperor's son didn't, but he was sworn to secrecy. However, he did want Phineus to realize something important. "Just a thought," he said. "But if he does, and we're seeing his magic, then maybe he knows you are here."

"Good point," Phineus conceded. "What should we do?"

"I think you should return to the capital," Ahad said.

"What? And leave you with Ruel and Crefen? That would be quite a party."

They both laughed. Ahad would miss his friend if they separated, but this was not working out the way they had planned. Silence descended, dramatically broken only by a huge roar and a trail of fire that seemed to come in their direction and left them both momentarily blind.

"What the he–" Phineus did not get a chance to finish his sentiment as Ahad pushed him to the floor and dived on top of him. "Ouch!"

When there was no more roars or fire, Ahad rose and offered a hand to his friend. Phineus was rubbing his ribs.

"That's no way to treat your–"

"A man should protect his *shadow*," Ahad cautioned.

"Still, you're filling out to be a strapping lad," Phineus smiled. "But I thank you. That was close."

Ahad shook his head and they sat in silence watching the sky. When nothing happened, Ahad asked his friend what he knew about Wycaans.

"There is a story of a magic lake where they went to replenish their strengths," Phineus said. "I used to think this was real."

"Why?" Ahad asked, waiting to see if his friend was putting it all together. He received his answer.

"My father doesn't age. He actually looks younger and healthier when he returns from campaigns." There was again silence as Phineus collected his thoughts. "My father goes away quite regularly."

"He's a busy man with a huge responsibility," Ahad responded.

Phineus turned to face him and he wore a deep frown. "Where does your loyalty lay, Ahad? To me or to my father?"

"Does it have to be one or the other? Your father asked me this question, as well."

"What did you answer?"

"That I have sworn oaths of loyalty to him, but that you have my friendship and the loyalty that comes with it."

"I bet that didn't please him." Phineus grinned.

"Actually, it did," Ahad said. "Don't underrate his love and concern for you."

Phineus snorted skeptically and fell back into his own thoughts. Ahad did not want to push his luck. No conversation with Phineus about the Emperor ever ended well. But Ahad wanted the Crown Prince to know that when he ascended to the throne, he, too, would have Ahad's loyalty.

"Do all Wycaans have white hair?" Phineus asked after a while.

"I don't know," Ahad replied. "We know the elf does. But I have also seen white-haired people that are quite normal. Why?"

"I don't remember ever seeing my father's hair. He always wears his turban."

Ahad's chest constricted, and he wanted to shake his friend or yell at him to see what was right before his eyes.

Another streak of fire crossed the sky, much further away, and they could not help but stare at it in wonder. When Ahad's night vision returned, he saw a ranger standing patiently in front of them.

"I bring a message from General Shiftan. He requests that you return to his camp at the pass."

Ahad stared at him. "How did you find us?"

"We're very good at our work."

"I know that," Ahad replied. "My father spoke highly of you. He also told me how you work in groups. How long have we been tracked?"

"You should take that up with Gen–"

"I'm taking it up with you," Ahad snapped. "Have you heard our conversations?"

A glimmer of fear crossed the ranger's face and he glanced at Ahad's assassin's pin. "If you know I do not work alone, then you know I'm not alone now. Harm me, and you will not return to the pass alive. We don't concern ourselves with any conversations save those we are instructed to hear. You have my word that my orders were to track you and nothing more. But my ord–"

The ranger's eyes bulged, suddenly, and a stain of blood spread slowly across his chest. In its center protruded the tip of a serrated knife. The ranger toppled over, and Ahad saw Ruel standing a few yards away.

A moment later, Ruel slumped forward, clutching his own chest, an arrow entrenched deep into his back. Crefen cried out his brother's name and charged in the direction the arrow had come from.

Ahad began to rise, his hand going to his sword. But Phineus grabbed his arm. "You won't get there in time," he whispered. "Don't move. You and I did nothing."

A moment later, they heard a muffled scream from Crefen and the dull thud as a body hit the ground.

Chapter Fifty-Three

Seanchai lay on his pallet and pulled a bearskin over himself. He put his hands behind his head and stared up inside the hollowed tree. It was still alive, he had to remind himself. Somewhere in the dark, the wood was solid, and life connected from treetop to roots. He sighed and felt his eyes close of their own volition.

The bears were walking uphill. No words were spoken. The great white bear from the ice flows of the north paced by his side, its paws treading in unison with his. Two small black bears walked on his other side.

He could sense others behind him as they climbed higher into the heavy air. The huge grizzly stood, waiting for them, and nodded as they neared. It led them to a ridge.

Beneath them was a huge forest whose trees reached up almost to the height the mountain they had climbed. It was dark and ominous below. The grizzly turned to face him.

"You are going there?"

"I am," Seanchai heard himself reply.

"We cannot join you," the grizzly said.

"I know," Seanchai nodded his large bear head. "But I must go, nonetheless."

The white bear growled his unhappiness.

"I have entered dark places before," Seanchai said to him. "I have walked alone and faced many tests."

"This will be the darkest," the grizzly said.

"And I am the most prepared I've ever been."

The white snarled, and Seanchai looked from him to the grizzly.

"He doubts that you're ready. Have you ever faced those who walk our path?"

Seanchai pawed the ground, staring down. "What choice do I have? I must face them, learn from them, and lead them back to join us."

The grizzly nodded. "Not all who walk our path walk as we do. Remember that."

Seanchai looked slowly at each bear before descending down the other side of the ridge, forcing one paw in front of the next. When he reached the entrance to the forest, he stopped and turned his head. The bears, fourteen of them now, rose on their back paws, threw their heads back and a loud moan, similar to a wolf's howl, filled the air. The sound flowed through Seanchai, and he rose on his hind legs and joined them.

"Outlander! Outlander!" Pyre's concerned voice came from outside the tree.

"Hey, Pyre," Seanchai called. "Is everything okay?"

"You were howling like a wolf. What ails you?"

"A dream, that's all. I'm sorry if I scared you."

He came outside, and she led him to a stream where he drank and washed his face. The water tasted rich and earthy. Then they climbed a spiral staircase up a thick tree to the second level of branches, where they reached an open area in a circle of trees. Elves sat on logs, eating from carved wooden bowls. Most had white hair as he did; a few of the younger ones did not. Perhaps they had not been tested yet, he thought, and his mind went back to his dream. The bear scar on his chest was hurting, a dull but noticeable ache.

"Come, take a bowl and serve yourself," Pyre said.

Seanchai noticed she walked taller now, clearly relishing her role as his guide. He smiled, enjoying her company, her energy. In his village, Seanchai had often looked after younger *calhei*. He wondered if any were still alive and quickly cast the thoughts from his mind. It was a long, dark path.

"What do we have, Pyre, bloodwood nut soup?"

"For breakfast?" She giggled. "Some credit please, Outlander."

"Call me Seanchai, please. So what is breakfast?"

"A healthy gruel," she said, "made, of course, from bloodwood nuts." She giggled again.

They took their bowls and sat in the crowded area. Seanchai watched it thin out and remembered what Pyre had said about the others' fear of him. It had never occurred to him that his own people would reject him so. He finished his bowl and followed her to a washing area where they rinsed and hung their utensils.

"A long way for the drops of water to fall," Seanchai said, looking down.

"There is a great mushroom patch on the ground under this and vegetables grow next to it."

"Thank you, young Pyre," a rich female voice said from behind them. "I will take the outlander off your hands."

They both turned to face a broad, muscular elfe; her white hair was curled into a rigid bun behind her wrinkled, but pointed, ears.

"His name is Seanchai," Pyre said, folding her arms across her chest.

The big elfe just stared at her, and Pyre blushed but maintained her defiant pose. Seanchai bent down. "I appreciate you looking out for me, Pyre. You are my first friend in the West. I hope that honors you as much as it does me."

Pyre beamed. "I'll look for you at supper," she said and skipped off.

Seanchai turned to his new guide. "I do prefer to be addressed as Seanchai. How should I address you?"

"Weapons Master," the elfe replied, staring after Pyre.

"Hey," Seanchai said, hearing the sharpness in his voice. "She's okay."

The Weapons Master smiled. "Yes, she is. You misinterpret my expression. Come. Tell me about your weapons as we walk."

"Why? Am I being tested at fighting?" Seanchai asked.

"I never mentioned testing you. My job is to teach you, but not only weapons. The way an elf yields his weapons and how he or she learns, can reveal a considerable amount about his personality. Maybe you are being tested, but not in the way you think, and not by me, for now."

Seanchai talked as they walked along a thin path to the ground. "May I see your blades?" the Weapons Master asked.

Seanchai drew them and handed them to her.

"They are truly beautiful blades, and ancient. The knowledge needed to forge these has sadly been lost. I am curious. Why Win Dao swords? Mhari never fought with such weapons."

"You knew Mhari?"

"Oh, yes," the Weapons Master replied, her voice breaking.

Seanchai saw tears well in her eyes as she turned away. She raised his Win Dao swords and began a beautiful and elegant form. Seanchai watched as she increased her speed, the blades soon becoming a blur. Seanchai did not recognize the form, but he knew the rhythm. He had channeled his grieving for Ilana and Mhari into his form. It was cleansing, somehow. Fortifying. When she returned to him, the Weapons Master's voice was soft and she shone with tears and sweat.

"The finest swords I have ever seen and probably ever will," she said, handing them back with sorrowful eyes. "Just as Mhari was the finest person I ever met, and ever will. Of that, I am sure."

Chapter Fifty-Four

Seanchai followed the Weapons Master to a wide expanse of flat ground surrounded by trees. As they approached, five white-haired elves, all dressed in similar green clothes, jumped to their feet and stood in clear expectation.

"Good morning," the Weapons Master said.

"Weapons Master," they all replied in unison, bowing their heads in respect.

"This is Seanchai. He will train with us. Draw your swords and partner up. Check your training sheaths are secure on your blades."

Seanchai was excited to see that they all had Win Dao swords. Mhari had told him that she did not possess the knowledge to make him a swords master with such weapons.

"Cheriuk. Please spar with Seanchai." The Weapons Master turned to Seanchai. "This is not a duel. You will begin slowly, matching his form. He will gradually speed up so that we can see what you know. Do you understand?"

Seanchai nodded. "But I have no training sheaths. I lost them somewhere."

Cheriuk rolled his eyes. "How careless," he said.

Seanchai stared at him for a moment, trying to decide if this was a test or the elf was simply arrogant. "I have lost a lot in the past year, battling in Odessiya. I have lost friends. People are far more valuable than objects."

He turned to the Weapons Master. "I have been on the move for a long time."

"Please." A thin elfe with pale skin almost as white as her tightly braided Wycaan hair stepped forward. "Use mine, if they fit. I will pick up a set when we break for lunch."

Seanchai's annoyance at Cheriuk dissipated at the elfe's smile. "Thank you," he said. "How should I address you?"

"Shathea," she replied. "It comes fr—"

"I know the name. One of my closest friends is a human called Shayth. His fa—"

"Are you planning to defeat your enemies by talking them to death?" Cheriuk taunted Seanchai, and there was a round of laughter. "Come, show me how an Eastern elf fights."

They began to spar slowly, with Cheriuk leading. Even though the pace was comfortable, Seanchai knew almost immediately that his opponent was better than him. As they settled into a rhythm, Seanchai struggled to swallow his pride and learn from his opponent.

Gradually, Cheriuk sped up and began to use new forms and combinations. Seanchai was clearly on the back foot, but managed to hold his own. The Weapons Master moved among the pairs, but spent a good deal of her time watching Seanchai. Finally, she called for a break, and everyone moved toward a table with water and fruit.

Shathea walked alongside Seanchai and Cheriuk. "You fight well," she said pleasantly to Seanchai, and Seanchai saw a dark expression cross Cheriuk's face.

"Not as well as I'd like," Seanchai replied. "My sword training was brief, and my teacher did not know the way of the Win Dao swords. Cheriuk here could have finished me quickly if he had wanted to."

"Then why choose swords that your teacher does not know?" Cheriuk asked.

"Often the Wycaan does not choose the sword; the sword chooses the Wycaan," Seanchai answered, keeping his voice pleasant. He might not have the skill of Cheriuk, but he had experience. "These swords claimed me at my. . .my transformation."

"You went through a ceremony?" another asked.

"Didn't you all?"

"No. We are natural born Wycaans. Our hair is white from birth and as young calhei we display certain characteristics in our abilities."

"It doesn't seem to be that way in the East," Seanchai replied.

"You went through a transformation, and then Mhari gave you the swords?" The Weapons Master asked.

"No," Seanchai replied. "They came to me during the ceremony, when I was under the water."

"I've never heard of that," the Weapons Master said, shaking her head. "They must be meant for you."

"Mhari said it was very rare, and she had never witnessed it either."

"And you have used them in battle?" another elf asked.

"Too many times," Seanchai answered. "They have felled common soldiers and pictorians, but they alone are not enough to face the Emperor."

"Pictorians?"

"They are often eight foot tall, with a horn on their heads and battle in their hearts. They served the Emperor until. . ." he trailed off.

"I have fought pictorians," the Weapons Master said. "They are fearsome enemies. Do they not still serve the Emperor?"

"No," Seanchai replied, suddenly aware of and embarrassed about how much he was talking about himself. "At the battle of Hothengold, I, um, I convinced the First Boar to remove his troops from the battle. Then, before Sellia and I came here, I went before their high council and persuaded them to join the Alliance. I am hoping they can keep the Emperor's forces busy until I return."

"Have you persuaded anyone else to join you?" Cheriuk's voice was cynical.

"The dwarf nation has risen. I was with them in the Bordan Mountains and at the Battle of Hothengold. The Aqua'lansis have also promised help."

"You've been very busy," Cheriuk replied.

"Perhaps, then, you can forgive him for losing his training guards?" Shathea rebuked Cheriuk mildly, and the others laughed. He forced a smile.

"Cheriuk," Seanchai said, his voice earnest. "My master, Mhari, said that my ability to create friendships, trust, and alliances was a more powerful weapon than anything else we Wycaans possess.

"The day will come when I must face the Emperor, and I will need to be the best warrior I can be. Can you set aside your derision while we train and at least help me master the Win Dao swords?"

Cheriuk stared at him, and Seanchai met his gaze. The group was silent.

"It's not about me, Cheriuk. It never was. There are elves, dwarves, and humans who live demeaning lives as slaves and serfs. They crave the freedom you take for granted. Put aide your animosity and help me. If not for me, then for the elves of Odessiya, who pray each night for the return of the Wycaans."

Cheriuk slowly put his water skin down on the table and wiped his mouth on his sleeve. Then he bowed his head slowly. "With the Weapons Master's permission, I will help train you."

They both turned to the Weapons Master. She nodded her head in accordance, and Seanchai thought he saw a new level of respect when she looked at him. If she was testing him in more than weapons, he realized this had not harmed his cause.

Chapter Fifty-Five

They broke after another hour of sparring. The Weapons Master and Cheriuk both offered Seanchai advice. Cheriuk, while still not exactly friendly, was at least helpful. Several times, he even acknowledged when Seanchai was able to parry well.

Pyre was waiting to escort Seanchai to lunch, and he was happy when she took his hand. He was even more thrilled when Shathea asked if Seanchai would join her for a walk after they had eaten.

Lunch was served in the compound with other Wycaans. Seanchai was still not used to seeing so many white-haired elves, but there were few willing to talk with him. He sat with Pyre and those he had trained with, and all ate in silence.

When he saw Shathea go to clean her plate, he turned to Pyre. "Are you allowed outside the Wycaan compound?"

"Of course," she replied. "When I'm not studying, I visit my parents and play with my friends. Why?"

"I was just wondering how my friend Sellia is doing. Would you check in on her?"

Pyre seemed excited at the prospect of a mission. She leaned in and whispered, "Any secret message you want to pass on?"

"No," Seanchai smiled.

"Can I tell her that Shathea likes you?" Pyre had a cheeky expression on her face.

"Definitely not. Just tell her that the Wycaans are being very supportive. Thank you."

He put his arm around her shoulder, gave her a squeeze, and then rose to clean his plate. He saw Shathea waiting for him and pondered what Pyre had just said. He liked Shathea, but needed no unnecessary drama.

They walked together away from the compound and out into the forest. Shathea asked many questions about Odessiya and what he had done before he came to their land. It occurred to Seanchai that she might be fulfilling a role with her questions, but he had nothing to hide.

They began climbing, and the tree growth became thinner. A river came into view, and Shathea led him up a rock face, an easy climb. When they reached the top, he saw that they were looking down on a waterfall.

Below, elves of all ages were swimming and cleaning themselves. Most were naked. Seanchai felt the tips of his ears grow hot and was sure he was blushing. He turned his attention further along the river. An elf was fishing like Denalion had. The technique fascinated him.

"What are you thinking?" Shathea asked. "Have I pried too much?"

"No," Seanchai replied. "I'm enjoying your company. The way your people fish fascinates me. Everything about this place fascinates me. Seeing elves who are free, proud, and unbroken is amazing. Your life here is so idyllic. It's a far cry from where I grew up."

"You will go back in the end, won't you?"

Seanchai looked at the elfe. He was surprised by the question. "Of course. I must. I have a responsibility, and so do your people."

"We won't give this up," Shathea said, her voice gentle, but certain. "We have worked so hard to create what we have."

"But how can you live here, knowing what's happening to your kin in the east?"

"We didn't know," she said. "Perhaps we still don't."

"What do you mean? Sellia and I are here. Mhari, my teacher, and maybe other Wycaans from the east have been here." He stopped as a thought crossed his mind. "Shathea. Are you certain that your leaders had no idea what was—what *is*—happening? They were part of it. Defeated, they fled and established elaborate defenses. Maybe they've known all along. Maybe that's why I'm not welcome and why they fear me."

As the thought hit him, a chill coursed through his body. "Shathea. Have the Elves of the West been called to arms before? Did those who came before me ask your people to help?"

Shathea pulled her hair behind her pointed ears and pursed her lips. "It's not about the fighting, I don't think. It's about opening ourselves up to a society we do not believe in. Look at us. There are no rich or poor, no starving or overfed. There's no crime here, and when any elf is sick, they receive the best herbs and treatment possible. It is an honor, not a privilege, to sit on the council. Do you understand this, Seanchai? Do you understand what we stand to lose?"

Seanchai looked at the intensity on her face. "I think I do, Shathea. But there are people, with and without pointed ears, who are suffering. What value can you give to your freedom when you know others are denied it?" He realized that she had not answered his earlier question. "Shathea, I need to know. Have the Elves of the West been called to arms before?"

"I have not seen anyone come from the east during my lifetime. But stories are whispered around the fire at night. The young and restless wonder what our people ran from and what we left behind."

Seanchai stared at her, and she could not return his look.

"You must ask the elders, Seanchai. Start with the Weapons Master, for it is rumored that she wanted to follow her mate back. Now her mate's student stands before her with the same request. If she regrets her decision to stay before, maybe now she will not allow herself to be refused a second time."

"The Weapons Master and Mhari. . ." He set the thought aside for the present. "Shathea. Will the Weapons Master be able to persuade the High Council?"

"I'm not sure that should be your goal," Shathea said with more certainty. "Maybe the council shouldn't decide for everyone. Make friends, Seanchai. It seems this is what you're good at. Make friends, and then ask the council to release those who want to come with you."

"Will they allow that?"

She turned now and put a hand on his arm. Her light blue eyes were hard. "If not, then it begs the question: how free are the free Elves of the West?"

Chapter Fifty-Six

S hayth couldn't believe his eyes. He had been watching Ahad and the Crown Prince for an hour, wondering whether to attack and how. He needed to get Rhoddan to a healer, and Ahad had unwittingly camped only a stone's throw from their small cave. If they were not going to move, he would have no choice, and he didn't fancy his chances alone against four men, all academy-trained.

He was about to return to Rhoddan when he saw the ranger approaching. He waited. He couldn't hear the conversation, but judging from the body language, there was a confrontation. Shayth glanced around. These rangers were so good, another one could be right next to him and he wouldn't know.

Then one of the prince's bodyguards threw a dirk into the ranger's back. As the ranger fell forward, Ahad and the Crown Prince both instinctively crouched, bracing for an attack.

Shayth didn't hesitate. He already had an arrow nocked, and he took out the bodyguard easily. He heard a roar and the other guard came charging into the brush, right in his direction. Shayth's second arrow ripped through the man at such close range.

Then Shayth looked at Ahad. The Crown Prince was restraining him. He watched as they both drew swords, but no attack came. Shayth wasn't sure if there were any rangers around, but if there were, would they dare attack the Crown Prince and a Master Assassin even if one of theirs had been murdered?

The two who were alive weren't the ones who had killed the ranger. Ironically, by killing the one who had slain the ranger, Shayth might have just saved their lives. Maybe taking out the guards was enough. Shayth picked up a small rock and through it over to Ahad's other side. When Ahad and the prince jumped and faced that direction, Shayth retreated.

It was two against one now, and Shayth was relieved. He heard movement, and the fire behind him was extinguished. Two shadows moved back in the direction of the Cliftean Pass. In the morning, he would be able to move Rhoddan out.

When he reached the cave, he heard Rhoddan panting. The fever had returned, and the elf was sweating profusely. He lay in both his own and Shayth's blanket. Shayth felt his pulse. It was too quick, especially for an elf.

He pulled the makeshift door over the cave entrance. It was kind of pathetic, he conceded, but for some reason it made him feel safer. He needed some rest. Tomorrow, they would try and reach the village.

Another roar came from whatever patrolled the skies, and Shayth looked into the darkness of the cave to avoid losing his night vision to the bright fire. They couldn't travel by night anymore, which would have made it considerably easier.

The dawn was still gray and unpromising when Shayth woke to Rhoddan gasping. He helped the elf sip water.

"You're a mess, my friend," Shayth said as water dribbled out of Rhoddan's numb mouth. "Do you understand me?"

Rhoddan nodded, though his eyes were glazed.

"We're going to move. Maybe the village we circled around yesterday has a healer who can deal with this."

Rhoddan muttered something incomprehensible and then shook his head.

"Either you're trying to thank me for being such a loyal companion, or telling me to leave you here to haunt these hills. Give it up. I don't need your thanks, and you don't need to waste your breath trying to convince me to leave you. I'm going to check if the path is clear."

He returned in a couple of minutes. Ahad and the Crown Prince had gone, but Shayth now wondered if rangers were tracking him. He decided not to worry about them, since he wouldn't find them unless they wanted him to.

He pulled Rhoddan up onto his feet and began walking, the elf leaning on him heavily. Just maybe, their luck would hold, Shayth thought as they passed through a small wood.

When they exited the other side of the trees, a sixer of mounted soldiers stared at him. Shayth groaned, and Rhoddan, who had been dozing, moaned. He laid Rhoddan on the ground against a tree and looked around for help.

The officer took a pace forward. His horse snorted a billow of steam into the crisp air.

"In the name of the Emperor," the officer called out, drawing his sword, "Come peacefully, and we won't harm you."

"I'm sure," Shayth snorted.

"I said *we* won't harm you. What General Shiftan does is his decision."

"That's refreshingly honest of you," Shayth said. "But I'm not going to be captured again while I'm still alive." He nocked an arrow. "You and I will go together."

"Well, I have no choice," said the officer straightening up in his saddle. "It is my duty. Know that I leave behind a loving wife and two small boys. You, Prince Shindell, should know what it means to be denied a father."

"Can you try to be a bit meaner?" Shayth grimaced. "I prefer to hate someone when I kill them."

The officer smiled, but his face was sad. "I take no satisfaction in your capture or from my own death."

Just then another soldier maneuvered his horse in front of the officer. He took off his helmet and let it drop, revealing a balding head and weathered face. The helmet bounced on the hard ground. "You can take me, Prince. I be old and can't stand by while yeh kill a good man. Jetha here be a fine officer and 'e saved my miserable neck enough times."

"Jeez," Shayth said wearily. He considered lowering his bow, but couldn't see another way out. "I'm not going to be captured again," he muttered more to himself. Then out loud: "Let's end it, then," he let loose the arrow.

The officer and his four remaining soldiers charged. Three fell to arrows that came from the trees behind Shayth, and he, himself, took out the fourth. As the officer reached him, Shayth stepped aside and knocked him from his horse with his bow.

The man rolled and jumped to his feet, but then froze. Behind Shayth, three rangers approached. Two had bows ready, and a third held a long knife. The officer sighed and threw his sword down. Shayth grabbed the reins of the officer's horse and offered them to him.

"Go back to your wife and children, Jetha. For these men's sacrifices, live an honorable life and teach your boys to do the same."

"Take your family to the dwarves in the mountains," one of the rangers said. "I can't say they'll be safe, but your sword will be useful."

"Take your sword," Shayth said, throwing it to the man, who was now mounted.

"Thank you," Jetha said, looking from Shayth to his fallen friends. "They were all good men," he said, and then turned and galloped off.

"Too many of them are," Shayth replied quietly before turning to face the rangers.

Chapter Fifty-Seven

"I don't understand," Shayth said. "Who do you serve?"

"That's of no consequence now. You avenged the life of my cousin back there when that scum knifed him in the back. He was merely relaying a message."

"I'm sorry for your loss; truly, I am. But if you were shadowing the other ranger, then you work for my uncle, and surely you've been given orders what to do should you encounter me."

"We'll help you get your friend to the village. There's a healer passing through. Rumor tells that she has strange powers. Perhaps she can help him."

"Thank you," Shayth said, as the biggest ranger knelt down, removed Rhoddan's swords and bag, and pulled the delirious elf up over his shoulder.

Shayth picked up the pack and swords, and they walked together.

"Are you really Prince Shindell?" the youngest ranger asked.

"My name is Shayth," Shayth replied.

"The tales you have left behind are as confusing as any trail a ranger can follow. Should I believe the good stories or the bad ones?"

"Unfortunately, both," Shayth said. "I went through a bad time after my parents were murdered."

"Murdered?"

"Yes. That's why I've chosen to fight against my uncle. Still want to help me?"

The ranger laughed. "We'll help you to the village, and then we'll forget we ever met."

"We'll forget we ever met, but I'll remember you came to my aid," Shayth replied.

They reached the road just outside a rundown village that Shayth and Rhoddan had passed through under the cover of darkness.

"Can you manage him from here by yourself?" the ranger asked. "Best we are not seen aiding you."

Shayth nodded, thanked them again, and let them help put Rhoddan on his shoulder. The elf was muttering again, and Shayth could feel intense heat emanating from his body.

He barely walked a few paces when a man rode by on an old horse. He stopped when he saw them and stared nervously at Shayth's sword and bow.

"My friend is ill, maybe dying," Shayth said. "Either help me, or let me pass. I'll not harm you or any in your village."

"Swear it to me," the man said, his voice shrill. "Swear it."

"I swear on my sword."

The man dismounted and helped Shayth put Rhoddan over the back of the horse before leading them into the village. Though it was still early, people were already busy preparing for the day's labors. They stopped and stared at the strangers. The man knocked on the door of a small hut.

"Mistress, I bring a man—err—an *elf* who is badly wounded."

The reply was muffled, but Shayth heard bustling inside. When the door opened, a small woman, slightly younger than Shayth and Rhoddan, with spiky hair, similar to his own, stood there with her arms folded across her chest.

Shayth gasped, but the healer just smiled.

"Maugwen?" was all he could say.

"It's a long story," she said. "First, though, let me work on Rhoddan. Tell me what happened."

Shayth recounted Ahad's quarrel and the resulting symptoms. As he spoke, they lay the elf on a table. Shayth removed Rhoddan's boots and wrapped him in a blanket. Maugwen laid steaming towels on his forehead and feet. Then she laid her hands on Rhoddan–one on his stomach, the other on his chest. She closed her eyes.

"Make yourself comfortable, Shayth. This'll take a while."

Shayth retreated to an upright log in the corner, sat down, and looked at Maugwen. He had, in truth, forgotten about her. She had been thrown in a cell with Ilana when they were all captives in Galbrieth. He had correctly suspected that she was a spy, but her attempts to extract any information were half-hearted at best. She had escaped with them, but left the group with some other refugees when they went to fight with the dwarves.

Seanchai had confided that when he and Mhari had scryed them in the dungeons of Galbrieth, Mhari had talked of another with power. Watching Maugwen at work now, Shayth could guess what Mhari had sensed.

She was still short, but not as round as he remembered. Her dark hair stood up like his, and this made him grin. Her big, green eyes were the same, but her body movements were more assured and confident. Gwen, the frightened little girl in the dungeon, had grown up fast.

It was late afternoon when Shayth woke. His neck was stiff, and he was momentarily disorientated. He smelled a thick, earthy scent and opened his eyes to find Rhoddan sitting up and drinking from a bowl.

"Hey, Shayth. Come. Gwen won't let me eat your food. This soup is great."

Shayth grinned and turned to Maugwen. "I preferred him delirious."

She laughed. "I missed you guys," she said. "Actually, I only missed Rhoddan. You were a mean–"

"He's improved," Rhoddan interrupted. "Not much, but he's headed in the right direction."

"They say a prince rides against the Emperor. Quite a change in direction, I think." Maugwen poured a bowl of soup and passed it to Shayth. "Is it just the two of you?"

Shayth hesitated, and Maugwen glared at him. "Still think I'm a spy?" she asked.

"Sorry Gwen," Shayth replied. "It's just the two of us."

"I go by Maugwen now as the Wycaan predicted. Did Seanchai and Ilana go to. . . go. . . where he said he needed to go?"

Shayth and Rhoddan exchanged glances. "I'm sorry, Maugwen," Shayth said. "Ilana is. . . Ilana is. . ."

He didn't finish the sentence. There was no need. Maugwen cupped her hands to her mouth, and tears welled in her eyes. Shayth put his soup bowl down and went to her. He put his arms around her and held her shaking body. It was a while before anyone spoke.

Finally, Maugwen turned and went to the water bucket. She washed her face and joined them, cradling her own soup bowl.

"She was so kind to me–so strong and wise." Maugwen's voice was quiet.

"We all miss her," Rhoddan replied, his voice just as soft. "Every day, we think of her. We'll never forget."

Chapter Fifty-Eight

Seanchai stared along the shaft of the arrow. He let out his breath and shot. To his credit, he hit the target, though only just. Sellia's arrow had almost hit the center of the log. He winced.

"Do you notice the breeze?" the Weapons Master asked, her arms folded over her chest. Seanchai glanced over to a nearby tree and saw the leaves fluttering. She continued: "That was the difference between Sellia's shot and yours."

"Good job, Sellia," she patted the elfe's shoulder. "If you want, I can help you find a Wycaan who shoots straight, one more worthy of you."

They both laughed. The teacher seemed a different elfe around Sellia, who had been allowed to join them at the archery training ground because it was outside the Wycaan compound.

Seanchai nocked another arrow, and this shot hit the target nearer the center, but it still wasn't as good as any of Sellia's shots. The elfe had always been very good with the bow, but now, with the elf-crafted tips she had received and the hours she spent on the range, she was even more impressive.

Many came to see her as she toiled hour after hour. There was nothing else for her to do, she had confided to Seanchai. He told her she was lucky. His weapons' training was intense enough, but after an exhausting day of it, he had still been expected to practice with the elements.

Two elderly Wycaans, the two who sat on the High Council, had taken him to different places to train. Dyfellian was the oldest elfe he had ever met, but though she walked slowly, she held her body erect with no need for a staff for support. She spoke less than her colleague, but when she did, her lessons were clear and effective. Seanchai could feel the wisdom exuding from her.

He had, thus far, directed water, controlled the wind, and moved stones, though his control over the stones was very tenuous.

Lymonia was younger than her colleague but still wrinkled. She watched as he worked with darkness and then taught him to create light in the dark.

Neither teacher was forthcoming about anything beyond the work they were doing. But they constantly asked him questions, as they analyzed every step he had taken since leaving his parents' village.

They neither criticized nor complimented Seanchai, but they did delve deep into each of his actions, thoughts, and decisions. Often, he would provide an answer that would be followed by a long silence. At first, he found this distracting and stressful, but learned to embrace and use it to his advantage, bringing water for the three of them, or stretching an aching limb.

He continued to spar with Cheriuk, who remained aloof, but helpful. Seanchai became frustrated that each time he raised his level, so did Cheriuk. Even more infuriating, the Weapons Master refused to teach him new techniques.

After a confrontation with his teacher about this refusal, Seanchai stormed back to face Cheriuk, who promptly sent him flying, not once or twice, but five times. His swords were faster than Seanchai's, as was his footwork. Seanchai glared at him, then the Weapons Master, and made to storm off.

Cheriuk was in front of him in a flash. "Glare at me all you want, *calhei*," he snarled, "but to the Weapons Master, you will show respect."

Seanchai considered several ways to send Cheriuk flying. None involved swords, and he did not doubt his chances. But as he looked into Cheriuk's hard eyes, he caught just a glimpse of. . . what was that? Disappointment?

He turned back to the Weapons Master and bowed. "I apologize. I must trust in your experience to teach me."

The Weapons Master did not move, but inclined her head ever so slightly. Then Seanchai turned to Cheriuk, who still stood at the ready. Seanchai extended his hands to his sides in peace.

"You're right, Cheriuk. I apologize to you, as well. You are a worthy teacher. Thank you."

Cheriuk, mimicking their Master, inclined his head, as well, but not before a smile escaped.

Seanchai left the compound and went to his tree. He slumped down against it and put his head in his arms.

A water skin was nudged into his hands. He looked up and saw Pyre standing there.

"Can I sit with you?" she asked.

"I'm not sure I'm much in the way of company."

"Is Cheriuk getting under your skin?"

"A bit. I just want to feel that I can beat him. No, I want to beat him. And I want the Weapons Master to teach me how."

Pyre laughed. "You *can* beat him, and if the Weapons Master won't tell you how, it's because she wants you to work it out for yourself."

Seanchai looked at the young elfe and nodded. "That makes sense. It's a test."

"Everything here is a test," Pyre said.

"What makes such a young *calhei* like you so wise?"

Pyre laughed again. "That's what I like about you. Everyone here is so serious. You make me laugh. But I'm not wise, Seanchai. I'm observant; that's all."

"You're smart, Pyre. Trust me. I know smart people."

"Denalion is smart," Pyre said.

"The dreamwalker? Yes, I like him."

"Then go to him for help," Pyre continued. "Many of us do when we're stuck in our training. He's a unique teacher. He's walked further afield than anyone else. He'll help you because, deep down, I think he knows that you were always meant to come."

"What makes you think that?"

"Everyone's talking about you, the Book of Prophecies, and the teachings of Master Tansu. Many say you shouldn't have been allowed in and that you shouldn't be allowed back out. There are a few who stand up for you because they don't want to let fear rule our lives. Denalion speaks as though he knows you—as though he has already decided to support you.

"And, Seanchai, you must understand. Denalion holds a seat on the High Council, but he rarely sits upon it and almost never speaks publicly. He lives in two worlds, the real and the dream, and it gives him knowledge and power. But it also makes him uncomfortable to be among us when he isn't needed. He seeks solace and meditation. But now he's in the thick of discussions and debates. And he stands with you. Always. *That's* why I think you should go to him, Seanchai."

Chapter Fifty-Nine

"I'm no Wycaan, Seanchai," Denalion said when Seanchai sought him out the following morning. "You should study with them for now."

"I need help," Seanchai said. "I need something extra to pass these tests."

"You need to learn from them everything you can, and, yet, you need to discard all they teach you."

"You speak in riddles."

Denalion smiled, then his expression became serious. "You told me that you enjoyed fishing, isn't that so?"

"Yes."

"Go ask the Weapons Master for permission to spend the morning with me."

"And if she asks what we plan to do?"

"Tell her the truth, of course. Tell her we're going fishing."

Seanchai found the Weapons Master eating. He waited until she had finished and cleared her bowl before asking her permission to join Denalion. The wrinkled elfe smiled.

"An interesting and wise choice, Seanchai. I'm impressed."

Seanchai was confused, but decided to cover his ignorance. "Actually, the credit goes to Pyre."

"Aah. Then I commend you for your choice in friends. That little one is very special. Wait a moment." She went to another elf, who was also eating, and whispered in his ear. He nodded, and the Weapons Master returned to Seanchai. "Ask Pyre if she wants to join you. Her teacher agrees, but impress upon her that she'll need to make up the classes she misses."

A half hour later, with stomachs full and holding long, slender poles, Pyre and Seanchai set off after Denalion, who had invited Sellia, as well. They walked north until the forest thinned, crossed a small stream, and then followed the stream west. It met a slow-flowing river, and here, Denalion put his equipment down.

"So, fishing for you is attaching some food on a hook and putting that in the water?"

Seanchai nodded.

"I'm going to teach you another way, okay?" When Seanchai nodded again, he continued. "What fish are we trying to catch?"

Seanchai shrugged. "*Tasty* fish?"

Pyre snickered and quickly covered her mouth. Sellia was smiling, and Seanchai didn't feel too much of a dunce.

"When you went out to fight the Emperor's army, did you stroll into the battlefield and see who might just happens to come along?"

"Of course not," Seanchai said.

"Then do not fish like that, either. Do not do anything that way. Be *intentional*, Seanchai." Denalion clenched his fist to stress his words. "Think like your adversary. Understand him and what he does. Come with me."

"Shouldn't we bring the fishing poles?"

"No," Denalion said. "Let's find the fish first. In this river are brown-spotted pikura. They are big and hungry, but also lazy. They won't expend energy swimming against the current to find their food. Where are they?"

Seanchai thought, and then walked along the riverbank. He pointed after a minute's surveillance. "Over there."

"Why?"

"The rocks break up the current. Whatever floats along is going to get sucked into that little pool. If I were a pikura, that's where I'd wait."

"Good," Denalion patted Seanchai's shoulder. "Very good. Now you may fetch a fishing pole."

Seanchai returned with a rod and some bread.

"You hungry?" Denalion asked.

"It's. . . for the fish," Seanchai said.

"That's very nice of you. Have you seen any loaves floating down the river?" Denalion withdrew a soft, thin square of cloth from his pocket. He carefully opened it and pulled out a dried beetle. "These fall into the river all the time. Quite tasty to the pikura." He took the bread from Seanchai's hand and stuffed it in his own mouth. "This is good, too. Thank you."

He attached the beetle to the hook and moved to the edge of the water to cast. He began rhythmically whipping the rod backwards and forwards, watching until the line extended far behind him, and only then casting it forward.

"Watch my form, Seanchai. It is no different than wielding a sword in a solo pattern. Learn the shift of weight, the angle of the rod, the rhythm. You don't need to go back and forth too much. I'm just doing this as an example. Now, I'll lay the bait."

He let the rod come forward until it was parallel with the water, and then locked his wrists. The line rolled out and landed upstream, imitating a beetle falling into the water. The bait floated downstream and into the pool. When it flowed back out, Denalion flicked it up and repeated the process. After three attempts, he called Seanchai to take the rod from him.

Having learned to copy forms in his exercises and combat training, Seanchai soon picked up the rhythm and principles. Denalion talked him through the movements, and, gradually, the bait flew gently to the intended spot.

Denalion brought another rod and cast next to Seanchai. Further upstream, Pyre was teaching Sellia. As they settled into the form together, Denalion spoke.

"Know what you seek in any exchange: to hunt, kill, or befriend. Know whom you seek: opponents, friends, potential allies. Know what you plan to do, but be ready to change direction if necessary. If one type of bait doesn't work, try another. Change tactics, set new goals, and be flexible. Do you understand?"

Seanchai turned to the redheaded dreamwalker. "Thank you," he said, and bowed.

At that moment, a fish took Seanchai's bait. They both laughed. Catching fish seemed unimportant right now. From out of nowhere, Denalion asked, "Do you only become a bear in the dream world?"

Seanchai was taken aback. "Is there another way?"

"Bears are very good at fishing, Seanchai. It's the mainstay of their diet. You must learn the other way, and learn it quickly."

"*What* other way?"

"You must seek this knowledge from the Wycaans," Denalion answered. "I hear you wear a scar—a claw mark from a bear pack leader. Is that true?"

"Yes," Seanchai said. "Why?"

"Was this the only time a bear confronted you outside the dream world?"

Seanchai nodded.

"The pack was expecting you to do something. Ask the Wycaans. Demand it, if you must. You need to know. Here might be your only chance to defeat the Emperor."

Chapter Sixty

The next week flew by. Following Denalion's advice to learn and also forget everything, Seanchai allowed himself to develop his own sword style. He pushed Cheriuk more each day, and the sparring became faster and more intuitive on both sides. The Weapons Master began to switch his opponents at increasing intervals, forcing him to adapt to each individual.

As time passed, Seanchai felt it all connecting, and he began to push each opponent back, taking less and less time to determine and execute his strategy. He left these training sessions aching, sweating, and extremely happy. On the fifth day, multiple opponents interchanged. Suddenly, Seanchai found himself facing an opponent far more than his equal. He retreated under a blur of strokes, all masterfully executed.

Faster and faster the blades swirled, and Seanchai was now defending with only his instinct. He felt strangely exhilarated and at peace. Backed against a tree, he considered using other tactics to free himself from the onslaught. But as this crossed his mind, his swords were whirled round, and a blade touched his throat.

"Yield," a rich voice roared.

Seanchai relaxed his arms and bowed his head. The Weapons Master stood over him, sweat pouring down her cheeks, hair splayed wildly, and face flushed.

"Remember. . . young Wycaan. . . there is always. . .
someone better than you," she said between panting breaths,
and then smiled. "But they will be far. . . and few between. . .
when you are finished. . . here."

As he walked to the log table of water skins, the other
students stood aside and bowed their heads. Cheriuk was
waiting at the log and handed Seanchai a skin.

"Thank you," Seanchai said, and as he glanced at Shathea,
she gave him a small nod.

Despite his aching arms, Seanchai went every day from
swords practice to the archery range. There, he met Sellia, and
it was she who guided him in integrating the lessons he had
learned fishing with Denalion. It was not just his accuracy that
improved, but also the fluidity with which he was able to draw
and shoot arrows in quick succession.

Just an hour or so after he had fought the Weapons Master,
Seanchai shot four arrows in a square around the center of the
target.

"Don't shoot the fifth yet," an old elf, leaning on a staff, said
from behind him. "Run to that rock there and back as fast as
you can. Then roll and shoot."

Seanchai obliged, remembering the instruction Uncle had
given him a lifetime ago. This time his step was sure, his roll
controlled, and his arrow flew true.

"Good," said the old elf. "Follow me. You have earned your
nocks."

Seanchai had seen this old elf watching him before at the
range. In fact, on one of the first days, he had felt Seanchai's
muscles and measured his arms. The old elf's touch was cold,
but it possessed an undeniable strength and nimbleness. Still,
Seanchai had dismissed it as senile eccentricities. He was wrong.

"I am Niewak, the Master Bowyer. I have made bows for more than two hundred years, and apprenticed for three decades before that. Ever since you came among us, I have been preparing bows that fit your stature."

They stood before a huge, hollow tree.

"Do your breathing exercises, young Wycaan. You may lift and hold each of the more than thirty bows inside, but leave here with only one. Each is imbued with magic of the forest and the Wycaans. My blood runs through each one, and I know them better than my own *calhei*, but you and the bow must choose each other."

Seanchai set his feet and breathed deeply. He felt the energy of the trees coursing through him. A few moments later, he stepped inside the tree.

It took a moment for his sight to adapt to the array of bows hanging inside. He continued his breathing and felt tendrils of energy from the bows probe him. Many faded, leaving just four to choose from.

"You are choosing me," Seanchai said out loud. "Come to me, then. I await your choice."

Now three remained: One was golden, thick, majestic, and strong. To its left, a blood-red bow that pulsated with energy. And the third—pale green, sleek, and glowing softly.

Seanchai looked at each before mentally thanking the golden one, and it faded away. He moved slowly forward and extended his hand to hold the red.

He could feel vibrant, powerful heat emanating from the bow, but he released it back to the wall of the tree. The green floated into his hands, and he felt the trees stir. *A gift from the great forest. A mighty warrior will yield the red, but this bow can only be harnessed by the wise.*

Seanchai's hands clasped the green bow. He looked to the red. "Thank you," he said. "You will serve a great master but it is not our destiny to walk the same path."

The red bow glowed brighter, and then slowly faded into the tree. Seanchai stepped outside and showed his bow to Sellia and the bowyer.

"It's beautiful," Sellia murmured as she caressed it reverently.

But the bowyer was shaking his head.

"You disapprove of my choice?" Seanchai asked.

"No, no," the old elf was stunned. "I did not make that bow. I have never seen it before, and I never hung it in the collection for you."

"It is a gift from the forest," Seanchai said, and the trees rustled their ascent.

The bowyer walked into the tree and returned with a green and beige quiver full of arrows with light green feathers. He presented it to Seanchai and took the bow.

"We usually make the bow string from the intestines of animals. But this is made of bloodwood vine. It is so thin, and yet," he pulled and then bit it, "it is the finest I have ever seen."

They walked back to the archery range. Seanchai drew an arrow and fired. He barely hit the target, but adjusted his technique under the tutelage of the bowyer. The last few of the dozen arrows in his quiver hit the center.

He went to retrieve his arrows, but the bowyer stopped him. Seanchai watched as the arrows disappeared from the target, and felt his quiver grow heavier.

CHAPTER SIXTY-ONE

W hen Shayth woke, he realized just how tired he must have been. Maugwen had assured him that they were being guarded and could each catch up on their sleep.

"They won't be able to stop the army if they come searching, but we'll be warned. It will be more effective than you sitting outside trying to stay awake."

He stood up and stretched. Maugwen was asleep in a big, round chair that made her look as diminutive as she had when they had met her in the dungeons. He had given her a hard time back then, suspicious of her prying questions even though she had seemed so lost; her parents had been forced to leave her behind and flee to find a way to purchase medicine her mother desperately needed to survive. By the time they had walked to the gallows, Shayth had begun to trust her, but he still had treated her gruffly.

Rhoddan was asleep on the bed, and Shayth crept over to him. The elf was no longer sweating, and his breathing was normal. As far as Shayth could see, Rhoddan was sleeping peacefully.

He turned, picked up his sword and scabbard, and stepped outside. It took a few moments to adjust to the sunlight, and, when he did, a small boy stood in front of him.

"What do you want?" the boy asked, more inquisitive than rude.

Shayth smiled at him, but the boy's eyes were riveted to his sword. "I'm hungry." Shayth said. "Do you know where I can get some food?"

"Is the healer your friend?" the boy asked.

"Yes," Shayth replied. "We go back a long time."

That settled it. The boy just nodded and offered him his hand. They walked down to a hut with makeshift benches outside and a big window for passing food through.

"The farmers have just eaten," the boy said. "Maybe we can find you something."

A heavyset woman came outside, wiping her meaty hands on a dirty cloth. "Can yeh pay?" she asked by way of introduction.

Shayth nodded and tapped his pocket. Coins jingled inside.

"He's a friend of the healer," the boy protested. "*She* doesn't pay."

"She pays by healing people and takes no money for 'er troubles. If 'e can pay, 'e should. We ain't rich 'ere." The woman put her hands on her hips, and the loose flesh of her upper arms quivered.

She turned back inside, and Shayth ruffled the young boy's hair. "Thanks," he said.

"Are you from a big city?" the boy asked.

"I was born in the capital, but ran away when I was just a little older than you."

"Why?"

"My mum and dad died." Shayth realized that he was able to say this without a boiling eruption of rage. Still, he preferred not to push it. "But I'd rather not talk about my past."

The woman had returned with a steaming bowl of food and stared at him as she set it on the table.

"Thank you," Shayth said. "How much do I owe you?"

"Ain't no need for yeh to pay, yeh majesty," she said in a mixture of awe and fear.

"Don't call me that," Shayth snapped. "And I insist on paying."

He slammed three draktans onto the table, an amount similar to what this woman would earn in as many months. Her eyes widened.

"I'm paying for the food and your discretion."

The boy looked from Shayth to the woman. "What does dicre-discretion mean?"

"That we continue to talk of 'im as a friend of the healer," the woman replied, "and nothing else."

"And he is the healer's friend," said Maugwen, coming up to them. She turned to the boy. "Would you sit with the patient while I eat? Call me if he stirs."

"Oh, I can do that. You can trust me." He turned to Shayth. "You can be my friend, too. My name's Miko."

"Thank you, Miko. The elf in there is a close friend of mine. Guard him well."

The boy sprinted off, gleeful with purpose. Maugwen laughed and sat down in front of her own food bowl. When they were alone, she leaned in to Shayth.

"I see the evil prince is dead. Long live the good one."

Shayth snorted. "I'm no better than I was, I just have more control now; that's all."

"I don't think so," Maugwen said. "People still talk about you, but now with hope instead of fear."

"Our hope lies with Seanchai, no one else," Shayth said, feeling tension gathering in his shoulders. "Tell me what happened after you left us."

"I joined a caravan of traders. At first, I stayed with a kind, old woman. She was a healer and taught me a few basics. I knew very little, but I suspect neither did she. She suffered from a pain in the liver. I don't know what it was, but once, when I tried to comfort her, I prayed to my gods—yes, those that I rejected in the cells—and a strange thing happened.

"Warmth flowed through my hands and into the woman. I couldn't heal her, but I was able to take the pain away. I think she even got stronger for a while.

"The caravan passed through a monastery, and I stayed there, learning how to heal with prayer."

"Wow," Shayth said. "Do you really think it is prayer?"

"I don't know. All I know is that I can help people. Then I met a woman who told me that the Wycaan had healed her this way, and I thought maybe I can develop my healing abilities with Seanchai."

"You were coming to find Seanchai? How did you know where to come?"

"The monks suggested I look for him. I had a recurring dream of this village, and one of the brothers knew the place. In my dream, I joined up with Seanchai and the rest of you. So it did not surprise me to see you. I think I will find my own answers from the Wycaan, and that is why I have returned to serve him."

They both ate in silence. Then Shayth sighed.

"What is it?" Maugwen asked.

"I hope you get the chance to work together and heal people. It is Seanchai's dream, and it will mean that we've won."

"You don't sound too hopeful," Maugwen said.

"Seanchai went to the Elves of the West, as I told you. No one has ever returned from there. If they even exist, they have never come to our aid despite how elves are treated in Odessiya. I don't know if even Seanchai can persuade them to join us."

"If anyone can," Maugwen said, as she wiped her bowl clean with a piece of bread, "it's Seanchai."

They sat together, each absorbed in their own thoughts. A few moments later, Miko came running up. "He's awake and sitting up."

"Did he say anything?" Maugwen asked.

"That he's hungry. Is that a good sign?"

Shayth grinned. "Hard to tell. He's always hungry."

Chapter Sixty - Two

I t was Rhoddan who sensed the danger first, while he sat with Shayth and Maugwen, outside Maugwen's infirmary. The sun was setting, casting warm hues that made even this dilapidated village look inviting.

The conversation had turned to what they would do next, now that Rhoddan was improving. It was clear to all that Maugwen would join them when they left the village.

"I want to try and cross through the Pass," Rhoddan said. "Seanchai might need us there, but it's also. . . well, I grew up hearing the stories of the Elves of the West. I'd like to see them for myself."

"How do you even know they exist?" Shayth asked. "They might only be legends, and you'd be wasting your time."

"They're real," Rhoddan said. "If they aren't, what's Seanchai doing there?"

"Searching," Shayth replied. "For the elves, for himself, for something to help him face my uncle."

Miko brought them a pot of stew and three bowls.

"Aren't you eating?" Shayth asked him.

"This is food for customers," Miko replied, matter-of-factly. "The meat's expensive. Sometimes I get to eat it on festivals."

They went quiet as the warm food made its way through their bodies. The meat was tough and leathery, Rhoddan thought. It would be scraps for the dogs in most other places, but here it was out-of-reach to this peasant boy.

He dished out seconds for Shayth and Maugwen. Then he filled his bowl and passed it to Miko.

"I'm not hungry," he said. "Still recovering, you know."

"Shayth said you're always hungry," Miko replied.

"Then accept it as a gift from a friend," Shayth replied.

Miko did not have a problem with that and the others smiled as they watched him wolf it down. The conversation returned to their plans.

"I cannot fight him," Shayth said. "But I can hurt him by taking out his son."

"Is the Crown Prince good?" Rhoddan asked.

"I wouldn't know. But he must have trained with the best teachers at the academy."

"I heard he's very good," Maugwen said. "Rumor has it that his problem is with his studies. That's why General Tarlach's son was brought into the palace. He's supposed to be the Crown Prince's tutor."

"Supposed to be?" Rhoddan asked.

"I also heard that the Emperor wanted Ahad close to him as a bargaining chip with General Tarlach."

"But Tarlach was loyal, wasn't he?" Rhoddan asked.

"Tarlach didn't have a problem with disposing of Seanchai," Shayth growled. "The Emperor was worried that Tarlach wouldn't be able to kill me because he swore an oath to my father to protect me."

"He was in a tough position," Maugwen said.

"He was an oath breaker and a violent killer!" Shayth snapped. "Don't let the intrigue in the public houses fool you."

Shayth's tone ended the conversation and they sat in silence. Rhoddan glanced at Miko to see if Shayth had scared him, and a chill went through his body. Miko looked. . . different. His face was set in an expression of an older man. His body had straightened and tensed. Most noticeable, the boy was no longer eating.

Shayth had not noticed and began to talk again. "I'm sorry for my outburst. Family isn't my favorite conversation piece. Anyway, it's not my cousin that worries me. He's probably a good fighter, but so are we. He may have better technique, but we have more experience. Facing him one-on-one, I think I could take him. I just need to remember that he's the son of the man who murdered my parents."

Rhoddan saw Miko's face twitch, and the boy's eyes hardened as he stared at Shayth. Shayth rubbed his spiky hair. "It's Ahad who worries me. He's not only a product of the academy, but also of the assassins. He was the one who shot you with the small crossbow, Rhoddan. I'm sure of it. Only a Master Assassin could hit from such a distance."

"Does he have much experience?" Maugwen asked.

"No. But the same fire that burns inside me fuels Ahad. He wants revenge on the man who killed his father. Sound familiar?"

Miko wore a wry smile now. As he turned and saw Rhoddan staring at him, the smile vanished. Rhoddan whipped out his dagger and pointed it at Miko. There was no fear on the young boys' face.

"Go ahead," said the deep, icy voice. "I have little need for the boy. He's just another peasant who will probably die of hunger or disease."

"Who are you?" Rhoddan demanded.

In answer, Miko looked at Shayth. "It is good to see you, nephew. I'm glad you remain as evil and violent as I remember. We are truly kin, after all."

The Emperor laughed through Miko, and it sent shivers through Rhoddan and the humans. The cackle was evil and alien to this innocent farm boy.

Maugwen was the first to recover. Her voice was even, though Rhoddan was sure she was straining to keep it steady. "Say what you have come to say and leave the boy. He's one of your subjects."

Miko turned to her. "I do not lack for subjects, little healer," the Emperor said. "He should be honored to let me use his body."

Maugwen's brown eyes hardened. "Do not harm him," she said.

Miko laughed again and then spoke to Shayth. "You will not kill my son. Not yet. Maybe in time, if you deserve to be my heir, but I am not convinced yet that you are worthy.

"As for Ahad, the two boys that accompanied them were instructed to sow seeds of doubts in him. By now, he probably realizes that his father was not the hero the boy thought he was. It is a shame that you curtailed their fine work.

"Your father became a threat to me by creating a close cohort of officers fiercely loyal to him. You're making the same mistake, Shayth.

"Your future lies with Ahad and my son, not in their death. Join with them, and win them over. Either become the future Emperor's right-hand man or take the throne from him when the time is right."

"You don't care if Shayth kills your own son?" Rhoddan asked.

"A strong throne in Odessiya is of paramount importance, elf. It could be that my son kills Shayth instead and proves himself worthy of succeeding me. Who knows?"

"Are you a Wycaan?" Maugwen interrupted abruptly.

The boy turned to her. "Why do you ask, little healer?"

"Because you don't fear Seanchai. He has considerable power and yet you don't seem too fazed."

Miko snorted. "You're sharp for a peasant woman whose father is a tax evader and deserted you." He paused, but Rhoddan saw how Maugwen kept her expression impassive. "I am far more powerful than your precious elf can imagine. I'll deal with him in time."

Maugwen frowned. "Aren't you afraid he'll return with the Elves of the West?"

Miko laughed. "He's a weak, young fool and they won't risk their diluted power against me. Once they leave their precious woods, they are no longer protected by their magic and just become fodder for my armies."

Maugwen smiled smugly. "Thank you," she said.

"For what?"

Rhoddan understood. "For confirming the legends," he said and smiled. "The Elves of the West exist."

The boy glared, but did not say anything.

"I still don't understand," Shayth said. "Why would you allow me to take the throne instead of your direct heir?"

"Why do you think? What qualities might you possess that he does not? What order would take precedence over my family line? Why have I indulged you all these years? Think, boy."

Shayth frowned and shook his head.

"Because, my dear nephew, the power I possess often runs in a family. Phineus has been tested. I even checked Ahad, illogical as that was. But you, nephew, have yet to take the tests. And that is why you still live. Until we meet again."

Miko began choking. His body shook, and then he slumped forward. Rhoddan caught him and knew he now cradled the little peasant boy.

Chapter Sixty-Three

Seanchai stood outside the elders' door for three days, sending energy into the tree trunk where they lived. He pulled power from the earth and from the trees around him. It coursed through his body, nourishing and sustaining him. He did not move to eat or drink.

Pyre brought him water, but he refused it. The young elfe brought him a blanket on the first night, but when he ignored her, she curled up in it herself. "If you won't sleep, neither will I," she had said, then yawned and promptly fell asleep.

The Weapons Master, Shathea, Cheriuk, and many other Wycaans hovered nearby, waiting in tense anticipation.

It was Denalion who bid them leave Seanchai to face the elders by himself. The red-haired elf stood guard over him, sending away those who approached, his back to Seanchai and the tree of the elders.

Seanchai was ready. He knew every day away from the rebellion in Odessiya was costing lives. He had learned more than how to fish, wield his Win Dao swords, and shoot an arrow. He had delved into the deeper levels of each art and absorbed all he could for now. The dreamwalker's words haunted him.

"I hear you wear a scar—a claw mark from a bear pack leader. Is that true? . . . Was this the only time a bear confronted you outside the dream world? . . . The pack was expecting you to do something. Ask

the Wycaans. Demand it, if you must. You need to know. Here might be
your only chance to find out."

Seanchai approached the Tree of Elders and requested entry.

"Not now," a voice called out from inside. "Return when
you are ready."

"When will that be?" he asked.

"Even the shortest tree in the forest took centuries to grow."

"I don't have centuries, or even years."

"And that is why you are not ready."

Seanchai remained where he was. After a couple of hours,
Dyfellian came outside.

"Why are you still standing here?"

"To demonstrate patience," Seanchai replied.

"It is not enough," she said.

"It's all I have." She stared at him, and Seanchai returned her
gaze. "People in the east are dying," he pleaded, "the elves are
dying. You don't have to send an army with me, but at least give
me what I need."

"We owe you nothing, yet we have already given you
much," she said, her tone sharp. "Who are you to come and
demand more?"

Seanchai was genuinely surprised. "Do you think this is for
my own gratification? I crave the life of a healer. I apprenticed
with a mother who is dead and lived in a village that was razed
to the ground for shielding me. I've lost my soul mate and my
teacher, and have the deaths of thousands on my conscience. You
have a lot of audacity if you're accusing me of self-gratification."

She held his gaze, and then nodded. "You are right, Seanchai,
son of Seantai. I apologize. But you haven't provided us with enough
evidence of your readiness. The elders will not grant your request.
Those who walk with you have not yet revealed themselves. Until
such time, you cannot become a Wycaan Master."

Seanchai blinked and glanced back at Denalion. Then he took off his shirt, revealing the claw of the brown bear. "This," he said, "should not have happened. It must not happen next time. I need to take the next step. Odessiya cries out and I must answer."

Dyfellian stared at the wound and at last spoke quietly. "The last Wycaan who came from the east attacked us when we refused him entrance. He breathed fire on us from the sky and nearly broke our defenses. He was too powerful for the elves. The strength of the forest alone blocked his path."

"I am not him," Seanchai replied. "The forest has embraced me."

"When you have such power, it can corrupt."

"He who attacked you has grown stronger still," Seanchai replied. "He will return if he is not stopped permanently. I am the one destined to confront him. When he transforms into the firebreather, how will I respond?"

When she didn't answer, Seanchai spoke again. "Wise Dyfellian, member of the high council. Go ask the elders this: when the firebreather comes, will he be met with claw or the ashes of our race?"

Dyfellian turned away shaking her head, but Seanchai hadn't finished. "When he came for you, the forest protected you. What if I have the will of the forest? What if the trees side with me?"

Dyfellian stopped and her old body seemed even more bent with the weight of responsibility as she turned to him. "You don't," she said, but her wrinkled face revealed fear. "They wouldn't." She went inside and closed the door.

And so it began. Seanchai took up the first position, breathing in the air of the forest, and spread his consciousness out, embracing the deep roots and tall trunks. His energy spread through the tree trunks, slowly encompassing the entire forest.

And gradually, tentatively, the trees responded. The energy Seanchai sent out was transformed, enriched, and returned inside of him. For the next three days, as light became darkness and then light again, he called up the ancient energy of the trees and channeled it. A brown shimmer began around his feet and moved up his body. By the second day, it was a foot thick, and green, crackling sparks left his arms, legs, and hands. On the third day, the crown of his head ignited with a beam of bright green light as the energy flowed out from him.

And then the shimmering of the leaves began. It was high-pitched and weak at first, but it grew and spread throughout the forest.

Thousands came to the borders of the elders' home, drawn by the vibrations that shook the leaves and then the branches, and finally the very trunks of even the mightiest trees.

As the forest vibrated, the elders came out of their tree. Several stood staring, and Dyfellian stepped forward. She leaned on her staff as she approached Seanchai. She reached out with her staff into the vortex of energy that swirled around him.

The light brightened, and many were forced to look away. The energy caught to the ancient elfe's staff as though burning it, eating its way up the length of the carved wood. Soon, Dyfellian was lost in the light with Seanchai. From its epicenter came a deep growl, and a cat's yowl answered it.

The trees gradually stopped shaking as the energy grounded and was sucked back into the tree roots. From the fading light, a young, sleek grizzly bear emerged, its fur rich and shining. It panted heavily, its flanks shimmering. The black panther nearby, its coat ruffled and patchy, shook its head and began to walk away. It stopped, turned, and hissed at the grizzly, which lumbered awkwardly after it.

When the two animals had disappeared into the trees, Pyre stood and walked over to Denalion.

"What did Seanchai do?" she asked, her voice quivering with emotion, "Did he just defeat the entire forest?"

The red-haired dreamwalker looked down and ruffled her hair. "No," he smiled. "He called upon the forest to choose, and the ancient trees gave him their support."

"Has that ever happened before?"

"No, Pyre, it has not."

"Will Seanchai be our leader, then? Is this what the trees have declared?"

"No, little one. Seanchai builds alliances. But your friend must leave us soon. He'll probably never return to the ancient forests of Markwin. But surely, he will never be forgotten."

Chapter Sixty-Four

S eanchai was panting. He could feel the cold rock beneath his naked chest, and yet the claw wound burned. He was cold and sweating. His muscles screamed at him in protest, each either contorted or torn.

He opened his eyes and took a few moments to adjust to the bright sunlight. Summoning his strength, he pressed his palms into the ground and pushed himself up. His arms shook from the effort as he sat up and he immediately fell back against the rock behind him. His head was pounding.

A familiar smell filled his nostrils. It was dangseng root, the herb that Mhari had taught him to cultivate and drink, to strengthen and recover his energy. He sighed deeply and allowed himself to sink into the rock.

"Here," the shrill voice of Dyfellian interrupted his dozing. She hovered over him with a mug of the root tea. "You should be serving me, by all rights, but you do look terrible." She chuckled to herself as she shuffled back to her seat. "Not bad," she said when he had consumed a few sips.

"Did I actually transform into a bear?"

"Of sorts," she said. "You were a touch melodramatic, if you ask me." She chuckled again. "And the trees, well, that was simply playing out, but it was quite effective."

"You aren't angry with me?"

"Angry?"

"For confronting the elders like that."

"Ah. Maybe we need a little. . . confronting. . . every couple of centuries." She poured herself a cup of tea and, though her movement was slow and strained, her hand did not shake. "Seanchai. I am almost six hundred years old. I could transform at an early age, and I was somewhat rebellious. I have been to Odessiya. I have seen the trials of our people in the east."

"But you did nothing?" Seanchai was shocked.

"At first, I tried to gather a force to go help. But I was afraid, as the other elders are. We have much to lose here, you know. But we should talk about you."

Seanchai suddenly realized he was naked, but that Dyfellian was not. "How were you able to keep your clothes?"

"There is a way."

"You could have taught me that first." He moved a hand to cover his groin.

Dyfellian laughed. "Now, why would I do that? I may be old, but I'm still an elfe!"

Seanchai smiled. "Okay. Have your fun, but tell me: what does all this mean?"

"In most cases, when a Wycaan reaches a certain level of expertise in the craft, when he approaches the level of master, it is possible to make a connection with his or her animal spirit. Usually, we're connected to animals that suit our character. I used to be quick and agile, smart and spoiled. A panther makes sense for me."

"But why am I a bear?"

"It seems to me that bears are strong, skilled, and deft, though they have much to learn as cubs. Most importantly, the bears of Odessiya are often family-oriented pack animals. As long as there are ample resources, they'll remain in large families. They're very loyal to each other and will fight to the death to defend their close ones, especially their cubs. Do you get the picture?"

Seanchai nodded and rubbed his head. The tea was easing his headache.

"No animal has complete dominion over the land," Dyfellian continued. "Some are strong, others smart, and others fast. It is important that when a Wycaan fights another Wycaan, whether in his natural state or animal form, that he employs all the techniques and knowledge that he has acquired in training. You may well have to confront him in your animal form to have any chance of succeeding."

Seanchai looked up at her. "Can a bear defeat a firebreather? What hope do I have, if not?"

"There is always hope, young one. You must seek whatever talents you have that he does not. You must discover what the core strength of the bear truly is. Come, change for me."

"Um," Seanchai said as he stood up. "I'm not sure exactly what I did before."

Dyfellian's cackle echoed off the rocks. "Well, I can't help you with that, I'm afraid. Perhaps you should go fishing with the dreamwalker."

Seanchai closed his eyes and began to draw up energy from the surrounding rock. This was considerably more difficult than in the forest, as everything around him now was inanimate. He felt the energy slowly grow inside of him, and he imagined becoming a bear. Though the energy moved through him and Seanchai felt vibrant, nothing happened.

He tried to imagine himself as the bear–his claws, fur, and massive haunches. He searched with his mind for the spirit bears, but something pulled him back. He heard Dyfellian softly snoring and looked around. The shadows had grown significantly. He gave up, stretched, and sat down, nurturing the fire and making more tea.

When Dyfellian awoke, it was her turn to look puzzled. "What happened?" she asked.

"Nothing," Seanchai replied. "It was like a regular standing exercise. What do I need to do?"

Dyfellian shook her head, then in a moment transformed into the panther and back again. When the elfe looked at him, Seanchai saw doubt in her eyes.

"What is it?" he asked.

"I thought you had it," she said. "Now I'm not so sure."

She rose stiffly and kicked out the fire. She emptied the small pot of tea into Seanchai's cup and packed up. Slowly, she led him down the mountain, her staff clicking on the rock.

Near the bottom, Sellia waited. Seanchai prepared himself for a comment on his nudity, but Sellia was staring at Dyfellian, and there was no humor on her face. When they reached her, Sellia took off her traveling cloak and wrapped it around Seanchai's shoulders.

Dyfellian waited, and then turned to him. "I told them that you should take the final test, even before we saw you change into your animal spirit. Some disagreed, but now that you have changed, I am sure they will demand it."

They resumed walking back to the forest, and the ancient elfe continued. "You want to go, and many will be glad to see you gone because of the fear you make them feel. The test will take place before the entire people. You must use what you are strongest at."

"The swords," Sellia said. "You're good at the bow, now, too."

"No," Seanchai said. "There are always better swordelfs and archers."

"You cannot risk the transformation if you aren't able to do it easily," Dyfellian said. "That would have been enough, but not now. Do you have other talents that I'm unaware of?"

Seanchai stopped abruptly. "I must use what I am strongest at?" He turned slowly and stared into Dyfellian's ancient eyes. A smile stretched slowly across his face. "You brought me out here to teach me what I need to know to pass the test, and you have done that. Thank you, Master Dyfellian." He bowed low.

"What is it?" Sellia asked.

Seanchai smiled at her and then turned back to Dyfellian. "It will take place before the whole nation, correct?"

Dyfellian nodded.

"As you said, the bear spirit chose me because we share attributes," Seanchai said. "When they came to me the second time, there was not one family, not just one kind of bear, but many. The great whites came from the north, and the little reds from the tropics. The black bears came from the plains and the brown bears from the forests. And the great grizzly came down from the high mountain peaks. They came, one and all, to claim their places in the Wycaan Alliance.

"This is what I'm best at: unity. I'll leave here at the head of a mighty host of elves, or I will leave alone. I am a builder of alliances, Dyfellian, and that will be my test.

"The Elves of the West will hear my call and decide."

Chapter Sixty-Five

Sensing Pyre's presence, Seanchai concluded his standing exercises; grounded the energy; and took deep, cleansing breaths as he stretched and opened his eyes. He sighed. He would miss the vibrant energy that this most ancient forest shared with him.

Pyre had brought him the nutty gruel they shared each morning, but her eyes were locked on his packed bag and bedroll folded into the bearskin. His cloak was folded on top of the pack, and his bow and swords leaned against the tree.

"You're really going?" she asked as he settled down with his breakfast.

"I must," Seanchai replied. "People are dying every day in Odessiya. I began something, and elves, dwarves, humans, and pictorians fight under my call. I have to finish this, one way or another." He paused to eat a spoonful of the smooth gruel. "I appreciate you taking care of me, and regret that leaving means our friendship cannot continue to grow. You've looked out for me, but I've given you nothing in return."

Pyre just smiled, but it was clearly forced. "Will you ever return?"

"I must go and face the most powerful army in our lands and confront the most powerful Wycaan ever. It's difficult to think past that."

"But you must go?" she said quietly.

"Pyre. All of us here are elves on the outside, our ears pointed and for those who are Wycaan, our hair is white. But inside, I fear, we're all different. I'm driven by a desire to stand with my friends, free my people, and allow all races to live free and with dignity. I couldn't stay here, knowing what was happening outside."

"I know," she said. "I think that's what I like most about you." She sighed and looked away for the moment. "They won't agree, you know. The High Council will hear your petition, but they won't risk everything we've built here."

Seanchai nodded. "I swore to my friends that I'd try. I can do no more. The Elves of the West have given me much. I will not walk away ungrateful, but I cannot yet say I will leave happy. And I'll miss the friends I have made here—you, especially."

Pyre jumped to her feet and leapt at Seanchai. He opened his arms and hugged her tightly. He could feel the energy she was expending trying not to cry. They held each other, and then Seanchai loosened his grip as he saw others approach.

Pyre also sensed their presence and pulled away. She picked up the bowls. "You'll have at least one supporter in the Great Hall," she whispered. "Look for me if you need a friend."

"But *calhei* aren't allowed to attend, are they?" Seanchai asked.

Pyre forced a smile. "Do you think that's ever stopped me? Look for me if you need a friend," she repeated, and left.

Seanchai watched her leave and then rose. The Weapons Master approached with Cheriuk and Shathea walking either side of her. They all wore tense expressions.

"We would be honored to escort you back to Bloodwyre," the Weapons Master said, "and to the Great Hall."

"Is this a security detail or honor guard?" Seanchai asked, immediately upset by his tone.

"Both," the old elfe's voice was just as crisp. Her hair was not in a tight bunch now, but hung down. A leather band with a green stone held her snow-white locks in place. She looked all the more imposing. "When you leave the Wycaan compound, you will need new wards to reenter."

"But you walk with friends," Shathea added, playing the role of peacemaker.

"It is so," Cheriuk confirmed, his body rigid and his voice formal as ever.

"Then let's go," Seanchai said. Before he picked up his belongings, he touched the tree that had been his home in gratitude. He thought the tree shimmered in response.

They walked in silence away from the Wycaan village, and Seanchai was too preoccupied to notice their route or surroundings. He was unaware when they passed through the magical boundaries and back into the great forest. He barely felt them ascend into the trees or register when they reached the outskirts of Bloodwyre. Only when they approached the main square did he start to pay attention.

The Great Hall seemed bigger. The walls of vine were rolled back, leaving only the great logs that supported the roof. Without the walls, the hall stood as one with the forest. Seanchai wondered whether this was to accommodate more elves or to allow the trees to bear witness.

He stopped on the edge of the square and looked at the stern faces on the High Council's platform. The previous time, a chair had been vacant, but now Denalion occupied it. Pyre had explained that he rarely sat in his place on the council. Seanchai wondered what to expect from Dyfellian and the dreamwalker.

The open-aired structure was full of elves, and more stood under the trees. There must be thousands he thought and a knot of fear clenched in his stomach. He began his breathing as the

Weapons Master put her strong hand on his shoulder.

"It is time," she said, and gently pushed him forward. As they walked, she whispered: "Learn from your friends, my student. Be diplomatic like Shathea, strong like Cheriuk, genuine like Pyre, and unpredictable like Denalion."

Seanchai smiled. "And what may I take from you, Weapons Master?"

"Love," she replied, her gaze firm and looking ahead, but her voice soft. "Remember those you love who have sacrificed themselves."

They stopped at the edge of the square. Seanchai turned to his escorts. "I should walk alone," he said. "Thank you." And the Wycaan from the East bowed low in reverence.

Cheriuk, Shathea, and the Weapons Master all bowed back. "Never alone," the old elfe whispered.

Chapter Sixty-Six

The Great Hall quieted as Seanchai walked to its center. He felt even the trees strain to listen and watch. He took up a position before the High Council and studied each of them in turn. Dyfellian gave him a brief nod and Denalion smiled, but otherwise, he saw no reactions.

He turned to speak, but the elfe who sat in the center raised her hand to stop him. "Before you begin, there is another matter of business. Step forward, Sellia, please."

Seanchai felt a wave of concern as Sellia stepped forward. She was also in her traveling clothes; her skin shone and her dark hair was resplendent. She stood next to Seanchai and frowned, unsure.

Two elderly elves appeared from the crowd. One spoke for all to hear.

"Dark Sellia, you were called by those in the east. People, even elves, viewed you with wonder or suspicion because of the color of your skin. Friends, you had; some, you even considered family.

"You came here to support and aid the Wycaan, and he is, I am sure, deeply in your debt. But you also came with a hope that you, too, might find answers. We represent a small order of academics and historians. At the request of Denalion, the dreamwalker, we have used our skills to discern your family line.

Step forward, House of Tryzen."

A group of dark-skinned elves stepped out, cowed by the attention, and one approached Sellia, a shy smile on her face. "You are the daughter of Senzia, my sister, who went into the east with her mate and never returned. I fear we won't have time to spend together, but you should know where you come from. This was a gift from my sister many years ago, when she and I parted. I give it now to you as something to connect you back to us."

She stepped forward and put a thin, leather band around Sellia's head. A family emblem and inscriptions were burned into it, and a small, red stone shone at the front.

The woman stepped back and raised her voice. "No longer shall they call you Sellia Without a Past, or Mysterious Dark Elfe. You are Sellia, daughter of Senzia, from the house of Tryzen. You have a past and a family, and wherever your path takes you, you will always belong."

As one, thousands of voices repeated: *Sellia, daughter of Senzia, from the house of Tryzen.* The elfe took Sellia's face in her hands and kissed the stone and Sellia's wet cheeks. Then she took Sellia's hand and led her to stand with her family.

Seanchai watched Sellia walk away. It occurred to him that she had a choice now, an alternative to returning to the unsure and dangerous path that lay before them. He started to imagine continuing without her, but the voice of the High Council leader brought him back to his own predicament.

"Dyfellian, is the Wycaan ready to be tested?"

"He is, Treewent," the old elfe replied, her voice strong.

Treewent turned to Seanchai, but all heard his words. "Are you ready to be tested to become a Wycaan Master? Traditionally, failure has meant death. However, given your responsibilities in the East, should you fail, you will be banished, and no Wycaan Master may ever teach you further. How do you choose to be tested?"

Seanchai took a deep breath. Now was the time. "I am Seanchai, son of Seantai, an elf from Morthian Wood. I have learned to wield sword and bow with your Weapons Master and Master Bowyer, to embrace my animal form with Dyfellian, and to apply my Wycaan training to all areas of life from Denalion. But I am a student also of the human Wycaan Master, Mhari, and the dwarf Wycaan Master, Onyxei. My ears are pointed, but I represent all races of Odessiya, in the east and the west.

"There was a time when a Wycaan would test with sword or bow, with elements or animal spirits. Many of your finest have bore witness to my abilities with these powers. But beyond these borders, I have led and won battles at Galbrieth and Hothengold. Most importantly, I have crafted something more powerful than weapons. I have brought together the dwarves, the Aqua'lansis, and the pictorians. The free humans will follow one who is bonded to me. The peoples of Odessiya have chosen. Now it falls to the people of the West. My test is also your test: I choose alliance building."

There was a murmur of surprise throughout the crowd, and Seanchai saw Denalion smile. But Treewent frowned. "State your case."

Seanchai turned to address the crowd. "When I came before you—"

"You should address the council," a high-pitched elfe beside Treewent snapped. "It is we before whom you stand in judgment."

Seanchai turned back to her. His voice remained steady, but he felt—and knew others could, too—an immense power building up inside of him. "I stand in judgment; that is true. But I do not stand alone this day. The High Council stands in judgment. The Elves of the West stand in judgment."

There was another wave of uneasy murmuring. Seanchai continued.

"When I first came before you, I reminded you of the teachings of Wycaan Master Tansu, recorded in the Book of Prophesies. He brought you into the west, but he foresaw a time when you would be called upon to return.

"You strive to create a pure society where energy is channeled into learning, cultivating crafts, and transcribing histories. At one time, this was correct; the elves were weak, defeated, and shattered.

"But it is a false culture—a flawed learning—because it ignores the negative energies in this world, even in our own Wycaan order. You know of whom I speak, for he breathed fire upon you and only the power of the forest protected you. You know of what is transpiring in my land, for some have witnessed the oppression and suffering beyond your border.

"The elves of the east are a slave nation—pitied at best, abused at worst, and it is usually the worst. The dwarves, our oldest allies, stood alone when your ancestors fled, burying themselves underground in fear, in shame, and in helplessness. They have risen now and fight with me in a new Alliance.

"The fierce pictorians forsook their proud warrior history and sold themselves to the thirst for blood, because they thought it was the only way to protect themselves. As we speak, they reclaim their heritage and stand once again for freedom.

"A prince is reborn who can unite the humans, and he stands with us. He has sworn his sword to me. Even the Aqua'lansis gather to answer the call, as all great nations did for thousands of years.

"I would like nothing more than to stay in this forest, surrounded by good elf folk–to delve deeper into the Wycaan arts, to learn more about my true passion of healing, and to take a mate and create a family the likes of which I have not had since my parents were slaughtered, and my village razed to ashes. Deep inside, I crave for what you have. Instead, I have been honored to call those who have joined me on my journey my family.

"My part of this test is to walk away, to leave this great forest and the Elves of the West, knowing I may never return. But I will go to the races in the east and face the one you fear. I will face him alone, if necessary, but know this: the destiny of the west is also the destiny of the east. What prevails in Odessiya will ultimately prevail here.

"I leave either way with a heavy heart. If it is my destiny to walk alone, my sadness will be for your shortcomings as much as my own loss. But I will pass my test, because I will leave and return to face the evil in the east."

He turned and stared slowly at all who had gathered. As he circled, he returned and looked at each of the High Council in turn. Finally, his gaze fell on Treewent.

"Are you ready to take the greatest test your people have faced in living history? Are you ready to choose?"

There was a tense silence as all eyes went to Treewent. He cleared his throat, but his gaze never left Seanchai. "We told you when you stood before us, young Wycaan, that your request would be denied. We will not risk the elven world of the west to help our brothers in the east. We cannot allow ourselves to risk everything we have accomplished.

"It is not us who have failed, for the test was not ours to take. You walk alone, destined never to become a Wycaan Master."

Treewent raised a beautifully carved staff in the air and poised himself to pound the ground with it. A steady voice stayed his arm.

"Hold, Treewent, my old friend. That is not the unanimous decision of the High Council. Seanchai will not walk alone."

Chapter Sixty~Seven

A thousand elves gasped as Denalion, long red hair and dark shining skin, rose from his seat at the edge of the High Council's heavy table.

"The Council has met and discussed this, honored dreamwalker," Treewent said, lowering his hand and the staff. "You had a chance to speak already, but were silent, as oft you are. Our traditions state—"

"Our traditions, wise Treewent, show us the past. These unsettling times that we all have felt are, themselves, unconventional. The future of the Elves of the West cannot be shackled by our past. This is why we have not grown. This is what has prevented us from flourishing.

"I chose not to speak at council because I am uneasy that the Council makes such momentous decisions for us all. What gives me the right to decide the actions and fate of the entire Elven nation? What gives you that right, Treewent?

"It is easier for you, dear friend, for all you see is what the forest offers. But my destiny has been to walk in the dream world, and I have seen the oppression Seanchai describes. I have heard the cries and desperation of our people. The pleas I heard in the dream world haunt me in this world, too.

"So the decision is not unanimous, Treewent, for I will leave with Seanchai." He looked at Dyfellian and Lymora. "My hair is red, but I know the inner being of a Wycaan Master. I know their values, their principles, and their responsibilities. Seanchai does not need this Council's consent or approval. I go now and stand proudly beside a Wycaan Master."

Denalion stepped from the stage and went to Seanchai's side. Seanchai watched him approach and then turned back to the High Council, but all other eyes were now focused on the Weapons Master, who stood at his other side.

"A Wycaan Master is motivated, above all, by honor and love," she said. "I have devoted my life to the service of our people, but I left my heart with another Wycaan, one who sacrificed her own life to help Seanchai. He is my only connection left to her. Once, this council denied me the opportunity to go with her. This time, I will not ask permission. I will walk in Mhari's path and continue to offer guidance to her last student for as long as I draw breath."

Treewent sighed. He looked to the council members on both sides and then back to those who stood before him. "You have both served us well all your lives, and we know you are compelled to do what you are convinced is right. You go with our bless. . . NO!!!"

Seanchai swung around. Standing twenty feet behind him was Pyre, accompanied by twenty other *calhei*, all her age or slightly younger. They wore traveling cloaks and had bags and weapons strapped around them.

An angry buzz circulated around the crowd, and members of the High Council had sprung to their feet. The children closed in together, frightened by the reaction. Only Pyre stood her ground.

"You are not of age," Treewent snapped. "You should not be here."

"Would you prefer that we snuck off in the dark?" Pyre replied, her young voice calm and even. "It would be fitting, for you have raised us in the dark. How can you teach us the Elven Code while ignoring the cries of those of our people who are oppressed?"

Seanchai did not wait for Treewent to respond. He turned and knelt in front of Pyre. When he spoke, it was for her ears alone.

"I cannot take you, my dearest friend. It may deny our people a generation of *calhei*, and it would endanger me."

"How?"

"I would be scared for you, knowing you are physically smaller and not fully trained. I would watch out for you and plan tactics around you. Ultimately, the Emperor would use you against me, as he has used my other friends–as he used my mate, Ilana.

"You would honor me by staying. Complete your training and be ready to rule in the new era. For when we have freed our people, they will seek out leaders, and those who ignored their cries will not be accepted. I'm our people's hope for the present, but you are their hope for the future. Stay. Learn. Train. And be ready to serve when you are called."

Pyre shook her head. "You told me just before that an elf's strength lies in the friendships he forms. I can't let you leave without fighters to help you."

"He will not, Pyre," said Shathea from behind her.

Seanchai looked up and saw she stood with others. Cheriuk spoke to Pyre now. "We will serve with him in your place," he said. "We swear to protect your friend as best we can."

Pyre stood up, her small body erect. "Then swear, Cheriuk, before the entire Elven nation."

The silence was thick with tension. Cheriuk took a step back and drew his Win Dao swords. The crisp rasps of metal from two hundred scabbards behind him, Shathea's included, answered. When Cheriuk spoke, his voice carried up to the tops of the mighty trees.

"We swear allegiance to the Wycaan Master, and to free the people of Odessiya or die trying. *Ashbar!*"

"*ASHBAR!*" responded a hundred voices.

Seanchai stared in wonder and gratefully saw the determined faces of rows of white-haired elves, including all who had trained with him, their swords held high in the air. He looked up to the High Council. Treewent had crumpled to his seat, but Dyfellian stood, leaning on her staff.

"Step forward," she said in her shrill voice. Seanchai did so, wondering what was coming now. "Seanchai, son of Seantai, you came to us with two goals: to train with us and call us to arms. You declared the way in which you should be tested.

"Look around you. Those who know you best have given their answer. You leave here a Wycaan Master at the head of an army. The Elves of the West have given their answer.

"Go, then and free the races of Odessiya. Unite the Elven nation and rebuild the Alliance as our ancients foresaw."

Dyfellian struck her staff on the platform, pounding the wood repeatedly, and the people took up the rhythm, clapping their hands in time. The beat reached a crescendo and then, as it began to subside, a high, shrill rustling came from the trees all around them.

Seanchai felt a surge of energy course through his body, a final gift from the forest. He bowed deeply and said, in a voice quivering with emotion, "Thank you."

Chapter Sixty-Eight

"I'm going after Ahad and Phineus. This changes nothing."

"Shayth, if you face them, then you'll face the Emperor, as well." Maugwen appeared the most composed of the three.

"Maybe you should give yourself up," Rhoddan suggested. "Let's find out if you are a Wycaan."

"Are you crazy?" Maugwen snapped, her composure snapped. "What do you think the Emperor will do with him? He'll either kill Shayth and eliminate him as a threat, or bend him to his will. Shayth might be a Wycaan, but he is untrained and will face a master."

"But, meanwhile, he'd provide a great distraction for the Emperor," Rhoddan continued, unmoved by her tone. "It would give Seanchai—"

"So you'll serve him up as bait? Is this your idea of friendship?"

"Enough," Shayth scratched his bristly hair. "We'll decide in the morning. Leave it be for now."

"Whatever we decide, we know one thing for sure," Maugwen said, her voice calm again. "We must leave the village. I wouldn't put it past your uncle to burn it to the ground for sheltering you. Can we at least agree to that?"

Rhoddan and Shayth both nodded, and each moved to his bedroll. As one, they both stood up again and spoke together. "We should post. . ."

"I'll go first," Rhoddan said. "I'm not going to fall asleep."

He sat outside the hut for some time, watching the sliver of moon climb into the sky. When he yawned, he stood and began to pace the muddy, brown furrow that served as a street.

As he walked, he went over the various options they had and realized the futility of each. Frustration welled up inside of him. They were waiting for Seanchai, who had gone into an unknown land to seek a people who had vanished into legend, be trained and tested, and then—hopefully—return. What if Seanchai was dead or lost? How long could they hope to hold out against the Emperor's vast armies?

He stopped at the end of the street and stared into the blackness. There was a small pile of rocks near his feet, so he picked up a few and threw them with all his strength.

"Don't do that," Maugwen said from behind him. "They plow these fields with oxen and kneel to weed and harvest. They clear the fields from stones, and you're undoing their work."

"I'm so useless," Rhoddan hissed. "I follow everyone; first Seanchai and now Shayth. Aaagh!"

Maugwen's hand went to his shoulder. "When we were in the dungeons at Galbrieth, I kept asking Ilana about you. I watched you train in the darkness. Your jokes and kind words held me together, and I craved your attention. You made me feel like. . . like somebody who mattered. Maybe you don't have Wycaan powers or a royal heritage, but you hold our little band together.

"You're brave and principled, Rhoddan, and you hold a mirror up to the rest of us, even when we have closed our eyes. History will record the Shayths and Seanchais, but those of us who live through it know your worth. We appreciate how important you are."

Rhoddan stared at her. Then she opened her arms and they hugged tightly for a long time.

Rhoddan walked in a land he had never seen, and yet seemed familiar. It was hazy and subdued, and everything shimmered around the edges: the rocks, the trees, and the stream he followed.

He walked around a bend and stopped, frozen. Further up the stream, a pack of bears fished and cavorted. Rhoddan knew there was something unnatural for he knew black and white bears weren't from the same regions. It seemed they were all trying to teach a young grizzly to fish.

Rhoddan silently climbed the rock and lay down to watch them. He laughed when the grizzly slipped and fell into the water, and was surprised to see the bear pack react as if laughing, too. The grizzly's big paws splashed the pack's two cubs, and they ran for refuge behind an adult black bear.

"He makes friends so naturally, doesn't he?" said a voice behind him.

Rhoddan turned to find a small, ruddy bear sitting on his haunches. He stared at it for a moment, trying to organize his thoughts. "Are you talking to me, little bear?"

"When you are awake, do you usually talk to animals, Rhoddan?"

"Um, no. As a matter of fact, I don't."

"And in your waking life, would you see bears like these together?"

"No."

"Do you know what you see there, Rhoddan? It is an alliance. Any bear there remind you of someone?"

Rhoddan looked at the grizzly in the middle of the pack.

"That's right," the red bear said. "Seanchai is in his animal form. I am Denalion, a dreamwalker of the Elves of the West, and I have

created this dream of yours. I do not know how to bring others with me so he is unable to see or talk with you. But you can see it is him."

"Why are you in my dreams?" Rhoddan asked.

"I bring a message from the Wycaan. Seanchai needs your help, Rhoddan—you and the one called Shayth. He asks that you make haste to Ballendir of the dwarves and to Umnesilk, First Boar of the pictorians.

"Seanchai asks that you mobilize to attack the army at the Cliftean Pass."

"There are many of them, and they have fortified the area," Rhoddan said.

"And I'm sure the Emperor is sending more troops as we speak. You need to engage them and try to draw some of their forces and, more importantly, their attention away from the Pass.

"We must get Seanchai through. He believes the Emperor saw him escape and might still be in the area. Seanchai needs to confront the Emperor so the soldiers no longer have a commander."

"Is Seanchai strong enough to defeat the Emperor?"

Denalion did a fair job of a bear sighing. "I don't know. He has learned much, but one key thing alludes him."

"What's that?"

Denalion didn't answer, but looked over at the bears in the river.

"Wycaans can transform into animals," Rhoddan said. "Is there something wrong with the way he does it? We suspect that the Emperor can become a firebreather."

Denalion looked back at Rhoddan. "You're very smart, my young elf. Most Wycaans will never find their animal form. Only the masters—the special ones—can complete the change.

"Seanchai should be able to. The bears came to him in his elf form and expected it. We have seen him change once, in a moment when he yielded great power, but he has not succeeded since."

Rhoddan looked across to the playful bears. "If he cannot change, and the Emperor does, he will be defeated, won't he?"

The red bear sighed again and looked away. "We can all only play our part, Rhoddan. There is time yet, so who knows? For now, you and Shayth must mobilize and attack. Can you do that?"

Rhoddan nodded. Then a thought occurred to him. "Does Seanchai come alone?"

"I cannot discuss this with you in case you are captured. He said you would understand. But I imagine you know him far better than I do, and I would not have asked that question. I think you already know the answer."

Rhoddan nodded, and then smiled. The ruddy bear began to chug—a rough, throaty sound. He was laughing, and Rhoddan laughed, too. It felt good to laugh. His pent-up frustration flowed out of him as he let his head fall back and released his emotions for the first time in ages.

Rhoddan heard others laughing. He opened his eyes and saw Shayth and Maugwen staring at him. Both wore broad smiles across their faces. Weak light filtered through the window. It was dawn.

"Someone had a good dream," Shayth said.

"You have no idea," Rhoddan replied. "No idea. Let's eat and pack up. We have much to do."

Chapter Sixty~Nine

Seanchai could not lead his small army back the way they had come; the magical barrier was one-way only. They had to take a roundabout route through the forest and out onto the Plains of Godrin, which would lead to the Cliftean Pass. At that point, the Emperor's sentries would see them.

"This will take too long," he said to his small group of command: the Weapons Master, Denalion, Cheriuk, Shathea, and Sellia. "It could take two weeks to cross the plain. I think the dwarves could engage the army within three days."

The others, Sellia apart, glanced at each other, and then Denalion spoke. "It will take two days to reach the end of the forest. We will then cross the plain in less than three days."

"How?"

"You'll see," the redheaded elf said. "Trust us."

"I do," Seanchai said. "I haven't thanked you all for coming. I didn't expect this."

"No, it's we who need to thank you, Seanchai," Shathea said. "We weren't thriving in the forest; we were stagnating. And you know what happens to water that doesn't move."

Seanchai turned to Cheriuk. "I thought you didn't like me. What made you come?"

Cheriuk frowned as he considered his answer. "Though you vastly improved, you have more to learn with the Win Dao swords. I am worried by the prospect of you being defeated by a lesser, but smarter, swordself."

"Your concern for my survival is gratifying," Seanchai replied drily.

"You miss my point," Cheriuk said, raising one eyebrow indignantly. "I treasure my reputation and that of the Weapons Master."

Everyone laughed as they dispersed. When Seanchai was alone with Sellia, he turned to her.

"Was he joking?"

She put her arms around his neck and kissed him. "That's for you to figure out," she said. "Come, we've spent no time together in ages. Let's go for a walk."

They strolled through the forest and were soon alone.

"How does it feel to know you have family and a history?" Seanchai asked.

"It's a lot to think about," Sellia said fondling her mother's stone. "But there's nothing I can do with it. I won't get to know my family, and I'm still left with many questions."

"Do you regret leaving them? Do you want to go back?"

Sellia stopped and turned to him. Her forehead creased. "Why do you ask? Don't you want me with you?"

"Part of me wants to leave you here," Seanchai said, eliciting a deeper frown from her beautiful face. "No, don't misunderstand me. I know you want to learn about your family. And I would feel lost without you, but I know that when the battle begins, you'll stay close to me, you'd give your life for me, and I might lose you. I can't go through that again."

Sellia pulled him into her arms and held him close. When she spoke, she whispered in his ear. "It will be different this time. I can't promise either of us will survive. But I can promise I will try and stay alive for as long as you are.

"Ilana was convinced she was going to die. She accepted and prepared for it. I am not like her. No prophecy or wise dwarf has condemned me. I have a luxury that Ilana didn't. I'm dreaming of a future, after you defeat the Emperor–a future that has us together."

"Mhari told me that relationships rarely work for the Wycaans. I'll be traveling around the land. You might join me at first, but if we have *calhei*, you–"

Sellia put a finger to his lips. "I said I *dream* about a future. For now, that is enough."

She moved her finger away and replaced it with her lips.

They reached the edge of the forest at nightfall the following day. Denalion and the Weapons Master approached Seanchai and Sellia as the others set up camp.

"You will sleep away from the camp tonight, and neither of you will eat," the old elfe said. "Seanchai, do your meditations and prepare yourself."

"What for?"

"For whatever happens tomorrow," Denalion said, mischievously arching an eyebrow.

Seanchai went through his standing exercises, and Sellia completed a series of slow stretches and movements Seanchai had never seen her do before. When they had finished, they wrapped up together in the bear fur.

"What were you doing before?" Seanchai asked her.

"While you were off playing swords and futilely trying to become better with the bow than me, I learned a form of stretching exercises that the elves here have done for centuries. It makes you more supple both physically and mentally. I will show you when we have time. . . afterwards. Now, go to sleep.

It sounds like we have a big day ahead of us."

"Do you know what's going to happen tomorrow?" Seanchai asked.

Sellia turned onto her side, her back to him, and feigned sleep.

"Fair enough," Seanchai said and, pulling her close, spooned his body around her. "I'm glad you chose to come with me, Sellia. I know what you've given up to be here."

Sellia snored softly. Seanchai didn't know whether she had heard him or not.

"Dream of our future," he whispered. "Keep me by your side in the dream world."

And with the scent of her hair filling his nostrils, Seanchai drifted into a deep sleep.

Chapter Seventy

Seanchai frowned. He had woken with the first lights of dawn and gone through his exercises, filling himself with the energy of the ancient trees. He was not sure if he would ever have such an opportunity again to feel the vibrancy of the forest. Now he stood staring out over the Plains of Godrin.

While not totally flat there were almost no trees and, more importantly, Seanchai could not see the Cliftean Mountains in the distance. The rising sun restricted his sight, but Seanchai could not sense them. He could feel something else, though. There was life on the plain, but this did not hold his interest.

Denalion had entered Rhoddan's dream two days ago. The dwarves would be ready to march and could engage the Emperor's army within another two days, maybe three. Seanchai knew he had to join them soon to have any chance of defeating a far larger, well-drilled army. He wondered if the Emperor or General Shiftan had decided to reinforce their defenses that faced west. He sighed. They would most certainly have done so.

He heard Sellia coming up behind him. He turned and gasped as the rising sun lit up her dark skin. The small, red stone on her hair band glimmered.

"You're beautiful," he marveled, and felt the tips of his ears burn.

She smiled and threw her arms around him. "I meant to thank you for packing up the bags," he said into her ear.

He felt Sellia's body ripple with laughter. "'You're beautiful works better," she said, then pulled away and kissed him. She stroked the tips of his ears, which, he was sure, confirmed he had blushed.

Denalion spoke suddenly from behind them. "Sellia. Please take your bags and join the others. They're over that way." He nodded back the way he had come.

"Seanchai, come with me," he continued, and the Wycaan followed the dreamwalker out onto the plain. They climbed a small hill and when they reached its crest, Denalion instructed him to put his bags and weapons down. "Have you prepared?" he asked.

"We fasted, and I've done my exercises," Seanchai replied. "These plains are immense. We won't get there in time to help the dwarves and pictorians."

"We will, but for now, put such thoughts aside. I want you to scry. Look for life on the plain and, when you find it, invite it in. It will be suspicious of you, so take your time. Let it probe if it tries. You have nothing to fear."

Denalion sat down and closed his eyes. Seanchai planted his feet and began his breathing. He felt the energy rising up through the ground, considerably less vibrant than the forest.

He allowed it to flow through him, and then he sent it out onto the plain, probing for life. He felt a soft tug at his consciousness, but when he tried to connect, it shied away. He moved his mind slowly in its direction and followed its trail without trying to catch up. The creature—no, *creatures*—moved quickly and lithely. He sensed them turn in a circle, and one of the creatures tentatively came forward.

Seanchai resisted the temptation to probe with his mind, and instead waited for the creature to approach him. He felt a warm sensation that resembled hot breath and heard panting of an animal that was wary and ready to take flight. He needed to ground his energy and allow the creature to decide.

The warm, humid breath entered his consciousness, and he could sense two flaring nostrils breathing on his face and into his body. It was strange, alien, and scary, but he kept himself still. He felt a layer of sweat on his face and a chill behind his neck.

You call upon us to bear you, but we are free.

"You are free," Seanchai said in his mind. "But I need your help. You have answered to the call of the Elves of the West in the past."

We have answered the call of the Wycaans, yes, but they are not what they once were. In times long past they were mighty leaders, masters of Odessiya. The age of the Wycaan has passed.

"No, it has not. The races of Odessiya have cried out for freedom, and the Wycaans rise again to lead them in the fight."

Denalion's voice piped up nearby. "Great one, before you stands a Wycaan Master. He has called my people to arms, and we have answered because he imbues the greatness you speak of. He has built an alliance in the east, bringing humans, dwarves, elves, pictorians, and aqua'lansis together. Now, he asks that you help in these dire times. Bear us across the Plains of Godrin with the speed of the wind. Only you can do this."

What awaits us on the other side of the Cliftean Pass? Our numbers dwindle, Wycaan. Great herds no longer gallop across the plains as we once did. This is the age of man, elf, and dwarf. We are from an age gone forever.

"A great battle," Seanchai said. "But I will not ask you to fight; only to aid us across the plains."

Oaths we swore to the great Wycaans. Ashbar, we said. We are obligated to answer your call.

The creature shook its mane and snorted with resignation. Seanchai took a chance.

"Transport us across the plains, and I will release you from your oaths. Fulfill them this one last time, and you will run free forever."

He was answered with silence, a pulling back. Then Seanchai felt a surge of energy course through his body and many voices melding into one.

The herd senses your wisdom and feels your spirit. Prepare yourself, then, Wycaan. We will answer your call as we answered your ancient ancestors. The Plains of Godrin will shake once again under the beat of our hooves. Prepare your people. The Shieldhei are coming.

Chapter Seventy-One

S eanchai felt their approach long before he saw them. He recalled these legendary creatures of great speed and strength from the children's stories his parents told. The ground indeed shook as hundreds of hooves pounded in a single, rhythmic canter.

He looked to the south, where clouds of dust rose. Denalion patted Seanchai's shoulder. "You did well, Wycaan. You are truly a builder of alliances."

"They had oaths to fulfill. They would have come."

"Ah, yes." Denalion swept his red hair back. "But they come now as proud, free creatures. It makes all the difference and is the magic of serving you. It fills us all, both sides of the Cliftean Pass, with hope for the future. The Emperor faces a weapon he cannot contend with. And it is exciting to watch."

Denalion started to walk back to the others. He had to shout over the sound of approaching hooves. "I'll leave you to meet alone. When you're ready, come to us. We await your lead."

Black dots became Shieldhei, which veered toward Seanchai's companions. Only one continued toward Seanchai, his gait long and powerful.

In moments, a great, four-legged beast stood before him. The Shieldhei were horses that had been exposed to Wycaan magic. They were silver, almost translucent, from head to tail.

Their haunches were larger and stronger than was proportionate. They were honed to gallop, and took great joy in feeling the wind on their faces.

Seanchai felt a wave of childhood excitement. As the creature approached, he saw its face was angular with a boney ridge down the length from its mane to muzzle. Its neck was also longer than a horses' and similarly ridged.

The great animal stood before Seanchai, breathing heavily, puffing warm smoke into the chilly morning air.

We have come, it said inside his head. *I am Amuranth, Lord of the Shieldhei. Only a Wycaan Master can ride me, and only then with my consent.*

Seanchai moved forward. "I am honored, Amuranth. Thank you. I craved the stories of the Shieldhei as a *calhei*, but never dreamed I would have the privilege to ride one. May I be worthy of your benevolence."

There was no saddle or reins. Seanchai tentatively raised himself up onto the animal's ridged back. They moved to accommodate him sitting down and then closed to secure him.

Amuranth turned and trotted east into the sun. Seanchai watched the herd close in behind him, carrying his friends. Denalion rode to one side of him and the Weapons Master on the other. Further back, Sellia rode behind Shathea on a huge stallion. And the great shieldhei and their elf riders stretched out in the shape of an arrow. It was a magnificent sight.

We ride in arrow formation so that none of us is denied the wind in our manes.

When the backline was in formation, Seanchai leaned forward and spoke into Amuranth's ear. "Lord of the Shieldhei: what is it like to feel the wind whistling in your ears?"

Amuranth nickered and shook his mighty mane. *That cannot be described in the stories of children. I must show you.*

Seanchai could not suppress a whoop as Amuranth flexed his mighty leg muscles.

Shayth crawled up to the edge of the soldier's camp. He needed to procure three horses, and quickly. If Rhoddan's dream was really a message from Seanchai, then they would be doing a lot of traveling in the next few days. Army horses were strong and well cared for.

The patrol was shouting and laughing around a roaring campfire, becoming increasingly raucous as more ale was passed round. The two on-duty guards seemed more intent on listening to the stories than looking for an enemy. Shayth moved silently to the one near the horses, waiting for him to stop laughing so as not to attract attention from an abruptly curtailed cackle.

The guard enjoyed the end of the story, which Shayth ensured was the last he ever heard. The soldier crumpled to the ground without even so much as a grunt, his throat split while a hand covered his mouth.

Shayth slowly crawled to the horses, allowing them to smell his hand so they didn't startle. He chose the three furthest from the camp and patted them gently. He had already procured three saddles from near the horses' feed. Now he untied the reins and crept away.

Laughter erupted from around the bonfire. *Laugh on, gentlemen,* Shayth thought. *Save some stories to tell when you walk back to your camp tomorrow.*

He turned into the tip of a sword "Canna a prince ney afford his own steed?" a gray-haired officer with a huge mustache asked.

"I'm planning to meet up with my dear Uncle," Shayth replied. "I'll be sure to return the horses then."

The officer glanced beyond Shayth. There was another wave of laughter from those sitting around the fire. "I served under yeh father for many years. I owe Prince Shindell mah life."

He was clearly struggling with conflicting emotions. Shayth waited and covertly held out his hand to stay Rhoddan, who was approaching from behind.

"Odessiya would be a different place if yeh father had become Emperor. Tell mah. This elf we hear about: is he feh real?"

"More than you can imagine," Shayth said. "He changed me from a violent, angry child to what I am today, without force, and almost without me noticing."

"And what have yeh become, Prince Shindell?" The officer challenged him with earnest eyes.

Shayth took a deep breath and stood up straight. "I am the son of my father. Or, at least, I strive to be."

"Aw, I could tell yeh stories about him," the officer said. "But as three of mah men here will discover, now is ney the time feh stories.

"The Emperor is strong, young prince—stronger than yeh think. If yeh defeat him, there'll be many within the army who'll rally to the son of Prince Shindell, but ney while yeh uncle lives.

"Go now. If yeh have become whom yeh say, and the elf is real, too, then meebe next time we meet, I'll tell yeh stories of yeh father and make yeh proud to carry his name."

The officer stepped aside, and Shayth led the horses on. Suddenly, the reins felt terribly heavy.

CHAPTER SEVENTY-TWO

"What do you mean, you won't come?" Rhoddan yelled at a scowling Ballendir.

They had known each other a long time and Shayth knew the dwarf wasn't used to being shouted at.

"Mah orders come from the King in Hothengold. I received them two days ago. All troops are ordered ta pull back. We leave in the morning."

"Why's he pulling troops back?" Shayth asked, anxious to calm Rhoddan. "Surely he knows that this'll bring the battle to him. Hothengold has not been rebuilt to withstand another assault."

"Mah king has lost faith," Ballendir said, lighting his long-stemmed pipe and sending up a cloud of smoke. "Seanchai came to him a broken elf after Ilana died. Now he has disappeared, and no one knows what has happened to him."

"*I* know what happened to him," Rhoddan jumped up from his chair. "Don't you believe me? After all we've been through, Ballendir."

"Settle down, laddie," Ballendir said, his voice sharp. "Drink 'n listen. Yeh described yeh dream, and I believe yeh had the dream. But I canna assume it ta be more than a dream, and, frankly, neither can yeh."

"But how else could he communicate with me from beyond the Pass?"

"Mebbe it was wishful projection from a desperate friend," Ballendir said and turned immediately to Shayth. "Has it occurred to yeh that mebbe the Emperor's behind this?"

Shayth pulled a hand through his spiky hair. He nodded. "I thought of that. I don't have an answer."

Ballendir disappeared behind another mass of pine-scented smoke. Shayth heard him sigh.

"Ballendir. We're going back to the Pass, and we'll do whatever we need to in order to distract Shiftan on the off chance that Rhoddan is correct. We need the dwarves and the pictorians.

"You know there is an opportunity here and that we must take it. What happens when the dwarves burrow underground again? The pictorians will head back north, and the Emperor will seek revenge with a massive army. He will pick you off, one stronghold at a time. You *know* that."

Ballendir stared at him, slumped in his chair, and gnawed on the stem of his pipe. "I need more than that ta disobey mah king."

They went quiet for a while. Immersed deep in his thoughts, Shayth gradually began to realize that everyone was looking at him. He stared back at them: at Rhoddan, Ballendir, and Maugwen.

She leaned forward. "He's right, Shayth. Perhaps it's time."

Shayth rose and moved away to a corner, his back to his friends. He could feel their eyes upon him still. One hand went through his hair, and he began to bite the fingernails of the other.

He recalled the villagers where they had returned the children all bending down on one knee. "*We will do the bidding of the prince,"* the village leader had said. He thought, too, of the old officer who had let him steal the army horses.

And then he remembered Sellia whispering into his ear when they had last said goodbye. He could feel her hot breath. *Be the person you were destined to be, Prince Shindell, and stop wasting so much energy trying to deny what everyone else sees so clearly.*

Shayth slowly returned to face his friends. When he spoke to Ballendir, he barely recognized his own deep, measured tone. "Send a messenger to the King at Hothengold. Tell him you have answered the call of the son of Prince Shindell."

Maugwen and Rhoddan looked at each other knowingly. Ballendir nodded slowly.

"Yeh ready? Yeh sure?"

"I don't know. But I need you, Ballendir, old friend, if I'm going to find out."

They caught up with Umnesilk and the pictorians late in the afternoon the following day. Their horses were exhausted from being driven relentlessly.

"Umnesilk! First Boar of the Pictorians. Where are you going?" Shayth called out. "Have you lost your battle spirit?"

The First Boar signaled for his small army to stop. There could not have been more than two hundred boars left, but their running still caused the ground to shake.

"White-haired one not return. Little people go into rock tunnels. What left here for us but to die in battle that serve no purpose?"

"Seanchai is coming," Rhoddan blurted out as he jumped from his lathered horse. "He has summoned us to attack the army at the Cliftean Pass, to divert their attention enough to allow him to come through."

Umnesilk stared at him. "Where he is, then?"

"On the other side. He went west of the Cliftean Pass seeking the Elves of Markwin. You know this."

Umnesilk frowned. His voice went deeper. "No one ever return from there. Pictorians have stories."

"He's coming back," Rhoddan said, his face reddening.

"He bring help?" Umnesilk asked.

Rhoddan didn't reply.

"You spoke with white-haired one, no?"

"Not exactly," Rhoddan said, his voice becoming despondent.

"You not speak with him?" The First Boar managed to frown even more. "Then how you know he return?"

Rhoddan glanced over at Shayth, but the latter shrugged. Rhoddan turned back to Umnesilk. "I had a dream, a very powerful dream."

"You talk with him in dream?"

"No, I spoke with. . . I spoke with another." Rhoddan winced. "He was red. His hair. . . or fur. . . was red."

The pictorians surrounding him growled in their own language. Umnesilk stepped up to Rhoddan and towered over him. "You met *Unsek,* dream spirit? What his name?"

Rhoddan thought for a moment. This hadn't been a detail he had particularly paid attention to. He creased his brow. "Den. . . Denali. . . I think. No, Denalion."

The pictorians erupted in shouts, growls, and roars. Only Umnesilk stood motionless, staring at Rhoddan. When his boars quieted, the giant pictorian turned to Shayth.

"Son of Shindell. We run with you to Cliftean Pass. If *Unsek* call for fight, pictorians give mighty battle."

Umnesilk called something out, and the company formed up, turned, and jogged back in the direction they had just come from.

Chapter Seventy ~ Three

B allendir's scowl was not a welcome sight so early in the morning. The sun had barely risen, and a thick mist had settled around the camp where the dwarves had set up their base.

The pictorians were higher on the mountain, and a messenger had been dispatched to call Umnesilk. They waited for him in silence.

Shayth poured himself a hot drink and joined Rhoddan on a bench, where he sat with his eyes closed. Shayth was wondering if his friend had fallen back to sleep when Rhoddan let out a short snore. The Prince shook him and gave him the tea.

As Shayth poured himself another cup, Umnesilk opened the flap of the tent.

"Thank yeh fer coming, First Boar Umnesilk," Ballendir bowed. "I regret the early hour."

"Dwarf leader have good reason," Umnesilk said, eying Shayth's cup.

Shayth offered it to him, and Umnesilk nodded in thanks. Shayth returned for a third cup. If it wasn't so cold, he might have given up. They waited for him to join them at the table.

"After I agreed to join yeh, I sent three dwarves ta Hothengold ta tell the king," Ballendir said, and looked at Shayth, "They met an advance party of soldiers 'n killed all but one. They. . . asked. . . the survivor what the patrol was doing."

Shayth winced. Dwarves were not known for their delicacy with prisoners. Since his meeting with the officer from whom he had stolen three horses, Shayth was having difficulty lumping them all together as a single enemy.

"They learned that the Emperor sent an army ta Hothengold, 'n while on its way, it received orders ta change direction ta the Cliftean Pass. It'll be here in three days.

"One of mah scouts returned ta tell mah. The other went on ta tell the king."

"And the third?" Shayth asked.

"Aye, he feasts in the halls o' our ancestors. He was a fine dwarf. I knew him well."

"I'm sorry for your loss," Shayth said.

There was silence as everyone stared at the map in the middle of the table.

Rhoddan, now wide awake, voiced all their fears. "We cannot get caught between two forces. We don't have the strength. We need to attack today and try to weaken Shiftan's forces."

"Maybe we can draw them away from the pass," Shayth suggested. "What if the pictorians attack from here—" he pointed on the map "—and then run north through the valley?"

Ballendir shook his head. "They might draw some away, but the General isn't going ta be troubled by pictorians when they're running away."

"His troops are stationed there to protect the pass," Rhoddan added.

"What if they were chasing me?" Shayth persisted. "Would I be more of an incentive?"

"You might draw out Ahad, but Seanchai is the bigger bait."

"Umnesilk," Ballendir looked up from the map to the First Boar. "What do yeh think?"

"Pictorians not good at tactics. We charge, we kill." He laughed in a deep, rasping voice.

Rhoddan sighed. "Maybe we're looking for something that doesn't exist. Right now, Seanchai needs a distraction, not an outright battle."

Ballendir nodded. "Aye. Their camp's spread out. We attack from different sides 'n retreat. Dwarves are better in the dark than humans. We attack at different times of the night ta make sure none sleep."

"Let's try to destroy their supplies," Rhoddan said. "Deprive them of sleep and food."

"Umnesilk. Can yeh boars attack from the south 'n reach the central area, here?" Ballendir pointed on the map. "I'll lead mah dwarves from the north, 'n we'll try 'n draw soldiers ta us. We'll attack two hours after the moon reaches its highest point. When yeh hear us engaged, yeh attack 'n try ta destroy their supplies."

Umnesilk grunted and nodded his massive head. Ballendir turned to Shayth.

"I'll give yeh a group of mah best archers. Yeh can make mischief of yehselves during the day. Mainly, I want ta prevent them from sleeping."

"What about the second army?" Rhoddan asked.

"I've sent some of mah dwarves ta rig the gorge they'll come through. It'll thin them out a bit, mebbe slow them down, but nothing more." Ballendir looked at them all grimly. "If he comes alone or not at all, we won't win this one."

The others nodded despondently, except for Rhoddan, who drew himself up straight and glared. "He will come."

Eleven dwarf archers joined Shayth. Their shorter bows didn't have the trajectory of his longbow, but made up for it with sheer velocity. He was impressed as they moved north along the periphery of the camp, taking shots through the rocks and picking off sentries before disappearing again quickly.

In the afternoon, they were chased away and split up. Several dwarves peeled off and doubled back. There was no distinct plan or chain of command, but a dwarf named Countradir occasionally gave orders. He and two others stayed close to Shayth at all times.

After a while, it was only the four of them, but their pursuers were dropping back and scattering.

"How do we regroup?" Shayth asked.

"We don't," Countradir replied. "They'll find their own way back. Once they leave yeh, they cannot return and join yeh."

"Why not?"

"In case they're being tracked."

Shayth stopped and glared at Countradir. "Do you have orders specific to my protection?"

The three dwarves looked at each other guiltily. Shayth didn't wait for an answer. "Come on," he said. "You're just following orders. Ballendir, however, is in for a tongue-lashing."

Chapter Seventy-Four

S hayth never got the opportunity to confront Ballendir. The dwarf had gone out on a scouting party ahead of the offensive planned for that night. Another officer told them to eat and grab some sleep while they could.

Shayth felt as though he had hardly closed his eyes before a dwarf woke him. As he sat up, rubbing his eyes and sighing, he saw the dwarf apprehensively trying to wake Rhoddan, who continued to snore.

"I got him," Shayth said, putting on his boots. "Where is Ballendir?"

The dwarf frowned. "He has led the main contingent of the army over ta the north side. They'll attack at any moment."

Shayth was instantly awake. "Why didn't he wait for me?"

The dwarf drew back, surprised at Shayth's ferocity.

"Yeh ta attack from the south with the pictorians. Their First Boar and Ballendir must have. . ."

"I'm sorry," Shayth said. "Just my adrenaline prior to battle. Pay no heed."

The dwarf nodded. "I brought yeh this black pitch to cover yehself and yeh weapons with. You leave in a short while."

Shayth thanked him and approached Rhoddan to shake him sharply. "Wake up, soldier. The night is still young."

Rhoddan took a few moments to pull himself up onto the edge of his bed. When Shayth started blackening his blades, the elf came awake immediately. They didn't speak as they worked, and were soon out of their tent.

"Maugwen's over there," Rhoddan mumbled. "She'd like you to say goodbye before we leave."

"Should I wake her?" Shayth asked.

Rhoddan shook his head. "I doubt you'll find her sleeping," he said and walked off to a fire with a steaming pot over it.

When Shayth entered the tent, he found rows of wounded and bandaged dwarves lying on cots. There was a stale, medicinal smell, and he had to fight the urge to walk back out.

Maugwen stood up and stretched. Strands of hair flailed wildly along with those standing up on her head. Her shoulders slumped, but when she noticed Shayth, she straightened up and tried to tame her hair by tucking it behind her ears.

"You look tired," she said.

"Have I rings under my eyes like you?" he asked. "When was the last time you slept?"

"I'm not even sure where my cot is," she replied looking around. "There's so much to do here, and after tonight, I'm sure there'll be far more."

"Then you should pace yourself," Shayth replied.

She laughed humorlessly. "Our soldiers are dying all around me, Shayth, and many more will die. How can I sleep?"

Spontaneously, he opened his arms, and she fell into his embrace. "Many will die or be wounded before dawn breaks, and I don't know if we'll even make a dent."

"This war makes no sense," Maugwen continued, her voice muffled in his chest. "I wish the Emperor would do his own fighting. Perhaps then he might not be so quick to send others to war."

"If the Emperor fights," Shayth replied, despondent, "there'll be far more casualties. Careful what you wish for."

They heard voices outside and cries in the distance. Shayth let go of Maugwen and touched her cheek. "Pace yourself," he said. "You'll help no one if you aren't able to move and think."

She nodded. "Be careful," she said. "I don't want to have to treat you. You probably make for a lousy patient."

"Oh, I do, at that. But don't worry. I've got Rhoddan watching out for me." With some effort, Shayth forced a smile.

"And you watch out for him, too." Maugwen turned away, unsuccessfully hiding the tears welling up in her eyes.

Shayth was momentarily glad to step outside into the fresh air, but gulped when he found the pictorians waiting for him. Umnesilk towered over them from the rock he stood on.

"We are pictorians. We know no fear. We know no mercy." He paused, and the sounds of fighting and shouting floated over from the other side of the huge camp. "We leave no one in wake but reach little brothers who already fight. Our grandchildren will beg to hear tales told of Battle of Cliftean Pass." He drew a huge mace, its blackness glinting in the light of the nearby fire. "Tonight, all will know the wrath of pictorian warrior. We fight! *Ungallah! Ungallah! Ungallah!*"

The warriors raised their axes, maces, and swords, and answered: *Ungallah! Ungallah! Ungallah!*

Shayth moved behind Rhoddan, who was shouting and thrusting his Elven broadsword into the air. He smiled and put his mouth to the elf's ear. "Do you even know what that means?"

Rhoddan turned, cheeks flushed, eyes hard. "I have no need for translation. I hear the cry of the warrior."

Shayth was taken aback at his friend's sudden battle fever. They turned together and jogged with the pictorians. Shayth breathed along with the rhythmic thudding of hundreds of boots.

His mind went to the Emperor, to the Crown Prince, and to Ahad. He allowed the image of General Tarlach to fill his mind, and he felt the hate and rage seep back into his body. He embraced the once-familiar feeling. He needed it.

He thought of his father and mother, relying now on fading memories. Betrayal and loss coursed through his blood. When the pictorians charged down into the camp, Shayth heard himself screaming: "*Ungallah! Ungallah! Ungallah!*"

And he didn't stop screaming even after his blade cut into the first soldier unfortunate enough to cross his path.

Chapter Seventy-Five

Rhoddan had trained for this all his life. As soon as he could hold a long knife, he begged his father and the other warriors to train him. Ever since, he had modeled himself after the brave role models around him, forcing himself to master not only the weapons he wielded now with such fluency, but also his mind.

When Umnesilk led his boars down the side of the mountains and into the army camp, Rhoddan felt his breathing settle and his muscles enter into a different state of tension. His breathing evened and his muscles tensed. As he swung his sword and charged forward, he felt like his warrior psyche had found its place. He stayed close to Shayth, as Ballendir had ordered, fighting his way through the tents and slashing ropes. The bigger pictorians felled the tents, sending their contents smashing to the ground.

Rhoddan and Shayth advanced beyond the sleeping quarters and found themselves in a more open area. Here, soldiers who had not been sleeping gathered to stand their ground in organized ranks. The pictorians set upon them, forcing the soldiers to retreat, shields and bones shattered in their wake.

Shayth moved efficiently through the fight. When attacked, he dispensed of his opponent quickly, and more than once interceded when a pictorian was outnumbered. Rhoddan followed, leaving his own wake of carnage. When they reached the main square, Umnesilk barked out orders. The pictorians split, with one group heading toward the Pass and the other toward the camp's south side, where Ballendir fought with his dwarf army.

Rhoddan and Shayth joined the smaller forces attacking the command tents and the Pass. At the main thoroughfare, a cry went up, and the pictorians formed a defensive wedge as they faced a line of disciplined cavalry.

The first front line of pictorians went down on one knee and thrust their shields into the ground at an angle. The shield tops' had two sharp points facing up and when the two forces clashed, the horses screamed as their undersides were cut open.

The mounted soldiers toppled into the second line of pictorians, who slaughtered them with speed and relish. A wave of arrows followed, but was mostly ineffective on the heavily armored pictorians.

The pictorians, Shayth, and Rhoddan advanced quickly and cleared the command tents, kitchens, and dining areas of the last few soldiers gathered, pausing only to torch everything that would burn.

"Most of the army must be fighting Ballendir at the south side of the camp," Shayth yelled in Rhoddan's ear. "We need to help them."

Rhoddan began to have a strong feeling that they were overlooking something important. Why sacrifice so much of the camp and especially the headquarters? And even if there was a reason, why leave the cavalry in such a small number?

He assumed that the cavalry had stayed on the broad paths because of the difficulty they would have maneuvering through the tents. By the side of a burning tent he knelt down and saw signs that horses and laden carts had moved out of here. He stared into the flaming tent and a growing unease gnawed his mind.

When they reached the junction in the camp where the pictorians had split, Rhoddan's fear was confirmed. A huge wave of cavalry was waiting for them. The pictorians formed a wedge again, but mounted horses swarmed from the other direction. They had walked right into a trap.

The cavalry boasted some of the best-trained and experienced soldiers, and they fought ferociously. They also seemed to know where the weaknesses were in the pictorians' armor. Battle was slow and deadly for both sides.

Shayth signaled Umnesilk for a horizontal retreat into the tent areas. Umnesilk struggled with his pictorian instinct to battle straight through to the death before roaring for his troops to do as Shayth requested.

When they were momentarily safe, Shayth addressed the First Boar, but spoke loudly to everyone. "There's an army behind them. It's a trap. The second regiment got through the ambush we set for them, and we're now in the middle. We must reach Ballendir and break out as a unified force."

Umnesilk nodded and led his boars, numbering at no more than a hundred now, through the tents. Suddenly, they were face-to-face with many confused dwarves.

"We got ta walk through," Ballendir yelled at Rhoddan and Shayth. "T'was too easy."

"The other army," Shayth yelled back. "They've broken through. We're trapped."

They stood, each looking at the other. Then Rhoddan said, "To the Pass. Their superior numbers won't matter in the narrow gorge."

Ballendir and Umnesilk led them west through the camp. But when they came to the main path, they found General

Shiftan's battalion waiting, and they were pushed back against the mountains.

Now both of the Emperor's armies closed in on either side, and the dwarves had nowhere to run. Ballendir saw the panic on his warriors' faces, and jumped on a rock. With his voice going hoarse, he cried out to his troops.

"We're here ta fight, 'n fight we will. If we die, we take as many o' the scum as we can. We're dwarves, 'n if we have ta, we'll walk proudly inta the halls o' our ancestors."

The dwarves turned to face the oncoming armies in a wide arc, beating their shields rhythmically as they had in Hothengold. They called it the Hiyenmut, but this time it was slower, in recognition of the reality of their situation. Rhoddan's eyes met Umnesilk's, and the pictorian nodded. He sensed it, too. He turned to his host and took up the pictorian battle cry, first matching and then speeding up the battle chorus.

The dwarves beat their shields harder as the pictorians cried *Ungallah! Ungallah!* Rhoddan drew a deep breath and turned to Shayth. "It's a fine day to die," he yelled.

Shayth nodded and opened his mouth to respond, but at that moment, a stout dwarf jumped onto the rock with Ballendir. As the Emperor's army charged forward, he drew a golden horn, raised it to his mouth, and let out three long blasts.

To their left, from within the Pass, came the response. A higher-pitched horn blew back three times. Rhoddan grabbed Shayth.

"An Elven horn," he cried, and, as he spoke, a hundred strangely proportioned horses, mostly black, with ridged backs and long heads, poured out of the Pass. Rhoddan recognized the legendary Shieldhei from the stories of his youth. He gasped as he saw they were mounted by white-haired elves, many brandishing two swords in the air.

Shayth pointed to the lead horse, where a huge Wycaan fired arrows from a glimmering green bow.

"Seanchai has come," Shayth cried, grabbing the dwarf and pictorian leaders. "Let's greet him on the battlefield with the alliance he built."

Prince Shindell raised his huge broadsword and, flanked by Rhoddan of the Elves; Umnesilk, First Boar of the Pictorians; and Ballendir, general of the dwarf nation, charged out to meet the enemy.

Chapter Seventy-Six

T he elves, mounted on the powerful Shieldhei, tore through the foot soldiers and headed straight toward the cavalry, which quickly organized and galloped out to meet them. A wave of fresh foot soldiers from the regiment that had just arrived charged in behind the cavalry, and their sheer numbers slowed the elves.

Still, the elves were stronger and faster. No one fought as hard and with such ruthless speed as Seanchai. When he saw that Amuranth was foaming at the mouth, he leapt down and pulled the mighty steed's ear to his mouth.

"Gather your herd and find safe pasture. Your oath is fulfilled. Ride free forever, Lord of the Shieldhei."

Seanchai let go and jumped back into the fray. Seeing the overwhelming numbers, he called the Markwin Elves to him, and, together, they progressed as a sharp wedge-shaped unit.

Advancing at the head, Seanchai turned the group, and they began to make their way toward the dwarves and pictorians. He could see mighty Umnesilk, head and shoulders above all others, swinging a huge axe. Other pictorians fought nearby.

The dwarves were not having it all their own way, but were holding their ground with the aid of the pictorians. As Seanchai led the Elves of the West into the fray, the dwarves were absorbed into the wedge and found a moment to catch their breath.

Cheriuk replaced Seanchai at the wedge's point so Seanchai could consult with Ballendir. If the Emperor's soldiers thought this might give them a break, they were mistaken. Cheriuk's swords were just as fast as Seanchai's, and Shathea and the Weapons Master fought on either side of him.

"Well met, elf," Ballendir said, pressing on an arm wound with an already bloody piece of material. "I was wondering when yeh might decide ta drop in 'n join us. I was worried we might be finished before yeh turned up."

"Did you doubt me, my friend?" Seanchai called back.

"Aye," the dwarf conceded. "But he never did, not once."

Seanchai turned and threw his arms around Rhoddan.

"They're real," was all Rhoddan could muster, tears brimming in his eyes.

"They are real, my friend, and they have come." Seanchai turned to face all who were close and cried out, one of his Win Dao blade flashing above him. "Now is the moment we turn the tide. Come! Odessiya begs to be freed."

A cheer went up around him, but Rhoddan grabbed his arm.

"Where is Sellia?"

"Around the periphery with a group of archers. And Shayth?"

The smile on Rhoddan's face disappeared, and he glanced at Ballendir. "I–I don't know."

Ballendir called three dwarves to him. They were quickly sent in different directions. When he turned back, Seanchai saw worry on Ballendir's face.

"What is it?"

"There's a master assassin wandering around looking fer the young prince." Ballendir called back. "They're boyhood friends but the prince killed his father. I doubt they plan to reminisce about old times."

Seanchai nodded. "Ahad. Then let's go find them first." He pointed a finger at Ballendir and grinned. "No matter how much trouble he's in, don't let him catch you calling him a prince. . ." He trailed off as he comprehended the looks on his friends' faces. His mouth dropped open in wonder and then a smile etched across his face. "Let's go find Prince Shindell."

Shayth moved toward the edge of the battlefield. With Seanchai leading the offensive, they had a good chance to win. This meant the Emperor would have to show himself.

It was his destiny to fight and kill the Emperor as he had killed Tarlach. The man had betrayed him, but the Emperor was directly responsible for the death of his parents. He made his way around the fighting, occasionally entering the fray when attacked or when he saw an opportunity to help an overwhelmed dwarf or a surrounded pictorian. But otherwise, he kept moving.

He caught glimpses of someone shadowing him, probably one of Ballendir's guards. The Emperor wouldn't hide like that and Shayth had to find him before he singled out Seanchai.

A robed figure ran in front of him, looked both ways, and disappeared into a gorge between the rocks. He was hiding something in the gorge.

Shayth followed, and, as the sky began to lighten to a dull gray, he found himself in a dead end. The figure turned, withdrew his hood, and smiled.

"Hello Shayth, my dear cousin. It's been too long."

"Young Phineus," Shayth replied. "I'm surprised to see you so near a battle, and all alone. Why are you creeping off? Did you plan to hide until your dear father cleans up out there?"

"You insult me, cousin. It has been a long time and I have passed through the academy. I left my fear back with my diapers. And you assume much if you think that, unlike you, I would be alone." He nodded behind Shayth.

"I've been waiting a long time to face the boy who bullied me all those years," Ahad said, removing black leather gloves. "Now that we have him cornered, he looks quite pathetic, doesn't he, Phineus?"

The Crown Prince laughed, but Ahad was serious. "I might not have bothered, but I heard you asked the elf to let you fight and kill my father. Did you really ask the Wycaan to let you kill him, Shayth? The Wycaan didn't force you, did he? You wanted it. Tell me true. I need to know."

"I did," Shayth replied slowly. "Would you also like to know why, Ahad? Your father was no noble knight from a child's fairytale. He killed tens of thousands of men, women, and children without remorse. He tortured and abused anyone who got in his way, including his own soldiers. And though he swore an oath to protect me as a boy, he stood aside when little Phini's father murdered his own brother to quench his thirst for power. Your father was a murderer and an oath-breaker. Nothing more.

"Yes, I asked to fight him, but I'm not sure if the Wycaan would have allowed me to if his mate hadn't been poisoned by your dear father. She lay writhing in pain at your father's feet. The Wycaan had to make a choice between surrender and the antidote, and he, dear Ahad, is no oath-breaker. He had sworn to Ilana that he would not sacrifice his work to save her, and he walked away from his soul mate. Only then did I step forward and fight your father."

Shayth stared into Ahad's eyes. "You know I tell the truth, don't you? You are not like him." There was surprise in his voice. "Ahad. Your father was responsible for all his choices. To his credit, I believe he would agree with me on that. He never begged for mercy, denied any accusations, or made excuses for his actions. But I don't believe he would want you to walk the same path.

"The Emperor is going to fall. He has a son woefully inadequate to take over, so who will rule the new Odessiya?" Shayth saw Ahad stay the Crown Prince, who was ready to spring.

"Do you think it will be you, Prince Shindell?" Ahad asked sarcastically. "I hear people drop to their knees before you. Rather premature, no?"

"Him?" Phineus said, circling Shayth cautiously. "He has left a trail of blood and violence in his path. All Odessiya waits for him to hang and will celebrate his death."

Shayth spoke only to Ahad. "I regret much of what I have done since my parents were murdered. But the Wycaan has changed me. It's the most powerful part of his magic. When you meet him, you will understand. He is the moral face of Odessiya, so unlike the three of us. Meet him, Ahad. I promise you safe passage if you leave him. I also give you my word that I will not claim the throne if you take it and become a just ruler."

"Why would you do that?" Ahad asked.

Shayth noted that Ahad had not questioned whether he could trust Shayth's promises. "Because I believe you struggle with what is right and wrong. Because I am convinced you have more of your mother in you than your father. But even your father was never purely evil. I believe he had many good traits, and I believe. . ." Shayth's voice broke. He was so shocked at the revelation and heard his own voice waiver. "I believe that he really regretted his choices. He loved my father, and I believe they're both up there in the next world rooting for us to form our own alliance."

Ahad didn't move.

"This is crazy," Phineus cried. "He's toying with you, you fool. I will kill him." He produced a small bow from his hip and aimed at Shayth. "My father will rejoice that I killed you, and, after you, I will find that pathetic elf and do what Ahad's father was too weak to do. I am the Crown Prince of Odessiya. I know what must be done. I was born for this."

He raised the crossbow, but the arrow he fired careened into the sky. The Crown Prince of Odessiya froze and, eyes wide open, fell backward, an assassin's shryken death disc protruding from his forehead.

As Phineus's body hit the dirt, a ground-shaking roar filled the air. Shayth turned to Ahad, whose throwing hand was frozen in front of him. "Get out of here. The Emperor comes to avenge the death of his son. I will face him."

Chapter Seventy~Seven

"Congratulations," the ice-cold voice came from behind him, and Shayth swung round. The Emperor of Odessiya jumped down from the rock he stood on and stooped to check Phineus' pulse in one fluid motion and gently closed his son's eyes.

"He could not have ruled after me, I know, but he was my son all the same." He covered the boy's head with his hood. Then he turned to Shayth and sighed.

"The irony is that, had he not been born, you and your father would have succeeded me in time. His birth set off a series of regrettable events that left none of us in a flattering position." He glanced at his son and sighed again, shaking his head.

"You have also sentenced Ahad to death and so prevented him from staking his claim. He, at least, had potential. So, Shayth, what do we do? I actually think I could train you and that you might even become a good leader for the people. Succession is back in your hands, and we are where we would have been if he had not been born. How ironic don't you think?"

"That roar," Shayth said, ignoring the question, "it came from you?"

The Emperor answered by slowly unraveling his turban. His hair was snow white, shiny, and vibrant. "I, too, am a Wycaan.

Another irony. You needed one to heal your wounds and bring you within grasp of fulfilling your destiny. You traveled so far to find one, and yet there was one in the family all this time."

He laughed, but stopped at Shayth's scowl. "I did not need any Wycaan, Uncle. I know little of your order, but I suspect there are good Wycaans and bad."

"Oh come now, Shayth. It's far more complex than simply right and wrong. But I concede, your friend seems to have certain qualities that maybe I don't. Still, in the end that will not prove to be enough. I roared because I wanted Ahad to run and, in truth, you as well. And I wanted the young elf to come scurrying to protect you.

"He comes as I wished, but you are still here. Don't fight me Shayth. I am infinitely more powerful than you despite your big heart. This is one fight you cannot take on for him. I am not General Tarlach, and he is not the lost elf he was back then.

"Walk away for now, and I will give him the chance to come with me to the palace. We are two Wycaans, and he needs a teacher."

"And if he refuses?"

The Emperor shrugged. "I will kill him."

"There are other Wycaans back there, you know."

"Yes, I have watched closely. Only one is a master. I can assure you that I will not underestimate her, but she is old and not my match any more, if she ever was. I roared, Shayth, but I can do far more than just make noise. It is the mark of a Wycaan Master. I am the only one who can sustain an animal form, and mine is formidable.

"The Wycaan approaches, nephew. Go with Ahad. If you both make your way to the capital, I will take you under my wing and maybe Ahad as well, for his father's sake. Go. This is not your fight."

Shayth hesitated, broadsword in hand, though he couldn't recall drawing it from its sheath. He flexed his sword hand. The hilt was comfortable in his grasp, but he knew he could not win.

"He's right, Shayth," Seanchai said, walking into the gorge, his voice calm and measured. "Please leave us. And take Rhoddan with you."

Rhoddan began to object, but Shayth turned to Seanchai.

"You sure?" he said quietly.

"If you are here, he will use you against me," Seanchai whispered. He put an arm on Shayth's shoulder and his other on Rhoddan. "Mhari warned me that my loyalties would be my downfall. I need you both safely out of the way."

"Can you take him?" Rhoddan asked. "Honestly, now."

Seanchai's smile was grim. "I don't know. He's more certain than me, but that might be to my advantage. Please go. Try to finish the battle while the Emperor and I fight. Then get everyone out of here. Okay? And Rhoddan, Sellia found her family back in the Forest of Markwin. Take her back there and help her make a new start."

Rhoddan nodded. Seanchai squeezed his shoulder. "Tell her I love her."

Rhoddan's eyes were full of tears. He was a warrior through and through, but at this moment, he was first and foremost Seanchai's closest friend.

"Promise me you'll go, Rhoddan. Say it."

Rhoddan took a deep breath. "*Ashbar*," he said, and let go of Seanchai. He drew his broadsword and ran back to the battle.

Seanchai turned to Shayth. "Is it true? Do they call you Prince Shindell now?"

Shayth nodded.

"What made you change?"

"You," Shayth said. "Even with the deaths of your parents, Ilana, and Mhari, you never strayed from your path. And—just maybe—this is the best way I can honor my own father."

Seanchai squeezed Shayth's shoulder. "Then whatever happens now, Prince Shindell, lead your people to freedom, and make your father proud."

They hugged, and, when they disengaged, Shayth turned to the Emperor. "If you kill him, I will come to the capital as you request. But it will be with my sword in my hand to avenge the deaths of my parents and best friend."

The Emperor shrugged. "I'll be waiting for you, young prince."

Shayth turned away and ran after Rhoddan, back into the thick of the battle.

Chapter Seventy~Eight

Seanchai drew his Win Dao swords and took a defensive stance. But the Emperor turned back to the rock he had jumped from and sat down.

"Not so fast, young Wycaan. We'll get to that, but first, let's talk. You have my word that I will not attack you while we sit here, unless you try first. *Ashbar.*"

Seanchai sheathed his swords and moved to sit. The ancient language sounded wrong when spoken by the Emperor, but he was Wycaan trained and therefore bound by the magic of the language.

The Emperor regarded Seanchai at length before speaking again. "So you made it to the Elves of Markwin and persuaded them to join you," the Emperor stated. "Well done."

"How does that make you feel?" Seanchai asked, anxious to grab the upper hand. "They let me in, accepted me."

The Emperor paused a moment and then shook his head. "It doesn't," he said simply.

"Lies will make this conversation meaningless," Seanchai said.

The Emperor raised his head, eyes narrowed. Seanchai thought they reflected a faint glimmer of respect, too.

"It hurt, didn't it? They rejected you, said you were not worthy. You even failed to penetrate by force."

A smile crept across the Emperor's face. "Very good," he said. "Yes, it hurt–both their rejection and my failure. That was the first time I was ever defeated. But I was young then, just a bit older than you. It was also the last time I ever lost.

"Do you ever wonder if they had accepted and taught me, perhaps I might have turned out like you?"

It had not, and the thought disturbed Seanchai. But he needed to store it for another time. "How did you discover you were Wycaan?"

The smile on the Emperor's face disappeared, and he did not answer. Seanchai pushed him. "You seem pretty sure that I'll be dead soon, so what does it matter?"

The Emperor relented begrudgingly. "The strain runs strong in my family. My grandfather was Etheral Martwell. Have you ever heard of him?" When Seanchai shook his head, the Emperor smiled a cruel grin. "Have you heard of the Black Emperor? He split the Wycaan order and destroyed the Alliance.

He was cruel to my father, who did not inherit the power. My father, in turn, took his frustrations out on me. Both were great influences on me. They made me tough and decisive. They taught me there must be a strong and clearly defined social order, that each race must know its place, and that those who rule must do so with clarity."

"Clarity?" Seanchai's brow creased in confusion.

"Look at you," said the Emperor. "One minute you talk about alliances and freedom for all. The next moment, you wield your swords and crush those who stand against you. Do you heal people with your powers?"

"I try to. I still have much to learn."

"And I bet you tell people that you would prefer to be a healer than a warrior."

Seanchai nodded. "That's true."

"No it's not," the Emperor hissed. "You delude them and yourself. Deluding them is fine, but deluding yourself is pathetic."

"That's your opinion. Where is this going?"

"Are you so eager to die?"

"No. I can sit here all day. It will allow my friends to escape your reach."

"They will never escape my reach, young Wycaan. Shayth will even come to me, apparently."

"What is this, then?" Seanchai asked. "If we are just passing the time, then why not do so over an ale? I'll treat."

The Emperor laughed. "I must know if you're worth keeping alive so I can break your spirit and have you serve me and my successors. A pity you're an elf and can't wear the crown."

"Why is that? Why can't an elf rule?"

The Emperor rolled his eyes. "I told you–rule with clarity. Everyone must know their place in the order of things. It would become complicated if the elves ever decided to restore their long-lost dignity. I don't want to give them any ideas. So now it's just a matter of who will take the throne–Ahad or Shayth. And if you are compliant, you could serve whoever rules."

"You'll never break Shayth."

"Oh? I can be very. . . persuasive."

"Shayth is like his father, and you couldn't break him. An arrow in the back is the work of a coward, following orders of a coward who has run out of options. He beat you."

The Emperor glowered. "Maybe you're right. But one never knows how a man reacts to torture or the thirst for power. That includes you, young elf. You have never been tortured have you? Maybe I should take you back to the capital and test your mettle there."

Seanchai shrugged. "You thrive on power. You breathe power, and it has intoxicated you—made you drunk and single-minded. I am strong and well-trained—powerful in my own right—but I still seek to create alliances, to build friendships. How is it you fail to understand this desire?

"We are both Wycaans, but our similarity ends with the color of our hair. I strive for peace and equality. You bathe in the pits of your own, lonely darkness. You are pathetic. I actually feel sorry for you."

The Emperor exploded. "You arrogant little pup. You can talk. Let's see how you fight." He took off his cloak and drew a huge broadsword and a thin axe.

Chapter Seventy~Nine

As Rhoddan reached the opening of the gorge and surveyed the battle, Shayth swept past him. Guessing that his friend was fueled by fear for Seanchai and rage for their inability to help him, Rhoddan sped up to stay close to the prince, worried he was anything but the calm, focused warrior he needed to be.

It was hard to see how the battle was progressing. The pictorians were pushing through waves of soldiers, making their way toward the cavalry that stood on the periphery, unable to enter the fray without injuring their own. On the other side, the elves were helping the embattled dwarves. Rhoddan felt a rush of adrenaline and pride at their fluent style and technique.

Rhoddan and Shayth headed to join the dwarves and soldiers fell to Shayth's sword. Rhoddan had never seen him fight so fast and fluently, and the elf was hard-pressed to keep up. Shayth made his way to Ballendir.

"We must finish this quickly while Seanchai fights the Emperor. If he loses, we need to be gone."

Ballendir looked around. "We'll fall back ta the north 'n disappear inta the mountains. Does Seanchai have a chance?"

Shayth shrugged. "I don't know. I have never seen the Emperor fight, and I don't know what Seanchai learned with the Elves of Markwin. We should assume the worst."

Ballendir summoned his horn-blower and orders passed on. The elves veered to clear a path, and Rhoddan longed to fight alongside them. But he had been ordered to watch out for Shayth, and he was disciplined.

"The pictorians," Ballendir called. "They've nae changed direction."

Rhoddan and Shayth looked over. "The command tent is up on the hill. They might be heading there," Shayth said. "I will go-"

"No," Ballendir yelled back. "Keep moving. They'll see us. If they choose to attack the command point, then. . ."

A huge explosion erupted near the pictorians. Bodies and boulders spiraled into the air.

"It's a trap ta tempt the boars," Ballendir shouted. "Keep going."

There was a second explosion, followed by a third, and then a fourth. The ground rocked around them. The dwarf with the horn tried to summon the pictorians, but Rhoddan realized that those alive might be temporarily deaf.

"He's killing his own troops," Rhoddan was astonished.

"That's my uncle," Shayth sneered. "Come on. We owe Umnesilk." He set off through the thickest part of the battle with Rhoddan and six elves close behind. For a moment the soldiers fell back, creating a few moments of respite.

A dark-haired elfe tapped Shayth. "You Shayth?" she asked.

Shayth nodded.

"I'm Shathea. Sellia told me about you. Shame about your ears; we could have been related."

She laughed and moved off before he could reply, her thin sword blades gleaming. Shayth smiled while a white-haired elf asked where Seanchai was. Shayth told him.

"Why did you leave him?" the elf snapped.

Shayth didn't answer, but an older elfe interjected. "Trust his decision, Cheriuk. Where are we going, Prince Shindell?"

"To the pictorians," Shayth replied, accepting the use of his linage. "We must bring them with us as we retreat."

The Weapons Master nodded and led the group on. Rhoddan watched, mouth agape, as the elfe's blades became a blur. The ones called Cheriuk and Shathea were beside her, synchronized in deadly precision and leaving Rhoddan and Shayth with little to do.

Twenty yards from the first pictorians, who were standing in a stunned group, the three elves veered around and in front of them. Umnesilk was wounded, bent on one knee.

"We head north," Shayth called to Umnesilk. "We'll defend further along the plain where it's narrower."

"Arrows!" someone warned, and the pictorians raised huge shields to protect from the aerial assault.

A scream. The arrows had been a distraction from three huge crossbow arrows shot from a line of ballistae. The first impaled the Weapons Master. The second grazed Umnesilk's shoulder and sent him sprawling. The third was meant for Shayth. Cheriuk dove across with incredible reflexes, and knocked him to the ground. Rhoddan fell with them.

When Rhoddan rose, Shathea was kneeling, cradling the Weapon's Master's limp body. He went to try and still the blood, but it was no use. The wound was huge and had gone through her stomach, but the old elfe was smiling.

"Tell Seanchai, I will send. . . his regards," she wheezed. She coughed, and blood dripped from her mouth. She tried to grab Rhoddan, and he leaned in. "Tell him not to mourn . . . I only ever wanted to be with her again."

The old elfe went limp, and Shathea hugged her momentarily. She looked at Rhoddan. "Take her swords," she said quietly, "and remember her message to the master."

Rhoddan was stunned by what had just happened. "Seanchai? A Wycaan Master?" He stared then at the elder as Shathea closed her teacher's eyes. "Who's she going to see?"

"Mhari was her lover and soul mate. She joins her now in the great forest forever." Shathea looked past Rhoddan. "Oh no," she gasped.

Rhoddan tuned his head, and saw Shayth bending over Cheriuk, his ear close to the elf's mouth. After a moment, he rose and another elf took Cheriuk's swords. Shayth put a hand on Rhoddan's shoulder and another on Shathea's.

"I don't understand. His dying words were to tell the Wycaan Master that he was ready to follow him."

Shathea nodded. "Not now," she said.

They headed north, two pictorians supporting Umnesilk. More elves arrived and surrounded them as they continued to fight their way through the valley. Then a mighty roar shook the ground around them, and the soldiers pulled back, staring into the sky.

"Keep going," Shayth cried. "Don't stop."

Another huge roar echoed in Rhoddan's ears. If the Emperor was coming, they couldn't get caught in the open. Then again, if the Emperor was coming, all was lost, anyway.

Chapter Eighty

Seanchai slowly drew his Win Dao swords. They produced a fine rasping sound which bounced off the rocks. For a moment he hesitated, a pit of fear forming in his stomach. He took deep grounding breaths, trying to pull energy from the arid, sandy ground, but it was scant. He felt the Emperor doing the same, and braced himself.

The Emperor flew at him in two unnaturally large strides. Seanchai raised his swords, and the two sparred. Gradually, the Emperor sped up until Seanchai felt he was fighting harder than ever. His adversary clearly surpassed even the Weapons Master with the sword.

Sweat dripped off Seanchai's face, and his muscles began to ache, but he matched his opponent blade for blade. As the axe swung toward him, Seanchai rolled and swung at the Emperor's back, dropping him to the ground, too.

The roll brought Seanchai back on his feet, and he found himself standing over the Crown Prince's body. He stared down at the boy's face. "He's no older than I am. Why did you let him come?"

"What makes you think he came with my consent? He wanted to test himself, to make a name, to impress me. He failed."

"Does your heart cry for him? Do you even have a heart?"

The Emperor screamed and leapt forward, again covering ground at a supernatural speed. His blows were faster and harder, but also more erratic.

Seanchai fended them off with considerable effort. "You couldn't even protect your own son," he cried. "What makes you think you're fit to rule?"

The broadsword and axe rained blows upon him, and Seanchai was forced to retreat. He stumbled, and the Emperor sent him crashing into a rock. Seanchai extended his hands and pushed with his mind.

The Emperor was lifted off the ground and shot back thirty paces, but rolled effortlessly back to his feet. Seanchai breathed heavily from exertion and took a moment to realize what he had just done. He had never mastered the use of the Empty Force.

The Emperor rose and sheathed his sword and axe. "Nicely done," he said. "But why do we fight as common soldiers? You have some skill as a warrior, I admit. But it takes more than that to become a Wycaan Master."

As he spoke, the Emperor began to shimmer and blur at the same time. His skin stretched, and he snarled with both pain and exhilaration. The intense brightness forced the elf to shield his eyes. Dust swirled around them, and, as it settled, Seanchai found himself facing a scaled, reptilian creature with a huge, spiked tail. It was a deep red but its eyes were still a cold, Wycaan blue.

The creature rose on its hind legs and flexed massive claws. A long, forked tongue flicked from its mouth, and a voice spoke in Seanchai's head. *This is the level that distinguishes the Wycaan Master from a Wycaan Warrior. The Elves of the West should have taught you if they could, or at least warned you. You shall feel my bladed claws before I incinerate you into dust. Prepare to go meet those who have died before you. They will know your failure even as they live with their own.*

Seanchai tried to block the voice and focus on transforming into a bear. He tried to recreate the tension with the forest of Markwin, but nothing happened. The firebreather sprang forward, and Seanchai slashed with both blades. The swords met impenetrable scales, and the consequential reverberations forced him to drop the blades.

"No," he gasped.

The creature sprang again, and Seanchai pushed out his hands. At the last moment, he ducked to his left and leveraged the creature's own propulsion to blast the firebreather into the rock.

The firebreather roared in pain and anger, but was soon up on its feet again. Seanchai strained to change himself into his own animal form before the creature leapt at him and smashed a huge maul into his side, sending Seanchai spinning across the ground.

Feel my breath, feel my fire.

A column of fire burst forth, and Seanchai instinctively rolled out of the way. Fire. Pyre. The young elfe's face filled his mind. *Just be yourself,* she had said. Her face was joined by others: Shayth, Sellia, Rhoddan, Mhari, Master Onyxei, the Weapons Master, and finally, Ilana. She was smiling, her eyes twinkling. *Just be yourself,* the voices said.

Seanchai exhaled a long breath and, as the firebreather leapt, he felt his body stretch. The grizzly bear roared and swatted the firebreather away just in time. It stood back up, astonished. Seanchai bared his teeth and snarled.

A grizzly! What hope does a bear cub have against a firebreather? Do you know the stench of singed fur?

Seanchai rolled away from the fire and sprung off powerful back paws, aiming his claws at the reptile's throat. It turned, and its massive, spiked tail smashed into Seanchai, catching him in his flank and sending him sprawling against the rock face. A sickening crack echoed, and Seanchai gasped, his side split open and he lay panting. He felt the cold rock, saw a ledge protruding above him, could smell his own blood, and, when he tried to rise, a sharp pain stopped him.

He grunted.

You had such potential, little cub. I could have made you into something spectacular.

Seanchai tasted blood in his mouth, and his vision began to blur. This was it, then. He would join Ilana, burdened with the knowledge that he had failed to form their Alliance—that he had not freed Odessiya.

"I'm sorry Ilana," he said, unsure of whether he had spoken out loud or not. He could feel his consciousness slipping away.

What did you say? An alliance? Such sentiments are your weakness. Only one can rule, and there can be no alliances."

The firebreather rose on its hind legs. *My claws will rip the life from you, but first, you will acknowledge that the Alliance is forever dead. There is no Alliance. There never will be. A Wycaan stands forever alone and now you die alone.*

Seanchai stared up at him, panting. The Emperor drew a set of long, sharp reptilian claws back, ready to strike. *Say it. Your final words will be an admission of defeat. Say it.*

The sun shone around the fire-breather's great body, making its giant stature even more imposing. Rays of strangely beautiful sunlight shone through the spaces between the claws. Seanchai took a deep breath, and, with all his strength, roared in defiance: "The Alliance! The Alliance!"

And suddenly, two moving blurs, one white, the other brown, blotted out the sun. Seanchai heard the growls, the roars. He felt the Emperor's pain and forced himself onto his haunches to watch, mouth agape.

The great white bear from the land of snow and ice sunk its teeth in the firebreather where its tail connected to its body. The grizzly clamped its jaws around the firebreather's throat. Blood spurted as the firebreather tried to shake his attackers. More bears appeared and entered the fray: two black bears, and a red–Denalion?

The firebreather shot out a ring of fire, emitting roars of pain. It shook off the grizzly and rained fire into it. It turned on the white, and blood smeared its snow coat. But a brown bear smashed into its back leg, and there was a loud snap.

Seanchai forced himself onto his paws and mustered his remaining strength for one last attack. The firebreather had freed itself, but was limping, and blood was spurting from its side. Seanchai roared and leapt. With all his might, he smashed into the firebreather and struck its jaw. A crunching sound, and the creature's mouth hung awkwardly.

The firebreather turned on Seanchai, blood flowing from its side, leg and mouth. It jerked its head, trying to summon the fire, but its broken jaw prevented the act. The firebreather raised its wings and, with a labored grunt, pushed off the ground. Blood splattered like rain, but the beast flew awkwardly into the sun and out of view.

Seanchai felt his legs give way. The sun disappeared, and darkness engulfed him.

Chapter Eighty-One

When Seanchai opened his eyes, his vision was blurry, but he heard sounds around him. Wood crackled on a fire, and a warm bandage was easing his pain on the left side of his rib cage.

Someone moved close to him, and he moved his head slightly, waves of pain riding over him. He used all his power to suppress the nausea, but through it, he could smell Sellia's hair.

"Stay still, my love," she said.

Seanchai thought he saw red hair, too. "Denalion?" he whispered.

"I am here, my friend, as I told you I would be. Now, stay still and let the healers close your wounds."

"The bears. . . and you."

"Me? A bear? No, I just walk in dreams. I'm no Wycaan. Why, my hair would be white, and how could I possibly live with that?"

Seanchai tried to laugh, but it turned into a wince.

"Don't make him laugh. I need to sow this up," a stern–yet familiar–female voice instructed. Seanchai frowned, trying to place it, but couldn't. He turned to other matters.

"Who lives?" he whispered. "Rhoddan? Shayth?"

"Both are alive," Sellia said. "They will join you soon. Umnesilk is badly wounded, but Maugwen is trying hard to keep. . ."

"Maugwen?"

"I am here, Wycaan. You rescued me at Galbrieth. Now I can return the favor."

"She's a healer now," Sellia said. "She has considerable skill and uses energy. You won't recognize her."

"Who died?" Seanchai said again.

"The Weapons Master," Denalion said, "and Cheriuk by her side. He sacrificed his life to save the young prince's."

"If they want Seanchai at this council, then you will all need to stop talking," Maugwen said. "Here, Seanchai, bite on this cloth. I don't want you turning into a grizzly and mauling me." He tried to laugh, but it was too painful.

"I can take the pain," he said softly. A moment later, he was unconscious.

Seanchai woke with the distinct feeling that someone needed him. He opened his eyes, and it took a moment to accustom himself to the darkness. Shayth sat by his cot, and he thought he could make out Sellia asleep on a chair.

"How are you doing, my friend?" Shayth whispered.

"I'll be fine. How long have I lain here?"

"It's been two days. Can you walk? I need to talk with you."

Seanchai reached up, and Shayth took his hand and put his other arm behind Seanchai's back. Seanchai clenched his teeth to avoid gasping from pain. When he was standing, he leaned on Shayth's shoulder.

"Slowly," Seanchai whispered, and they moved out of the tent and toward a fire on the camp's periphery.

A few soldiers in tattered uniforms sat chatting quietly. When they saw Shayth and Seanchai, they jumped to their feet.

"I need to talk to my friend privately," Shayth told them. "Please make sure no one knows we're here." The soldiers nodded stiffly, and Seanchai thought they were trying hard not to salute. "Please also bring my friend some ale," he asked of one soldier.

"Yes, my prince," the man said, beginning to bow, stopping himself, and apologizing as he scurried after his friends.

Seanchai looked at Shayth and arched an eyebrow. "Soldiers?"

"Once the Emperor was gone, the battle ended," Shayth began. "Many soldiers lay down their arms and went back to their villages. Others came here, and, well, I guess are our prisoners, though no one is guarding them or making them stay. I have Shiftan and a couple of his officers in a tent and the pictorians are guarding them. Rumors abound that the Emperor is either dead or badly wounded."

"What will you do with Shiftan?"

The soldier returned with a flask of ale and a plate of bread, cheese, and some roots that Seanchai didn't recognize. He wasn't hungry, though he nibbled on the bread. The ale, however, gently dulled the pain.

"No one will disturb you, my prince," the soldier said. "We guard your perimeter." He disappeared into the shadows.

"I'm not sure. I don't think of Shiftan as a bad man. He was in my father's secret society. I would rather have his experience helping me."

Seanchai smiled at his friend. "You have grown, Shayth. Do you feel the weight of responsibility upon your shoulders?"

"Very poetic," Shayth said. "And yes, I do."

"What can I do to help?"

"In the old days, the Wycaans served the kingdom by advising the ruler. You all seem to think I can be king, but I'm not so sure. I'm still the wild, young kid you met all that time ago. I dread returning to the capital."

Seanchai nodded. "We were all young not so long ago, my friend. Life never allowed us to finish our childhoods. You barely got to experience any of it to begin with. But we still have roles to play. What do you ask of me?"

"Ride with me to the capital. If I'm to become king, help me formalize the Alliance we formed with the other races into a peacetime alliance. Be there to advise me."

Seanchai took a swig of the ale and nodded. He stared into the fire. "We must find others to advise you how to rule, older and wiser politicians. I don't have the knowledge, the experience, or the desire.

"But I can help you unite the races. Now, tell me. What do you think happened to the Emperor?"

"Those who saw say he was badly wounded. He could not fly straight, and blood fell from the sky in his wake."

"Do you think he is dead?"

Shayth hesitated. "No, I don't. And I think assuming so would be at our peril. I do not want you to go after him in the state you're in. Why not send other Wycaans? Shathea said there are more in the West."

Seanchai sighed deeply. "They are old, young, or not fully trained. I would like to create a school for Wycaans of all races, one where we not only train with weapons, but also delve deeper into our own potential, into the world of healing and leadership." He looked at Shayth. "That's not going to happen, is it?"

Shayth smiled. "Not immediately, but it will do no harm to begin planning. First, though, we must establish an order of rule, and then go hunt down the Emperor. Maybe there can be some other form of government, where the races all send local leaders to the capital and make decisions together."

Seanchai laughed. "So I'm not the only dreamer."

Shayth put his hand on Seanchai's shoulders. "The dwarf king will be here soon. We will hold council together with the Elves of the West, and Umnesilk will represent the pictorians. Humans, dwarves, elves and pictorians, will all sit together in council.

"I want you to stand by my side when I formally request their support to transform the Alliance into a civic society. Can I count on you?"

Seanchai put his hand on top of Shayth's. "This is something I've dreamed of all along. How can I refuse?"

They sat together and stared into the fire. Eventually, Rhoddan, Sellia, and Maugwen found their way over. Ballendir brought more ale and some fine pipe weed. Umnesilk joined them, limping, and a short while later, Shathea completed the circle.

Members of four races, for so long alienated from each other, sat together around the fire. In the ensuing weeks, there would be much to discuss and negotiate. Agreements would be brokered, and pledges and alliances solidified.

But for now, there was no need for words. There was pipe weed, ale, and, best of all, friendship. The fire, crackling in the night, was the only sound.

Epilogue

H is body was weak and bloodied, but though bones were broken, his spirit was not. The Emperor, in his animal form, flew far into the south. In the warm, volcanic swamps of Elbereth near Mount Grogin, he rested and slowly healed.

He had allies outside of Odessiya–ones who could be tempted or bent into service, seduced with a false promise of power. Odessiya was his. He would bide his time while he healed, carefully planning his return.

He had made a crucial mistake. The Wycaan elf had won because he had built alliances. The Emperor, though head of a great army, had stood alone. In the end he had faced the elf and his allies, and not only from the four races. The bears. That was unheard of.

But the elf probably did not know the entire history of the Wycaan order. Few did and they rarely spoke of it.

Those who had won had ruled. But those who had been vanquished had not died out. They were just waiting to write the next chapter in the history of Odessiya and the Wycaan Order.

He had written much of the recent past. He would yet write the future.

Author's Note:

Dear Friend,

I trust you survived this battle relatively unscathed. I hope you laughed and cried with Seanchai and his friends, as I have. We have come a long way together, and perhaps it is time for some to rest. But as one chapter closes, another opens, and Seanchai will return with some old friends and some new. As I write this, the first draft of Book 4 is completed. It will be very different. Seanchai, Sellia, and the others are not as innocent as they once were. But who among us is?

The world of epic fantasy thrives, and there are many great authors producing fine novels to choose from. I thank you for taking the time to read *Ashbar* and the Wycaan Master series.

If we meet upon the road or at a tavern, let us meet as friends and tell tales of old times: of battles won, love lost, and alliances formed.

If we do not meet, feel free to contact me at anelfwriter@ gmail.com or sign up for my weekly blog post at http://www. elfwriter.com. I also tweet at @elfwriter. Please consider leaving a brief review of this book online.

Thank you again,

Alon
http://www.alonshalev.com

Non-Fantasy Novels by Alon Shalev:

Unwanted Heroes (Three Clover Press, 2012)
A Gardener's Tale (Three Clover Press, 2011)
The Accidental Activist (Three Clover Press, 2010)